Cary J. Lenehan is a former trades assistant, soldier, public servant, cab driver, truck driver, game designer, fishmonger, horticulturalist and university tutor—among other things. His hobbies include collecting and reading books (the non-fiction are Dewey decimalised), Tasmanian native plants (particularly the edible ones), medieval re-creation and gaming. Over the years he has taught people how to use everything from shortswords to rocket launchers.

He met his wife at an SF Convention while cosplaying and they have not looked back. He was born in Sydney before marrying and moving to the Snowy Mountains where they started their family. They moved to Tasmania for the warmer winters and are not likely to ever leave it. Looking out of the window beside Cary's computer is a sweeping view of Mount Wellington/Kunanyi and its range.

Warriors of Vhast Series
published by
IFWG Publishing International

Intimations of Evil (Book 1)
Engaging Evil (Book 2)
Clearing the Web (Book 3)
Scouring the Land (Book 4)
Gathering the Strands (Book 5)
Following the Braid (Book 6)
Approaching the Source (Book 7)

Warriors of Vhast Book 7

Approaching the Source

by

Cary J Lenehan

Approaching the Source

Book 7, Warriors of Vhast

ISBN-13: 978-1-922856-71-5

Printed in Times and LHF Essendine font types.

IFWG Publishing International
Gold Coast

www.ifwgaustralia.com

Foreword

It has taken a while, but you now hold the seventh book of the Warriors of Vhast series in your hands (or on your screens). Covid has a lot to answer for in lost sales and delays. Thank you for continuing to read the stories. There is only one more to go in this series.

Having said that, I am working on two other series. One is contemporaneous and deals with what happens in Freehold as the Mice are looking after the rest of The Land. The other is set several thousand years before at the end of the last Age.

With Patreon (*https://www.patreon.com/user?u=3009225&fan_landing=true*), the stories now extend for many thousands of years of the history of the planet and I have more in mind as novellas that may take it back even further in time as well as forward. I hope that you all get the chance to look at the various maps, eat the food from my recipes and, now, even play a character behind the scenes in Ashvaria.

Whether you have bought the books, borrowed them, or read them through the library, I hope you enjoy this latest offering, and that you share my world with friends. Please also feel free to leave a review anywhere you can (even a few words). For writers working through small press publishers, these are vital.

Feel free to talk to me and ask questions on my Facebook writer's page or through my website. I am more than happy to answer them.

Cary J. Lenehan
nipaluna/ Hobart

A cast list, glossary of terms used in this novel, and an annotated map of Mousehole can be found from page 353. I advise strongly using them when you start in Vhast.

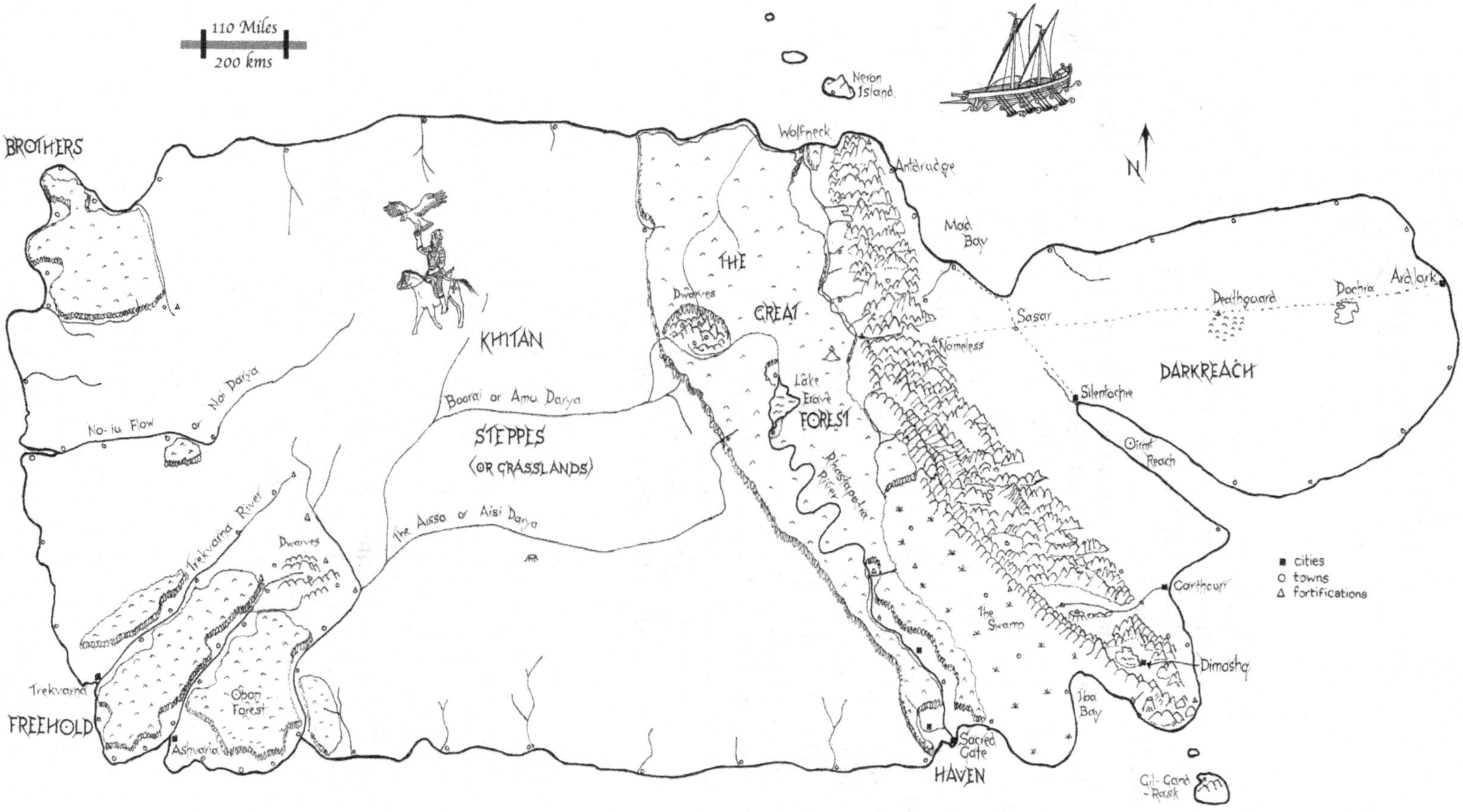
110 Miles
200 kms
Neron Island
N
BROTHERS
Wolfneck
Antarudge
Mad Bay
KHITAN
THE GREAT FOREST
Dwarves
Sasar
Deathguard
Dochra
Ardlark
Nameless
DARKREACH
Lake Erave
Silentochre
Boorai or Amu Darya
No-iu Flow
or Noi Darya
STEPPES
(OR GRASSLANDS)
Oirat Reach
Rhastapootra River
The Aissa or Aisi Darya
Dwarves
Trekvarna River
cities
towns
fortifications
Carthcurr
The Swamp
Dimasha
Trekvarna
FREEHOLD
Oban Forest
Ashvaria
Sacred Gate
HAVEN
Iba Bay
Gil-Gard-Rask

My wife, Marjorie, continues to be my rock and my support. Without her I would not be doing this. She is very patient for a start.

Once again I thank Pip Woodfield for the beta reading she has done for me, checking my continuity errors and knowing many of my characters better than I do myself.

I respect and acknowledge the Muwinina people, who are the traditional owners of the Nipaluna Land where I reside and write my stories. I give thanks to the Tasmanian Aboriginal people and to elders past, present and future. I acknowledge that they never ceded the land where I reside.

The Caliphate

Map of part of the Southern Mountains area

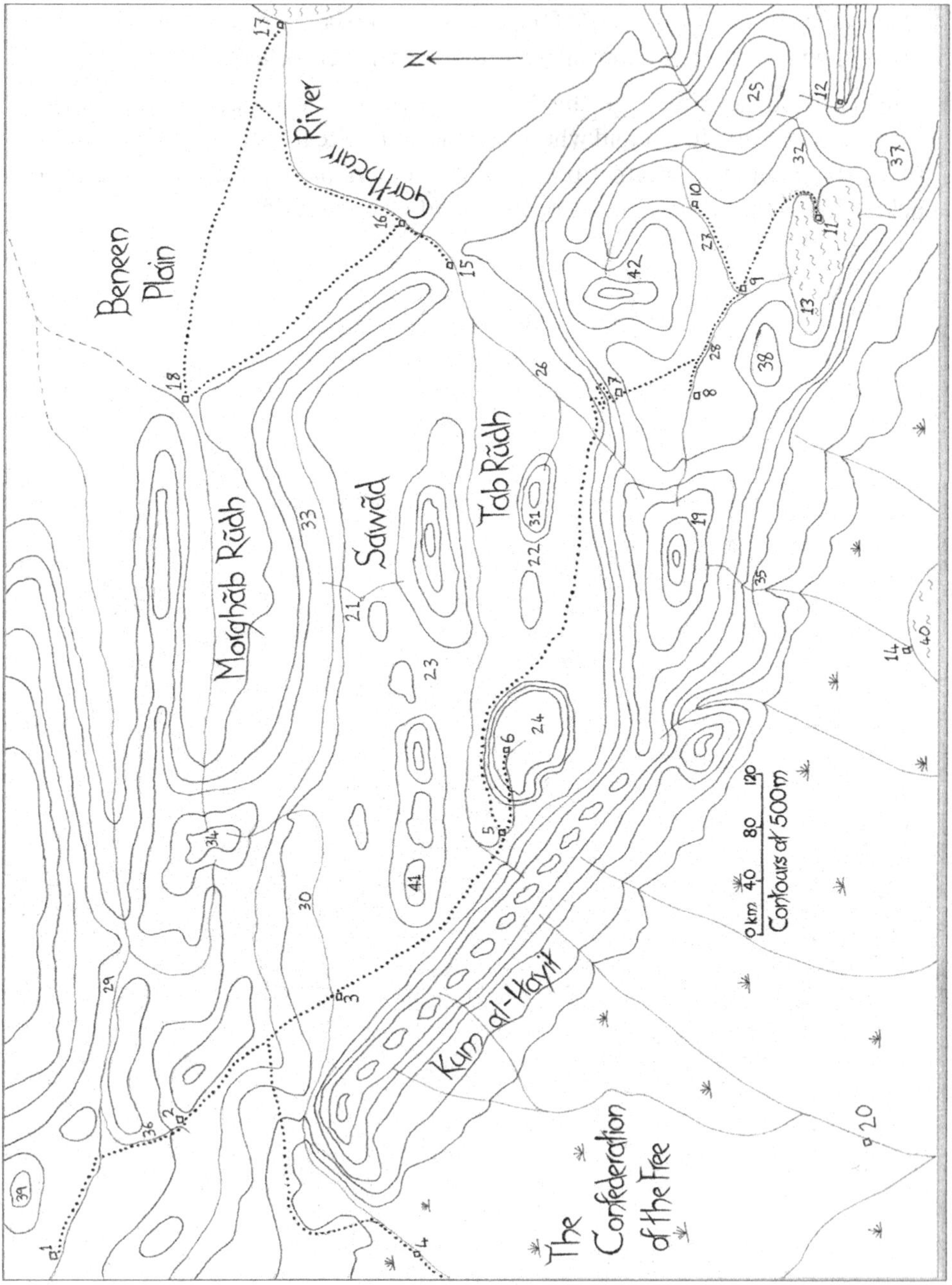

1. Yãqũsa: most northerly town in the Caliphate on the Khãbũr Rũdh
2. Ubulla: northern town on the Hasbani Rũdh
3. Ta'if: a small and new village on the Ziyanda Rũdh
4. Caer Gwyliwr Ddwyrain or Eastguard Tower, a heavily fortified town in The Swamp
5. Yarmũk: a town in a bend of the Tãb Rũdh
6. Misr al-Mãr: a village, holy site, and main base of the Ghazi
7. Bab al-Abwãb: a village in the northern pass into the Rãhit
8. Ashgãbat: a town in the Rãhit on the Hawrãn Rũdh
9. *Jebrael: a town in the Rãhit at the junction of the Litani Rũdh and* Hawrãn Rũdh
10. Ma'amir: a town in the Rãhit on the Litani Rũdh
11. Dimashq: the capital of The Caliphate
12. Chamãn: small village on the southern flank of Jabal al-Jais, on the Musaqara Nahr, it guards the southern pass into the Rãhit from Darkreach
13. Buhairet Tabariyya a large freshwater lake
14. Glawdans or Rainjig: a small and isolated village in The Swamp
15. Wheoh Grass: a small Darkreach village in the mouth of the Sawãd, here the Tãb Rũdh changes to being called the Garthcurr River
16. Rebelkill: a small town in Darkreach
17. Garthcurr: a large town in Darkreach
18. Doro: a small town in Darkreach. Here the Morghãb Rũdh becomes known as the South Lost River
19. Jabal Kartala or Snowcap
20. Bloomact: a town in The Swamp and its capital
21. Badr: well, small oasis, and battle site on the Sawãd, the site of failed ambush of Darkreach forces
22. Uhud: well and battle site on the Sawãd, site of final defeat of Caliphate forces (after Badr) in last war with Darkreach
23. Khotal Tamuru: a pass in the Kũm Hadramawt, a range of hills in the northern Sawãd, the plain of the Tãb Rũdh
24. Hadbat Rih al-Ed a large, cold and mostly barren windy plateau
25. Jabal al-Jais: large mountain east of Dimashq
26. The Orontes
27. Litani Rũdh (on the Rãhit from Jabal Tahat to Buhairet Tabariyya)
28. Hawrãn Rũdh (runs down from Jabal Kartala to Buhairet Tabariyya)

29. Khãbũr Rũdh, which becomes the North Lost River in Darkreach
30. Ziyanda Rũdh, which becomes the Buccleah River in The Swamp at a large waterfall known as Kabeer Ma'a
31. Jabal Misht: a mountain in the Sawãd above the Orontes
32. Kadisha Rũdh (on the Rãhit) to the Buhairet Tabariyya from Jabal al-Jais
33. Kũm Hejaz: a long ridge with many peaks elsewhere known as the Grey Virgins Range
34. Jabal Umm: a mountain where the Ziyanda Rũdh starts
35. Snowcap Rivulet
36. Hasbani Rũdh, a tributary of the Khãbũr Rũdh
37. Jabal Hermon: mountain south of Dimashq
38. Jabal Sawda: a small mountain north-west of Buhairet Tabariyya
39. Jabal Shams: or Mountain of the Sun above Yãqũsa
40. Iba Bay
41. Cheekda Dar: most westerly peak of Kũm Hadramawt, the others on that part of the ridge are Driba Karltira and Jabal an Nabi Shu'ayb
42. Jabal Tahat: major mountain east of Bab al-Abwãb

A Rubaiyat
from Ayesha bint Hãritha

By mountain path and through the sky
On horse and by swift saddles fly
Into the mountains on task so solemn
Set light to dispel us of dark we try.

Our seers give direction by foretelling
Come together now in futures slow jelling
Respond to threats upon our valley
An evil-rooted tree, it needs a felling.

My own people, my teachers, do foully betray
An attack in the night ends in deadly melee
Victory for us comes at greatest of cost
The death of a ruler makes great disarray.

Preacher and teacher filled full of bile
The holiest of holy he does now defile
Bloodshed or heresy that is the pick
From hardest of choices we cannot resile.

Chapter 1

Theodora do Hrothnog

26th Primus, the Year of the Water Goat

It is only the day after Astrid so summarily dispatched Ith and Athgal. As well as any other issues we may have to face here, I have now been left with a dilemma. We are no longer being quiet. We are unmasked and out in the open. I am still determined to take the Mice on to all of the other villages of the Swamp, but should we avoid the fortress and town of Eastguard Tower?

It is, after all, where many of the dead from our last raid had come from. The story of how they were tricked, and who had tricked them, will soon get there. Is it really going to be worthwhile for us to risk any of the Mice by going there, or should we hope that we can let the people of the Swamp settle that one for themselves?

I feel that I may have made a mistake in asking Astrid for an opinion. It has made the girl smile that predatory feline smile of hers. "I want to go straight there. If we wait too long, they might flee and I will not get a chance to take some exercise. What is more, it will mean less revenge for our people who might want it." Theodora gave her a pained look.

So much for us being cautious in our approach. I really do suppose that it was too much to ask for. Perhaps we can have some sort of a compromise.

"We will first go to all the other villages of the Swamp and check them for Patterns and, by the time that is finished, the word should have reached Eastguard. Perhaps the issue will have resolved itself by then. Maybe tempers will have abated or the guilty fled by the time we get there. Who knows? You may still get to fight someone."

Astrid looks quite disappointed at that and is not bothering to hide her feelings. I suppose I should explain why I think it is a good idea. "You will have to be content with that, I am afraid. At least, if we go there as the last stop of our journey through this area, then we will be doing so guardedly and cautiously, as we have been advised to do."

Bishop Christopher Palamas

The Princess may well be off talking with Astrid about what to do next, but I need to get on to finding out if, despite the compulsion on him, Athgal was able to lie about a Pattern here. He began to set up and cast to determine if there was anything new. *At least none dare say anything contrary to me as I work. We have them worried.*

There are no new ones here in the village. Unless there is one set up in a nearby hamlet or farm then the messages coming to him must have come from somewhere else by hand. I suppose that, in a way, this should have been obvious. If they were coming from somewhere nearby, Athgal would probably have been warned of the start of our visit and not been caught by surprise.

Theodora (later that day)

At least that is good news and some relief. Given what had happened, I had felt sure that another Pattern was out there, even if Athgal didn't know about it. Unless he got his instructions from a fast messenger there should be a pattern somewhere. But, as Christopher said, it cannot be too close by or we would probably not have had surprise when we arrived.

We keep forgetting to ask the right question until afterwards, when it is too late. We should have asked Athgal where his instructions came from. Still, we have to move on, and I will try and remember that question if we get another chance. Our next call will be at Bloomact, the capital of this wretched place. More and more I am coming to agree with my husband about the Swamp.

Some of its people are fine, Father Kessog is a lovely man and all of our Mice from there are agreeable girls, sometimes a little odd, but charming none the less. I think that it has more or less been decided that we should stay on here for another night. We can fly on in the morning when Christopher is fresh, but I should check this with someone.

If we stay, I can try being a diplomat and see if anyone in this place, apart from Father Kessog, is worth talking to. I wonder if this time I can get some sense out of their Reeve, Urfa. Last night I was not able to. It might be that he is still in shock from having the events of the world around this village revealed to him and to the others present.

On the other hand, it might not. He might have been against the war itself, but before he had heard the story, he still voiced his smug world-view of isolation and self-sufficiency. Now, his worldview has been badly shaken. To top that off, I am not too sure about how firm his grip on the world was even before it was shaken by us. He seems a bit...scattered in his thoughts.

Goditha Mason

Father Kessog has been taken out of the village on a saddle to gather what remains of his flock together and to bring them back to the village. I am going to give him a surprise. Taking some of the others to help her, Goditha started doing what she could to clear the ruins of the church while he was away so that at least he could start out from a clean slate in the rebuilding.

By the time he had returned there was a small pile of re-usable timber and stone to one side and a larger pile of rubbish was already being thrown in the river. *At least we agreed that he can be told that he and his wife will be taking over one of the rooms that we Mice are in once we leave. Bianca has already paid for it until the church and its presbytery are rebuilt.*

Basil Akritas

Everywhere that Astrid goes in the village there is a shadow following behind her. She has very pale skin and long straight raven-black hair, held back from her face in a ponytail that hangs most of the way down her back. She has a snub nose, thin eyebrows, and the sort of face and ears oft described as elfin by those who have not seen a picture of one of the Eldar or read a proper and real depiction of them by one who has. I have read such a description at least. We are trained to look for them.

She is also wearing a lot of leather, even on her arms. Trotting alongside her is a creature that sort of looks like a grey possum except that it has a black mask across its face and has black bars on its tail. When it sits up you can see that, while it is clearly an animal, it has almost human hands on its front feet. It even has thumbs on the hands, but the hands look deformed somehow. Basil looked more closely at it.

Its hands lack a digit. It has only four actual fingers as well as the thumb.

When the small creature is watching you, it seems to follow the conversation, looking from one person to the other as they talk. While most of the people in the village are in terror of Astrid and will quickly stand clear or walk the other way if she comes near them, the witch Ia follows her everywhere.

Basil noted her follower with amusement. "If you are sick of me and want to change direction, there is one who only needs to have a single word said to her." He was rewarded with a glare from his wife.

I have to admit, quietly and only to myself, to having quite some amusement at this. While my wife may be confident and self-assured when facing someone in combat, she doesn't know how to act towards or even react to the presence of her follower.

In desperation, she has even tried pointing out to the girl that she is married and very happy that way. She should have asked me about that first. She managed to make the situation even worse as it brought the matter into the open and she is now followed at an even closer range. She was more circumspect before but now Ia makes no pretence at being only co-incidentally there.

The young girl eventually, through her shyness, pointed out the marriage of Bryony, Adara and Stefan to Puss. I saw and heard her go so far as to ask them about their relationship. She blushed as she did so at her breach of etiquette. Even in the Swamp, it is an unusual arrangement that they have, but who holds whose hand or leans against the other or gives a quick kiss leaves little room for imagination as to its nature. Basil just grinned.

Puss loves to tease others and she is rarely caught out herself. The grin moved to his wife's face for a little while when, in a quiet street, Ia turned to him. "Basil, do you find me attractive? Wouldn't you like a second wife?" It took all of his self-control to keep a straight face to that question without his wife bursting out laughing at his turn at discomfiture.

Damn her for that question. The girl is beautiful. She will know if I lie, but if I tell the truth Puss will be upset with me. While he stumbled for a diplomatic answer, she opened her jerkin wide so that they could better see her charms and what she had to offer. *She has a small body but a very nice shape. Thank God I don't have to answer, at least for now. Here comes Theodora with a question. I am rescued by the very heavy cavalry.*

Theodora

What is that witch-child doing? She has managed to make Basil blush and that is not easy to do. I am sure that his eyes were cast down the length of her torso at least briefly. Even Astrid looks more than a bit surprised.

The girl's back is to me, and I was some distance away when I saw them, but I could have sworn that the witch-child had her wrap-around jerkin wide open when her familiar animal pulled on her long coat and chattered to let her know that someone was coming up behind her. At any rate she is fastening it now and Basil seems very glad to see me.

Now, what did I want to ask? That is right. "Do we go on now or tomorrow? It is still before lunch and, from the map, we could easily reach Bloomact today."

"It will be raining before we get there and we will be flying into the village soaked and bedraggled," said Astrid after a moment's thought. "What is more, if we come to combat for any reason, Christopher has already used most of his mana for the day." *As usual, it seems that she has her finger on the pulse of everyone's activities.*

"He, at least, would like to stop here for the night. Goditha is off at the church, and I know that she wants to finish clearing the site and to talk to some of the local builders for Father Kessog. She doesn't trust him to bargain or to know what to insist on in the rebuilding. In addition, Adara and Bryony are having far too much fun introducing their husband around the town, and talking up his exploits, all of them, and they are showing off their jewellery."

"As for the rest, Ayesha is still asleep and she said, before she went to bed, that it would be best if she told the tale for a second night here." *She is not saying anything about herself, and the young girl is hanging off her every word.* "Everyone seems to have assumed that it would be tomorrow and, while the Khitan are at the tavern with the saddles, most of the others are scattered around. All in all, I think that we are best going tomorrow and leaving a few hours earlier."

Theodora nodded. *Without my husband here, I have to rely on the people that she talks to for advice. I did feel the same, but it is best to check. The whole time I was talking to my Mice, the witch-child stood there without moving as if she had a perfect right to be included in what is being said and decided. Astrid might try to ignore her, but she refuses to be left out.*

I have never been this close to her before and my senses itch almost as if the girl were a Mouse, she carries that much magic on her. This young witch is carrying more enchanted items than even most experienced mages do…there is one pouch that has to be full of wands and that is the least of it. There is another similar pouch that I cannot feel anything from. It probably holds more wands and I have just not picked them up. She probably made them all herself.

Attached to a strap bound around her head and holding her hair back is a small hexagonal piece of timber…that will probably be elm…set within a ring…that has to be made of chrome…which is set with six hexagonal cut pieces of amber that have insects embedded in them. It shows to anyone that knows that she works in the Air realm and has been born under the sign of the butterfly and that it is there to enhance her casting.

It is also highly magical as well. It is probably also being used to store mana for her. Her leather garment, at least one ring and a main-gauche complete her obvious magical equipment. I am not sure about her sword and there is something else about the girl that I cannot work out. I am sensing a sort of magic that I have never felt before.

At any rate, if she has enchanted all of that lot herself...as a priestess of the Air in a way...she might be young, she has barely stopped being a child, but she is also good...very, very, good and, like I have done myself since I have left Darkreach, for some reason she must have taken big risks to do so much. Theodora turned and left to seek out the Reeve.

Astrid the Cat

At least I know why she wears so much padded leather. The little black and grey beast climbed her body and then settled onto Ia's shoulder. Its claws dug into the padding as it kept its balance. *The creature may have hands, but the hands have non-retractable claws on the fingers, and it seems to climb her whenever it feels like it.*

She must be stronger than she looks. She hardly tilts at all from its weight. Unconsciously the girl reaches up towards the animal to scratch it behind its ear as it seems to speak, in turn, into her ear.

"You need not answer now. Maeve..." *that must be the animal's name* "...and I will wait on your answer and in the meantime, I will talk with your priest. If you are to have this school and pretend to be independent, you will need a Priestess like me to look after any students who are from here or who look to the Mother.

"Some will want to stay firm to the way they were brought up in the knowledge of the genatrix and her power..." her eyes flick across to where Stefan and his wives are visible "...and not all of us are evil. I will see you again tonight." She smiled at them both and moved off quietly swaying. *Which one of us is she trying to seduce?*

Eventually Basil spoke. "I think that she wants to drag one of us into bed... and while at first I thought that it was you, now I am not at all sure which one of us it is. At least we are sharing one room with all of the others, so the brave warriors should be kept safe from the little girl until we can leave this place."

He smiled "After that we need to work out what to do if she is serious in what she claims and does come north...did you see the tattoo that she has just under her breasts? It is sort of like the one the priests use and yet it is also like the one the mages stand in. I think that she has had a casting pattern put there as a tattoo and it is very detailed so it should be very powerful."

Astrid

Again, we have a tavern that is full as new people, and some of those from the night before, come to hear the story. Despite the crowded room, the girl Ia has somehow managed to get a seat. How did she get one right beside where Basil and I are sitting near the door?

"She is determined," Basil whispered a practised low volume, "are you sure you don't want to keep her?" A low growl, like that of a cat giving warning just before striking, was the reply.

"If you want to be private in what you say..." said Ia as she leant across. *She has put her hand beside mine where it lies on Basil's leg, only a little higher, so that she touches us both with it* "...you will have to be much quieter than that...my hearing is very, very good.

"I will not be kept or let go by any another, but I do know that I will be following you and in time we shall see what we shall see." Her eyes looked from one to the other. "I really do believe that you two are the answer to some of the things that I saw ahead of me as my future when I first bought my crystal ball some time ago."

Something may have been foretold about me? Astrid winced inside herself. *I do not want to be a part of any prophesies like that. Such a geas has happened for Hulagu and Ayesha and for Theodora and Rani as well. The foretellings seem to have worked out for them. However, I am very content as I am with my accidental lover and husband.*

It was evident that Basil felt the same as both of them were so distracted by that piece of news from Ia that they forgot for some time about the hand lying lightly there holding on to both of them as if it also belonged there.

Chapter II

Astrid

27th Primus

The next morning, once all were up and about the saddles were brought out and they were preparing to leave. *Dear Saint Kessog, I cannot escape. Ia is there with her animal, her raccoon. It even has a belt around its waist and a strap so that it can be tied on. She has a long bow and a backpack and appears to be ready to leave with us.*

Another young girl has just given her a deep kiss and is leaving her without looking back. She has turned and is now standing talking to Verily and it is obvious that she intends to come along with us when we go. Astrid came over to her. "What are you doing here?"

Ia smiled at her and answered calmly, "and good morning to you as well Astrid. I told you what would happen when we parted. I looked at the immediate future before I saw you last. When I left, I went and spoke to your Bishop and he agreed that I was needed in your village. I am going to be flying with this kind lady as she is very light and so are Maeve and I. Until Basil lets me travel with him, I will fly with her and just think of you."

Verily has a puzzled look on her face as she looks from me to the girl and back again. "I thought that you knew," she said. "Christopher asked me to carry her with me until we have returned home. Is this wrong? Is Ia not supposed to be here?"

Astrid scowled at Ia before turning to Verily. "It is not your fault, and I am sure that Christopher is right in what he has agreed to. I just wish that someone else had asked him if they could come or that he had been able to choose another person for the task."

Ia is pouting at me and putting the back of her hand to her forehead as if playfully saddened by my rejection. She may think that it is funny. I don't. Then, seeing Basil coming out of the inn, she smiles warmly in his direction. *At least he is even more uncomfortable about her than I am...but he never answered her question.*

Astrid

half an hour later

This time we are flying directly away from the river and down south into the depths of the Swamp. As we fly away from Rising Mud, it can be seen that the ground begins to gently rise as we move to the south. It looks to be such a long and gentle rise that, if you were on the ground, you might not even notice it.

It does not take us long to pass over the crest of the low ridge that runs along the river from the mountains to near Garthang Keep. The rising land and the resulting ridge really only become obvious from on high. As we follow the path that lies below, often obscured by the trees, it is easy to see that ahead lay a number of small streams and below us is the wildlife of the area.

If anything, the land is even wetter looking here than it is along the Buccleah. Now we are roughly following the course of what must be the Delta River, or at least one of its major branches, as it grows beneath us. By the maps I have seen, it is not a very long river, but a lot of water flows down it.

Small herds of the giant lizards can be seen on either side. Some are so tall that they dwarf the trees around them. Several times some of their giant predators could even be seen, Thunder Lizards and the like. Even as they flew the cries of birds and lizards could be heard and sometimes there were glimpses of bright plumage and, sometimes, other arboreal creatures were glimpsed in the tops of the trees beneath them.

At one stage a screeching flock of leather-wings, all brown skin and bright plumage, rose up from a patch of tall trees towards them, although it was easy to avoid their sluggish flight just by rising higher and the Mice quickly out-flew them. *It must be their nesting time for them to do that. Usually, they are only aggressive if you go after them.*

It was soon possible to see that ahead of them the trees abruptly diminished in size and soon, marking that change, it was possible to see Bloomact come into view on its island where the real river disappeared and fragmented into the braided water paths and deep bogs of the actual delta. *Long bridges go from the island to each side of the river.*

Unlike the other settlements that we have seen so far, there is a comparatively large, cleared area on each bank of the river near the village and long clumps of dense planted trees act as fences for it. These cleared areas seem to be largely filled with fields of rice and sugar, although any higher ground shows rows of fruit trees and breadfruit on it, often alongside paths and roads. A large stone circle with the usual two arms is visible and a flat grassed area alongside the river has some normal-sized animals grazing on it.

Bloomact is a much larger village than Rising Mud...at least twice the size and a small town really...and it is only built on one island instead of being scattered over five. It is, nonetheless, built along the same pattern as the smaller settlement with timber pilings driven into the river mud. More mud and dirt have been piled inside them and houses put on top of it all.

The long bridges and their opening sections also look far more substantial than those at Rising Mud. Even from here you can see that they sit on piers made of solid timber trunks, not just branches only a hand or so around. Around the edge of the island several small wharves can be seen empty or with a river boat or a canoe or punt tied up there.

As well I can see that downstream a pair of long piers are enclosing a proper wharf. It is obvious that a large number of craft can be tied up here to trade, to fish, or just to carry people about. I wonder if we can get the River Drag*on up here. It is far inland, and there is no well-known river. They would have to be coming up through a maze of channels. Should I ask around and try to find out? My sister will want to know if it is possible, but will anyone here want to tell me?*

Bryony flew up to Astrid and began pointing things out. "That is the sports area", she said referring to the grassed area. "It is sort of like the sports area at Freeport, but without the open intent for the spectators to have sex with the winners. Each year there is a competition. It is as well you are getting Harnermêŝ to teach you his way of wrestling. When this is over you can come here one year and collect all of the prizes. I am sure that with your strength you should win easily."

Astrid smiled. *That is a fun idea; especially the idea of it all being over. For now, however, it is back to business. Below and ahead I can see that people are starting to move around quickly as if they are expecting an attack. It is time to move into our contact formation and to bring our speed and height down.*

Soon they were moving along at a trot and, indeed, were flying not much higher up than a rider would sit as they moved south along the western bank. *Having lost altitude and speed it is now a lot more uncomfortable. The temperature has soared as we lose the cooling breeze of our transit. Ahead of us in the far distance the clouds of the afternoon rains can already be seen moving up from the distant sea to bring some welcome relief.*

As proof of the more significant nature of this village there is a solid gate at the end of the bridge. If needed it could quickly close off the start of the bridge, at least until it is forced, along with a much larger guard house that is made of stone and would be defensible for at least a little time. Today it has three guards to occupy it.

It even has its own landing platform, with a small boat out of the water on a frame, behind it. Adara has no problems gaining entry for us however and this time we fly along the bridge, which is wide enough for a full-sized cart to travel along it and, along its length of a hand of filled hands, there are even two spots wide and long enough for two carts to pass each other.

Basil

We get to fly over a wagon, and I soon wish we had been further away from it. It is well laden with stained barrels each of which has a fastened down lid with a hinge on the side. The stench that we fly through, rising up from the cart, tells of its purpose as it goes out to the fields to deposit its daily load.

As we fly over it, and happily and quickly leave it behind, I am reminded about the old children's joke about what has two wheels and yet also flies. I am very glad that we have proper sewers at home in the valley.

Theodora

Adara turned around and called back to Theodora. "I am going to take you straight to see the Reeve. He is in charge of his whole area just as you are in charge of our area, so it is only polite. You will need to talk to him at some stage anyway."

We are flying down the streets above the people, and I can see into upper windows that have been left open, with only screens of light gauzy cloth to cover them, screens that will allow any breeze to enter and yet keep the insects out. As least we have our Dadanth ointment on. Below us people look curiously up at us passing over the heads of even the few riders on horseback.

If we need any proof that this is more solid than Rising Mud, once we are away from the edge of the island, many of the houses here have a first floor of stone and, looking ahead it is possible to easily see our destination. It is a building raised into the air on stone colonnades with cloth stretched on frames that extend out from its side. They expand its shade further over much of the surrounding area.

Ayesha

Allãh wadhu, I can hear the call for prayer for Dhurhr coming softly from one of the buildings. It is not called out proudly and loud for all to hear, but it is there, and it is not hidden. Praise be to Allah, the Patient, it looks like Imam Iyãd will have at least some good news to hear from our visit. She noted the building that the call came from. *I will return here later.*

Theodora

As we approach the odd-looking building that the street leads straight to, where it sits on the highest spot in the village, it can be seen that this focal point is also the business hub of the town. Many people stand or lounge around here. They stand and stare, interrupted in their affairs by the sight of our flying approach.

People have set up tables with sheets of paper on them and other people wait to see them. Those are scribes. They really do not teach their people well if a place of this size needs so many scribes to read and write letters or to witness contracts. Some of the people there are very prosperous looking, and most of them seem to be talking to others who look to be farmers but there are also others who look even more disreputable than is usual in this place.

In a corner a street entertainer looks to have been holding sway, but he has now, like everyone else, stopped to watch us approach.

They came down to land in the large open space in front of the building under one of the awnings and Adara hopped off her saddle. "Wait here until I return," she said to the Mice. "It will be best if we give them a warning before we all go upstairs." Turning she climbed the three steps that extended around the perimeter of the platform, before beginning to push her way through the crowd of people between the columns.

Most of the people around us are now just standing silently. They are all watching us, even if they don't ask anything. Adara is moving towards the more solid rear of the building where, through the shade, a set of stairs can be seen going up into the top section of the solid stone structure that all the cloth roofs hang from.

Astrid

She may have been born near here, but we need to send Basil with her. Astrid signalled for her husband to follow Adara to make sure nothing happened to her. *Damn that girl. Ia is following him. If the girl was going to come with us, she will have to learn some discipline and when to obey and do what she is told.* Astrid was unconscious of the irony of her thought.

Around us a curious circle of faces is being formed. They stay just out of the range of a hand weapon or even of a spear, at least they think that they do. The gazes of the onlookers seem to be divided between our women, the saddles themselves, and what we are equipped with. I can see quite a few looks that appear to be appraising if we can be relieved of anything.

Looking up to the building above and around the upper levels of the square people can be seen looking down at us from behind their screens. Having stopped moving, the heat and the humidity are now even more oppressive, and I can feel sweat beginning to trickle slowly down my back and appear under my tits.

Astrid

It took only a few minutes for the three to be seen coming back. Before she could be upbraided, Ia held up her hand. "I know that I should have asked, but I just realised that Adara would not be known here, and I am in a little way. The Reeve is a sort of second cousin of mine by marriage. We are not close at all, but there is a connection. There wasn't really any time to explain."

"At any rate," said Adara. "I will take the Princess and the Bishop upstairs with anyone they want with them. They are waited on. Ia can go with someone else and can find us an inn so that we can be inside before the rains start." She turned to the girl "the Pure Doe if it is possible." Ia nodded. Adara looked up at the sky, "and hurry."

The group began to sort themselves out. *I get to stay with the saddles, while Theodora and Christopher take Hulagu, Ayesha, Dobun and Bianca and go back upstairs with Adara. Someone has to go with the girl and, unfortunately that means Basil. He is the only one we have along who is trained to look for trouble.*

Stefan can go along with them as well. His job, as usual, is to be the manly and upright figure, the more obvious one for trouble to look at. One day he will get sick of that role, but so far, he realises how he is being used and seems to take it in good grace, and even with some amusement at times.

Chapter III

Ayesha bint Hãritha

In many ways this is the most unremarkable start to any of our visits in the Swamp. No-one has died and there has been no panic. Now our credentials are established, places at this Pure Doe obtained, and our saddles put away and guarded we can begin to scatter through the town to see what is here.

Ayesha took Atã and Tãriq with her to the small mosque where they found that the local Mullah, Uthman ibn Hakam, was a man who would have been more suited to preaching in Darkreach than in the Caliphate. They introduced themselves to the surprised man and asked how he had come to be here.

"The youngest son of the Caliph, praise be to his name, visited this area and realised that we have many people of the Faith living here...through choice or otherwise." He shrugged. "Inshallah...the Prince granted money as sadaqah, charity. It was enough to send a Mullah out and to keep him here for several years."

"I was, I am sure, chosen for this task as the Imams and Mullahs in Dimashq thought that I had far too much levity for them to find a place for me in the Caliphate and so I would be the one who would be the least missed if I was killed by the kãfirũn. Since then, while I still get packages with money, I have heard nothing from them. I send them many letters but..."

"It is nice to see that I am not the only one to be sent away as being inconvenient. I had heard that you had started training before I left." *He has a broad smile on his face as he looks at me.* "So, all is not as we have been told in Darkreach then," he added looking at Atã and Tãriq. "I am not surprised. This place is very different to what we were told as well."

"I was half expecting to be killed for my beliefs, but if I die it will only be out of boredom. The rulers here ignore me completely and my small flock are free to do what they want the same as anyone else is. I have less than twenty to care for although, Allah willing, we are working hard to correct this…" he stopped in mid-sentence and a smile appeared.

"Your most eminent connection cannot send me some girls can he? I am not the only one lacking a wife, so we need at least half a dozen…them we need more than anything else. For me I do not ask that she be as beautiful as you are, although I will not complain if she is. We have money and so do not really need that…three of my people are both prosperous and generous and my needs are small."

They settled down for a serious discussion until it became time for Asr prayers after which Uthman took them around the corner to a kaf house. *It makes me think of home, even if it is crowded with the people of the Swamp.* They stayed at the kaf house until it was time for the Maghreb prayers after which the Mice returned to the inn.

While they were there Ayesha told Christopher what she had found out from Uthman. "There are at least as many Christians living in the area as there are Muslims…but they lack a priest." The three then went back to the mosque for the last prayers of the day at Isha.

By the time that Isha was finished they had met most of the Mullah's flock. *Several, indeed, all of the women except one with a baby on her hip and other young around her, are pretty girls, but they are all slaves from brothels.*

Uthman told several of his men that perhaps wives would be coming for them, but as for when, Inshallah. *The girls look disappointed at that news, but they make no complaint. They have known since they arrived what their lot was to be for at least several more years.*

Ayesha made sure she had a talk with Uthman about the slaves. *It turns out that one of his men is actually in love with one of the prostitutes and spends all of his spare money on buying her time. The others…even if the girls were free…they cannot return home and they will have to see what will happen. Allah, the Merciful will provide. Perhaps we can provide some aid to that.*

Ayesha took a long look at Atã and Tãriq. It was a meaningful look. The two men quickly took the hint that they had been given and were quick to offer their opinion on the subject and went directly to talk to the local men. *I thought it likely that the two had been well schooled by their wives on this subject.*

Ayesha thought about how much money they had with them and paid a quick visit first to see Theodora and then to two of the brothels with Stefan to bargain for her. *I may not have Shilpa with her skill to bargain for me, but at least Stefan has some of the right experience to draw on. At least he is a lot better at getting a good price than the daughter of a Sheik is.*

Ayesha

After the evening meal the story was told in the maqhaa, the kaf house, called the Fragrant Bean, rather than the inn. *A small, but important, audience has been invited to hear it here. The Reeve, Gowan, along with the chief druids and wiccans and mages are all here along with some other men and women who are prosperous looking, but it is hard to pin down just what they do.*

Maeve is not the only animal present and, indeed, is not even the only raccoon. It is important that we have set up here for the tale. Uthman has a valuable chance here to increase his prestige and act as the host and many of the Mice are scattered around the room to explain points and to serve as examples.

Uthman ibn Hakim

This may be my best chance that I will ever have to show my important connections and so aid my small flock in the village. The spare spaces are filled with the local Muslims, some of whom help with serving, including four of the five girls who, praise Allah, the Merciful, are still in shock over their newly purchased freedom.

When Ayesha takes breaks, they, along with some of the Mice, also provide music and dancing to keep the visitors occupied. The last girl, along with our blacksmith, is useless for anything except to sit in a corner where they pay attention to each other. I am unsure if they actually have heard more than occasional snatches of the tale. That man, at least, has needed no prompting from the Mice as to his fate.

It is hard for me to stop smiling. I even have a supply of money for the mahr, or bride price, of each girl, but except for the blacksmith, who only found out after he had made clear his intent, the men don't know that, and each will be sworn to secrecy when they find out. This ghazi does not seem to have a problem with the newly freed girls and nor do the two men with her who have married their ilk as, it seems, has their old Emperor.

It is a pity that the ghazi is not free, but should I make one of the girls an offer myself before they are all snatched up? They are all beautiful and all speak the local tongue. I know what my superiors would say, but should I ignore them and instead attach my fortunes to a more distant Darkreach than to my home?

If more Mullahs do arrive from Darkreach for the other villages then they will regard me as the senior Imam of the Swamp and perhaps it will be better, in the long run, to have a superior who is powerful, even if harder to contact, rather than one who is ignoring me even when they are only a few weeks journey away. It is a hard decision to make, but perhaps waiting will make things clear. Inshallah.

The position of Darkreach will be reinforced here if the Christians from there send some of their priests into the area along with the Imams. It seems that the Christians are destined to become my unlikely allies and, if what we have heard in the story is right, the Princess of these Mice is one of Hrothnog's get as well.

Astrid

To my relief Basil and I are almost completely free of Ia tonight. Theodora has monopolised her services. If the girl is coming with us, she has to prove herself and work. Tonight, it is her job to show her usefulness and to keep her distant second cousin supplied with kaf and happy to stay and listen to what is said.

From where I sit, I am pleased to see that most of Ia's time is spent doing this while trying to avoid his wandering hands. His nickname might be 'the Enchanting' but his distant cousin seems to be less than spellbound with his charms. Ia has ended up perched on a stool directly behind him where he can talk to her when it is needed, but he cannot reach her without getting out of his deep chair.

It was fairly early on in the night and the tale scarce begun that Astrid felt a tug on her trousers. Soon Maeve had climbed the couch to land in her lap and then to curl up and go to sleep as if she had a perfect right to do so.

Basil may be amused that I don't know how to react to that. I am not, but what can I do. We don't want her trodden on. The animal ended up staying there all night only waking to delicately take some food when she smelt some pass by, although she wrinkled her nose at kaf.

Basil only pointed out to me, now it is all over and we are returning to the inn, that by accepting the animal so willingly, I have also given a tacit acceptance of her owner. Astrid floundered for a reply for some time. She was about to give one when Ia started walking alongside them. *Suddenly it is already too late for me to retort that my acceptance, even if that is what it was, implies his acceptance of the situation as well.*

It was arranged that the general people of the town will all have a chance to hear the story on the next day. It will be told from where most announcements are made and all-important information spread..from the steps of the Marchnaty, the colonnaded building in the centre. It is the practice that they are accustomed to here and the place even has a town crier to make sure that only one story gets out to the people.

It seems that, over the years the Reeves have found that this helps to minimise rumours and makes it easier for them to rule. However, it has also been earlier deemed that the important people would be best told where they could be relaxed and comfortable in the kaf house and will be sure to hear it all and not at the same time as the common folk.

Ayesha

28th Primus

Early the next morning the crier went around the town telling the folk what was about to happen and, although it was Tetarti and so a workday, a fair-sized crowd quickly gathered.

There are enough people here to fill the square as folk take their ease, food vendors begin to gather, and runners from taverns take orders. Although I may not like doing it, I will use the loud talker from the Brotherhood today. I have to hold it a little distance away from my mouth so that I am not too loud but, without it, those at the rear of the crowd will soon grow restless.

With the curiosity about the saddles and attention I am now getting I soon have people appearing at windows and there are even a few sitting on roofs. With a few short breaks the story took nearly all day to tell and was only brought to a conclusion a few minutes before the afternoon rain started.

The nature of the tale held their attention and, over the day, rather that grow bored with me, the number of listeners even increased. It is interesting to see that they are more amused with some of the things we have done here than angry. As for some of the things we have done, I am not sure if they actually believe them all.

Christopher

I got to start the day differently to the others, but predictably. It is good to know that there are no patterns within range of my detection prayer. I have also found some of the lost Christians in the area. Most are slaves of one sort or another and are treated the same as any other. Only three are free. Two of them are poor farmers who are share-cropping and the third is a carter who only has a wheelbarrow.

All three received alms that would make life easier for them and were promised a priest at some time in their future, at least as a visitor. *Hearing what Ayesha did, I have sent Stefan back around the brothels and I now own the contracts of three of the girls from them. Now, what do I do with the girls until their final fate is worked out?*

From a lack of someone of the Orthodox faith to look after them they were given into Uthman's charge, until a priest could arrive. *He may have been surprised by this, but that is how they would do it in Darkreach. We need to be like there and act together on our principles, not apart as enemies when we all have the same goals in mind.*

Basil

I get to spend the day questioning the newly freed girls of both faiths about who captured them and how they arrived there. The three Christian girls show no obvious pattern. One came from Freehold and two from the villages along the south coast. From the timing it seems likely that all of them were captured to re-stock Mousehole and were just sold here once that was shown to be impossible.

The others were all brought down from the Caliphate. Before I started, I didn't think that the questioning would give us anything useful, but it is something that I do all of the time out of habit. I ask questions and then later write down everything in my tiny script in the rarely used tribal tongue of Insakharl in the small book that I carry with me at all times.

It is one of things that you do as a part of the Antikataskopeía…gather as much information as you can in the hope that one day one tiny piece will fall into place with another and that the two will then lead you to something much bigger. I wonder if this time one tiny piece may have just done that.

The Caliphate girls have all reported being taken from different places, with most having been bought openly, and only one of the girls having been taken from her home outside Dimashq by force. However, once they were in the hands of a trader, they have all passed through the small and fairly new village of Ta'if.

Although for the rest of the trip they were treated well, while they were there, they all reported having been inspected, and indeed used brutally, by a strange young man who seemed to enjoy the pain that he gave to them and the terror he made them feel. He did it without actually marking any of them permanently. He gave each of them, before he took them, to understand that he had the right to kill them outright if he wished.

That had made their terror worse as, in order to stay alive, they had to accede to all that he did to them for the whole night and it had been a whole night of pain and terror that left them all weak, drained, and unable to walk the next day. What made him strangest and most memorable to the girls was that his eyes were golden, and he had a deep and terrifying voice.

Basil smiled to himself remembering what little his wife had said about her visit to Hrothnog. *If you add that to what I just heard and to Dobun reporting a place of resistance in the Caliphate that he had been unable to pin down, then it is just possible that we have located one of the Adversaries.*

I will wait until we are back in the valley before letting the Princess know what I think, although I will leave out the part about Hrothnog and, of course, about the golden eyes. I will share that with my wife, but no-one else needs to hear that at this stage.

It does fit well with everything else that we have found out and it explains why there is no Pattern listed in the Caliphate. One of the Adversaries could have been based there all along. From there one of them could even easily and quickly send a messenger down into the Swamp with any instructions he had if he wished, or even into Darkreach itself. After all, it is likely that he has access to a carpet.

Chapter IV

Theodora

29th Primus, the Feast Day of Saint Gildas

The next morning they left Bloomact and flew west and on to Squamawr. *This village sits on the eastern side of a river and like all of the other villages that are not isolated on islands, it has a tall fence made of whole trees that are set into an earthen rampart. Some of these uprights are not even logs. They are real trees, alive and growing. It looks like every fourth pole seems to be alive and an anchor to the rest. New ones are even growing up between them.*

In Squamawr's case the fence is incomplete with the river side only having a tall timber-faced levee which seems to be of more use for controlling a flood than stopping a rampaging herd. When asked, Adara pointed down. "The river is both deep and fairly wide above and below the ford. See, there is the ford below the village and there is nothing placed near it. You can see the trails leading to it. You can see that not just people use it."

As well as the usual stone circles and shrine, that looks like a mine could be seen a longish walk away on the east side of the river. "Cinnabar," said Adara.

The entry to the village was, unusually, at one of the corners of the palisade where two of the great fences didn't quite meet but each ended in a great wooden tower built around the final tree of the fences. Platforms rose up the trees and ladders connected them. Light structures and rope bridges even bridged the gap between them. Each of these towers supported a massive wooden gate.

The Reeve here is Conaire ap Molloy and it seems that he, as the village next closest to Haven after Dolbarden, has some paid troops, not just the usual village levy, at his disposal. Just like those at the other armed village,

I am told that these men and women seem to regard their tenure here as an opportunity to get rich at their neighbours' expense.

It is, apparently, a more limited opportunity to raid Haven from here though, as the trip is both longer and through terrain that is harder to travel quickly through to escape pursuit, but it is still an opportunity, and one they enjoy, although they are careful not to raid too hard or destroy too much when they do so.

It turns out that the garrison here was nearly unanimous in opposing war. As well as being well placed to raid, they would be the settlement that is most vulnerable to any retaliation. The city of Sacred Gate, and the large army that is there, lie only a bit over a week of hard travel away to the west and this village has only a fordable river and their levee and wooden wall as a defence and only a few mages to help them.

It seems that there is no Pattern here either, but there are a lot of slaves, mostly Havenite, but some are Christian and brought from the south coast or else born here. Most of the slaves seem to be used in the boring but easy work of cultivating silkworms. Many possibly even have a better life here than when they had been free.

According to Astrid even the girls in the brothel seemed quite unconcerned about their fate. Their owner treats them very well and even allows them to keep their tips. It seems that they will most likely be fairly wealthy women from what they take from the garrison when they finally gain their freedom.

The tale that night was told to an audience who were relieved to find out why people had been acting so strangely and imperilling their livelihood.

I am now much more attuned to my husband's prejudice and am fully disgusted with the locals, although I cannot say it. All that the hard work, risk and sacrifice of we Mice means here is that the unruly residents are now able to go on with their life of theft and low-level raids without interference from an actual war or impinging armies.

It is obvious that they don't care at all about the wider implications or even about the larger struggle that people are dying for. It seems to be the case that they are not likely to ever stop their exploitation of their wealthier neighbour either through trade to the city along the coast or by raiding its outlying areas.

Chapter V

Astrid

31st Primus

There was little to delay us at Squamawr, or to induce us to stay any longer. They flew east and north to Flyjudge, near the head of Iba Bay. *There is no doubt that we can land here to trade. The village may not be visible from out on the sea, but that is only because the island that it is on is so large and the trees hide it from view.*

It stood well offshore and the village faced the land, or at any rate it faced the mouths of several streams that emptied into Iba Bay at this point. Two short wharves were on the landward side, and a few river boats similar to those used on the Rhastaputra, or those that she had seen at Bloomact, were docked at them.

I was not able to get anyone at Bloomact to talk about the possibility of navigation down to the delta, or even to acknowledge that it happens, but from the look of these craft, I need ask no more. It is unlikely though that any of the locals will be willing to part with their navigation secrets. The River Dragon *might be able to make it up the river, but the locals are not likely to want such a large competitor doing the run.*

The wharves flanked a beach where outriggers and dug-out canoes were drawn up on the sand. A large stone circle with long two-stage arms lay behind the village and Ia indicated where the grove was near the coastal shore.

Except for the grove and the trees along the shore and mangroves that run from them out to sea, most of the land of the island is cleared as are many large and small islands that we saw inland among the branches of the delta. It is very obvious that this area grows cotton, and lots of it. It seems that most of the slaves brought into the Swamp end up here.

As they came lower the village looked more like Freeport on Gil-Gand-

Rask than any other part of the Swamp. *Even the houses are unusual. They are quite different to all of the houses that we have seen so far on this trip with thatched roofs and broad veranda roofs on top of what have to be whitewashed wattle and daub walls.*

The Mice had come in low over the water to see an excited military preparing to defend the village as people rushed around in confusion. *What a disorganised mob of idiots.* During their stay they were never able to find out who the village expected attack from…or rather everyone had a different opinion on who would be the ones to attack them.

Ia pulled some wands out that could be kept concealed and volunteered to go to meet them while the rest stayed out of range. *Both Adara and Bryony are more than happy to let her take the risk, so we can let her be useful.* Astrid waved Verily and her passenger on. In the end her wands, whatever they did, were not needed and she soon waved the rest in to see Niam verch Firlan, the Reeve.

Nothing here has two storeys and the windows also have the screens of gauze that were typical at Bloomact. Now we are here it is obvious that the name of the village comes from the swarms of stinging flies that only go away with the setting of the sun to be replaced by other insects. If anyone forgot to rub the Dadanth cream on their exposed skin, to keep the insects at bay, they will soon remember.

That night, after the rain, the tale was told from the veranda of the large wooden hall of the Cotton Producer's Guild with the audience sitting on the grass in front. *Flyjudge is so out of touch with the rest of the Swamp that they have only heard sure news about the possibility of war a month ago. Rumours of its failure have also arrived, but no news that is regarded as certain.*

Unless they suffer a raid from the sea the only concern that they have here is as to whether a war will disrupt their sales of cotton. As long as they are left to their farming the people of this village, free and slave alike, are more than happy to completely ignore the rest of the world and its concerns as being of no importance to them.

Christopher

I am able to attend to many of the flock here as, of all the areas that we have been to, this one proves to have the most Christians. Almost all are slaves, although apparently there are a few families made up of freed former slaves living on the mainland although no-one knows exactly where. They just grow cotton and bring it in on punts to sell.

Regardless of the difficulty, it now seems that Cosmas is going to have to find priests from somewhere. By now it is obvious that at least five are needed to attend to the needs of the Swamp. Even that number assumes that only one is sent to each village and more than that will be needed here. What was more, we still have another two villages to pay a visit to.

Chapter VI

Astrid

32nd Primus

The next day the Mice flew east and north over the pellucid expanse of Iba Bay.

The volcano is making a few comments into the air from our steerboard front. Even if I was not able to get a clear answer from anyone about the access to Bloomact, at least I have its name...or one of its names...for Olympias' map. What anyone else calls it I still don't know. It is now written in Basil's book, including how it is pronounced.

I hope that they have an easier name to call it in the Caliphate so that we can use that instead. Here it is called something like Llosyfyndd yr Aderyndân and every time that I try to say it, the locals smile broadly at my lack of skill with their language. It is not even just my clumsiness with their words, the people here in the south seem to have a different way of saying it to the way that Bryony and Adara say it, although they all insist that it is spelt the same.

The Mice were seen some distance away and, when it became apparent that they were headed for the bridge a single person could be seen running to try and cross it before they arrived. In the end they had to wait for him. When he arrived, he gaspingly introduced himself as Saccius ap Nemglan. *It seems that he is quite disappointed that we have nothing with us that is intended for trade and that he can tax.*

It appears that he is, all at the same time, the Reeve's armsman, the local tax collector and even the bridge repairer, street sweeper, the town crier, and indeed the only staff for the Reeve, Samthann ap Dufgal. All of this I find out from him as he cheerfully leads us over the bridge into the village. Well, he crosses it and I fly beside him. I don't want to set foot on such a flimsy thing. It is also so close to the water that no large craft would pass under it and even a person in a canoe would have to duck if they went underneath on a high tide.

Rainjig is the smallest village that we have been to. It only has a few hundred people living there and in the area around it. Despite not being the furthest south of the villages of the Swamp, it has the distinction of being both the hottest and yet also the driest. Here it seems that rain is unusual. I am now told that the clouds that cover the rest of the Swamp seem to avoid this area. The mountains behind the village drive the clouds away. I am sure he will have to draw breath at some stage. She looked around as she listened.

Like Flyjudge the village is on an island, but there the resemblance ends. For a start it has only one river emptying near it. As well the sea breaks some distance from the island. It seems to have a reef, like those at Gil-Gand-Rask, which covers most of its seaward side. An arriving ship will have to sail up towards the river and nearly reach the shore before it can turn into safety behind the reef through a narrow passage.

In addition, instead of cleared areas covered in fields, most of the land around here is made up of low-lying and swampy marsh. This contains a series of lakes each of which are surrounded by the white fringes of drying salt. Some of these lakes have shelters beside them and tracks lead there, often over bridges. From what Saccius says, each month, at the highest tide, these shallow lakes flood and they then spend the next month drying out.

Drying and packing salt is the main industry that is practised here, although I can see several people in outriggers throwing nets around them and there are a number of fish traps very visible in the river and along the coast.

The Mice found out that the locals collected the poorer quality salt from the margins of those lakes and made the better-quality product in metal pans beside them. Once the brackish water was put in the pans, they were slowly heated by magic to drive out the remaining water.

From what I saw from the air its Druidic shrine is, apart from the circle itself, only just begun and the grove, unlike all the others so far, lacks the long groomed and well-tended look that the ones we have seen so far seem to usually have. Only one druid and one Wiccan priestess tend these. Along with the mage who doubles as the Reeve, they are the entire spiritual and magical complement of the island.

Theodora

It seems that, on its far coast this village, they call it Glawdans, is very isolated. A couple of times a year a caravan makes its way down from the Caliphate to buy barrels of salt and a couple of times a month, when the sea was calm, their one merchant loads his outrigger canoe with as much salt as it can carry, carrying it in the fine barrels that are made here to keep it dry from sea and rain, and he sails across Iba Bay to Flyjudge before loading up with what he can find there and then coming back.

The salt gradually makes its way from there out to the rest of The Land, even being sometimes seen in the far north. Occasionally another boat will call in, sometimes even from Haven, and will be able to unload almost anything that they have on board onto the villagers, and that is all the contact that they have with the rest of The Land.

It must be hard for Samthann the Reeve to run a village with so little. "If you don't object, we will pass the word to Southpoint in Darkreach. It is just around the end of the mountains. Surely that place, just as isolated as you are, will be able to send one of its fishing boats around here at least once or twice a year. One place has salt and the other has sugar and lots of foods. It would have to be worth it for both of you."

If whoever makes the trip were to toss in a trip to Gil-Gand-Rask, then someone who has a sea-worthy and capacious boat could make a very good living setting up a nice triangular trade, once they work out who needs what.

Astrid

After a small, light and rare afternoon shower, the people of the village began to gather. *They see so few people as visitors here that the visit is accepted by everyone in the area as an occasion to down their tools and have a party. It also seems that they greatly approve of parties here to break the boredom of their isolation.*

The few people that live in assarts have, apparently, been told by messengers or by the sound of a large drum that was beaten on our arrival in an odd rhythm. They are even now starting to arrive and greet each other. Most are coming in canoes and outriggers from the coast or the river, but some ride ponies or walk.

Astrid stood and watched one group come across the bridge. *Somehow neither the pony nor the protesting young bull that they are leading has put their foot through the planking or fallen off.* She felt someone beside her and went to take the offered hand until she realised that it was Ia, and not Basil who stood there. Abruptly she blushed and dropped the hand before quickly turning and striding back towards the buildings.

Christopher

I wondered about that. It turns out that the bull, like everything else on this island seems to do, has two duties. In the first case it is a sacrifice for the Druid, who has promptly taken it away with some worshippers and quickly dispatched it in thanksgiving for our arrival. They then came back with the dead beast in parts and its second role became apparent; it will be the meat for the village tonight.

There may be quite a few passages about that practice, but we may need to ignore them for the while. Paying too much attention to them will, most likely, be seen as a grave insult by our hosts and they seem to be nice people from what my broken Hindi lets me understand. After all, it was not sacrificed by us to strange Gods.

The carcase was quickly prepared for its second role as others put fish wrapped in leaves into a pit that was full of hot rocks. While this was done laughing children climbed trees to bring down coconuts and other fruit.

Astrid

I can see that Ia may be talking to the island's priestess but I am still making sure of whose hand I am holding as I look up at the mountains outlined in the Eastern sky. I have Basil's hand firmly clasped in my own and I am sure of that. I want Saccius, in a brief time when he is not organising the food, pointing out what can be seen.

The great peak that lies almost north of us is Snowcap, the mightiest peak of the southern range and, with a lack of imagination on the part of whoever had given it a name; the river that is nearly in front of us is the Snowcap Rivulet. It stops being navigable to anything that is not a canoe almost as soon as it leaves the shore behind, even though it carries a lot of water from the melting snow through its shifting stony banks.

The peak of Snowcap is always white; never losing its snow, even when the area shakes from the many small tremors of the ground that afflict it. That white top is how it gained its name and a small glacier can even be seen coming down from the tall peak. The rivulet winds its way up the mountain to start at that river of ice. It is a steep run. One waterfall can even be seen from the village. There are sure to be more.

Apparently to the left and north of the mountain lay the village of Yarmũk and the ghazi base of Misr al-Mār. The road passes behind the peak and then to the right is the new village of Bab al-Abwãb. The mountain directly east of us is called Giant's Drop and then there is the mountain of fire that I cannot pronounce.

Behind it, from here, lies Dimashq on the shores of its mountain lake. Going north from Snowcap lie a long range of near identical lesser peaks which trail away into the distance. The very tips of each bear a small white wreath of snow. Together those peaks are called The Wall, and Saccius may know all of their names, but the long list he recited has disappeared from my head almost as soon as I am told.

On the other side of that, in a valley where the Buccleah starts, lies the new village of Ta'if. Finally, well beyond that, is the village that is the furthest north of all of the Caliphate, Yãqũsa where, presumably, Ayesha's father still rules. Just below the end of the wall in the Swamp lies Eastguard, where we will be going to next.

Christopher

The local priestess is in a deep conversation with young Ia well away from the rest of the village. Their two familiars are looking at each other cautiously as the two women sit and talk, they seem to have decided to co-operate to intensely discourage any others from coming near their mistresses. They seem to be a lot more intelligent than a normal animal.

The local woman has as a companion an odd boxy-looking quadruped, black and covered with white spots and with very strong looking jaws. She called it a Devil-beast. It keeps making odd rumbly-growling noises at the raccoon, which sits in front of it and chatters back at it. These two growl and chatter at each other for quite some time. It is almost as if each knows what the other is saying and makes proper reply.

Now the women are finished talking and Ia has headed off somewhere. I can get to work with the local Priestess and the Druid and look for a local Pattern. It seems that my two supposed spiritual rivals are very keen to ask me about what I am doing and why.

As I expected, with such an isolated place and with no writing even remotely pointing this way, there is nothing in evidence. Now to get on to my other task...

...and there are no known Christians in the area, which explains some of the interest of the priest and priestess as they have never met a Christian priest before and my rituals are so different to theirs. What is more there are so few people here that Caractacus ap Comyn, the druid, and Dianan verch Erin, the Wiccan priestess who is apparently his sister, know every one of them by their name and genealogy.

I am coming to understand the way that names are put together in the Swamp now. Apparently, unless they have an epithet due to some characteristic or their trade, it is usual for the men's names to say whose son they are, while the women's names usually tell who their mother is. It is rare for it to be the other way around, but it does happen.

Ayesha

It seems that there are a few people of the Faith here, but only a very few; one small family of freed slaves and two men who will stay in that condition for several years. Our Christian priest has let me know and I have them join in prayers with me and the other two Mice. It is a pity that I cannot promise them a Mullah of their own.

"I will try and get one to visit you occasionally." In the meantime, she pointed out that they could do their prayers themselves and told them what she had learnt from Imam Iyãd about how isolated groups conduct themselves.

The locals are even more interested in seeing the Hesperinos service and are surprised that anyone is welcome to attend it. To them most of their services and ceremonies are secret with only the initiated among them being allowed to even watch what happens. The fact that we allow Maghreb to segue into a Christian service surprises them even more.

Theodora

Around the main square of the village the trees have strings draped through and between them. From each string small stones are hanging, each in a basket of their own string. I did wonder, but their purpose is apparent when night falls and the Reeve activates them so that a glow spreads around the whole village. He is still a young man and apologises for what he has done:

"I am afraid," said Sammthan, "that they are only as strong as I can make them. As well, my realm is of water. That is why I have had to have so many of them shedding their lesser light. One day I will be able to make stronger ones, but that time is quite some way off."

I speak only half out of politeness. Many villages have far less than this. We should think of something similar, something not too bright. "The glow which leaves things only half revealed adds to the ambience instead of bringing out the harsh brightness of day," she said diplomatically. They settled down to enjoy the food. *Although it is obvious that there are no professional cooks here the simple food is good and tasty. The fish is excellent. I miss fish at home. We have it too little.*

As Ayesha told the tale to a rapt audience, who were sitting around on woven mats in the warm night, Theodora's mind wandered from the familiar tale.

It is only six days since we left Rising Mud. Is that allowing enough time for word to reach Eastguard Tower of what we did in that village, and who we killed and why? If we go straight there tomorrow it is still quite likely that most of the residents will not yet have heard the facts, or even the rumours.

She was roodling and staring into the fire when it came to her. *The people here seem to be nice people. Certainly, they are the nicest that I have met yet in this horrible Swamp place. Even Christopher has noted to me that they lack the feel of other villagers here. There is no-one who is a career criminal or a raider. As well, Southpoint lies far nearer to this village than Eastguard does.*

I can send Astrid and Basil there to tell Basil's parents about this village and let them know that trade is welcome. They will then have to stay the night and that will add two days before we have to leave on our next leg. That also means that I can have Ayesha and Hulagu take people up to the mountains to try and quietly have a look down at the Caliphate.

I heard that funny man, the one who it seems does everything that needs doing, talking to Astrid earlier. If we keep low, from Snowcap, and with the telescope, we can possibly spy out most of the Caliphate to add to what we know for when we have to go there. That is not far off. I can go up there as the mage and so see for myself what lies ahead for us.

That leaves Astrid and Basil. They can take the witch-child with them on Basil's saddle. She may be young but she has more power in casting than anyone else we have here. I am not sure what is happening between the three. Astrid seems to be out of sorts about something, even if they do seem to stay close, but I like the girl anyway.

When I took her aside and asked her about her magic, I discovered that she has thought of how to make Air-magic, apart from just bolts, that is useful in battle. Those wands I didn't pick up, although there are only three, are very powerful in their own way. They will cause a group of people to panic. The girl is unfortunately not strong enough yet to make wands that she can recharge, but we will work on that when we get her home.

The witch-child has also shown me the tattoo on her stomach…another interesting innovation…and it is kept charged. That could be a problem if she is hurt there in a battle, but otherwise it makes her casting so much easier. That would be what she showed to Astrid and Basil in the alley, although why the girl did that I have not asked.

The rest of the Mice can have a day off. I have heard a few complaints from those who are not normally used to being cavalry about some stiffness from being in the saddle as much as they have been for the last few weeks. A day swimming in the warm waters of the lagoon or talking to the villagers here will be a nice break for us all. I am tempted to stay here myself, but I have to do my duty and see the lie of the land that we will have to go to soon…

During a break in the story, while Verily was playing a new harp she bought at Bloomact, she went to tell the others. *The witch-child says that she already knew that she would be going*. "I saw it in my ball", she said. *Astrid does not seem pleased, although she flashed a brief grin at her husband when she was told of the travel arrangements.*

Hulagu wants to take the entire air group with us. "There has been very little chance to exercise them as an ergüül, a patrol, on this trip and I want to take this opportunity."

Theodora thought for a moment. "Yes, that was a good idea."

Ayesha wanted to cry off from the trip. "I want to spend more time with the local apothecary and the midwife. You should not need me to point anything out. There are so few settlements that it should be obvious." Theodora over-ruled her by playing on her sense of duty.

Theodora pointed out that Basil would be heading to Darkreach and left it dangling as to who would look after her. Ayesha took the point. "We will go for just one day," she grudgingly admitted. "That will still give me a day with the others."

That night most of the Mice slept on a veranda.

Except for those who come here on ships the island has never had this many visitors before and they do not have anywhere to put all of the extra people. Luckily it is a warm night and we have a supply of the Dadanth ointment to keep the insects at bay. There are so many biting bugs in the area that the next major watercourse to the south is even called Fosgitoscilfach which means Mosquito Creek in their tongue…and apparently with a lot of justification.

Chapter VII

Theodora

33rd Primus

After Orthros, the two parties set off. *In case there were any Caliphate carpets about the flanks of the mountains Hulagu is keeping his party low as we follow the rivulet up into the mountains. Every now and then we stop and use the detection device taken from Skrice and the telescope, but nothing is to be seen in the sky above us.*

Despite the speed of the saddles in open flight it takes us as long to get to the real base of the mountain as it did to travel to the village from Flyjudge. As the land began to rise, we flew into a thick and tangled forest. It looks as if it has never seen a person passing through it and, from what we can see, there are few tracks for anything else of any size. None of the giant lizards can have come into the bush here. It is far too thick for them. Surely there is a market for this timber.

Even though we are following the course of the rivulet, we have to travel above the trees as the vegetation meets over the watercourse in the middle of the stream and forms a low green tunnel for the runnel to pass through. This belt of trees is only a few miles wide though and, as the land rises further, most the trees begin to lose their height, although even on the steep slopes some of the giant eucalypts and myrtle beeches that we have at home still grow.

Eventually we enter the domain of the smaller deciduous Fagus and then, as the stream comes down a series of small but spectacular waterfalls in leaps and bounds, the alpine vegetation takes over. We still cannot pick anything up of interest when we stop even though a sliver of Buhairet Tabariyya, the lake that Dimashq is built on, is now visible over the ridge that leads south from Snowcap. We are travelling up a valley and, from what I saw from below, should soon reach the bottom of the glacier.

When they reached the glacier, they travelled to one side, keeping the blackness of rock as a background behind them. *If we move up over the glacier and anyone happens to train a telescope on that feature we will stand out as a series of dark dots on the whiteness. For the same reason we stay below the snowline, once we reach it. We allow the bulk of the peak of the mountain to soar far into the sky above us.*

Cautiously we circle around as we fly, staying almost at ground level until we have a good view of the south of the Caliphate and even, in the far distance, a hint of the Tãb Rũdh that flows from Yarmũk down past Rebelkill in Darkreach to enter the sea as the Garthcurr River at that town. It is indeed an imposing view that we have from these chill heights. I see that we should have brought the warm cloaks with us.

Almost directly below us the new village of Bab al-Abwâb can be seen and it seems to earn its name, 'Gate of Gates'. It sits astride the ridge that divides the broad flat valley of the Tãb Rũdh from the far higher mountain valley of the Buhairet Tabariyya. Near us to the south is one stream that you can follow with your eye. It starts near us in the snow and flows until you can see where it ends at the lake.

Just to the north and left of us another can be traced down, although I lose sight of it in a few places. It will end up in Tãb Rũdh and thus travel into Darkreach. Bab al-Abwâb dominates the ridge between the two watersheds and, once its walls are completely rebuilt, even though Ayesha says they are mainly made of fired brick, it will be easily possible to deny anyone transit over the ridge on the ground.

There is only one way up to the ridge and only one way down the other side of it and the village sits square in the middle of this pass with a stiff climb to approach it from either side. At present, using the telescope it clearly only has one wall, one that faces north, and a population that will only be as large as that of Rainjig. It is, however, clearly not isolated. Caravans can be seen on the roads that wind down from it leading both to the north and the south.

There are only a few small fields clinging to terraces on the slopes around it and grain would have to be brought in, but several flocks of goats or sheep, perhaps tended by children are visible on the nearby hillsides and the few small shelves of land that are there show where people are trying to scratch out a living with at least a few plants in the cold of the mountains.

There is a quarry for stone that is visible just off the pass to the east and another site much further up the opposite ridge and around a narrow mountain path that Ayesha says is a mine for the crystal that is used in balls and for jewellery throughout The Land. At least it all only has to go downhill from here.

When I turn to the right the huge fertile plain of the Rãhit that surrounds Dimashq is laid out below me. There are several towns to be seen. It is covered in square fields marked by stone walls and palms and other plants and it is dotted with hamlets and farms. All around the plain on the slopes are more villages. I can see straight lines of greenery running across it. Ayesha says that they mark what she calls qanats that bring water underground.

Before The Burning their lands may have extended much further, but it is obvious that in this valley lies the real strength of the Caliphate. It is why little Bab al-Abwâb that lies below us is so important to them. As long as they hold this area, even if they lose all of the rest of their land, they can rebuild.

On the lake small boats can be seen moving around. Some are fishing. I think that I can see nets, while others apparently bring produce across it to Dimashq from the settlements clustered around the edge. "It is often easier to use a boat than to bring it around by land," said Ayesha. "Dimashq even has two gates on the water...one for the traders and produce and one just for the fishermen."

The city sits on a flat mount in the lake with a short peninsula connecting it to the shore. Even though the city is a very long way away the telescope lets me clearly see the minarets of the mosques. "We have six. The Mosque of Sulieman is the most important and the most holy. It is the one in the centre and is a part of the Alhambra...the palace."

"What are they?" asked Dobun suddenly, pointing away from Dimashq towards Giants Drop. *In the distant sky I can see several large flyers. They must be very large to be seen from here.*

"They are a type of dragon," replied Ayesha. "We know little of them. They are much smaller than the one that we killed and do not live near as long. However, we do not bother them and they rarely bother us. Sometimes they come into the Caliphate and eat a cow or two, but only if it is a hard winter. Mostly they graze on the beasts of the Swamp. If you ask the people of Rainjig they could probably tell you more."

When everyone had seen all they wanted they moved on around the mountain, again staying low and slow as they headed north under the snowline. *Soon we are looking north-west along the line of peaks that are The Wall. Now, below us, but a little further away than the village was, lies the fortress and temple complex of Misr al-Mãr on its plateau. Here is the place where Ayesha trained. The village of Yarmũk is invisible from here, hidden as it must be by the far edge of the plateau.*

More of the huge flat valley of the Tãb Rũdh can now be seen. Only the just finished conflict between Darkreach and the Caliphate has stopped this place from filling up with people. It is, however, not a safe valley like that of the Rãhit. It is far larger and its broad mouth allows easy transit to armies and to raiders coming from each direction.

It was only a bit over thirty years ago that Darkreach broke a major push out into its lands by the Caliphate. I remember it well. Granther nearly lost a whole army in the last battle of that war, but somehow the tables were turned. When I lived in the Palace, I admit to not listening to those sorts of events all that well.

Hulagu pointed out something tiny that was moving quickly. *Well below us a carpet moves through the sky. It stays fairly low to keep in the warm air.* They watched it for a while. *More caravans can be seen moving along the floor of the valley as tiny specks. Along the route the caravans are taking stand a few isolated buildings. Some have patches of cultivation around them as tiny flecks of green.*

"They are caravanserai for travellers," said Ayesha. "One day some may become villages, but now they are simply places to spend the night. Although it is still thought of as being perhaps a little risky, setting up such a place is also regarded as being a way to ensure a chance of wealth for your children's children. It is not an easy way, but it one of the best that a person without much in the way of prospects may do."

"Inshallah then all they need to make a start at it are some supplies and tools and a few goats and a willingness to go hungry for a few years while they build a place that others will stop at. I believe, from something that my father said, that it is becoming popular now while there is hudna, truce, in al-jihad al-Akbar, the Great Struggle." *So, it is only a truce, even if it lasts a century or more. That is interesting in itself.*

Several peaks stand in the middle of the valley and a long ridge marks it from the valley of the Ziyanda Rũdh which runs the other way past Ta'if and becomes the Buccleah River. Snowcap is so tall that, from where we are it is possible to even see, to the north and north-east, the start of the vast flatness of the Beneen Plain and possibly even Garthcurr. It is tall enough that I am finding it harder to breathe.

I wonder why, given the view that we have from here, the Caliphate does not have the equivalent of Forest Watch in place here to keep tabs on all that happens. With the telescopes that Forest Watch has, and some magical support, they could see any invasion long before it even enters the valley. Even the Khitan would take two days of hard riding to reach the road that climbs to Bab al-Abwâb from the valley mouth.

Ayesha doesn't know the answer to that question and has never heard, in the past, that it has ever been used for such a role. They have always used the carpets to fly over the land and to spy out what is happening. Maybe it took having the saddles available to change the way that you view the world. At the very least, the Caliphate has grown complacent in their mountains.

Flying carpets are rare and magically difficult to make and their mages have a near monopoly on them due to the skill of their people at making ones that are long-lasting and durable. Once the saddles become well known and their implications have sunk in, I am sure that a watch will be placed up here.

Eventually everyone had looked their fill and they continued travelling slowly around the bulk of Snowcap until the Mice returned to where they had started at the valley of the glacier and they went down again to Rainjig. They went faster this time, returning to the little settlement well before the light faded.

Chapter VIII

Astrid

33rd Primus

Unfortunately, the only way for us to travel will be with Ia mounted behind Basil and tied down there with her arms around him and her hands free to stray. We worked out how to deal with this. Basil mounted and, once Ia took her place, and before she could object, he took Maeve and put her in front of him.

It actually is the only place the raccoon can ride safely for such a long way. It also serves a second purpose of giving no place for wandering hands to go. Maeve made a noise and tried to go elsewhere, but Astrid had quickly tied her down with the fastenings below and out of her reach.

"Do not try and undo those." *I feel silly talking to an animal like this, but Maeve is feeling at a strap and I want to stop that. Parminder seems to be able to communicate with her animals; perhaps Maeve is reading me the same way.* "If you do you will fall off and die and I am sure that Ia will not want that." She turned and looked at the girl. "Do you? And you won't do anything that is likely to let her fall, such as distract the person who is doing the flying, will you?"

"I will be good," said Ia. *That was almost meek.* She continued with a more determined look on her face. "I have seen what I have seen and while all of the things I saw are not definite in any way and the path itself is still unclear, I know that I have to stay with you both. So…yes…I will…behave as you wish. There will be time later."

The other Mice have left and are now headed up the rivulet. Now it is our turn. Keeping fairly fast and low we head south-east along the shore. Already ahead of us I can see a hint of the top of distant Tor Karoso on Gil-Gand-Rask peering above the horizon.

We pass the watercourse called Fosgitoscilfach. We were warned not to stop there under any circumstances. Not only are there many of the mosquitoes it is named after living there, but the area also has a very bad reputation for diseases. The locals rarely come here and think that the creek and the dense foliage that surrounds it form their main defence against any invasion from Darkreach by land.

Basil

Ia's hands may not be wandering, but she is making sure that she sits close enough that I can feel her breasts pressing close. To add to my discomfort, I spend time worrying if this raccoon will have an accident where it is. At least it is not trying to get loose now. Astrid called out something and Basil slowed to hear it. *She is pointing left.* "What are those?" she asked.

"Dragons," said Ia. "You should know…I thought that you had killed one of them?" *That is what they think a dragon is?*

Astrid and Basil both laughed loudly. "Not little tiny things like those," continued Astrid. "Even the biggest of them is scarce bigger than the *River Dragon*…our ship. These are only an overgrown naked leather-wing with a horse's head. The one we killed was many, many, times that size. It was at least two hands times larger. Besides, those are all different colours. There is a gold one and that one is darker…almost bronze and that is brown and those are blue and green."

"Those, or the solitary red ones that sometimes are seen that are the same size, are what we mean by dragons. Only the red ones, we call them Cymry for some reason, breathe fire. I suppose that everyone has assumed the same as I, that you have exaggerated the size of the one you killed to make what you did sound more heroic."

"Then we must tell them otherwise," concluded Astrid. "The head of the one we killed was longer than the largest of those beasts. You will see its skeleton when we return to Mousehole."

From her muttering behind me Ia does not seem to know whether to be dubious or impressed. I do have to admit that I had difficulty believing any animal could be that large until he flew over us when we were on the way to Dwarvenholme.

They continued past the volcano and the watercourse that flowed from its flanks. *According to what we were told it is called Quiethaven. It enters the sea in that small bay and can provide shelter from storms if a boat is driven well off course. It is the only real shelter that can be found on this coast.*

They next came to a pair of mountains. *Ia has no name for them and we are beyond where she has ever been to before. As we pass them a valley is revealed. It runs behind the three peaks that Olympias used to navigate by.*

"I have not been here, but I know that these are usually called the Three Sisters, but there is a story about them that uses different names," said Ia. "Those who call them sisters call them the East, West and Middle Sister, but the Wiccan story calls them the Crone, the Mother and the Maid. One day I may tell you the tale. Southpoint is supposed to lie at the other end of this valley."

Basil and Astrid looked at each other. "It will cut an hour off the trip," Basil said.

Astrid nodded, "Let's," she said and peeled left. *We are flying over a lush valley of dense jungle with the Sisters towering over one side and the unnamed pair on the other. Once again, we are out of the swamps and into forest. The trees grow higher and the lizards grow to match them. This unseen world is more like the north of the Swamp than the area around Rainjig.*

Soon, ahead of us, I can see the three smaller mountains that lie behind Southpoint and that Demaresque Creek springs from. It is a sight of my home that I have never seen before. The ridge on their left disappeared and was replaced by a last projection of the Southern Mountains. It did not take long at their highest speed for the Sisters to give way to the last peak before Southpoint.

"I have never seen it before, but that must be the peak called The Tempter," said Ia.

Basil gave a start. "That is what we called it as well." *That is odd, that we both have the same name for it. There must be a story about that, but who would know it now?* Ahead Southpoint was now in view and Basil pointed at it.

"That is where I grew up. I have never before seen it like this. We will be late for lunch, but the crabs will make it worthwhile. I wish my sister hadn't told me about Gundardasc trailing them behind the Dragon in a box to keep them fresh and alive until they reached Ardlark. I have been hungering for a taste of them ever since."

When they reached the village, they stayed high, well out of bowshot and then, moving out a bit they gradually circled down to where people waited. *Ia is already undoing her straps while we are landing. She is impatient. She immediately springs off the saddle and moves towards mother as soon as we touch down.*

"Greetings mother," she said in Arabic. *Mother looks surprised. It was accented, but clear. I suppose that she has had no chance to learn Darkspeech, but it is obvious that she is not from the Caliphate.* "I cannot talk now, but I urgently need a place to…" she waved a hand vaguely. *I suppose that I should untie Maeve…too late.*

Anna pointed towards a building. "The customs house, ask there," she said. *She has a bemused expression on her face.* As Ia ran off, she turned to Basil and Astrid and then noticed the small animal that had climbed down and had also sought a place to relieve itself. "Who is that girl," she said, "and why did she call me mother?"

Basil sighed. "You will have to ask her for the answer to the second, but she is a Wiccan priestess who is now travelling with us. It is all my wife's fault. If she had just had the patience to wait for another couple of weeks to kill someone, we would not have her with us."

Mother is looking at me with a look that I have not seen for a long time. "Is that supposed to be a real answer? Why are you here with just the three of you? What are these things?" She points at the saddles. *That is right. We did not bring them out last time we were here.* "And do I have more grandchildren as yet unseen?" *She concludes in a complete non-sequitur that, I am sure, would make sense only to mothers.*

"It can all wait until we have eaten. We left Rainjig early this morning and have only had a nibble as we flew and I need crabs and lots of them."

"I need something else as well," said Astrid suddenly as she headed off to the Customs building. "But it has been a long trip and we will explain all… Oh…her name is Ia and despite anything that she may say nothing is fixed and we differ from her in our opinion." She headed off, leaving her bardiche on the saddle. *Oh great. That comment only makes it worse.*

Mother is just staring after her. I am not saying anything to make it worse. "I guess that there is an explanation and I will hear it in due time, even if both of you are being evasive." *I am still staying silent. She can hint all that she wants to.* "I will meet you at The Happy Man…" Anna said into the silence "I will go ahead and order. Is Astrid still eating for two?"

Basil nodded. *Since we went to Darkreach the last time Puss seems to eat for two the whole time. When she is actually pregnant, she somehow manages to eat even more.* His mother left and he moved the saddles one by one to sit outside the Customs building where they were out of the way. He had to call to Maeve to get her to come along.

She has found some crab pots stacked on the quay to be fascinating and is intent on investigating their smell.

"Do not go away from us." *Talking to animals…still, my wife talks to it and it seems to understand her. I may as well do the same.* "People here do not know you and do not understand about your mistress. You need to stay close to one of us all of the time."

Just then Ia came out of the building. "Where did your mother go?" she asked.

I am ignoring the question. We need to get our conversation back onto a professional track. "How did you know that she was my mother?"

"I use a crystal ball for my prophecies. I believe that the other Princess that I haven't met yet uses cards and the Bishop uses holy books and that the horse shaman uses a trance and drugs. They are all good, but I like the ball because you get pictures with it, even if you can hear nothing.

"Sometimes you do not know what they mean exactly, but I have found that when you see what was shown, then you will know all about it. I saw her face at the same time as I knew that I was coming on this trip. I knew that she was your mother, but I didn't know her name so I called her 'mother'. Does that answer you?"

"Yes, but you will need to explain it to her like that. Please do not talk about your other ideas to her."

"But I have seen them as well, and they are far more definite now" she said stubbornly. *It is such good timing. Here is Puss as coming out and reaching down to the saddle for her weapon.*

"Seen what?" Astrid asked.

"Puss, you don't want to know. Now let us go for lunch," and he headed off with the others behind him. *Maeve is trotting along behind us all with her nose held high sniffing around at the range of new aromas as she does. At least she is now staying close.*

Basil

Over lunch Basil's parents were first updated on the important things such as family changes, the arrival of the twins Anna and Thorstein, of Olympias' marriage, and the later arrival of Thalassa. They moved on to the Synod and what had happened there and then to Rainjig and the possibility of trade from there with both them and Freeport.

Georgios Anoteron, Basil's father agreed to talk to some of the local fishermen to see if one of them could be persuaded to change his trade.

Having an outlet for trade goods that is as close to Southpoint as Mistledross is, but with more exotic items to offer could tempt at least one of them into the decision. The land trip north into Darkreach is longer than the sea trip around the cape would be, although not as dangerous, but none here have thought of being a trader that father knows of.

"Besides," he continues, "fishing is good here as the currents sweep around from the west and we always seem to have a surplus of fish in the village. Mind you, this surplus of fish does mean that some of the boats struggle to pay enough to feed their owners...except in fish and eventually one gets sick of having nothing else."

His face took on a thoughtful look. "What is more, a reliable source of salt would help them keep more of the fish for sale instead of a lot of it going to waste. Sometimes unwanted fish is just dumped on fields and ploughed in."

Astrid

Ruth and Kaliope have given me strict instructions on what to do if a case like this comes up and I now need to go and see the local moneylender and talk about loaning her money so that 'there will be more capital available' as Ruth had put it...whatever that means. It is all gibberish to me even if Kaliope agrees with her about it.

Ia explained, with a straight face, why she had called Anna mother. *At least she can obey orders. I should have kept my mouth shut. Anna cannot get any of us to explain what I said, but it hangs over us like a cloud. Ia just sits back and looks smug and Basil and I are evasive. I cannot believe that even Basil has difficulty lying to his mother as she looks at him with a mother's stare.*

I need to change the subject totally. There has to be something...oh yes... why I eat so much. Astrid talked about what had happened to her in Ardlark and what she could now do. *It works. Georgios is insisting on me coming with him after lunch and showing some of his Starşiyrang what I know.*

At least we all enjoy the crabs, especially Maeve, who insists on washing their claws and legs in the bowl of water that she was given before eating them. She has climbed onto either Ia's or my lap several times to see if any of the big people somehow have pieces of crab that are being neglected for the delicious bits that might lurk in corners. Eventually it is time to finish.

Basil

After lunch Basil's mother took Basil to see Father Maro at the Church of the Holy Trinity. *It seems that they were bypassed here on the return home and the results of the Synod are, as yet, still unknown in this remote outpost. To receive direct word on the proceedings so quickly has made the elderly priest, the senior in the village, very happy.*

He will have to confirm it with his Metropolitan, as the priests will be leaving Darkreach and entering the jurisdiction of the Metropolitan Cosmas, but he has two priests who are more than ready for a parish of their own. The Church of Saint Phocas has one as well and, he will have a word to the local Mullah. He possibly has a couple of young men that he can spare to look after neglected souls as well.

It seems that the first boat to the Swamp will carry more priests on it as paying passengers than it will real trade goods. At least that guaranteed money should tempt someone. I pointed out to father at lunch that the local rum from Southpoint will not take up much space and will be well received in the west. I really have not been impressed by what I have tasted in the way of alcohol in most of the Swamp. They might be proud of it where it is made, but it is really very ordinary to me.

Georgios

Astrid and her father-in-law walked to the garrison post. *That young witch is staying close and following behind as if she has a right to do so. I will let my wife worry about what is happening there. I have found my new daughter a practice bardiche in my armoury. It is only a Human-sized one, far smaller than hers, but let me see what she can do with it.*

She is absolutely devastating. It is like a twig in her hands. My daughter-in-law has demolished several of my best soldiers one after the other and then in groups. Now, after a few potions to fix the wounds of practice, she is taking them back over what happened and showing them how she did it.

I am impressed. I have heard my son talk of the prowess of my daughter in law but admit that I thought that it was the exaggeration of a fond husband. Hearing how she has killed two of the Insak-div on her own, and now watching her in action is interesting and shows that there has been no exaggeration.

I can contrast her size and strength and exuberance with my small and quiet son and wonder how the two manage the disparity. I, at least, know that Basil is good at what he does. His rank and the confidence that the Emperor shows in him prove that, but they seem such an odd couple. They are the very contrast of fair and dark, of the large and the small, and the loud and the quiet. Perhaps that contrast is what they thrive on.

He then looked aside. *Now see how Ia stands and the way she is watching Astrid. I am starting to wonder even more about what is happening there. I will tell my wife all about the practice and what happened in it, but I will not mention the expression upon that girl's face as she watched, not the soldiers, or even the combat itself, but my daughter-in-law.*

Astrid

Astrid finished in time to go and see the moneylender. *I have been given a few purses just for this purpose and have not had a chance to use any of them yet. Luckily, before we left the valley, Theodora got Ruth to write out her message in several languages. That is why you have Princesses, to realise that none of us going along have a clue to explain to anyone what Ruth and Kaliope want...me least of all.*

The woman, Rhea, read the note and nodded. *The woman is interested in what it says. She is nodding as she reads it. Apparently, it makes complete sense to her. I can see her mind thinking about what to do with the money already.*

She has agreed to take the money on the terms that Ruth outlines in the note. She has agreed so quickly that I suspect that we could have easily asked for a lot more in the way of profit for the valley. I must remember to point that out to Ruth.

Together they went to see Anna to get an agreement witnessed. *I want to go home and show that I have done as I was supposed to, even if I do not understand it. I will leave not one, but two bags with her. Rhea seems pleased and is now off to see my father-in-law so that he knows to send the fishermen who may be interested in a new trade to her so that she can finance their venture.*

Astrid
a few hours later

They took two rooms at The Happy Man that evening and, once they were installed in their room for the night, with Ia being placed in another, Basil not only locked the door, but he then took the key out. He also put something solid on top of where the key lay so that it could not easily fly away with an enchantment, after doing that he also put a chair and a wedge firmly in place to further prevent the door being opened.

I thought that he was being overly paranoid, but obviously he has had experience with mages like her before. He is rewarded in his caution.

They had just finished making love, something there had been no opportunity to do for a week and were starting to drift off to sleep when there was a soft 'snick' noise as the lock was opened and an attempt was made to open the door. It failed and, after a short while the person, presumably Ia, went away.

Astrid giggled. "It looks like we will have to work out a way to lock ourselves into our own house when we get home."

Astrid

34th Primus, early morning

As they ate, Astrid put on an innocent face and turned to the young witch. "Ia, were you unable to sleep? Did you feel a need to stay up practising your spells last night?" *My reward for that catty remark is a look that confirms exactly who it was at our door, not that I doubted it in the first place. It was worth it though.*

Having said their goodbyes, their trip back to Rainjig was uneventful, although they went back along yet another path, travelling behind the two unnamed peaks and even closer to the volcano.

The vegetation in that second valley is the same as in the one further south behind The Sisters, but from this angle a long tongue of molten rock can be seen coming down the slope of the glowing peak and the smell, as we go close to it, is of burning sulphur and rotten eggs and it lingers in our nostrils well after it was left behind. Maeve is continually sneezing from where she sits on Basil's saddle.

Chapter IX

Theodora

34th Primus

I miss my husband, not that she would happily go into the water naked with men all around her. She was brought up very differently to me. At least the two days of relaxation are being welcomed by the Mice. Most have never swum, or even splashed, in the sea before and Harnermêŝ is very busily engaged in convincing them all to try it. It seems that he has missed this part of his home more than anything else.

The locals at first were very amused by the reluctance of the Mice to experience such an activity. The shoe is on the other foot now and they seem to be very shocked by the reaction of those who choose to swim. Public nakedness is not normal in the Swamp. For various reason, we are used to it in Mousehole.

The girls, Verily, Goditha and Tabitha, were in the water before we returned from the mountain. Having been slaves in Mousehole before it was freed, they have very little left in the way of body modesty and also have a conservative approach to their clothes getting damaged so, rather than get salt water on anything they strip and go swimming naked as a first option.

Apparently, Aziz was next although Christopher and Simeon draw a line at the idea. Now we are back from Snowcap, Bianca is going in with the rest of the Khitan. She makes sure to stay in the middle of them until they are in the water. They take to it as readily as Hulagu had apparently taken to the bath in Evilhalt. For an hour or so it is as if a large number of small children have been dumped into the lagoon. I am not missing out.

With me joining in, eventually even the five men from Darkreach have been talked into coming in. While my family may bathe naked, it is not a common practice in the Empire and they, particularly the two Muslim men, have difficulty with knowing where to look and end up in a group just drifting in the water away from the others and looking out to sea while a small riot occurs behind them.

Goditha

There is the druid Caractacus. "I cannot but notice that thy temple stones are incomplete. Mayest I help thee to dress some of those I did see lying rough and untouched. They doest look to have been lying there waiting for a mason and the right tools in their long grass and in a pile. I doth happen to be one myself and I hath the other at hand." *He seems shocked that I would do that.*

Once he realised that she was serious he accepted eagerly. *Of course, I have my tools with me. What if I had to erase a pattern etched in stone? I could not do it with my fingers. Finding me now without my tools nearby is like finding Astrid walking around without her huge meat cleaver.* It did not take her long to dress several of them and he assured her that he would get his people to put them up.

He seems embarrassed in that he cannot let me see the ceremony as it is one of their mystery rites, but at least now their circle will at least have the ends of its arms in place to mark the positions of the solstices and a couple of the stones placed in the middle to show the future intent. They will need to get more stones to the island in order to do anything else. I am not doing that.

Theodora

Most of the Mice have spent the two days just sitting around or playing instruments, although several have started either doing the exercises that Astrid is teaching them or those that Shilpa teaches. I am doing the second. I need it after all of that riding. I am out of practice again and I am quite sore.

Astrid and Basil have returned to us. They have reported what arrangements they have made to both me and, when we found him, Samthann. That means that we have done our job of joining people up for trading and generally being peaceful. We should also make money from what has been arranged and Ruth, and now Kaliope, will not need to look hurt when I say that this not very important for us.

It seems, from what they have to say that the locals think that we killed one of those little dragons we saw in the mountains. We need to make them understand the real size of the dragon that we killed at Mousehole. The sheer size of it will add to our prestige. What is more, as far as I know, it was one of the only five large ones that were left.

Now that they have reported, Astrid and Basil are off to the water and others are going back in as they use the excuse of exercise in order to swim some more. Being used to the sauna Astrid has no difficulty swimming naked and as for Basil, I rarely get to find out what he thinks, but he goes in as well.

Ia

Just by them going into the water, I am no longer with them and it is for the first time since we left my home. I have the same upbringing as the rest of the Free and, as I have to explain when I eventually managed to force myself, public nudity breaches many of our local ideas about privacy. I think that my blushes, on their own, are quite revealing of my struggle. I didn't know that I could get so embarrassed so easily.

Once she had taken the plunge, it still took her nearly until they were getting ready to emerge from the water to get near Astrid and Basil.

Everyone, particularly the junior mages, wants to look at my tattoo. Verily says that she can smell the mana embedded in it and is excited by the idea. Goditha wants one but is reluctant to get it done until she has talked to her wife. She is another of their woman who has a wife? How many of them are there? How is it different to the Princess having a woman husband?

I would not believe there was so much interest. The Hob priest, Aziz climbed out and talked to the Christian Bishop and then came back in to his wife. It seems that he and Verily can get one done on each of them as soon as they work out the exact designs that they want and have the time. Apparently, there is a Hob town in the mountains somewhere that is called Dhargev. They trade with it and there is a good tattooist there, so there is no hurry.

Maria and her husband Menas are in two minds on the subject: his, and hers. He heard what I said about the risk of damage to the person wearing the tattoo if it is broken and does not want her to take the risk. She wants to take the risk for the increase in her ability to safely cast a spell. I can understand that in a war mage. It seems that this is a discussion that could take more than a little while to sort out.

When Ia broke free and came near the other two, she actually behaved herself and stayed slightly apart from them. "I have to be honest with you about it. Unless we are all publicly agreed on our love, doing anything in public that I want to do in private with you both would be harder for me than this appearing naked is. It is hard. You may deny it, but I know how we will end up."

I am looking with jealousy at Stefan and the cousins holding each other and happily taking turns in diving under the water and upsetting each other and playing other games and at the other partners sharing the water and each other's company. It is not just Astrid and Basil. It is Verily and Aziz, Maria and Menas, Jennifer and Harnermêŝ, Hulagu and Ayesha, Tabitha and Neon, and Dobun with both Anahita and Kãhina.

Although I was told that nearly everyone was in the water in the yesterday and in the morning, Goditha and I are the only ones in now without a partner with us and, after examining my tattoo and looking at the situation around her, Goditha has left the water to dry herself once she has enjoyed a bit of a splash.

This leaves me floating around the vicinity Astrid and Basil looking downcast as I have no real purpose for being there. Having taken the huge step of making myself naked in public, I find myself left out. I must look so disheartened at this. Astrid has just laughed at me and it was a laugh that was just humour.

"You wait until we get home," Astrid said, "and get to be in the sauna. You will get used to being like this very quickly. Maybe someone will see your body there and decide that they like you and you will see them and decide that you like them."

When I tried to protest and talk about what I saw, Astrid just pointed towards the others who were floating nearby. Saying more where it could be overheard would be too public, too wrong. I will hold what I want to say within myself and go quiet.

I will take consolation from floating around and looking at the others. Of all of these Mice that are here only Harnermêŝ can actually swim, although he is trying hard to teach his wife. The result is, at least, more comical than successful and it results in a lot of spluttering noises from Jennifer as she frequently sinks under the water with her arms and legs thrashing around.

That night, this time celebrating the idea of having a trader possibly visit them soon, the villagers held another feast. At this feast the stories that were told and the rest of the entertainment were the simple ones that could be found in any good tavern.

Astrid helped things along by pulling out two flagons of rum that she brought from Southpoint. I may as well drink lots of that. Harnermêŝ pointed out to our hosts that they have the right attitude to having a party and recommends them visiting Freeport. I would like to do that as well. After hearing the stories of their visit there, I want Basil to run for me.

Theodora

Now is the right time to do it, before she gets drunk. Theodora came up to Ia and moved her away from the rest. "You have not been quite honest with the Bishop, have you?"

"What do you mean?" was the rapid reply from Ia. *There is a note of panic in her voice and she is desperately trying to project an appearance of innocence as she looks around. I have made sure that we are away from the others. No-one can hear us. Basil may think that I am blind to such things, but even I can see that she is trying hard to evade my question.*

"You are not yet qualified to be a full priestess of the Mother away from any others and in charge of your own grove, are you?"

"You have talked with Dianan, haven't you?"

Theodora nodded. "You are still a Maid. As it was explained to me, you do not have to be a mother to be a priestess in charge of your own grove and doing all of the rituals, but you do need to be no longer a virgin with a man. Is this correct? I have that right?"

Ia unhappily nodded. *She is obviously uncomfortable having to explain herself.* "I am trying to fix this," she said. "I have selected the man I want to initiate me, but he doesn't know this and it is complicated by his wife, whom I want to take to bed as well and who will possibly kill me if I approach it all wrong."

The honesty of her reply somewhat shocks me. I need to not show my reaction. I have to recover from that and probe further as to what she means. This could well be very important for all of us. "You mean Astrid and Basil, don't you?"

Ia nods despondently. "Can you talk to them for me?" she asked. Theodora nearly choked on the rum and coconut milk mix that she was drinking. *Ia continues without seemingly noticing my discomfort. That is not something I wish to repeat.* "You are their Princess, aren't you? They will do what you say? It is important as there is so much, I cannot do until I am no longer the Maid."

It took some time for Theodora to explain the exact relationship of the Princesses to the rest of the people of Mousehole, particularly in regard to Astrid. Others would take a command, but with Astrid 'suggestion' was a much more accurate word to use than 'command' in almost all of the circumstances that applied to her.

I also have to make sure that she fully understands the old expression about never giving an order that you are not sure will be obeyed. Actually, in this case, that is not even the case. It is one of those orders that I am very sure would not be obeyed. Even Basil is more than likely to say no and, as for Astrid…

I need to deflect attention away from me doing something stupid. I have an idea. Who knows, perchance it will mitigate things and even help. I will explain Christopher's role in our village. "Although he is of a different faith, he will be happy to talk to you and give you advice…not that I am at all sure that the Bishop will be able to do anything more than I can to help in this particular case." *At least it takes the problem away from me.*

Chapter X

Astrid
35th Primus

We get to leave early in the morning, refreshed by our stay and waving goodbye to our hosts, most of whom have delayed starting their work to farewell us…or have at least used that excuse to have a lazy morning after drinking the rum all night. I admit that it is strong stuff. Heading quickly aloft and waving people into position, Astrid immediately led them north until they were under the morning shadow of The Wall.

We fly over the tall trees along the foothills and with the peaks a constant presence looming on our right. When we reach the mountains, we turn left and fly north-west along the length of the Wall. As we fly, I can easily count two hands of near identical peaks. Even in summer the very top of each of them is gripped by snow.

The cliffs that The Wall presents below its peaks, at least on this side, are nearly vertical and so they literally do make up a wall that prevents travel in either direction except for the very hardy. All along the base is the rubble of fallen rock. No wonder the rain just drops out of the sky here north of Rainjig when the winds hit the peaks.

Thord
an hour later

Those rock faces look good and I have never seen their like anywhere before. They stand tall with only faint dips where the occasional waterfall cascades down a precipice from between the peaks. Some streams fall so far that the water never even reaches the base, but simply becomes a mist that hangs around and re-joins the clouds or that coats the trees below.

The cliffs here are indeed the tallest that I have ever seen. This might be an interesting place to bring my new bride to get away from everything after the wedding. With the saddles at our command there are possibilities that open up to us that no other Dwarf has a chance of enjoying. I can give her something unique as a present. I may as well take advantage of that.

Theodora
several hours later

All of the villages of the Swamp are either on an island or are fortified. To a large extent, this Eastguard Tower, or as they call it Caer Gwyliwr Ddwyrain, is both. I do have to wonder if I have its pronunciation even vaguely right. Hopefully I do not offend them, although at least generally the people here seem to find our attempts to say their place names hilarious.

As soon as the place came in sight, they stopped the saddles in the sky and examined it with the telescope. *A village of several thousand people, at least. sits on its own, quite large, island in the Buccleah River. It is well upstream from Rising Mud and at the upstream end of a reasonably sized lake.*

The island is really more than just large and I can see that a stone wall, not as tall as the wooden ones of the villages that are on the land, but still over thrice the height of a person, extends right around the island enclosing land that is well above the water. From what I can see from here, by the look of the stone, and the shape of the towers in it, different parts of it may have been built, or at least rebuilt, at many different times.

There is a stone bridge on each side of the island and the one furthest from us seems to have a wooden opening span to allow boats to go further upstream. The village itself, including a stone shrine with arms, sits on the downstream end of the island with docks on the outside of the wall. On the end of the island closest to the Caliphate there is a massive square keep which is surrounded by a tall diamond-shaped castle wall and with a gatehouse facing each bridge.

Any normal attacker would first have to land on the island and get through the curtain wall, and then they would have to conquer the castle and lastly, the keep to get to the village. Platforms for artillery are scattered around the walls on towers and there is even room for herds to graze around the shrine. Next to Fort Island in Sacred Gate and possibly Garthang it is the most formidable construction for many weeks travel.

It is obvious though that the three sets of walls all date from different times from the way that they are built. Despite its strength against any normal army, it is just like Peace Tower was for us. From the air, it is vulnerable. Using our molotails and our magic it can be reduced and taken in a very short time.

The sacred grove lies, not on the island, but on the southern shore behind a tall fence of trees and a track can just be seen leading further away to a mine that has created a gaping scar opening into a mountain.

"There is a thick seam of malachite," said Bryony, "they use it as it is and they smelt it for the copper." She pointed to where a plume of smoke rose into the sky. "There are other rocks in a thick layer below the malachite, much more of them, but they yield less metal. Most of the copper that people use comes from here, whether the people outside know it or not."

She pointed to the north of the lake. "See those tall fences..." *There are a series of fences made of whole trees, some living, dividing a series of large fields up into huge squares. Some necks and heads of lizards can be seen in them browsing on the trees fencing them in.* "Those are their sale yards. Here they raise some of the giant lizards as meat and leather animals and they need the tall fences to contain them when they bring them in and to help lead them to near the river for slaughter."

She again pointed to what she meant. "The northern shore is for meat and the southern for crops...see the rice fields there...they grow a lot of that here as well."

Bryony and Ia and Verily are given protective amulets and, while Bryony is not openly ready for combat, Ia has one of her panic wands in hand and I have given one of my strong Air wands to Verily. Any attempted ambush should backfire but, with the news going out from Rising Mud, such an attack is going to be possible.

Astrid has brought us all down to horse rider height and halted us a hand of filled hands away from the southern bridge while the other saddles go forward. She holds her bardiche ready in case she has to go forward to help. Several times I can see her edging forward. It is taking a long time for us to be waved closer.

Both Bryony and Ia appear to have had separate arguments with different people. Then everyone sits and waits for another person to appear. It looks like first one person, a man, and then another, a woman, had to be brought from the inside into the discussion.

Astrid has us formed up in two lines, ready for combat if needed with Stefan's and Astrid's groups in the front, on the left and right, with the archers and mages behind and above them. Once Bryony has finally turned and signalled, and Verily has moved through the gate, Astrid is moving us all into files as she leads us forward. "Keep your eyes out for treachery," she said just loud enough for all of the Mice to hear.

Astrid

A woman waits at the bridge with Bryony. "The guards lost several friends and relations at Rising Mud," said Bryony in Hindi, "and the man, the one who has just left, their captain, lost his brother who was the captain here before him. He wanted us to leave the saddles outside and for us to come in to the village unarmed…I refused…this is Blanid verch Barita…she is the Reeve…she overruled him and he has stalked off in a huff."

She changed to Darkspeech, "Bishop, you and the other priests should try and check him…and as many others as you can…I don't feel very safe here." She changed back to Hindi. "Blanid, this is our Princess Theodora and the woman with the axe thing is the one that you heard about who killed Ith so quickly. She will probably want to offer an open challenge to any who might bear a grudge."

"Can I do that?" Astrid injected eagerly. *I thought that allowing the news to come up here would rule out any chance of combats*. "I thought that I had ended that."

"As the champion for me and Aine and Dulcie and Adara and I suppose even Ia to an extent, yes you can and, seeing that it is an open challenge, not against any person directly, but against any who are aggrieved, then you get to set the rules."

"In that case I do."

"It is not as simple as that," said the Reeve, in a flustered tone. "It must be announced so that all can hear who you are and why it is issued. For now, come inside. We have heard much in the way of rumour and Urfai has even sent me a letter, but it is confused and I want to hear more about what he speaks of more directly from you."

With Theodora explaining matters to the Reeve as they went, they were led to a tavern which the sign revealed was called The Copper Cat. *I like that for a name at least*.

Astrid
a short while later

When they had been installed in rooms Theodora came to Astrid. "You are going to have to do your own announcing, I am afraid," she said.

"They have no crier here."

"I think I can manage that." Astrid grinned. "Just make sure no mages are hidden anywhere while I do it. I have an idea." She grinned even more. *Which I will put in place before Theodora has a chance to ask what that means and tries to spoil things…*Astrid turned on her heel and strode off. *Theodora is left, concerned I am sure, in my wake and she has to hurry if she wishes to try and catch up.*

With most of the Mice watching, although the Khitan were staying with the saddles, Astrid strode out of the tavern and down a street into the large, cleared area between the castle wall and the village. *It is an open grazing common with the stalls of a market still set up along the village edge. I have my bardiche in hand and can use it like a staff as I go.*

I can see people following me with their eyes and I can hear conversations die as I approach. I wonder if my description has reached here along with the gossip. When she had reached a likely looking place, she halted and raised the loud-talker to her lips. Facing the castle, she nodded back to the Mice. *Some cover their ears.*

"My name is Astrid the Cat and I am from the village of Mousehole in the mountains to the north." Her voice, speaking slowly in Hindi and amplified loudly enough to be heard over a whole battlefield, echoed off the wall of the castle and around the village.

Some of the local people in the market area who are close to us are now covering their ears as well. I am at full volume. I am sure that the people at the mine, out in the grove or even in the animal yards must have heard me. Most of those out on the lake must know what I am saying soon. Good. Now that I have their attention…

She allowed the words to sink in so that people stopped what they were doing and turned to see what she would say next. Then, still speaking slowly so that she could be clearly heard despite echoes, she continued.

"On behalf of all of the people that they had kidnapped and raped and killed, in particular among the murders those of Conan ap Reardon, Dafydd ap Comyn and Trystan ap Dafydd ap Comyn, and among those who were kidnapped Bryony ferch Cathan, Adara ferch Glynis, Dulcie o Bathmawr and Aine verch Liban, I have taken part in the execution or killing of Glyn ap Tristan, Conrad, Gwillam, and of a man called Cuthbert…whose families I don't know, but then most likely they didn't know who their real fathers were either."

"Then I helped kill a lot of these so-called patriots…who I name as being complicit in rape, abduction and murder. Most recently I have killed Ith ap Tristan and Athgal Dewin in challenge. These people all, whether they knew it or not, worked for some of the unquiet dead who call themselves the Masters and, through them, some other creatures that are called the Adversaries."

"On behalf of those I stand for, I still seek to find any others who were involved in these crimes and who worked for either the dead men, or the Masters, or more directly for the Adversaries. I issue an open challenge to any that wish to declare my statements of guilt false, or who wish to claim revenge for a relative or friend that I have slain in challenge or in battle, to meet me in trial. I will meet one at a time or even two at once if they wish."

"If there are any that hear these words and who fail to take me up on this and try their hand at me later or by subterfuge or ambush, I believe that the custom of this land is to have them declared coward and outlaw and I call that doom upon their heads."

"If you wish to meet me, I am staying at The Copper Cat and tonight our bards we will tell everyone the full story of what has happened and how your so-called patriots were either wicked men themselves or else just unwitting tools of evil creatures from outside the Free who were not even men. Again, if any challenge the truth of our tale that is told, then I am the nominated champion who stands for the integrity of it all."

Astrid was about to finish when she added to it the idea that she had while talking to Theodora. *I have to admit to a bit of glee over this. I think that I know how it will be received.* "What is more, if any have information of any who has worked for these men that I have called then I will pay near a year's wages for a good tradesman for any news that leads to the person's capture. I believe that will be ten guineas of your money on the head of each captive brought to me."

She grinned. *Before I have even finished, I can see people starting to talk about their neighbours. I thought that offer would appeal to these people.* "I thank you for listening and remember, Astrid the Cat who is staying at the Copper Cat. I am the woman with the teeth." She gave a smile and, turning, a short bow to the people who were actually in the market area and staring at her, several with very wide eyes. She then turned again and went back to the inn.

Basil

She didn't notice although, standing in the shade of a stall with Ia, I did. One woman actually fainted before she even finished. I wonder which one she is related to. After Astrid left Basil kept looking around for a little while to see if any wanted to try an ambush, but either the threat she had made was effective or the announcement had caught any enemies they had unprepared.

When no one made a threatening move, he turned and hurried to keep an eye on his wife's back. *I can sense the young witch-girl trying to copy my movements behind me and there is no doubt that the raccoon will be following close behind both of us.*

Astrid made it back to the inn through an almost stationary village. *Most of the people are just standing and watching her blankly, but some are whispering to each other. My trained eyes can see some of the onlookers looking at the others around them and wondering who to denounce. That offer my wife made was priceless. It has converted a hostile town into a town full of informer-allies looking to make some money.*

I have quickly come to agree with Rani. Until I came here, I thought that the scum that live on Anta Dvīpa were the most dishonest people that I have met. Now I know that most of them are merely trying to make their way through a bad situation that life, and their own upper castes, has dealt to them. I now think that most of the people in the Swamp are so mercenary that selling your own parents into slavery would be seen by many as a good way to retire.

I still cannot believe that they are so open about their theft and other activities. They have no shame and no concept that hurting another, anyone who is not one of theirs, is wrong. It will now be up to the Mice to sort out the real denunciations, if any come in, from the false. That is not my problem. That is what priests and mages are for.

Theodora

Blanid seems to be nearly as confused as Urfai had been. She has revealed that, like him, she succeeded to her position when her predecessor died. Before that she was just one of the local Wiccan priestesses and she was elected now because she was seen as being above the turmoil. She has had no training for the role and no inclination to keep it once everything is resolved. Good luck to her on that.

She wants to go back to her quiet life. She has added that the man who stalked away, Figel ap Machute, had been her main rival for the position of Reeve and one of the main reasons that she had agreed to stand. He apparently does not have a good reputation with the women of the town, particularly among the slaves in the brothel. He has to go there for sex as no other woman in the village will now have him.

Just like Bianca at home, it seems that anything that any woman feels or hears soon comes to the attention of the priestesses and that means affairs of love and lust in particular. The same applies to the Wiccan priests, but they hear things from the men's side. She has declared that, if any come to fight Astrid, it will be him or someone who he has prompted to do it, and if anyone is denounced, she suspects that it will be him as well.

Basil

Some of the Mice, with Stefan along to pay attention to the people who might watch the shoppers, are going to see what the village has to offer in the way of trade, while I want to go the rounds of the taverns. I may have a few words of Faen now, but there is no chance of my posing as a local. Despite her reluctance to do so, my wife is sending Ia along with me.

I wish she hadn't. The girl has taken the opportunity to hang off me and stand far too close, whispering the words 'we must be believable in our act' into my ear as her hands stray. It does not help that she is right and that we are getting nothing that is actually useful in the way of gossip. At least I can watch who it is that watches our shoppers.

Trust Goditha. She cannot resist the urge to buy metal. When she returns, she has several ingots of copper being carried along behind her for Norbert or even Eleanor to turn into useful things. It is just as well that we are headed home very soon as these ingots will nearly take up all of our ability to carry anything extra with us.

Astrid

"It's as well we'll be headed home," Thord said. "I am getting a sick of beer made of rice. I want some real beer, not poorly flavoured water." He made a joke about the local beer and making love in a canoe that set her to laughing.

Bryony and Adara are back with some new long bows. I wonder if I should get a new one. "No reflection on Robin," said Bryony, "He is a good bowyer, but these are even better. I had forgotten about the man who makes them until I saw him packing up for the afternoon. He is the best in the Swamp."

Astrid waited in vain. *Several have come to claim the reward, but already it seems too late. Even before I first started speaking to make the announcement, our Figel proclaimed that he was leading a patrol out to 'check on a few things from the Caliphate'. The patrol has not returned and every name that anyone has mentioned to us has been in that patrol.*

As each person is turned away, they are told that, if they can produce the person that they have named then the offer will be doubled and will still stand until two weeks after the next New Year. Basil says that excited groups are already sitting around in inns trying to work out in which direction to head or if those named, or their relatives, will offer more not to pursue them.

Ayesha

Tonight, I tell the story once again. This time I make sure that I emphasise the size of a real dragon. I must tailor the story to this audience and the part of the story that involves the Brothers, Skrice and the North can be cut down. What has happened locally needs to be the most prominent. As I tell the story I stress the security and power of the Mice. We want our people to be safe when they go out in the world.

Theodora

No-one wants to stay around here or linger on the trip so, the next day, although it makes for a very long flight, we are returning to Mousehole with only a short stop in Birchdingle to eat a late lunch. It is a welcome return to the village for many. At least Ia learns, on seeing the skeleton, that she had indeed badly misjudged the size of a real dragon.

For once we bring back no more children for the school, although that might be an idea that will take a while to come to fruition and, oddly, as I told my husband, it will most likely be one of the children from the smallest and poorest of villages, Rainjig, who will be our first when Samthann decides that one of them might have some potential as a mage, or at least it may be worthwhile sending one of their children to actually receive a real education.

Chapter XI

Gamil
the 17th of Jadwig, the Year 546,984 since the Spread

I can look back through the file after file that I have layered on the screens ahead of me. They fill an entire wall. She moved her gaze between them and brought one to the fore and sent others into the background with a touch. She pulled holograms out and rotated them in the air before her and overlaid them and compared them. *I thought that was the case.*

Even though they were discarded from the original selection, the people who appeared in the short list kept adding themselves to the final group. The sister…the cousins…the Hobgoblin and now the witch…and there are others as well. She started checking on the behaviour of some of the other discarded ones.

So far, they had yet to move from the path that they should be on, but then they had yet to have a serious interaction with the main players. Would this change? The thief is one anomaly. She was supposed to be in the village when it was freed, but she avoided that. Now she ignores the pull even after having seen and heard the main players and the story.

Even though the preliminary work had been done on all of them by the motivators before I made my decisions, once a person is discarded in these matters and they receive no further prompting, all of the texts say that they are supposed to return to their own path and work out their own personal destiny without any reference to the main line of the fating.

It is analogous in many ways to the path of a braided stream returning to the main flow of the river. It was only those who are chosen and further prompted that are supposed to be permanently diverted to end up as a part of the main flow. Her wing tips fluttered in agitation.

It is, particularly with such a limited selection of people, always possible for that path of one of the rejected to intersect with one of the chosen, but it is supposed to be almost a random matter and they should not attach themselves and become a part of the story. All of the texts say this and all of the experience on other worlds over millennia has shown this to be the case.

Anything else is against the rules that have been established as being the ones that work. Having said that, I have to consider what is happening here. For example, for the wolf-priest to join up with the main group he needed to have travelled to another continent to take his place. It is one of the reasons that I rejected him from the short list in the first place.

Now, his home village moves into a synchronicity on its own. It is moving and reacting almost as if they knew what he was doing. The people there are starting to shape the conflict on their own continent. It is even getting harder to see what is happening there just as it is in other places of interest. I can still see most things, but not all.

How many other strings in this New Found Land and elsewhere will resonate with the events set in train by my chosen actors as time goes by? Will they actually resolve their own fate as an echo of the events to the east? How about the ones on what they call the Long Realm? Will they change the course of centuries despite the inertia of their cultures?

My people have a limited ability to travel in time…to look at events and to pull things through time would be a more accurate description. That is largely how Vhast was built as it is. It is a very restricted form of travel and it can only be done once, and in only the one direction, for any given creature.

What is happening is almost enough to make me think that someone has worked out how to make travel go both ways and is, in light of what is now known, tampering with the fates that have already been set in motion, providing additional stimulus to almost the entirety of my short list to get them to join in the main stream.

Maintaining motivation on so large a group is quite hard. The size of the group that I was working with is considered to be near the largest that is practical. I acted on as many as I thought could be safely set in motion as it was.

I will have to look at the probabilities. They have to be very low, but I am sure that there is at least one research paper waiting to be written about what is happening. The question to be answered now is whether what is now happening on this world has begun to subvert our long-established practices and knowledge. Magic seems to be moving towards having stronger and stronger primacy over the technology that enabled it to flower in the first place.

Just as the teams that are working on the way that religion seems to work here have discovered that now things are happening in the field that are well outside their design parameters, such as the Intervention that one of my subjects somehow achieved long ago on the stairs of Dwarvenholme.

That is still causing heated arguments as to how it happened and it is likely that it will continue to do so for some time. They discussions are getting so heated that one whole group of my religious researchers are not talking to another group except in heated notes and articles in learned journals. At best they are barely polite in tone. It is a matter that will be a bone of contention for centuries to come.

What if an actual Destiny or Fate or indeed a reification of Dharma, as one of the cultures here calls it, has risen into being? If it were, that will shake my entire profession to its core, perhaps even cause it to disintegrate in turmoil, even though it could perhaps be viewed as a possible, or even probable, logical result or perhaps synthesis of our Experiment.

Hindsight is marvellous, but almost useless. I will have to think long and hard about the ramifications of this. Any paper that I write on this will have to be extremely watertight and not just speculation as, if I am right, almost my entire field of study will have to be rewritten. Who should I get in to help with the research on this? How will we even do the research?

Chapter XII

Rani

Ist Secundus

It is well past time for me to go over my lists to determine who should take part in this next trip out. Should people be given a break from these expeditions and not taken along? If I am going to leave people out, what rationale do I use to determine who shall go and who shall stay?

According to my wife Astrid has grown more than a little…irrational may be the best word…by issuing challenges to a whole village not only once, but twice. She was successful, but it seems to have been a huge risk. She must have gotten lucky in that fight if the man was so big and had been so successful all the time until she met him.

Goditha went along on the last trip, now I am planning on taking Parminder away. Although she is not needed on this trip, should Goditha and their children come along anyway, just to give them some time together? On the other hand, the village buildings, in particular the Basilica, need Goditha. Does her wife need her more? I know that I missed my Princess very much and that was only a couple of weeks of separation for us.

At least I am glad that we now have the River Dragon. *It might be cramped and with little chance for privacy when everyone is below deck, but at least we have our own place to sleep and we can bring babies along if we need to. I am even getting used to mine…a little bit. I am still worried about dropping her, but my wife has laughed at that and said that, apart from Robin, all of the other husbands in the village apparently complain about the same thing.*

Then there was the matter of taking people from the Swamp to Haven. Stefan will go no-where without his wives and we need him along. Can the women pretend to be from somewhere else? I suppose so. That only leaves the problem of Ia. I wish that Christopher had not brought her back, even if my wife is enthralled with her abilities.

Is it something about Air-mages…or in Ia's case an Air-priestess? She and Theo-dear both seem to be able to make marvellous spells that no-one has thought of before. All I can do is make bigger fireballs. Even Astrid only thinks me good for that when she suggests that the weapon of light has a limited range and that we might need a really long-range blast against the Adversaries.

She, the one who I am sure is the most completely non-magic casting person that we have in the village, even had the audacity to ask me if I could make my most powerful enchantment reach out to the horizon.

Mind you, if I am to be honest with myself, Astrid is right about us possibly needing a longer-range weapon. I suppose that what I am really irate about is that she didn't think to ask me if there was another way to do the same thing. She had just made the connection of Battle Mage and large explosions in her head. Rani would never admit to herself that being annoyed at Astrid being right was what most irked her.

At least thinking about the beam did make me think of a new spell. Others have used something similar to what I have thought of, but not the way I am putting it together. I am still working on it…but it certainly has the range and it packs a big punch and should be suited for what is likely to be needed if the other has too short a range for what we may need.

It may even be more useful than my wife's spell that had crushed the roof of the Brotherhood keep and certainly it has a far longer range. Once I have it all worked out, I will need to try and practice it and perhaps even actually cast it carefully, if I can work out how to, until I am smooth in my delivery. Making a mistake with a spell this powerful will surely kill me.

Aaaand that brings me back to Ia. Do we bring her along or not? We cannot do without Astrid and Basil. If it becomes a case of upsetting them or of losing Ia, then Ia will have to be convinced to leave our village, and do it quickly.

The only other choice we have is for her to stay behind in the village on her own. My wife has told me of the other problem as well, and that is a problem that even makes her completely useless for the very real task that she was actually brought into the village to perform.

It is typical of the problems caused by having a Swamp priest involved in anything. All they can do is cause more problems for people. At least I still have a week or so to work out what to do. I can afford to delay a decision on the trip while I look at people and think about it. Maybe I should have a talk with the girl.

Astrid
a while later

It was a good exercise session with the Brotherhood girls, but I need to go home now. Somehow, I forgot to get some clean clothes and bring them with me. I need to get them before I head out to the bathhouse. What I have on me now is not fit to put back on a clean body. Suddenly she felt a tugging and heard a chattering sound. She looked down to see Maeve at her feet. "What do you want?" she said to the small animal.

Having been noticed the little beast stopped pulling at Astrid's breys and ran away down the village towards an alley that led up the side of the little valley to some of the unoccupied houses...suddenly she stopped and looked back at Astrid and chattered again.

I wonder what is wrong with it. It wants me to do something. I can tell that much, but what? "Do you want me to come with you?" Maeve made a chattering noise and began moving and coming back.

I wonder what is happening in an area where no-one lives. Astrid went after the small beast. *It is running ahead and stopping and checking that I am following. There is no-one living up at the front of the valley near the wall. The houses have only been very minimally fixed up here, just enough to house people briefly for the Synod. It will be the next Synod in five years' time before they are going to be needed again.*

She looked around. *The windows are just oil cloth, and the doors were put together quickly out of still-green timber. Most of the houses that are occupied now have tile or slate roofs, or are getting them, the roofs of these are just a light thatch and they'll stay that way for some time.*

She followed the raccoon up the slope past a few houses until they reached the last row, hard under the wall of the valley and with the bare rock as the rear wall of the dwelling. *Our house is really only a few alleys away and down a level, but it is much closer to the head of the valley. This one is closer to the wall and directly behind the workshops. No-one wants to be here if they can avoid it.*

Norbert's hammer rang loud on the anvil and echoed around. Ahead she could see an open door, while her ears picked up the muted sound of weeping. *It sounds serious, as if someone is in considerable pain.* Cautiously she moved forward. *Maeve has stopped and is looking in.* Astrid moved forward and peered in. There, in a corner, rolled up into a ball hugging her legs to herself and with her back to the door, lay Ia.

Maeve was chattering again and went over and patted at Ia, but was ignored. She looked at Astrid and chattered again. *What has happened? I cannot leave the girl like this. Once you have saved someone's life you forever have an obligation to them.* She put her bardiche against the wall and went over to Ia. Tentatively she went to pat her as well. *No, that is wrong. Ia is not a nervous animal, she is a girl who is somehow hurting.*

I need to do what I did with Verily when she had finally let go of her pain. It seems to have helped. She sat down on the hard floor beside Ia and leant forward. As gently as she could she picked up the smaller girl and, awkwardly, lifted Ia into her lap. The witch girl uncurled enough to throw her arms around Astrid and to bury her face into her breasts.

Astrid started to react, to reject an advance and then she realised. *There was nothing sexual about that move at all. I think that she may not even realise that it was me who lifted her up. For now at least she is just a hurt child who needs consolation.*

Ia kept crying and was just seeking comfort. Today the object of her desire may as well have been the mother of a very small and lost girl who seemed even smaller in her desolation. Again, thinking of Verily, Astrid began to quietly sing and slightly rock as she now did for her own children when they were upset or had hurt themselves.

Astrid looked at Maeve. "Get Basil." The animal had been doing something to Ia's head but it stopped doing that and made a chattering sound at Astrid and headed out of the door.

It was quite a while before Basil appeared at the opening. Astrid had not been able to get a single word out of the girl in that time. Each time she moved away a little and tried to ask anything the crying increased.

I am not an expert at these things, but there is nothing happening now in the village that could cause this much pain. Whatever has happened here, it must have just been the trigger that has unlocked something deeper. There must be something else as well.

Basil stood waiting. He looked at Astrid curiously. *I don't want to upset her more. I will use Darkspeech.* "I didn't cause this, or at least I don't think that I did. I have another class. You have to take it. But first you will need to get Sin to look after the children for us...somewhere away from the house would be best. Take my bardiche home with you."

"I will try and get her back home without anyone noticing us when she has calmed down a bit and when people are back in their houses...I think that it would be a major breach of their ideas of what is right for her to cry in public. I am sure that being seen would make it even worse for her and it is probably why she is here and not back in the barracks."

Basil nodded, took the bardiche, and started to leave. "Umm". He turned back. "Move quietly and look at her wrist." Astrid had been trying to lift the girl around and she had dislodged and moved aside one of the bracers that Ia always wore on her forearms.

I can now see why she wears them. Her inner arm was exposed. An old jagged scar ran up most of its length. "Look at that…she must have somehow kept this hidden when she has been naked. She has tried to kill herself before this. She has pain bottled up inside her and we have added to it. What do we do?"

Basil

I realised long ago that my wife may be a hunter and an extremely practised killer, but she also has a very real soft spot for anyone who is in real trouble and a strong sense of duty to the weak. If she had not been like that then Christopher would most likely not have been saved and none of the subsequent events that flowed on from that would have happened.

He shrugged and shook his head. *I have no idea about things like this.* His wife continued. "What happens if she wants to kill herself now? If she did, I would feel responsible. She seems such an innocent little thing to have such pain." Her face shows her concern.

"It is useless to say that she is not our problem, isn't it?" *Puss is nodding. She has worry written all over her face. For a start we need to get her away from here.* "Then bring her home and I will take a long time getting there. I will get Sin to take the children to visit their uncle and aunt for the night."

I really don't want to say what I am about to say and I am not sure what paths it will lead us down. It may be a bad idea, but it is the only idea that I have.

"If you can do it, you may need to soothe her however she needs to be soothed, as long as you are at ease with that yourself. Once it is done, we will all go and see Christopher later." Astrid nodded and began gently stroking Ia's hair and making soft shushing noises as Basil left again. "Come on Maeve," said Basil. "You can come with me."

Astrid

It is taking a long time for the sobs to start to settle down, but she still refuses to talk. She is still crying, but it is softer. She is exhausted. I am getting a cramp. I may be well padded, but this floor is hard and very uncomfortable. She looked outside. *It is getting darker and most people will be eating. It is time to take her home before we both catch our death of cold.*

Standing without using your hands and while carrying a person who was two-thirds of your own weight is not easy, but Astrid was strong and managed it. Ia threw her arms around her neck. Looking back, she noticed an earring on the floor. *We can come back for that.*

Taking care not to bang her load against the doorframe she moved outside and, keeping alert to see if anyone approached them Astrid moved around the pathway between the houses and then, when she was behind their house, she came down to that level. *The door is ajar. Does that mean that someone is home? No, Basil has just thought of me trying to open the door while being loaded down.*

I do love him. He might pretend to be hard, but he really isn't. Christopher was right in what he said on our wedding night. Maeve now came out of the door and looked at them both. Astrid entered and pushed the door closed with her foot. *Now, where do I put her?* She sighed as she looked around. *None of our chairs are big and certainly none are comfortable enough for two adults to be in together. It has to be our bed.*

Astrid carried Ia into the bedroom but left the door open. Carefully she sat on the bed and tried to pry one of her boots off with the other foot. *That doesn't work. The bed can be cleaned later.* She wriggled over to prop herself up against the backboard while she still held the girl. *Ia is starting to stir and pay attention.* Maeve jumped up and sat on the end of the bed. Astrid waved her off and the animal eventually disappeared.

"Brica," she said. *That is a name, I am sure, but as for the rest...Faen is gibberish to me.* Astrid said nothing, but returned to her soft almost wordless singing. *The crying has stopped at least. That is the most important thing for a start.*

It must have been an hour later, and she was starting to get a cramp in her arms, when the girl in her arms gave a start and tried to struggle away. "You are not Brica...you are Astrid...I am sorry...I promised that I would wait...let me go...I won't bother you...I promised...just look after Maeve." Frantically she started to fight to get free of Astrid's embrace.

There is no way I am letting go of her now. Those last words bring that old scar into a fresh light. She is determined to kill herself. She sighed within herself. It seems that my husband is right, as usual. *There is only going to be one way to make the girl safe for the moment, at least until she is no longer completely flustered and is thinking properly.*

Saint Kessog, please accept that I am trying to do the right thing here. I am trying to save a life instead of taking it. This time, instead of one you can see, I am fighting a monster that is inside someone, and one that is tearing her apart from the inside. I am about to do what may be wrong to try to do right. Please forgive me.

She bent her head and gave Ia a deep kiss on her mouth that silenced her panicked talk and slowly calmed her struggles as Ia's arms again sought Astrid's neck, but this time in a different, and far softer, but still urgent, way.

Two hours or so later Basil came home, making sure that he was noisier than usual when he opened and closed the door. "Everyone is having an early night…so I had to come home," he said loudly from the outer room. *He speaks in Hindi. I will stay in Darkspeech, she knows Hindi.*

"You can come in. There is nothing happening at present that you haven't seen before. It is lucky though that you stayed out. I need to talk to you, but I am famished. Can you please see what there is that you can feed to me and then can you make kaf for us? Ia is asleep. She is exhausted. The crisis is over, at least for the moment." Basil looked in the room.

He can see what we have been up to. The bed is a mess. I am bare-naked and propped up against the pillows. Ia is at my side, tucked under my arm and also naked, but revealing nothing beyond her rear and the curves of her body. One of her arms is thrown over me and a hand is cupping my breast. Clothes lay scattered from one end of the room to another.

He ducked out and returned with a tray. "The fire was out, so although the kaf is on it will take a while to heat. Now Puss, tell me if I still have a place in this house while I feed you."

"Duffer." As she spoke, she had to stop occasionally as little bits of food were put into her mouth and she chewed and swallowed. "I gave you a vow and I will never break it. I love you. I don't love her, but she is pretty and she has suffered a lot and Rani was her usual insensitive self towards the lesser beings. From what Ia said she probably meant well, but it came out all wrong."

She gently turned Ia's arm so that Basil could see it. *It is the other one to the one he saw before. This one bears two broad scars. These ones are across it.* "She has had a bad past. I think that she has used disguise magic to hide these and some other scars. There was an earring on the floor where I found her. Doesn't Theodora use an earring for one of her disguises?" Basil nodded and Astrid went on.

"They might be good for disguise magic for all I know. Three times at least she has tried to kill herself with a blade and someone has walked in and saved her in time. She is only a virgin in her mind because she has not voluntarily had sex with a man. Apparently, that counts the same as not having had sex for her, but she was raped as a child and her mother was raped and murdered in front of her as it was happening."

"Her father died when she was very young and she once had two older sisters who disappeared as children. I am willing to lay any odds that you want that it was Thorkil who had her first and I think that, from what she said, it may have been Conrad as well when he was very young." She stopped and looked at Basil.

"It seems that she cannot be a proper priestess until she has a lover. She needs a man as a lover not another girl. She won't take one on as a casual affair. That is wrong for her people and for her role as a Priestess as it is usual for their first partner to father at least one child. She needs a husband and the vision that she had is very definite about you as her partner."

"I also think that if we throw her out, she will succeed in killing herself this time. I could not have that on my conscience. Those attempts were made when she was still really a child. She knows so much more now and is more likely to get it right. What is more she has had a firm vision in her ball. She has clung to it for years, like a drowning sailor clings to the wreckage of her ship, and it is all that has kept her alive. Having it dashed by us has almost completely destroyed her."

"I have to be honest and admit that, although it seems odd to me, I do not mind making love to her and she is good at making love back, even if I will always prefer you and...and she is very beautiful, much more so than me. I know that I said it in jest a while ago, now I am being serious, can we keep her? We know that Christopher will not mind, although it will certainly shock my brother." Astrid looked at Basil. He stayed silent and returned her gaze.

Basil

I know I was the one who suggested what just happened in our bed, but I only meant it as a stopgap. It was something to keep the girl alive for the moment. I should have known that would not work. Surely there is something else though. "Are you sure? It seems, I don't know...extreme to take her like this just to stop her killing herself."

"Do you have a better idea? I have prayed and prayed to Saint Kessog and this is all that I have." *There is desperation in Astrid's voice as she replies. It seems to me that she must have been lying there looking hard for an alternative for a while.*

"I am sure that allowing her to commit suicide when we could so easily stop her would be a bigger sin for us. I don't know which one, pride perhaps. What good is it keeping our virtue at the cost of the life of someone else? I will need to ask my Confessor that one. She has already talked to Christopher and he has not been able to do anything."

She desperately wants me to have a better solution, and I don't have anything for her. "No…I don't have anything better. I have nothing at all… but…"

Astrid nodded and continued in a practical tone. "I said that I have been thinking and praying while I have held her just now. It seems to be coming fairly normal here for important men to have at least two wives. Even Denny will have two and he is just a shearer."

"You are an important man. This one seems to have her talents and she is quite lovely, even if she does have small breasts and I know you like larger ones. I suppose that the important thing is whether we are both comfortable with it. Although it seems that she has developed a love for me, I don't love her…"

"…and I don't either," said Basil. "Is it enough to just marry the girl out of kindness? Will she be able to handle that I love you and do not love her? Don't get me wrong. I saw her naked in the water and she is at least as beautiful as Theodora is. Making love with her would not be a chore…" *I am starting to not make sense, or at least I am going places that I am not ready to go.*

"My beloved Puss," he finally continued. "I guess that what I am trying to say is that if you want to take her on to keep her alive, then I will be happy to do as you wish and marry her as well as you…I wonder what mother will say." *At least we are both smiling at that one although I have to admit that is actually a matter I should be concerned about, I think.*

Astrid

I am so not going to be the one who does that explanation. I don't even want to be around when it happens. That will be up to you, although…"I somehow think that your father guessed that something was happening…so she may already know."

Just then a voice spoke up. "What are you two saying? I am sorry Basil. I didn't mean to…ohh…" *Ia has just realised where her hand is resting. It darted away and now she is struggling to draw away from me and we are not going there again.* Astrid's arm didn't allow that to happen. *Ia looks anxious.*

"Don't worry little one." Astrid held Ia tight as she stroked her hair. "We have been talking about you, but it may not be bad." *Ia still looks anxious.* "You know that, although we just had sex and I was able to make you happy for a little while, or at least help you stop crying, I do not love you." Ia nodded. "And neither does Basil." *She nods again.* "I need to ask you; do you still want to marry us knowing that?"

That is a very definite nod for yes. "Love could happen between us later," the young witch said. "I am told that it often does where a marriage is fated or arranged. I would be willing to take that risk. I first saw my vision when I was only ten and it was a very strong one. It was soon after the last time I tried to kill myself and soon after I started learning how to see the future."

"My vision showed me with Basil and with another woman. Your face wasn't clear and it kept changing. Sometimes you had dark skin and looked more like you were from Haven and carried lots of knives, and sometimes you were shorter and dressed more like the teacher Presbytera and even sometimes dressed like the Bishop's wife does. It was as if fate hadn't decided on exactly who you were, even if it had decided on him."

Basil and I share a look at that. "That vision is all that has kept me alive..." Ia stopped talking as what she had been asked sank in and a tentative and shy smile appeared on her face. "Does that mean that you will marry me?" *She is looking at Basil. She may not realise it, but her face has taken on the look of an adoring puppy as she does. I hope she does not use that look much. Who could say no to it?*

"Yes," he said with a deep and resigned sigh. "Now I can smell the kaf that I set to brewing and I will bring more food for us all. We need to get to know each other if we are to be married."

It turns out that, although it can be done more formally if there is another priest or priestess available, to be married by her rite all that is required is agreement between the parties and a witness. Basil and Ia have already agreed and I can act as the witness and so they can already be regarded as married.

Basil
1st Secundus

Well, this is certainly a different way to wake up. I am lying between two very different but beautiful women whose hands are clasped on top of me. Carefully, trying not to wake them, he slid out from between them, put on some breeches and went out to get some breakfast for them all. At the doorway he looked back.

Already they have filled the hole I left and are now holding onto each other. Maeve was waiting for him in the kitchen. He looked down at the creature. "It seems that we need to work out where you will sleep."

She chattered at him. "...and we forgot to feed you last night." *She is looking up at a bench and pointing. The bread box is open and now she is pointing higher. One of the small salamis was missing.* "I guess that you made yourself at home and took care of that yourself then." He got a breakfast ready for them all. Maeve went to follow him.

Two women sharing my bed is one thing. I draw the line at familiars. "You can wait out here and tell us if someone comes home." *Maeve may be looking at me reproachfully, but she has gone and curled up in front of the door on a lap-rug that she has dragged outside. It is normally on one of the chairs. From the way it was mounded, that looks as if it is where she spent the night.*

When Basil returned to the bedroom, they were still asleep. *One is so dark and the other so fair, one with the dark-green eyes of the northern forest and the other with the violet of flowers. Ia's scars are still visible. We have to get her earring back later, but for now there is stirring as the smell of kaf penetrates their brains.* "Wake up wives and please at least try to remember that you have a husband."

Astrid's eyes snap open and she looks at the person she holds as if seeing her for the first time. "We said yes...didn't we...it wasn't a dream."

"Do you regret it?" Basil had switched to Darkspeech. *I don't want to offend Ia if the answer is wrong.*

"No," said Astrid. *She is speaking in Hindi,* "and until we have taught her a civilised tongue...we still have to get a book from Ruth...we should not speak in anything she doesn't know in front of her. It is nekulturny. I may be very surprised at myself and what I asked, but I do not regret our decision. I think that we will get along well together. We may not love her but we have taken her in and we need to be kind to her and to respect her and make her a part of us.

"If her visions are correct, and they have been on at least the main point, then you are going to be the father of her babies. Personally, I don't like all this prophesy. Normal people don't have prophesies about them and about who they are going to marry and have children with. They just get on with their life." *She is unconsciously stroking Ia's dark hair as she said that.*

Basil grinned wryly at her. "And exactly who said that we are normal in any way?" Astrid grinned back broadly.

Astrid

"Thank you," said the priestess softly and drowsily. "You cannot know how much it means to finally belong with someone." *She is hugging me as if she will never let go, but we have things that we need to do. I may want to stay here and purr all day, but I cannot.* Astrid gently disengaged herself and with a kiss on Ia's lips to show that she was not being rejected, sat up and started eating.

"Now we need to eat quickly and I need to be off to see about things. Sin will have the children home soon. I need to head them off and I will get your earring so that your scars are hidden." Ia gave a start and looked at her arms.

"I was right about that wasn't I? Don't worry dear, we will try and stop anyone hurting you like that ever again. That is why you have a big scary sister-wife and a much smaller but just as scary husband. Now Ia, you need to make sure that he eats lots. He has two of us to keep happy now and we don't want him running short on energy.

"Basil, I will take your men's class for now, and I will stay clothed. You two get to stay in bed and to act like any other new-married couple today. Even though I am jealous of that and feel like crawling back in to bed with you both, I am only the sister-wife and people do need to be told. It will be best for me to tell them. I am also going to see the Princesses."

"If I don't kill Rani for what she said to Ia then I am going to demand that they cast you a spell later. If you don't mind, that is my sister. I can see now why all of the girls in our village who follow the path I am now on are smooth down below. I also need to see about you getting some marriage jewellery." *This is going to cement things for her.* She opened a small box on top of a dresser and pulled something out.

"For today you can wear mine." She leant forward and fastened her rubies around Ia's neck before kissing her and sitting down naked and getting back to eating. "Stop crying…Basil…kiss her thoroughly and make her stop crying."

My…our husband is spluttering. "I am not sure how these things are going to work but think about how Stefan kisses one of the cousins. He doesn't hold back just because the other one is there…well he doesn't now." She cocked her head to the side. *We won't mention the first week or so of that relationship. Now it will be his turn to be amused at us.*

"I cannot afford to get jealous, or anything else, when there are things to be done and I have to admit to feeling both at present. I want to make love to both of you and have you fuck me all day." She popped some more food in her mouth as she started grabbing clothes and donning them. "Stop staring at me like that both of you. Ia…it is what you wanted…isn't it?" Ia nodded.

"Basil, look at her. She is very pretty. Remember what we agreed. Be tender with her and make her forget her past and anything else. Now have fun together and I will come back later. If I hear from you at all today it is only to be a cry of pleasure that I hear. Basil...she is crying again...stop her."

With that she slipped out of the door and let Maeve out of the house, bringing a chair with a woven reed seat out and putting it in the sun with the rug on it. "You get to keep people away for the day. I will call and bring food, but you have to make sure they are not disturbed at all until I have told everyone."

She looked back at the door before heading off. *I am still not entirely sure about the wisdom of the path that we have just taken, even if we could see no other course forward for us. The boat is certainly well and truly launched out now, and there can be no turning back for us. I pray that it works out and we will see what seas we will travel in good time.*

Chapter XIII

Astrid

2nd Secundus

I have talked to Sin about keeping the children elsewhere until tomorrow morning. Talking to Sin can be interesting. Her only reaction to the news is to want to know if she will be kept on. With the way the men in the Brotherhood treat women, it seems that the only surprise to her is that Basil had felt it necessary to marry Ia rather than to just take her.

Kaliope is more surprised. She may be from the Brotherhood, but unlike Sin, she is not from a slave background. Thorstein is absolutely flabbergasted. He looks even more stunned than he did when I appeared in the church, although on this occasion he hasn't fainted. "Try to think of it as getting another sister. You will no longer be the youngest of the siblings."

"Don't worry," Astrid said. "I know what I am doing...I think...and she is really very sweet even if she is not a believer. I think that their priests and priestesses have to make a choice when they start to actually practice. Only the good ones get to stay in the villages. The bad ones may try and hide it, but soon they flee and they often end up with everyone's hand raised against them.

"So, just like we know for certain with Simeon; we also know that she is not an evil person. How many can say that about their partner honestly?" She looked at her brother. *He needs more.* "I promise that I will work on her faith, although I do not think that I will have much success. One of the reasons that it had to be this way was because of her beliefs."

Astrid
an hour later

Of all the ways for me to announce the way that things now are, this has got to be one of the most dramatic. Astrid had reclaimed the earring, put it in a pouch, and then gone to the hall. She strolled in and looked around a hall full of near naked men.

Most of the men of the village are gathered and waiting for Basil. They look surprised but are waiting for me to speak. "I will be taking your class today. For a variety of reasons Basil married Ia last night and they will be very busy all day."

Now they are far more than just surprised. The expressions on their faces are so dramatic that I am almost tempted to go out and find another wife just to see them again. The next reaction from the men was so funny that she burst out laughing herself. After exchanging looks with the others, Robin complained: "But we didn't give him a send-off party."

"Then," said Astrid, "I will try to make sure that he is free tomorrow night. You can have him then if we have not made him too tired." *Not tonight though. You cannot have him at all tonight.*

Astrid
after the class

Astrid went to see the Princesses. *I was really incredibly angry with Rani. It is only by good fortune that Maeve led me to Ia before she stopped crying and actually had a chance to do harm to herself. At least, now after I have finished the class, I have burned off much of my rage and have calmed down somewhat. A little bit at least.*

I have to acknowledge, to myself at any rate, that the rejection by Basil and I had played a greater part for Ia. Rani only served as the one who actually set off Ia's despair. I think that their reaction, even though they knew of Ia's feelings, was almost as good as that of the men. Theodora has quickly agreed to cast the spells when they were wanted. She even gave me a kiss on the cheek in congratulations.

Rani

Astrid has finally left. The girl upbraided me in no uncertain terms and she did not give me a chance to interrupt her to explain my reasons or defend what I said. How dare she? I am her Princess and a Kshatya mage as well. She is just a hunter. She really does not have an idea about what her place is.

"Just what did you say to Ia?" Theodora asked. *Now even my Princess is telling me why having referred to the girl as being 'dispensable', particularly in the tone that I admit to using when I am addressing any person from the Swamp, might not have been a good idea in the circumstances. Is everyone going to tell me that I was wrong? It seems so.*

"She volunteered to come with us," Theodora said, "and she is still the only woman, who had not been rescued at any rate, to actually come from there. She is now one of ours. It is our job as Princesses to look after all of our people. Still, it seems to have worked out eventually, even if Astrid is now fiercely protective of the witch-child, well witch-woman or, I suppose, technically even a witch-wife now." *At least that solves the other, and for us more important, issue with Ia.*

Astrid

later

Christopher and Bianca are only mildly surprised and their quick looks at each other show relief on their faces more than anything else. She explained about the lack of ritual to Christopher. *He does not seem too concerned. They are taking it so well that it is obvious that they have been aware of the issue and discussing what might happen next.* Bianca came over and hugged Astrid tight. "Are you happy with this?" she asked.

It is so very clear that they have obviously been talking about us. I may as well be honest. Neither will gossip about what I say and I need to tell someone. "She has told you about her past." *Both nod.* "I think it may have been a lot worse for her than she ever let on to you. I will admit to you only that, at first, we married her out of charity...really it was to keep her alive. Now I am still not sure how I feel.

"I think it has always been obvious that I really like making love. Even if I prefer doing it with Basil, Ia is certainly good in bed and she certainly knows what to do to make me happy there and she is very beautiful, She is far prettier than I am. I only hope that we have not taken her as one might take a stray animal as a pet."

Astrid looked directly at Christopher. "I did pray about the decision, for an hour at least. I didn't just do it on a whim. Even though we care for her, we don't love her, but it feels right somehow. I don't know why. It is like there is some sort of completeness inside me.

"I need to talk with Ayesha about how she felt when she accepted Hulagu and, when I have settled down a bit more, to talk with the Princesses again. I have come to think that maybe the whole thing is destined for some reason, and that makes me more than a little nervous about what we have just done. I don't like being so important that I am involved in prophesy."

Astrid

later

Now I have to go through a whole day with people coming and congratulating me and asking questions. Lãdi wants to know about a wedding feast. We didn't even think about that. Astrid set two night's time for that. She explained about the men taking Basil tomorrow.

At least I don't have to chase up Eleanor. The jeweller came looking for me as soon as her husband told her. She may have some suggestions about wedding ornaments, but I have given thought to this and already have some very specific ideas in my mind. They have left our jeweller grinning. This will be something new for her to make. She needs to get to work.

Astrid

The warmest greeting has come from the cousins. I suppose that was predictable. Now they are not the only three who are openly in a group where everyone fucks each other. I suppose that we are in a thrupple as they are. They are very happy for us newlyweds. Not only is Ia from a family that they knew, but they have apparently seen how she has been around me, even if they said nothing. From their own experience they knew what such looks meant.

They are full of advice about how three people may behave in bed, some of which, I admit, made me blush deeply, although they will be fun to try at least once. There are quite a few things they have suggested that would not have occurred to me, and they have said that they would make sure that Stefan talks with Basil.

"You don't have to be as open about things as we are if you don't want to be," said Bryony.

"But that is up to you. After all, we had each other before Bryony found Stefan," added Adara. "You had Basil first…just make sure that you give Ia some public displays of affection, even just holding her hand. She cannot feel left out in that way."

"…and you will come to enjoy shocking people, I am sure. Sometimes it is good to just have someone to hold." *I hadn't realised it before, but when the two are together like this, their fingers just brushing against the other and with no-one else around, they are almost like one person with two, admittedly very nearly identical, voices.*

As she walked away an amusing thought struck her. *I wonder if, in time to come, Ia and I will start thinking alike.* Astrid grinned widely and nearly broke out laughing. *That could be very interesting the next time that we are in Darkreach. Hrothnog may never recover if that were to happen.*

Rani

The matter of Astrid and Ia overshadows what I wanted to talk about. I had wanted to show my wife my ideas for a new spell, but the way it now works it is possible that it will only ever need to be used once, and so I will have to suffer the fact that, as a new spell, it will be harder to cast.

I am proud of the way that I have now rejected my earlier idea. I am not used to thinking like this, but I have a modified version of the final spell that I can practice, so the final is not too far away from something I am familiar with.

I don't want to be scolded. I want my logic applauded. If the light weapon, or one of our existing spells, will not be enough, then the Adversaries will most likely be fleeing or attacking in a ship or on a carpet, or at least something like that. If I can destroy what they were in, or on, then I can, at least, stop them so that people with other spells and weapons can get within range.

I have made the spell so that it will attack, not the Adversaries themselves, but whatever they are using for their travel. If we are very lucky, they will be on a carpet and their fall may even kill them. As a consequence of limiting the spell so much in what it will affect, I have been able to boost, in the trade-off, the power of the spell when it hits.

The range is now as long as I need it to be. It is now a case of being able to hit anything that I can see well enough to target. When Astrid had been irate with me over Ia I tried to defuse the matter by telling her that I had the spell she asked for at least. That had, at least, partly deflected the wrath from me, but it did take away something from the surprise and congratulations over thinking of something so new.

Astrid

During the day Olympias came up from the *River Dragon* to talk to Rani and to shuttle more stone balls down to the vessel for the arbalests to use. *It is sweet of her. Now she has found out about what has happened, she is more concerned for how I feel than for her brother. Him she is not worried about at all.*

"He is a man," Olympias said, "and he has two beautiful women of his own who he can make love to legally. If he is awkward in any way now he will get over it very quickly. He will probably be over it by the time you get home although it may last until the next time you climb in bed with the two of them. However, if I ever catch you being unhappy while he looks smug then I will give him hell."

Astrid had to assure her that it had been her idea and she ended up telling Olympias more about her new sister than she had meant to. *She may need to know, she is my sister after all. I am getting to have quite a large family… aren't I? I now have two sisters and a sister-wife nearby as well as the men.* Olympias left promising to send Denizkartal up for tomorrow night and to be there herself for the feast.

They have been on the ship working on new weapons. My sister is proud that now there is an arbalest on each corner as well as a light weapon set up, for the present, under deck…but now they are finished. Our little River Dragon *now probably has a lot more bite on it than anything else that is floating on the ocean that is of its size. The big ships may still be able to beat us, but not if we are smart.*

Astrid

2nd Secundus, the Feast Day of Saint Amand

The night was a roaring success for the men. *It is even a good and appropriate night for a party and the drinking of wine.* Astrid and Ia spent the night together much more quietly, talking about their past and future as much as making love.

It is strange to spend as much time in bed just holding my sister-wife as I have doing anything else. As Ia has opened up more about her past, once again she has fallen into weeping. She has never told anyone all that has happened to her. She didn't notice Astrid's face growing harder and harder when she talked.

Ia had only just, by slipping off her bonds and running into the bush alone as a four-year-old, avoided the fate of Verily. It took her two weeks as a small child alone in the jungle avoiding becoming food for hungry beasts to make it back to the village. She was not able to describe her attackers well enough then for them to be taken.

It was only once she came into her powers and was able to use her ball to look back to that time that she gained a sense of who they might be. This reliving with me has been both good and bad for her. While she was a captive she was already healed twice in the same manner as Verily had been healed. I am sure that the warlock-priest of the bandits, the one with the raven, was the one who did it.

Without saying anything to Ia, I am now certain that her other, and older, sisters who went missing have probably had the same fate. They were not able to escape and, if we searched for them, we would probably find that their bones now lie somewhere down the path of our river. My poor dear little witch-lover, it is now up to us to show you the affection that you have never had.

In return, as she held her, Astrid told Ia all about her story and the family she now had through Astrid and through Basil. *I even told her the story of me killing the bear from when I was growing up and still almost a child. I have to admit that it is a long time since I even thought about that. I am not sure I have even told Basil.*

As well, by marrying Basil she has gone from being an orphan with nothing to having parents and more than a hand of brothers and some sisters and lots of nieces and nephews and far more cousins than I have ever met and I am sure that there are even more in Darkreach that I have not heard of yet.

Astrid
3rd Secundus, the Feast Day of Saint Agatha

The first light was trying to make the sky pale over the mountains to the east when Basil re-appeared back at his house. *It has been a while since we last heard the noise of the party after all.* He was brought to the door by Denizkartal and Thorstein, slung between them in a very lop-sided way given the height differences.

But then all three of the brothers-in-law are very lop-sided anyway and, when they left Basil, the other two needed to support each other as they moved away. I will bet Thorstein will be in trouble from Kaliope when he gets home and he will have penances from both his wife and his Confessor for some time.

Apparently exercise class for the men is cancelled for the day and even Christopher and the other priests are a little quieter than usual during the service. It is only us women who seem to be doing much in the way of work, particularly noisy work, around the village today. Some of the women even seem to be making even more noise than they really need to.

Astrid
much later

That night the wedding feast went well and, even if the marriage had been consummated already, the dancers all enjoyed themselves with eight women doing the Khitan dance in two sets of four.

It was pronounced by all to be an auspicious occasion for a marriage feast because, half way through, Bilquis gave a cry and had to be carried out by her sister-wife Yumn, Lakshmi and the priests with Fear in attendance. Tariq was hopping from foot to foot around her as her waters broke.

Most were back within the hour. The birth of the girl Zainab was cheerfully celebrated as being a proper part of the wedding celebration.

Chapter XIV

Astrid

4th Secundus

It has taken until now for us to crawl out of bed for long enough for Ia to begin to seek a place to put her grove. She is looking to the future and has already rejected the standing forest on the other side of our rivulet. "Until the bridge is put in it is too hard to get to, and once it is put in the area will be used for other things…it will lack tranquillity," she said and she was definite about that.

Now she is leading me up the valley below the path to the falls. The floor of the valley past the mine is too narrow to be used for much and even the animals seem to stay out of it. Fallen stones mean that anyone travelling up it has to scramble over them in a couple of places. We need to look out for snakes warming themselves on the rocks in the summer sun.

We will need to work on the area to make a path. However, now we are past the rocks, there is a nice flat area here. It is framed on one side by where the waterfall of warm water that comes cascading down from the path above and splashing off rocks into first a small pool and then a larger, placid, one before it drains down another small cliff into the river. She looked around at the markings on the rocks. *At least we look to be well above the spring flood level.*

All around are fern trees, the smallest of them is the height of a person and some are three times that size. We passed through a small patch of Leatherwoods and forced through some Whitey-wood and Mountain Laurel on the village side. Apart from the sound of the falling water, it is silent. There is only the occasional sound as a bird and or an insect speaks. Although it was not all that far away, the village behind its wall makes only a very faint and distant noise that you have to listen hard to hear at all.

Looking up an overhang hides the view from the path. Ia seems happy with what she sees. "This place seems to be fine. It is not the size that is important, but its feel. This has the feel of peace, of serenity, of being a part of the earth around us." *You can certainly see nothing else in the way of people from here, not even much of the uncleared area on the other side, except at its very upper end.*

"It perhaps needs some extra trees, but it has the huge tree ferns already and beds of moss lie underneath them." *She is waving her hands and indicating.* "Ferns cling to the cliff along with some rock orchids. The water is warm, but the area here is cool in the summer heat and it feels right." Ia sat down on a rock.

She is patting the damp moss beside her to indicate that I should sit there. It seems that it is damp bum time for me. Maeve is sniffing around the ferns still. "This will be my shrine. I will dedicate this as its first priestess. Here I will be in charge."

Opening a pouch at her belt Ia pulled out a tiny crystal sphere only half a hand across. "It is all that my stepparents could afford for me," she said. "I have been spending my money on weapons and other things. Getting a better one of these was to be next on my list. It will not be cheap." She took a small biscuit that she had baked that morning out of a pouch and held it up in both hands and closed her eyes.

She has begun praying in, what I assume to be Faen. Do I have to learn that now? Now she is eating the biscuit, holding it in both hands and nibbling at it like a little squirrel. She kept her eyes closed for a while before opening them and turning to Astrid. "Hashish," she said and began talking for a while.

Her voice is getting dreamy and her pupils are growing huge. She has only eaten one, but she is only small. She has made a whole box of them for the trip that lies ahead of us. Sin looked at them this morning and asked if she could have one. I admit that they do smell delicious and I was tempted as well. Ia quickly told her why it was not a good idea.

Now she is feeling the biscuit start to take hold. You can see that in the smile on her face, as if she were dreaming a pleasant dream. Her eyes are drifting. Ia held her hand up for silence and again began to pray. Eventually she opened her eyes and picked up the tiny sphere, again with both hands.

Again, she is behaving as if she were a little squirrel. She has it balanced on the tips of the fingers of both hands and is holding it up close to her eyes so that she can see into its depths. She is staring into it and humming to herself. All that I can see from here is that the little sphere seems to have grown cloudy, but that could even be from the light around us.

After the space of half an hour or so Ia put it away and pronounced herself satisfied in a dreamy voice. "It was a very good foretelling. I saw myself, ten or more years away, here with my children and several others gathered around. I will not have a large group to care for, but we will be happy and safe. I will need Goditha to help me. There will be a slab of stone there," she pointed at the ground, "...and there, there and there for us to sit on and a small altar carved into the rock there and a few other things."

"I don't even know some of the trees that will be here though and I will need to go back to an established grove to see another priest or priestess to get some other things." Smiling happily into the future of her vision she took Astrid's hand. *She may be more than a little unsteady on her feet, but it is not just that.* Together they went back to the village.

Astrid
late in the afternoon

After school had finished, Ia gathered up Ir, Fullon and Arlene, the three children in the school who came from the same sort of tradition as herself, but from among the Bear People, and took them off to the new grove to be.

They have taken some fruit with them in baskets and gathered up flowers and some dry sticks as they went past where the Khitan had left some. Soon a wisp of smoke can be seen going up. Now it is my job to forbid Ruth from going to watch by standing in her way. They came back only just before the others had finished eating their dinner.

Lakshmi
6th Secundus, the Feast Day of Saint John the Apostle

Over the next two days Rabi'ah and Asad have had a son, Rāfi, while Zafirah gave birth to Sughdī as a son for Atā.

Again, Fear has made these first births easier for the mothers and she has been right as to the sex and health of the babies. She has even warned that Sughdī is turned around the wrong way before the serious contractions start. It is as well that the men are already outside. Zafirah needed to be given a tincture of opium.

Now that we can see the opium taking effect, with Zafirah's sister-wife Umm anxiously holding her hand, with me instructing Fear in what to do inside the mother and, even more importantly, the aid of doing her own listening to the baby, Fear has been able to turn the baby around in the womb.

It is lucky that it looks like she will always have small hands and delicate wrists. The mother will still be sore for some time. At least the boy has been delivered safely without anyone having to make an incision in the stomach and so creating a bigger risk for both mother and son and without needing a miracle to be cast.

"She will make a great midwife," Lakshmi told Fear's proud parents. *After the delivery was over, and as soon as she had washed, I hear that Fear ran back to school and insisted on telling everyone about it, even if the boys really didn't want to hear the details and apparently some of the girls looked horrified at what they might have to look forward to later in life.*

Rãfi has also been an auspicious birth. Rabi'ah had gone into labour during the wedding of Nadia and Erika. *No-one is sure, with no brothers or other male relatives around, how the two girls can have a child themselves. All have to agree, however, that the omens are definitely good for them to have a family. Nadia looks pleased, although Erika is a little more cautious in her optimism.*

Theodora

Now that I have cast the spell that Astrid wanted, it is time to take Ia aside and check things. Before she arrived here, but after she had announced that she was coming to the valley, she was not able to ride a saddle. Now, and to her delight, the marriage seems to have made her a Mouse. It seems that the valley itself has accepted her. She is now able to do to ride a saddle. I admit that I may have thought to try it, but I really was not expecting the result.

I am more than a little shocked at all of this and its implications. Her mind worked on the ramifications of what had just happened for her conceptions of magic. *I had thought it possible, but now I will be testing our students, and even the later arrivals, on the first set of saddles and whether they can use them.*

Does this acceptance of Ia by the magic of our valley mean that the effects of the Horse charm will also apply to her? It has taken me only a little experimentation to show that the shield charms work for her, so it is more than likely that the magic of the Horse will as well.

Now, what does it mean for specific magic that is limited to a small group of people if it can grow and change like that? I have to lay that problem before my husband. Why has no-one commented on this before? Surely someone has noticed it at some time. Why has my husband not been taught this at her University? Indeed, why was I not taught it when I studied in Ardlark?

Christopher
14th Secundus

Christmas has come and gone. It is even possible, although it will still be largely incomplete, that by time the next Christmas comes to Mousehole the Basilica of Saint George will be able to be used for our celebrations.

With the aid of our magic and even with people just helping when they are free, the building is proceeding far faster than it would have with a full workforce of skilled workers without our aids. A good portion of the walls is nearly complete around the nave and even some of the parts of the roof near the altar are done.

The first of the small half domes around the edges of the great dome is even starting to take shape now. The artisan that had been brought in from Ardlark, Leo, has just been helping with general construction so far. Now he is starting to prepare the areas that he will work on when he can. Once the small domes are done the first part of the main dome will be the next part to be worked on and, once it is done, things can start being painted and laid and installed around it.

Only then will the rest of the building be completed. As it is, the building presents a strange appearance. On one end it is starting to look like it is nearing completion although at the other end, at the entrance, there is a front wall that is not even as tall as a single person. The entry doorway more resembles the wall around one of the fields than what its final form will look like.

Without our magic it would all have looked like that for very many years, even with a far larger workforce, but with the enchanted objects that we have available, and Goditha's daily enchantments, the building work is going far faster than anyone could have predicted.

Seeing that she will be posing as a Christian when she is in Haven, Astrid has made sure that Ia is starting to attend services. She has to seem comfortable posing as one of us. In particular she needs to know the correct things to say if she is asked.

She is very reluctant to come but Astrid is able to point out the other women of different faiths who are there, some just keeping their friends' or husbands' company, although some do join in with parts of the service, particularly the singing. Everyone usually enjoys the singing once they learn the words.

It was hard not to laugh when I heard the two. "Your voice is so much better than either Basil's and mine is. I think that you will have to do all of the singing for the family when we are in Church." *Astrid's face shows a huge grin at the horrified look that was returned to her. It seems that Ia will not have it all of her own way. For a start it is obvious that she has yet to learn when Astrid is making a joke at her expense.*

Basil

Before we are due to leave on our next trip out Stefan, it seems at the request of his wives, sat me down along with Hulagu, Norbert, Denny and the Muslim men. The more experienced men, as we had a few quiet drinks or kaf, gave a few pointers to Denny and I about how it is possible to survive a marriage as the permanently outnumbered partner.

Somehow it seems to me that it is far easier tracking plots in taverns than this way of being married is. What am I in for?

Rani

I have finally decided to start by taking the same group out to Haven as we took last time to the Swamp. I will be adding myself, Parminder and the other women that were born in Haven as well as Ariadne and her husband, Krukurb, to help look after the arbalests and Nikephorus, who has insisted on coming to look after us.

Lakshmi is unsure as to whether she should stay or go, but the next births due are those of Thomäis and Irene anyway. Both of them are crew and insist on staying on board the ship, even if they are restricted in what they can do. Olympias has reasoned that at least they can keep the log if nothing else. The former Brotherhood slave-prostitutes are really needed in their new role as sailors on this trip, although everyone will work the ship if it is needed.

Now that Christmas is over we can begin to move everyone down to the River Dragon. *Several of the couples and thrupples who are going have decided to have an early night. There will be little privacy to be found for them over the next few weeks. At the same time all of the mages and priests are doing all of the last-minute practising or worked on wands or other spells that happen each time that we set out.*

Christopher
14th Secundus

It is odd getting news as a Bishop. Aziz and Verily return with their children from Dhargev and I get a report. The visit was a great success and having four priests in the valley was a boon over the holiday for Father Michael.

He reports that, thanks to the stone working tools, the first and smallest church is already nearing completion and will be dedicated to Saint Fergus. It is already too small for what they need and several others are being planned before it is finally expanded.

Theodule is also told to expect another vocation or two to come down to start training soon, perhaps even while we are away on this trip. It seems that, unlike much of The Land nowadays where there is so much in the way of other opportunities, being a priest is now considered to be a prestige occupation among the Hobgoblins and, with the examples of Father Cyril and Father Aziz before them, several young men are starting to think about the priesthood as a good career move.

With everything that has happened, it slipped my mind that one of my roles as a prelate is to train my own priests. I cannot rely on just taking them from another diocese. It looks like at least one of the spare classrooms at the school might need to be used for adults, and not just for the language classes. With the Hobgoblin priests we will have to start with language training and writing before we can even get onto theology and the practical aspects of being a priest in a parish.

Ruth and Theodule have assured me that that they will start to put together a syllabus while I am away. It also seems that I have a secretary, We Declare Unto You Glad Tidings, who is known as Glad. She is one of the Brotherhood girls who just appeared one day in the building I am using as an office and storage area until the Basilica is finished and she just started working.

She promises to have them all written up neatly for me to look over by the time we get back. I have never gotten around to asking her how she has happened to take up her new role but, despite my earlier objections, I have found that I really do need her and she has soon made herself irreplaceable.

Neither Theodule nor I have ever heard of a priest with a tattooed pattern before, but I admit to curiosity in seeing how it works for Aziz. There are still so many things that are new to Simeon about the church here that this is merely one of them.

Even if it all goes well Theodule reckons himself as being too old for one.

"My skin is starting to get old," he said. "Soon the wrinkles that I am starting to show would make the shape unrecognisable, even to God."

I hear from my wife that, when they had unpacked from their visit and settled the children, Verily went looking for Ia to show off her new tattoo and she was very surprised to discover where she now is. It took a long talk with firstly my wife, and then she had to take her to talk to Astrid, before she fully understood why the changes had happened.

I have to admit that, when we discussed it in Confession, Astrid's point about rejecting Ia being a matter of excessive pride was, surprisingly, a very good one. It reminds one of Ezekial: 'Now this was the sin of your sister Sodom: She and her daughters were arrogant, overfed and unconcerned; they did not help the poor and needy.' Ia was very much in need of Astrid's compassion.

Chapter XV

Shilpa
15th Secundus

Tomorrow we leave and today a caravan from Freehold arrives in Evilhalt. Now I have a chance to pick up some trade goods, ones we have not produced, that we can take down river with us and make a good profit from. She hurried to their campsite and purchased their entire load of goods and arranged for it to be delivered to the wharf.

The traders are a bit surprised and are now looking around the village to see what they can take back home, but are finding little of note. They were thinking that they would use up profit while they waited to assemble a load, but to their relief one of our last saddles down from the valley has brought us word of a caravan coming down from Darkreach.

It will be here within a week. When I told him, the Freehold merchant was very pleased. If he is able to buy a load of goods from it, instead of travelling all of the way to buy items from Haven, then he will have cut well over a month from his trip and he will probably have some even more exotic goods than he usually has to take back across the plains.

Now that I have gotten Basil to spread the word through the village, the good citizens of Evilhalt are more than happy to be a trading point, instead of just a waypoint. Now I have a couple of people investigating loans to set up warehousing and wholesaling facilities. Haven may rue this in the longer term. This settlement is far better placed as a trade centre than my old Kingdom.

What I have bought from the caravan has given us a very mixed load of Freehold produce, with woollen goods, leatherwork, berry liqueur and even some illuminated books as some of the more prominent items. Bianca saw the load as it was being brought on board and it nearly caused her to cry.

Bianca

I looked at the manifest Shilpa was checking and it is very nearly the same load of goods that Francesco's caravan had been carrying when it was ambushed. She went to look at the caravan and had to hurry back to her husband. *The caravan has carts and packhorses, animal tenders like Rosa and I, and even a similar mix of guards, but I feel no treachery from them.*

It is so nearly a copy of the one that I was once part of. I look at the young girls working in it with the animals and see myself as I once was. The memory is burnt into my mind, although so much has happened since. I need to be held tight and made to feel safe. I thought that I was over the dreams, but I am again hearing the rapes and seeing the sights in my dreams. She began to shake.

Hulagu

Hulagu took himself off to have a talk with the tribesmen, who were back among the guards, both for the sake of information and to allay Bianca's disquiet. After they had gotten over the shock of being hailed by such a famous man, and a Ta-khan, they told him how quiet it had become crossing the plains. *It is very odd to be thought a ülgeriin baatar and deferred to.*

It seems that there are only the normal dangers of travel, wild beasts and perhaps a few of the younger members of the local tribes who were seeing what they could lift from inattentive travellers. The Örnödiin are not covered by the Compact, nor are they ever likely to be, and so the caravans with their merchants are now the only ones that are regarded as fair game by all.

It has become a game between the guards and the tribes as to whether things can be stolen without being noticed or not. It is just like often happens between tribal groups, without the chance of a feud happening. The Örnödiin haven't realised this yet and it is regarded as a great joke by all among the emeel amidarch baigaa khümüüs. The Örnödiin merchants still think of the plains as a very dangerous place and so they pay their guards accordingly.

Theodora
16th Secundus

We set out three days after Christmas into a fine summer morning. I can stand on the quarterdeck with my husband's arms around me as the River Dragon *heads out into the lake with the green light box almost unneeded but still showing the way. The wind is low, just strong enough to set the light from the cloudless sky playing in sparkling highlights on the surface of the water.*

We have the Freehold goods on board, as well as a mixed load from the north of the lake with some bags of wheat, barley and root vegetables, mainly as ballast, although I am told that good large onions always find a ready market in Haven. We have some jewels, some rosewater and some potions as well as Gasparin from our valley. What we will take from here to Haven as a regular item to justify our ostensible trade mission is unsure, and that is my job to determine.

Eventually I hope to have more caravans ending in Evilhalt or Erave Town, with merchants selling everything there to let the goods be taken down the river by boat, just as we are doing this time with the Freehold load. For a normal river craft that cargo, even without adding in the grain and vegetables would have made for a very full load.

If the wind is with us, the entire trip by river will take a quarter of the time it will take travelling one way by land, even allowing for the harder up-river leg. While we were in the Swamp, my husband reached a tentative agreement with both Baron Sigihevi and with Mayor Cynric about their river traders using the facility that we are trying to set up, once it is established.

The latter only agreed because of the influence of his Metropolitan, but the important thing is that he had finally agreed. My dusky beauty was probably a poor choice as a person to do the negotiation even though the end result of such a move will be a reduction in the numbers of Havenite traders and an increase in their own river traffic for the two villages, without them losing anything in the way of tolls.

It was hard, given her origin, for my husband to play this point creditably to people who are used to how the Havenite realm treats outsiders and I have had to make my own visits and go over the same ground to strengthen the point and stress the disinterest of Mousehole. I am getting heartily sick of local rivalries when there is a bigger picture for us all to contend with.

It is not as if the trade station is even so important. After all it is just being set up to serve as one pretext to send priests in and to have observers there all of the time to keep an eye on what Haven is up to. Surely the two men can see that. The fact that it makes financial sense for us all is surely just a bonus to the political gain.

At any rate, Metropolitan Cosmas knows what is really happening and Fathers Eustathius and Hilarion are waiting in Erave Town for us to take on to Sacred Gate as its first priests, while Father Kostas should already be finding his own way into Bloomact on a river trader.

Soon, after this expedition, and before we go on to the Caliphate, a trip will need to be made to give him, as well as any priests who might have come into the Swamp from Southpoint, money to build with and to live on until they can become established and able to provide for themselves, if they are ever able to. Those who live outside the Swamp may have to support the churches that are established there for quite some time.

Astrid

One who is very glad that we are on board the River Dragon *is Maeve. The racoon has obviously been waiting for her entire life to be given a ship of her own to play with and she is frequently running up and down the rigging, even hurtling down stays head first and hanging beneath them. It turns out that her hands are just the right size for the ropes.*

Unlike the last animal that was on board, the monkey that we will not mention, she is a delight and, just as in the village, she makes no messes for people to unexpectedly find. Although there are no children to play with, there are many unoccupied adults who can be easily convinced to provide a lap or to use the comb that she brings them. It is obviously a hard life for my sister-wife's little creature being the only familiar in the village.

Olympias

We need to take no soundings nowadays on the lake if we cross by the most direct route. With all of the practice that we have made over it, the whole lake is now almost familiar territory and my charts are now nearly complete for here, at least on a large scale. I have made us explore almost every corner of it, at least sketchily and even if the rowing boats have to be used.

As a part of our charting, I have even taken the River Dragon *down the Rhastaputra a little way and brought her back multiple times. Thus, although it is a river, and so changeable enough that we will always have to be careful, fairly confident charts exist for a bit over a day's travel south. We have even practised docking time and again, sometimes a dozen times in one day.*

Now that we are using the saddles openly in most of The Land, although if we do bring them out on this trip it will be the first time that they will appear openly in Haven, the navigation of the river is, as it will be for almost any unknown water, so much easier. Our Princesses have still not decided whether to be open about them in the city, but saddles will be openly used at least as far as first settlement above Garthang.

Olympias

later in the day

I can stand here almost silent and proud. Our docking at Erave Town shows the smooth handling of an experienced crew who have all done it many times before. The onlookers who are standing around watching the manoeuvre are now here more to watch the pretty girls of my crew than out of curiosity about my ship.

Here the tax man is ready and again goes away largely disappointed. We pay a passage fee only. Shilpa will be buying goods here but has nothing of interest to sell. Mind you, she is excited by the prospect of trade with the far side of the Swamp opening up and is quick to head off to talk to her contacts among the merchants and traders about the possibilities.

Here we will take on barrels, always a good item to take to cities, as much rose water as we can buy to add to what we have, and even some good ironmongery that was made by the Mayor himself.

Christopher

I have the priests and our wives quickly off the ship and headed off to Saint Sophia's where the missionary priests are waiting. Both are younger married men, who will be leaving their youngish children behind to be safe until they are called for. Their wives both need some support about the whole idea of travel to such a strange place.

The priests going to Haven have been provided with six armsmen who will be coming with them. It has been decided that holiness is all well and good, but some more physical protection will also be needed for priests who are living down there among the thieves. They will be good targets with their own goods and with money for building a church.

Cosmas is considering doing the same for the Swamp churches and I agree with him on that even more than I do for Haven. That is a far more dangerous place to be an outsider. Seeing that so many are in the group going down the river the priests are even bringing a cook to look after them all and they have a clerk with them as well.

Theodora

Although there is not much to say, I need to take my husband to see the Mayor at work out of politeness. He tries to hold himself aloof, but I have not given up on my seeking to make him more actively interested in what we are planning on doing in Haven.

My husband, even now, still has difficulty with the concept of a ruler doing such a manual trade, but I have made her wear her shipboard working clothes so that we can sit in his smithy and talk while he keeps working. I told my love that it is only by her obviously accepting him as he is that she can show that she has broken free from her past in Haven.

Astrid

The River Dragon *has barely tied up and Ia has taken me by the hand and, while our husband, and that still sounds odd, is headed to the taverns with Zeenat, Lakshmi and Ayesha, we are quickly on the way by foot to the sacred grove that lies well outside the village. As an unbeliever I will only be allowed into the grove because I am a sister-wife and there are no rituals being done now.*

It will, apparently, not do to fly to one of them on such a visit. How Ia has worked that out when the saddles are quite new to everyone is a mystery to me, but she already has a protocol firmly in mind and apparently flying to the grove to visit on a saddle was not a part of it. Maybe you cannot ride a horse to one either.

The senior Wiccan priests at Erave Town are Fiachu ap Maglorix and his wife Crida verch Ninne. It turns out, despite being them being several years older than Ia, and with a couple of children, that they are not much more experienced in casting than my young witch-wife-sister-whatever, if there is indeed any difference at all.

It seems that the more that a person crams into their life, and it does not matter whether it is painful, or if it is good, and the more that they are forced to perform and stretch themselves; the quicker they gain in their strength in regard to both magic and faith. I admit that the same seems to work physically with me, so I don't see why it wouldn't be the same with magic.

The pair of local priests admit that their life has been fairly uneventful living at Erave Town and tending to their small flock. That is something that they are both more than content with and they both hope that it stays that way. I guess that it takes a special person, or perhaps just a stupid one, to always seek danger and upset.

Ia spends time in discussion with the other two about what she needs back in Mousehole and arrangements are being made to pick some things up when we return. I just get to sit quietly and look around at this quiet and pleasant place. It is very similar in its feel to the area Ia has selected. It is like a Church, full of quiet and a balm for a busy soul.

I have to admit that the couple seem unlike most of the people that we met in the Swamp. They are both polite and cheerful for a start. They also seem to be open and lacking in the greed and dishonesty that we saw so much of. When we talk about what is happening in the broader world Fiachu admits that, when he was younger there was less of that selfishness and the growth of such attitudes is one of the reasons that he and Crida had come to this grove when they could.

They get along well with Cosmas, their children are being raised happily in the openness of the Lake villages and they promise to think of Mousehole for their children's schooling as they grow older and need something more than they can get here. Theodora will be pleased to hear that we have done our job here.

Ia turned as they were walking back. "I didn't tell you, but I brought you along to see if you will be accepted as my sister-wife. I am happy with what I have done and not all of the partners of priests and priestesses have that role themselves, but I have never heard of a partner who is not at least of the Wiccan way."

Basil

When we went out into the taverns we found that the word is still out with more rumours of trouble from the Swamp. We had to work hard to counteract this. It looks like the legacy of the late unlamented Athgal Dewin is still spreading its poison. What is more, there was no reason for them to believe me or someone from Haven.

Now we have brought Ia and the cousins, as first-hand players, to different taverns to tell of what is happening there and to be pumped for information. That they are all beautiful gives them a ready audience who then have to be dissuaded from following them back to the ship when they leave looking for more than talk.

We are finding so much to do that it looks like we will not be able to leave to go down river until tomorrow morning. At least that means that we get to spend another night ashore in a bed in a tavern instead of in a hammock in a stuffy hold. I was surprised with how much I liked having one wife. Now I am quickly getting used to having two.

Christopher

23rd Secundus

We are far slower at passing down the river this time. I have convinced the Princesses that we need to stop at the towns of Garthang, Peelfall, Vinice and Shelike, all of the major towns of Haven that lie along our route. I need to teach Simeon, and indeed Fathers Eustathius and Hilarion, how to look for a Pattern as we travel.

Simeon has to draw on Aziz for help and Eustathius draws on Hilarion but they are learning by performing the ritual safely and with aid. We also can look for any co-religious who might live in the river towns, but there are none to be seen or heard of in the settlements when we ask at the temples. Of course, they may not know, or more likely not care. It may take more looking.

Lakshmi, Shilpa and Zeenat are likewise unable to hear rumours of them. In the river towns Basil says that it is not worth his while to even start to ask. Apparently we get some respect from others simply because we are priests, but so many people shun the casteless man from outside that it is useless for him to think of trying.

As it is I cannot be sure if we have missed a pattern as we go because we have ignored the many villages and hamlets that dot themselves along the river bank between the larger towns. Eventually there are clustered so tight that they are within easy walking distance of each other with only a couple of fields separating one from the next.

Shilpa

I have paid duty on almost my entire load at Garthang, reserving only some rosewater and some of the items from Mousehole in sealed boxes, and I am glad that I have done so. Most traders from outside Haven go straight to Pavitra Phāṭaka. They lack a local person to find a market and do the negotiating for them.

The normal merchants simply don't trade in the river towns along the way. For them they are simply places to stay on the way to the market. However, it turns out that this is probably an error. The smallest of them is still bigger than any of the settlements of the North and the largest, Vinice, is bigger than any other town in the west except for Pavitra Phāṭaka itself and Trekvarna and Ashvaria in Freehold.

By the time we will arrive at Anta I will have disposed of a lot of what we brought with us and one hold is already beginning to fill with rice and boxes and barrels of herbs and spices to sell on. The sheer numbers of people in the small area that is Haven makes it a ready market for most goods. The authorities just prefer to control the trade of paradēśī by encouraging them to come straight to the capital.

When they were not actually tied up Shilpa spent most of her time studying what Ruth and Kaliope had written out for her and sharing it with Zeenat and Rakhi. *I have traded a lot before, but for me it has been more a matter of instinct than a science. The two women in Mousehole have given me a list of things to consider in my costing before I accept a price.*

It takes a lot of money to run the River Dragon, *and Ruth and Kaliope have insisted that this has to be taken into account when I am bargaining. Now that I am working through some of the prices that I had asked for and had been given last trip I see why some of the merchants in Ardlark were so pleased with the prices that they had to pay. I certainly made a good profit on the trip, but now I can see that it is nowhere near as good as it could, or should, have been.*

Astrid

I should not cause the Princesses to be upset with each other, even if Rani deserves it. Basil was sitting on a hatch cover holding Ia when I came up to the others with some kaf. The Princesses were talking about something inconsequential, but I could not help seeing that Rani was looking at my little Ia with a disapproving expression on her face.

"Will you two be telling Rani's parents about Aikaterine? Will your daughters expect a sister after this visit?" *Basil has reproved me over that.* "I cannot have Rani looking down her nose at my sister-wife while she ignores the issues in her own life." Ia half-rose. *She leans over our husband and shyly gives me a kiss, one that is a kiss of thanks rather than anything else.*

Astrid
24th Secundus

Now we are near to Sacred Gate and the issue between the Princesses is still not solved. All aboard soon knew about it, as it is hard to keep any such issues secret on a ship. It is like having an argument in a small house. There is nowhere where you can go to avoid hearing all about everything, even if you would prefer not to hear.

Theodora still wants Rani's parents to know everything about her, their marriage and about the children, whom she loves. It seems that until I used my big mouth to raise the matter, she had not thought of getting pregnant again, but now that the issue had been raised...I am really regretting having raised it and not just because I am undergoing a penance for it after having made Confession as to my reasons for making the remark. It was very nekulturny of me to do so.

Having seen a lot more of the world at large since we were here on our last visit, we are all now viewing the city with new eyes. We come through the islands with those who have been here before pointing out the sights to those who have not. As soon as it is in sight Ariadne is looking hard at Kilā Dvīpa, the fortified island, with very professional eyes.

She is looking up and I can see she is wishing that she could get above it and look down, but she is not allowed to. Rani has assured her not to judge the island too quickly. Only a fraction of the island's defences will be visible and she, herself, only knows a small fraction of them. Supposedly no single person, except perhaps the Maharajah, knows about them all. This fortification will have some of the very strongest magic known to back up its mere physical defences.

When we come opposite Hāthī Dvīpa, where Rani's parents live. For different reasons, several people on board have fallen silent. I think that I can see a faint hint of a tear in the corner of Rani's eye, but if it was there, she has quickly wiped it away. Once again I am hard at work kicking myself for what I so cattily said. She is trying hard to change and she is actually getting much better.

Chapter XVI

Shilpa
24th Secundus

We have reached Anta Dvīpa and easily found ourselves a vacant berth. It does not take long for an avid customs and port official to attend on us and find his way onboard. I can see him looking at how deeply the ship is laden. He is looking to dip deep into the duty we pay to line his own purse. It was a delight to show him the manifest, with only Havenite goods and goods that are under seal on board, at least openly. His face was marvellous to watch.

He can charge us very little for the visit, just the docking fees of two hundred Anna and no more. He is soon strongly hinting to me that this foreign ship that I work on will have its clearance held up, with no-one able to leave the ship to do anything, unless there is a payment made to help facilitate the paperwork.

He will personally make sure that things go smoothly and will pass on the payment to the right people. It is amazing how quickly his tone changed when Rani and Parminder, both now dressed as Kshatya battle mages, and with Rakhi unfurling an umbrella above them, come onto the deck and Rani started to ask why there was a delay in an imperious tone.

Rani

It makes me angry to see such blatant corruption. Put that on top of the whole issue that Astrid raised and it is all just getting to be too much. I know why I cannot introduce my wife properly and as I want to. As soon as I do that I will never be able to come through here again except in disguise and no-one respectable will openly deal with me. I will have lost all caste. I will be like a Harijani to them.

How can I explain to my wife the mindset of my family? It is the same mindset that almost all of the rest of my caste will have and one that the Brahmins will have even more abundantly. Everything has to be kept secret from them. Unfortunately, the Brahmins are the ones that we will have to deal with if we want anything to do with moneylenders.

Seeing they were forbidden from doing any physical work, banking and money-lending are the natural provinces of that caste. This is often done through an intermediary so as to avoid the contamination to the higher caste that could come from touching money that a Harijan or the wrong Sudra has touched, but it will be Brahmins who would be our customers.

Likewise, if we are able to buy property it will most likely be a Brahmin we buy from. Now the task for us will be to find one who will sell. Most of them only want to lease property. That way they can keep collecting rent and continually putting it up each year if any venture on their land turns out to be profitable. This way they squeeze as much as they can out of each transaction without having to do any labour to earn it.

Even out in the country this is the case and many of the farmers throughout the whole of Sharan work all of their lives for an absent landlord, some of them are handing over up to half their crop for the privilege, in addition to their taxes, while they live in penury and subsist on scraps in order to get the next crop in. I know that my family has land and this is what we lived on.

This once seemed completely normal to me. Now I have travelled and have seen lands, like Darkreach, where taking one tenth of the crop is regarded as being a very high charge and one that would only apply to one of high risk. At one stage Ayesha shocked me completely by saying that, in the Caliphate, loans are made on a different basis entirely and no interest at all is charged. There it is both illegal and immoral to do so.

Olympias

This visit we have docked a little further back along the wharf and more distant from the sea than they were on the last stay and the fort is not as clearly visible as there are a few small masts in the way of the view. Despite this being the so-called foreign wharf, most of the ships that the masts belong to look as if they do not travel away from here very often; or indeed that they go very far when they leave.

They all belong to Havenite masters and have local crews. From their appearance they might perhaps only go to Saltverge or some of the nearer southern villages or up and down the river. This end of Anta Dvīpa has buildings beside us that are even less prosperous looking than the ones nearer to the mouth of the river, where we were docked last time that we were here.

The local wharf on the other side of the island is, I am sure, far busier. I am sure that there is little sea-borne trade that comes through from any distant port and Jennifer has confirmed this. There are only a handful of vessels that trade further away than a few days transit. She contrasted the sight here with the far smaller, but always fully packed and busy, merchant port in Ardlark.

Basil

It is time to go to work again instead of enjoying myself. I will take Ia and we will start with this warehouse beside us. It seems that my Butterfly has some of my skills and some of those that Puss has as well. We have been surprised by how well the three of us fit together, in so many ways and not just the physical. Even Astrid is starting to think, very reluctantly, that perhaps it really was fated for us all.

All we have found is an empty, dirt and rubbish-filled space that has seen no goods stored in it for a very long time. It mainly serves as a haunt for beggars and other people who have nowhere else to go. We spent most of our time reassuring these people that we were not about to rob them of what little they have, nor are they to be forced out.

It is very depressing so see such degradation, but now we know what is in there, we can take steps to secure our flank. Next we get Lakshmi and Shilpa prepared to go out off the island and start investigating what they might find in the city.

Theodora

Lakshmi will take Zeenat with her and they will be going to see the lawyer that Zeenat knows. Hopefully he will act for us and they can start him off, for a start, with looking for the owners of the buildings near where we are docked. Lakshmi gets to play the part of being a wealthy Sudra who wants to put out feelers as to what may be for sale.

Vishal has been a keen attendee at Basil's fitness classes. Having oiled his upper body and hair and donned his weapons, he looks most impressive in his part as their guard. Just as Stefan does in other areas, he will serve as an obvious guard for onlookers to focus on. Once they are off Anta Dvīpa, where they are obviously too prosperous to fit in with the other people in the streets, they should blend in easily to the rest of the swarming people of the city.

Ayesha will also be going along with them as a less obvious attendant, but she will not walk with the others. She will just happen to be in the same area as them. She is now dressed like a Havenite beggar and is deliberately very disreputable in appearance. Any observant Brahmin will cross the road to avoid her shadow as soon as he sees her.

Shilpa is taking the less obvious route to finding land for sale while, at the same time, being the more visible. Her group stands out from the normal people of Haven like a Cow-lizard would in a herd of cows. Some of us will again be posing as Darkreach merchants. On this visit it will be easier to do now that we have actually sold off a load that we collected from Darkreach as we returned from Skrice on our last trip.

Astrid, Denizkartal, Gundardasc, Krukurb, and Aziz are all escorting Olympias and I. There are traders in the markets now who will eagerly talk to the translator of the Darkreach merchants as several traders must have made quite a good profit from our previous trips. Shilpa is there as the local escort and there is a wide space around us as we walk the streets.

Simeon is even along with us in his wolf form, trotting along at my heels, his nose seeking anything of interest. Ia and Basil are supposedly following to see who is interested in us. It has to be assumed that, if there is still a hidden web of people serving the Adversaries in Sacred Gate, anyone from Darkreach, and any ship as distinctive as the River Dragon, *will be suspect and investigated by them.*

We are not really supposed to do much but, as merchants, and obviously of interest, we simply are going out to try and draw unwanted attention away from Lakshmi and Zeenat, who follow quietly behind all of us on their mission, and to let Basil see who is interested in us as we look through the markets.

Bianca

This leaves me, as the person most used to the streets of a big city, to try and do the same sort of work back on the ship. At least, with my innate ability to sense treachery, and my experience at growing up in the poorer areas of Ashvaria, we hope that I can, at least, be able to notice something that is threatening. My husband sits beside me dressed as a simple sailor. He was better off being disguised as a wandering Hindu holy man last time.

At least we get to sit with our backs against the mainmast enjoying the sun. It is hard for me to stop Christopher from taking Eustathius and Hilarion to see if they can start work on healing and converting the beggars who are nearby. After all, it is what they are here for and the two new priests are both keen to get into their life's new vocation.

On board Harnermêŝ has been left in charge and he has Jennifer asleep below for the next watch. Rani is also below, but I doubt that she is sleeping. Several others of the crew and passengers are also supposed to be sleeping so that they are fresh later, while others lounge around on deck.

We are hoping that a casual observer will not necessarily have noticed that, on the deck and concealed by the ships' side or under something, each person has a weapon hidden near them as well as the openly carried belt knives that one would expect.

A rack of falchions has also been added to the ship around the base of the mainmast and, although they are only plain weapons, they gleam in the sun. The arbalests are covered but people sit near them and one group, made up of Brotherhood girls, is even using the one at the front as a table to play cards on. Denizkartal has been training them in how to use it.

Unfortunately, they look far too pretty to be normal sailors. Even though they are trying to learn how to sail and handle weapons and they have also been learning how to play cards, the bare feet, the shortened trousers and the loose shirts tied under the breasts which they favour, are more than a little unusual on most ships.

The clothes that the Brotherhood girls wear are actually practical for their work, but are also very distracting to passing men. Some of the women among the regular crew want to copy their comfortable style, but they may have to wait until they have been delivered of their children to do this. Having already had her child Galla is already working on this, getting back to fitness with Astrid driving her.

At least, after several weeks of training, the girls' skin has lost the pallor of the north, has gone through the stage of being burnt by the sun, and is starting to look more like the convincing brown of a person who works outdoors for a living. If any looked at their hands they can also see convincing calluses starting to form.

In many ways these girls have travelled the furthest of all of the crew, and not just in a physical sense. They are all from the brothel in Warkworth and, having left behind the timidity and ignorance that was forced on them, they have slowly, but inexorably, moved in exactly the opposite way. While there are men looking at them from the dock, the women are often also looking at the men and sizing their potential up.

It was obvious that this makes some of the onlookers uncomfortable.

Although none of them has taken a man yet, they have told me that they have heard about Jennifer's past and have almost taken her as their role model, in respect of her rejection of traditions. I am not sure that, as a Presbytera, I actually approve of that amount of lasciviousness. On the other hand, as a Khitan, I applaud their strength of character.

Bianca sighed as once again she thought about the split between her two halves. *As well, all of them have taken what Fire has done to heart and, just as she has become Kaliope, so they have become Mary, Anne, Cecilia, Catherine, Winifred and Bridget. In an ironic reference to their past, and as an acknowledgement of how they have chosen their new names, they have taken to calling themselves the Saints.*

Theodora

We, the supposed Darkreach merchants, are the first to return to the ship. What is more we come back with porters and their wheelbarrows trailing behind us. They are loaded with parcels and packages. Our ship will leave here even more deeply laden than when it arrived. More merchants will be following us later with silk and other bulkier items.

Our open enquiries about land have not yielded much news, although we have been asking about sea-front land. It seems that no-one wants to sell there; even though on our way off the island we went down the road the house we raided was on. Apparently it is called Vilāsita ka Mārg, the Path of Luxury. That is an irony. We saw many obviously empty and derelict properties and others that are probably only occupied by squatters. Hardly one house alone the street has obvious owners inside.

It seems that my husband is right. Once a landlord has hold of a property they are reluctant to let it go. If someone wants to buy it, then the owners seem to think that they might make more from renting it out. We will need luck to locate a Brahmin who will sell because he is short enough on cash, and who is also not willing to let their situation become too widely known through borrowing from others.

Theodora
soon after

At least the group that went to the lawyers had more luck. He has agreed to act for us. Gentle enquiries are now floating around, not necessarily traceable to any one party. That, after all, is why an honest intermediary is so useful. There are two sets of enquiries that have gone out, and he has sent them out through different people, one is about land and one looking for people who might seek additional capital.

It is also possible that, even as early as this afternoon, we might know who owns the land that is adjacent to us. Our lawyer has said that this just requires a search through the records office and, although it is supposed to be private information, anyone working in the records office is notoriously poorly paid and it is understood by everyone that the people who work there need to supplement their income somehow.

Like many things in Haven, although it is illegal, it seems that no-one in Pavitra Phāṭaka regards such simple peculation as immoral in any way. It is just the way that things are done. An office worker with a gift and a note has been sent away to visit a contact immediately and a reply will not take long to arrive. Theodora had shaken her head on hearing this. *I cannot believe that such a place as this can actually function.*

Chapter XVII

Rani
24th Secundus, night time

Having changed their clothes, rested and eaten Lakshmi, Zeenat, Rakhi, Shilpa and Vishal are now heading out again. I may not have missed the heat and humidity of the day time, but I have missed these warm nights back in Mousehole.

On this trip Parminder and I are going to be accompanying them as well. Our purpose this time is very different and our dress is suitably different as well. I have gotten used to openly associating with people of other castes at home, but somehow it is harder for me to accept now we are back here.

Vishal has changed to being a less obvious guard wearing a decorated heavy silk sherwani over his silk pyjamas, but still with a sword. The rest of us have a selection of concealed knives and wands between us. We are all now dressed and outfitted as if we are Kshatya…and that concerns me. To all intents and purposes, we are a party of wealthy young women going for a frivolous night out.

To preserve modesty and, thankfully, anonymity, as young women sometimes do on such occasions, we all have a veil. To emphasise our modesty, we have Vishal there to act as a suitable male chaperone. We seem to need to have a male relative there to watch over us. No-one will be certain exactly who we are, but that is the purpose. May Devi forgive me, we look the part.

Seeing that no-one will expect a person to dare to so blatantly break caste in their dress and behaviour, we should be safe. If not, to ensure our safety, I have the loud talker with me. In a dire emergency it should be possible to hear that from the ship from where we are headed to and so Hulagu has his group of flyers assembled below deck in a hold to immediately fly to our rescue if it is needed.

Basil

Ja and I are going to the same destination as the others, but we are travelling a little apart from them. We are now dressed more as wealthy Freeholders, but well-armed ones. I was worried that my little Butterfly is not as good at combat as I would like her to be, but she makes a point by pointing at her pouches of wands. She has even left her sword behind and has only two main-gauche as her physical weapons.

Astrid is worried about us both. She has reminded me about the man Ayesha had to fight. Is the Temple of Kali still involved? Simeon and Bianca are travelling with us as another foreign pair and Theodora is taking Bryony along as her partner for the night. As Freeholders we are all only speaking in Latin or a very poor Hindi such as a merchant on their first visit could have.

Our two groups will be going separately by foot across the Merchant's Island to Rājā kē Dvīpa, the Rajah's Island before taking a ferry back to Ānanda Dvīpa, the pleasure isle. There we will be seeking gambling areas, preferably ones where there might be a Brahmin playing. We have been told that any Brahmin that are at one of these establishments will most likely be loose with how they regard caste, at least while they are there.

We are hoping that one of our groups will find a gambler who is losing heavily. If we need to gamble, and make sure that we win, then Bianca is good with cards, Bryony is even better and none of us will play with Theodora at all if there are serious stakes.

I have seen her take a deck of cards, look at the order the cards are in and then to deal them out to other players with the cards ending up well out of the sequence they had been in and then tell people what their hands are before they look at them. Apparently there is no such thing as a friendly game in the Imperial family and card games among them are often energetic and brutal affairs even without magical intervention.

As well, if other games are being played, both the Princess and I are good at chess and I can play draughts more than competently. The other group is less well equipped in this regard, although Lakshmi has some experience with various other games of chance. Still, it matters little whether we win or lose if we find what we are looking for.

She does prefer playing with dice, however. Nonetheless, and much more importantly, she is also very quick to work out the odds for any game of chance and she has the self-control to follow these without letting her feelings get in the way of a profit. If we can find a person with land and a passion for gambling, we may be able to get him to eventually stake it in a game.

Lakshmi

Although we are alert for problems the only followers that we seem to have are the usual array of petty thieves who fancy their chances at picking a pouch. A look that tells them that they are noticed as they pass by usually discourages them, but some need a hand on their arm as they attempt something. I am, however, becoming very annoyed with one particular young man.

He is ignoring every hint that we give him and he is persistently trying to get near to Rani, who has an obvious, and quite fat, purse. Eventually, after getting Zeenat to provide a distraction, Laksmi used her belt dagger to steal his purse. *He was so very confident of his own skill as a hunter that he ignored the idea that he might become the victim in turn. I suppose that he assumes that he knows who to look out for among the other practitioners of his art in the street.*

He is wearing his kurta tucked in and so, now he has been relieved of his purse we reverse our roles and, now that we are passing through a crowd, I can bump against him and Zeenat can move past and, in the process, slit the waistband of his pyjamas so that they fall down. It is only as he is recovering, to the amusement of the passers-by, that he notices his purse is missing.

Then we are gone and, by the time he has regained his pyjamas, if not his pride, it is too late. His empty purse has been discarded and who would suspect a party of upper-caste young ladies of doing such a criminal thing. He is floundering around looking for someone who may have done it and we are gone. Lakshmi noted that he had been very successful with his work until then.

Several paradēśī must have been among his victims as the coins we gained vary from local ones to two Freehold gold nobles, several Caliphate gold dirham and some gold hyperion of the north as well as a large supply of silver from different places. If he had not been so greedy, going after the obviously fat purse that Rani carries, he could have gone home with many thousands of Anna. Instead he needs a new pair of pyjamas.

We are on a different ferry to Ānanda Dvīpa to the other group. We women are trying to appear flightier than we are accustomed to being. I have to admit that it is easy pretending that we are having a rare and long-awaited adventure out of customary seclusion. The ferryman appears bored with his job, but he is more than happy to overcharge us. I need to stay and pay what he asks without demur. I can use the money from the would-be thief freely.

Basil

The ferryman is trying to overcharge the foreigners. He is demanding fifty Anna for the six of them on the short trip. We are supposed to be hard-nosed merchants, except for the pair of flighty women of course. I refuse to be overcharged. I wonder aloud what happens if a rich person calls a person of authority to report a poor person. From his reaction I thought I knew what would happen.

My offer of twenty-five Anna is about to be accepted instead. I may have thought that giving Theodora the role of a flighty young woman was well within her capacity. She is so far over-acting that she almost parodies herself. I was hoping, when I gave her the role, that she would just be her normal self, but Bryony has to keep reining her in with whispers in Darkspeech.

Whilst foreigners might normally be despised or ignored in Haven, on this island they are made as welcome as anyone else with the right amount of money would be. With what we obviously have, that is very welcome indeed. Around us I can see many people enjoying themselves. The aroma of perfume and incense fills the nose just as the music from the musicians hidden behind screens in the establishments fills the ears.

Some of the crowd around us, particularly the women, wear veils to keep their identity hidden, or at least unacknowledged. It seems that the other party of Mice will fit right in with the current local practice. This growing custom of a veil, seen now through much of The Land, gives a very useful degree of anonymity.

Lakshmi

We have settled into a routine of losing small amounts and letting it be known that this is our first night out of several and that we are willing to talk to anyone, of suitable rank, who approaches us. Several young men, and one young woman, are left wondering who we are, but I think that we are giving little away beyond the concept of coming from that usefully vague and ill-defined place, of 'outside the city'.

We are seeing people win and we are seeing people lose, but none of them are likely to be suitable targets. It is always possible that any Brahmin who is out tonight is in fact visiting a randē in one of the other, and more clandestine, establishments on the island, the sort that Parminder and I were more accustomed to work in and one that we will now avoid. Perhaps they are even seeing a veshya in her house.

Basil

We are not being very successful at all. Although we play in high stakes games, few people are interested in talking with us. Even I am growing quite bored. Most of these gaming houses seem to have side booths. It gives a place to just sit and eat, or even play chess or backgammon with any who approach.

While the others continue in the high-stakes games I will try a change of strategy and take up the occupancy of one of those. As long as we order food and drinks, it seems we can sit as long as we want. I leave a chess-board sitting in front of me in open invitation.

Butterfly can sit beside me. She is obviously a decorative non-player. An occasional person, usually elderly, comes up and plays a game or two for small stakes of a Rupiya or an Anna and even, in one case, for just a single Dam, the smallest copper coin.

It seems that my constant games with Theodora must have improved my play quite a bit since I left Ardlark. It seems that I am winning much of the time now. Before I left Darkreach I was, at best, only ordinary.

Lakshmi

It is late in the night before we begin to retrace our route home. Of course I am careful to check for anyone who might be intent on following us. I notice that Basil's group are on the same ferry this time. Now, when we are on Rājā, and heading to the Vyāpārī bridge, a small group of young and well-armed bravos appear behind us from an alley as they attempt to get close to the us without being noticed.

Lakshmi smiled and indicated them to Zeenat. *It is our acquaintance with the slit purse. He has obviously worked out what happened to him and has assembled a few friends to try and help him to gain some revenge. I think that his disappointment will be intense.* Lakshmi passed the word and the half dozen followers were only about ten paces away when the Mice turned.

Vishal has a sword and a main-gauche out, but the rest of us have a main-

gauche in one hand and a wand in the other. Our wands are prominently displayed. The young men have stopped very, very, quickly and a couple have already taken a pace back. It seems that they have not even noticed the other group behind them, or at least have not connected them with us.

"You were given a warning earlier," said Lakshmi in her most threatening voice. "Why are you ignoring it? If you are not careful we will kill all of you and take everything that you have earned all night. Do not think that we cannot do it. Just because you are used to taking things from wealthy women who cannot protect themselves, do not assume that some of us women are not well aware of your tricks."

I hope that I sound angry enough. They are starting to look around them and some are starting to edge away.

"Karma has turned upon you and you may not survive the experience of learning." She then sighed deeply and shook her head. *I need to sound truly regretful about what I am about to do.* "We had just wanted a quiet night out, but if you insist on making trouble you have a choice. You can either try to overcome us, or I will just count to six before we kill you."

She began a slow count "...one...two...three..." *I don't even need to go on to four. They are all fleeing. Some even push their way past the other group in their haste to get away from us. They make no attempt to pause as they do so.*

Chapter XVIII

Rani
25th Secundus, the post-Christmas Feast of Twelfth Night

Today has been generally quiet, although a trip to the lawyers has revealed several names as the main owners of land on Anta Dvīpa. It seems that enquiries are now discretely proceeding about them and their desire to possibly sell. Our people are preparing to go out again tonight after the Christians have quietly celebrated their Festival.

There seems to be no official interest in us and our various watchers saw no-one showing untoward attention towards the ship. The more that we have moved around Anta Dvīpa, the more we get to realise that the area is in serious decline. Gradually, as people became accustomed to our presence, some of the Mice are starting to talk to the people who live around the ship.

I had never noticed it before I left, but now it is obvious. While the rest of The Land, or at least the areas that we have been to, is in a ferment of activity with trade opening up more than ever before and people happily looking forward to growth, the residents of this area see only a slow decline happening around them and continuing decay.

Is it just here that this is happening, or is it just the same all over Pavitra Phāṭaka? Is it that way over Sharan generally? The reports from Basil and the others all tell me of talk of businesses closing and the owners moving to the villages and smaller towns to start anew. Perhaps it is only in the cities, or perhaps that is just where it starts.

According to what we are starting to hear, some of the owners of land are supposedly even just abandoning what they leave behind in the city, but most owners have agents of some sort still looking after what little was left of their interests on the island. Are we starting to see the death of the city? Is it too large, too rotten?

Laksmi

Once again we headed out to Ānanda Dvīpa. I soon saw some of the young men of last night, but this time the bravos were staying well away from us. They cast nervous glances at us as they do so. One tripped over in his eagerness to flee as he turned a corner and nearly ran into Zeenat. He quickly scrambled away casting looks over his shoulder as he ran away.

Although I have no better ideas about what to do, I am not sure if this is the way to go about our quest. Once again it is a fruitless night in terms of our goals. At least this time we made a little more than we lost at the games of chance and skill. It can be a lot of fun being a rich and idle woman in the city, so at least there is that to commend what we are doing.

Basil

Once again it is a quiet night. I get to see some of the same people from where I sit, including the sad older man, a Brahmin I think, who again will only play for a symbolic dam, but who is happy to sit and talk idly while he does so, nibbling on the bowl of chevda that I have sitting on the table and giving up his seat if another comes near and looks to sit.

He seems to be a very sad and lonely man. Even though he plays, he spends even more time talking of the past glories of his house. He seems to be a person in the late autumn of his life who sees winter fast approaching, although he looks to still be hale. So far I cannot even get his name, let alone any detail about him.

Christopher
26th Secundus

The Princesses may not be happy about it, but we have been here three days now and we have to do something and not just watch. Around us people are dying. The beggars who live here are starving and several are sick, not just with the deformities that they earn money from, but with fevers and coughs and probably with worms and other parasites as well.

It is easy for us to convince some of them to listen to what we have to say in return for a meal for them and their family and for being prayed over. Truly it is a case of whatever you do for the least of these, you do for me. There must be no more wretched people than those I see about me here on this island. Many have not only lost all hope, but they have almost lost their lives as well.

There is one small family, a man, his wife and their two surviving children, people who live in one of the abandoned buildings beside us, who may be the worst off of them all. They have gone so far down in life that the adults were just sitting in a corner, holding their emaciated children tight, and waiting to die when we found them.

The parents have admitted that they hope that, when they all die, that at least their children will be reborn into a better condition. I would be false to my vows if I left them to die like that without doing all that I can. They are so far gone that they barely have more flesh on them than a skeleton when we carried them on board the River Dragon.

We washed them by hand with a solution of Guthog's Blessing to rid them of the lice and other vermin that can be seen running openly over their bodies and when they are given food it can only be a weak soup at first and they are nearly throwing that up. I do not know if we can save them, but I have to try.

Astrid

Christopher cannot be stopped. I have found myself sitting all day with one of these beggar children in my arms, dribbling teaspoons of thin soup into her mouth and then letting her sleep to repeat the feeding when she stirs. Her loins were wrapped in a dirty rag when she arrived. My sister-wife does the same with her younger brother while Maeve chatters at us both and fetches things.

Lakshmi

The eyes of the children are open but they seem not to see the women who hold them. Their parents are little better off even if they can talk and listen. They try to object that they are harijani, but it is being ignored. I have made sure that there are strong medical herbs in the soup and the first thing I have given the family is a potion of Darada. It is called Worming Potion for a good reason.

I have made sure that they have all stayed clad in their rags until the effects of this become evident. There was so little in their bodies that the medicine has gone through the family within hours. Their rags are then thrown in the river and we can put a dhoti on them, even on the woman, but she can have a child's choli as well. The dhoti can be changed and washed easily.

Caring for the whole family is like caring for sick babies, although the wide and blank-eyed little ones lack even the energy to cry that a baby normally has. I saw a lot of poverty when I was growing up, but never have I seen people as poorly off as these. Has it grown worse here in the heart of Sharan, or is this place really the worst we could see?

Chapter XIX

Basil

the night of 26th Secundus

It is yet another night and once again we are sitting in a booth on this Pleasure Island hoping almost forlornly to get a nibble from the fish we seek. This time I have gotten my elderly Brahmin to open up a little more. I have, at last, found out his name. Despite his experience Basil could scarce restrain his excitement when he heard it.

No wonder the man has declining fortunes and is only filling in time. Chăch Ghoshal has the largest landholding of all of the names on our list. We don't think that he even has any other properties, apart from those on the island, to sustain him with rent. He must be near to starving himself. My Chevda may even be his main meal.

However, Basil was about to discover that the matter went further than simple poverty affecting one of high caste and formerly great wealth. Basil now ordered real food and drink and insisted that his guest had to eat with him, as inappropriate as it may seem. He discovered that the man needed to find a large sum of money.

It is amazing what people say when they are offered both kindness and a ready ear with no visible agenda behind it, even from a non-Brahmin foreigner.

"One would normally live with such," he said. "It is fate after all. Although I have tried to live a good life, I must have a heavy karmic burden to dispose of." He smiled to take the sting from his words. "Sitting talking to aśud'dha paradēśī, and sharing their food cannot be helping that." *He has paused and sighed. He looks even sadder.*

Now that he has started talking, I think that he is going to continue without any further prompts from us. It is obviously a blessing to him to unburden himself to one who would not judge him on the basis of caste. I think that this time, all that I need to do is to listen and just nod sympathetically at the right places.

"My family were once great, how great I cannot say as we lost much during The Burning. What we have left, in the way of records and scraps of records and family legends says that once we were rulers...another town and not here, perhaps not even in Sharan, but we know not where."

"As a part of these legends there is a story of how, long ago, one of my ancestors ordered some jewellery for his wife. Every family of note has tales like that, but some of ours are written in books and parts of them but not all have survived. One part has a drawing of this fabulous set of rubies..." *He is describing my wife's, my first wife that is, Astrid's necklace.*

"It has been passed down through the ages as prophesy that, were the jewels to be found, our fortunes would be restored and we would again become wealthy. Thus our family has always spent what little resources we have to spare to search for them. I had given up on this as, a little while ago, I received what I thought was a good lead, and I used my last real money to send some men to the mountains.

"They disappeared and I thought that it was over, but just last week I have received word, from a contact in the Swamp that I trust to tell me the truth, that the jewels themselves have been seen there. But this is my problem and I should not burden you when you are seeking to enjoy yourself..."

"No," said Ia breaking in for the first time and smiling and using her eyelashes to effect. "It sounds like a fascinating story and one that is so romantic...a tale that has come out of the legends of the past. I entreat you to tell me what happens next."

She passes the wine over and Chăch smiles at the pretty young girl who shows an unfeigned interest in the meandering tale of an old man. Ignoring any caste implications, he takes a sip of the wine and continued.

"A man, whom I had not met before, has obviously heard the same as me and he came to me and said that he knows where the necklace is and has offered to get it for me. He named a figure, one that I cannot even begin to afford, or in the alternative he has offered to take my property in exchange for him getting me the necklace.

Chăch sighed deeply. "It is a parcel of property that is more of a drain than a blessing and why he wants it I do not know..."

It may just be an attempt to own an island, but it may be more. I am not going to say anything at this stage. We will have to see.

"He will not take part of it, but only the whole parcel. Then I will be left with nothing but the necklace and a prophecy. That is assuming that it really does exist. I am caught in a dilemma of having to risk all in one last throw of the dice over what may just be a rumour. I may destroy what is left for my family over nothing if I am not careful.

"So," a smile appeared on his face that lacked any humour, "you see why I am so sad and must sit and play chess without anything to venture on it. For the sake of my family I try to maintain an appearance, for that veneer is all that I have left as I am sitting talking to vidēśiyōṁ and eating their food and boring them. I am sorry..."

He is standing to leave. We cannot have that. I need one of our traders to be here. What do I say next? "Please sit, sethji. I believe that Karma must be moving in your direction and using me as its vessel. Would you mind if I ask you a question?" *He nods at least.* "Is this land on Anta Dvīpa?" *Chăch is nodding again. This time it is with more interest, and perhaps curiosity.*

"What would you say if I said that I know someone who will buy the same land...I cannot say why...I am sorry...they will want to buy all of it as well but they will give you a fair price. It will be enough for you to buy some good income producing land with enough left over to send someone reliable after the necklace?" He held up his hand.

"You would in fact do me and my friends a huge service if I could do this for you. I will not set the amount for the sale. If you can name a proper price, I will ensure that the person, a suitable Kshatya of my acquaintance, will have the money for you tomorrow." *The expression on the man's face is of sheer incredulity. I will press further.*

"What is more, you can see my friends and I are well armed and we have more than enough magic at our disposal. You seemed to imply that you did not trust this other person to do what they said. I am willing to put my friends and myself at your disposal to make sure they do not just rob you when you arrive with the money for the expedition...is it a large amount that they want?"

The man nodded. "They want ten thousand mohur." Basil forced himself to give out a low whistle and Ia looked shocked. "The necklace is worth ten times that at the very least" said Chăch. "I am sure that you cannot match that."

"My friends need to buy a lot of land for what they want. How much land are we talking about?" *I know that we have a lot more than that in coin and gems on board. It may not all be Haven money, but it is money.*

"Fifty virgates...it is nearly a quarter of Anta Dvīpa, although it exists in various pockets. I am sure that some of the buildings are useable if they were repaired but some need to be torn down and a new building put there. I can afford to do neither.

"Many years ago it used to all be prosperous land but it has declined in value over the years and there was recently a scandal with some of my tenants that drove out the others that paid rent as they did not want to be seen to be associated...and," a wry smile appeared on his face "...let us just say that I am not yet regarded as being fully aśud'dha."

"Do you mean a scandal with a sea-front property?" asked Ia innocently.

"See, even your young lady has heard of it and she is not even from here," Chăch said bitterly. "If I could sell for a good price and move to Vinice or another town with my family...even if I never saw the necklace again...after all the legend only said the jewels had to be found. It did not even say that I had to have them.

"I would prefer to leave them with whoever has them now and to use the money to repair our family...but the only offer to buy that my agent has received any word of so far has been the one that includes the return of the necklace."

"The money that you would get is Kshatya money...I assure you of that... you can handle that without an agent?" Chăch nodded.

"If I can have your address, I will get my friend to come and see you tomorrow. You have set an amount, she will make you an offer and, if it is favourable to you then you can sell and she can buy...but the offer still stands to talk to this other man for you if you fear what he might do. My friends and I are used to tight situations and even if he were a Thug with the temple behind him we would back you. Through my friend we would owe you a lot."

"But he implied that he had much magic behind him and..." Chăch tailed off. *Ia is smiling openly. She does have a pretty and open smile.*

"My young wife here is a strong air mage. We have several friends who are stronger and one friend who is possibly stronger than any who is currently working in the University here. Do you know what it means when a person has golden eyes?" He added casually as if in an aside. Chăch nodded. Basil indicated nonchalantly towards Theodora. "Then look at the lady over there and look closely at her eyes above the veil."

The man looked intently and then gasped. *By the look and sound of him, he might have known the answer to that question as an academic item learnt perhaps long ago in school, but he was not expecting to actually see someone like that across the room.*

In the end it was agreed and the old man went back home. *Already there is a spring in his step perhaps for the first time in many years.* Basil quickly gathered the others of his group and headed home, having gotten Ia to pass the word to the other group. Soon they were all on their way back to the River Dragon. *Having had that piece of good fortune, we need to make sure that nothing goes wrong now.*

When they had arrived at the ship Basil got them all to either change clothes or head straight to sleep. *I think that it is vital that we need to be off to Chăch's house to keep watch in shifts until the deal is completed. He lives on Gupta ke Dvīpa, two islands away.*

I am concerned that Chăch has not said anything about hearing of us asking to purchase the property. It implies that his agent is not an honest man at all.

He knows the plight of the old man and yet has not quickly gotten word to him about the offer. I am even more concerned about who the other potential buyers might be.

It is possible that they are just trying to get the land cheap and waiting to sell it dear later on. They are assuming that they can steal the necklace from Puss. However, I think it more likely that, if his agent is dishonest, then the supposed agreement to trade the land and the necklace will, in the fine print, actually be a binding contract regardless of result and the old man will end up either with nothing at all or perhaps even dead, along with all of his family.

Ia

The others can go straight to sleep, but I want to check on the young boy. He is still with Astrid and Maeve. My cydwraig looks patient, but tired, and my familiar is looking reproachful. They are still sitting and tending the children. Their parents lie nearby on the deck, exhausted and asleep. Ia agreed to give them a chance to sleep and wake them in a few hours.

"You will spend yourself for others' won't you? It is why you agreed to marry me isn't it? You wanted to stop me killing myself...which I probably would have ended up doing soon one way or another. You could not have borne that could you? I hope in my heart that I will never make you sorry for that decision." She kissed her older sister-wife tenderly and thankfully.

Chapter XX

Shilpa
27th Secundus

It seems that, with Zeenat in tow, and my husband as a guard, we are headed towards our lawyer to fetch him, while Rani will meet us on Gupta ke Dvīpa with the money and a contingent of Mice. It has been agreed that we will give these other people a chance to buy first. We only step in if the other arrangement falls through or if treachery is attempted.

Personally, I am hoping that something unexpected will happen and that the other offer falls through. The money that we are being asked to part with is more than we expected to pay, but then we are getting a lot more land than we expected to own as well. We have discussed it and I think that the price will be fair, in the long run.

This purchase will be the first to drain a significant amount of the cash money from our village treasury, but it is just sitting there at present anyway, and we have at least as much again, or more, in coins as well as much more in the way of jewels and precious metals that could be sold. This has a chance of giving us a return, not immediately, but over time.

As well as some scattered properties elsewhere, such as the one that was raided last visit on Vilāsita ka Mārg and the one that we spied from, and some of their neighbours, we will own most of the land around Videshē ka Ghāt on the path to the sea and even the Chamadee, the whole northern tip of the island except the temples of course, some of the land around Ashuḍh ke Pul, some of Khoya Kshetr and almost all of Manoranjan Ke.

If we can clean our properties up then, not only will we have land for a church and warehouses, but also houses and other buildings that can earn us several hundred mohur each year. If we do it right we could earn even far more from it, perhaps even a thousand and it is better to use the money like this than to leave it sitting in a cave to just look at and admire its colour.

Of course we will still have to convince people that we own their houses and then collect the rent, but that is a problem for later. The main thing is to get the deeds to the area in our hands, and to do it so that it cannot be questioned.

Astrid

We have reached Chăch's house very early and well before we are due to be there. The area around the house has ample supplies of lush vegetation and our watchers have been hiding in it. Spreading trees, groves of bushes and beds of flowers are everywhere both between the houses and along the streets.

Over the whole island that we have passed though most of the houses have walls around them, or at least fences of some sort and there are park-like gaps between some of them with trees, flowers and shrubs growing. Perhaps there were once houses there, but that would seem to be a long time ago, perhaps since the start of The Burning over a hundred years ago. Some of the walls and fences can be seen through, but others are well over the height of a man and solid.

The air is thick with the smell of flowers and even with the sounds of jungle birds. It is almost as if the jungles have come into the city. It is not like the places around where we are docked at all. It is hard to believe that this is all a part of the same city. Despite it being day, it is easy for us to find places to hide in and stay. Most of us are still out of view around corners and in ambush in bushes.

We now wait for our lawyer. Those near the house are trying to stay out of sight and inconspicuous as we do so, although it is hard with such a large armed group to seem to be innocently there if someone actually sees us in the bushes and behind trees and connects the scattered and waiting people together. Hopefully no-one calls the local Guard. I know that there is supposed to be one, even if we have seen little of it.

A nervous looking man has eventually arrived at the house along with a younger man with the look of a clerk who is carrying a box and another older man who is armed and looks competent. The older men are looking around at the neighbouring houses behind their walls, where they can, however it seems that they have failed to notice any Mice.

I am thinking that will be the agent, his servant and a guard of some sort. That box will hold the title deeds and all of the papers that are to be signed.

The agent stopped and looked all around the street as he went to go in. *He didn't just look once and he even moved to look up a side street. He has a disappointed look.*

It seems that he hasn't seen what he is looking for…or perhaps who he is looking for. He is obviously not searching for anyone who is hidden in ambush, but just looking for someone who will be waiting for him and not seriously hidden. After having spent their time looking around they went up to the house and were soon let inside.

Now it is the turn of Shilpa and her group to arrive with our lawyer. It is time for Basil and Ia to gather Rani and together they can all go inside to start their negotiation over the land. I am now the one who is in charge outside. Surely it is time for things to happen. It is time to move our people up into the more immediate area.

She dispersed them around close with orders to stay as much as possible in shadow at corners and under bushes and behind trees. *If anything is about to happen, it will be now.*

If the dishonest agent is expecting someone, they might still arrive before the money is handed over. Luckily this is a higher caste area and the streets are lined with these gardens. We are fortunate that in fact the whole island has a greater resemblance to houses set into a park rather than to gardens in a city. We have many very good choices of places to hide ourselves.

It was another ten minutes before Astrid saw Verily waving to her… *someone is coming…*she softly called out to the others and everyone came to alert.

A group of men came within sight. *One is a mage…those pouches are a dead giveaway…another is harder to work out. He is probably an armsman of some sort, but he has a wand pouch so he could equally be a mage who is used to handling weapons. We have a few of those ourselves. At any rate he seems confident and walks with a hand on the hilt of his sword. The two have a gaggle of people behind them.* Astrid heard a soft hiss behind her. She turned…

"Our friends the cutpurses," Lakshmi whispered to her. Astrid nodded and turned to Theodora.

"Can you knock them out?"

Theodora nodded. "The mage will resist of course, but then we will see how powerful he is. Get ready for him if need be." Astrid nodded back. The group were nearly upon the gate to the house as she heard Theodora's voice murmuring behind her.

They seem to be very confident and apart from a few casual glances over the apparently empty street, they don't look under trees, behind bushes or into the gloomy patches left by tall walls. This is lucky for us as most of these spots that are near the house now have at least one person concealed in them.

One of the cutpurses was just reaching for the handle of the small gate for people when Theodora finished her chant and went silent.

The cutpurses collapsed so quickly to the ground they may as well have been hit by sling stones. The silence is broken by the sound of them striking the ground in their fall. The mage, however, is just swaying. His knees are starting to give way as he tries to raise his hands. He is still trying to cast something as he loses consciousness.

The surprise package was the other man. *He is standing and looking around him in surprise as the others fall. He is obviously wearing an enchantment that will turn magic away.* Astrid motioned as she leapt and, almost without making a noise, the Mice sprang forward out of their concealment to take them all and bind them before any recovered from the spell.

The last man looked up and gave a brief cry, trying to draw his weapons, before he was felled by Astrid using the flat of her bardiche. *He might even survive that.*

"Quick, get them under cover in case anyone heard his call." Astrid ordered softly and there was another flurry of activity. They quickly dragged the bodies into Chãch's yard and were crouched behind the fence. "Strip them of everything…blindfold, gag, and bind them…someone tend to his head. We will want to question them all in detail later."

She looked at Theodora. *She approves and is nodding*. Soon an array of weapons, wands, rings and other jewellery were being put into a bag or tucked into belts.

Christopher and Simeon had consulted over the fallen. "The mage and the other man are evil," said Christopher. "There is no doubt about it and they both had one of those rings on that lets us know exactly who they work for. The others…well they have just the normal small evils of everyday villains, although several of them have lots of those."

"Thank you, Bishop. We apparently already know about those boys. They are the same set of cutpurses that you have Lakshmi doing a penance over. It seems that they are more than just pickpockets today. They have moved up in the world so they are at least low-rent sell-swords…with your permission," she turned to Christopher, "and yours," as she faced Theodora, "I am sure that Lakshmi will be well able to deal with them in a satisfactory and suitable way."

Astrid moved the rest of the Mice back outside. *Now that all of the intruders are secure we can afford to wait. More people of interest might even yet arrive, so we should stay hidden, and there are still the occasional innocent person moving about as well, and we don't want them noticing us either.*

Lakshmi

I am looking forward to this. Lakshmi grinned widely. *Such men lord it over the girls of the street, stealing their money, raping them and often making them live lives of fear. Every one of us has lost something to them at some stage*. "Bring them outside and under concealment." She pointed. "That thicket of bamboo looks secluded and private enough."

She made sure that they were firmly bound and unable to see a thing. The six were then lifted from the garden and brought outside. There they were leant against a side wall that bordered a small park. They were under the cover of trees and shielded from anyone looking from the street by a stand of bamboo.

It is nice and dark here and the azaleas are so dense behind the bamboo that I very much doubt we can be seen from the street no matter what we do. She pinched one of the bound men on the arm. He did not stir. *They are still dead to the world. I would say that our Princess has used all of her mana for the day. The spell lies heavy on those it has hit*.

Astrid

Eventually there are signs of movement. The man Astrid had stunned woke first and made a muted sound through his gag as he struggled against his bonds. Astrid kicked him and leant down. "Be silent and do what you are told and, who knows, you might even survive." *He is not moving, but I can see him trying to keep testing the rope on his wrists*. She kicked him again. "Be still I said. I did those knots. You won't get free."

The mage was the next to recover. He tried to speak and cast, but he was too well bound. *Lakshmi has even bound his fingers onto some sticks so that he cannot bend them to make some pre-set spell and so escape*. "Darling," Astrid knelt down and whispered in his ear.

"You are going to be very quiet and then, when I am ready I will ask you some questions. If you answer properly you may live and, if you answer very, very, well you will even be able to see as well. For now you are going to be as still and quiet as you can be. Someone with a sharp knife is watching you." She nodded to Bianca who stuck a sharp blade into his buttock quickly and withdrew it.

He thrashed a bit and tried to scream as it went in, but then went quiet as he realised that it was no use. *Soon a growing smell tells me that he is one of those who is a coward in their heart. If it were light the dampness of his trousers would have been apparent.*

Astrid turned to Theodora. "They are taking a very long time." *She is nodding.*

"We need to send someone in," she said. *She is right.* She looked around.

"Simeon, you look innocent, and our man has seen you already. Can you knock and go inside please. See Basil and tell him what has happened quietly. Watch what the agent does. You may need to restrain him...or we may need to when he comes out." Simeon kissed his wife and slipped off back to the yard and then went in along the curved path through the azaleas and up to the door.

Simeon

I guess that I just knock on the door and ask. Simeon knocked on the door and a thin elderly servant came quickly to open it. *I can hear voices from one of the rooms inside. One of them seems to be raised and agitated.* "I am here with a message for the visitors," *My Hindi may be very heavily accented, but he understands me.* The servant ushered him inside and bid him follow.

They came to a room. Rani, Shilpa, Zeenat, Basil and Ia, together with the lawyer stand on one side of a table and an elderly man, a middle aged one and two young men stand on the other. "A messenger for the visitors," said the servant. *The middle-aged man looks up with relief on his face only to have it fall when he sees another person he does not know.*

"Your pardon," Simeon said as came over and whispered in Basil's ear in Darkspeech in an update of what had just happened.

Basil nodded. "Well," he said to the middle-aged man. "It seems that the people whom you were expecting will not be coming. We hold them fast and we already know that two of them, at least, serve a set of evil demi-gods and the other six are scum of the streets who rob passers-by. They were not coming here honestly."

"The price we are talking about is good, and is even what your client asked, and your client wants to settle so that he can take his family and his servants and start a new life away from here. Are you going to allow him to settle now or will you keep delaying?"

"Yes, Mulraj" said the old man. "Why are you delaying?" Another question has occurred to him and he turned to Basil. "...and what do you mean that you are holding people?"

Basil looked at him. "Remember that you said you were concerned that you would be robbed? I too thought it likely so I arranged for some people to see if anyone would try and do anything untoward when the money was handed over…I will let Father Simeon here…he is one of our Christian priests…tell us all the rest of what happened."

Simeon sketched what had occurred and how they knew the cutpurses. *I need to keep my eye on the armed man, not the agent.* Despite his caution, as he was describing how he and Christopher could sense the evil in the two leaders the guard quickly drew a dagger and moved behind the old man, putting the knife to his neck. *I was not alert enough. He moved far too quickly.*

"You are going to regret that," he said. "Now we are going to go outside and they are going to be set free. We are going to take the money and…old man… you are going to sign the documents now and Mulraj will witness that you did it. That way your family will stay alive…you…" he is looking at Rani. She is as tall as Astrid and cannot hide what she does. "…stop moving your lips…all of you gather over…over…" suddenly he yawned and fell over. *Basil has dived on top of him and is tying him up. I should look to the others.*

"So much for him," said Basil. "Well done Ia…that was you wasn't it?"

"Yes…I made a sleep wand as we came down the river. It is not strong and only has a few charges…" The man is already awake and struggling against the shackles that Basil already has on his wrists and he is trying to prevent the gag going on, "…but it is better than nothing."

"With your permission Master Chăch, so that you are not soiled by it, we will take these scum elsewhere and we will question them and find out what it is all about. If you like I will come by later…or I will meet you at our table… and you shall get a full explanation."

"Let us sign the papers first. I need to get a new agent to care for me as I presume Mulraj was complicit in what has happened here." He addressed the lawyer whom the Mice had brought for their side of the transaction. "You sir, will you act for me now as well?"

Mulraj was edging towards the rear of the room and an open door, but Zeenat has brought him back into the centre of the room with a blade held to his kidney. He is protesting his innocence but none believe him. I am beside the young man, but he has hardly moved at all and his jaw hangs open in surprise at what is happening as he looks from person to person.

Simeon moved closer to him. *He just looks at me. His face shows his confusion. He does not feel evil or even really naughty. I think that he is just a normal person and a clerk as he appears to be. He has a belt knife, but he has, as yet made no move towards it.* "I believe this one is not evil." He looked at Basil. "What do we do with him?"

"Blindfold him, so that he cannot see where we take him and then he can witness the questioning. Once he has done that, if he proves to be innocent, then he can go and report what he has heard or…if he more sensible…he will go a long way away from these men's friends as they will want to know why he is alive and they are not."

"Tell me if he is fully innocent and then he can come with us," said Chãch, showing his generosity. "We will need servants to help us move and, if we are going to start all over again, I will once again need the services of a secretary."

The wide-eyed young man allowed himself to be blindfolded and was seated in a corner while the other prisoners were stripped of anything that might be useful and put with those outside in an outbuilding and guarded until night fell. Gradually most of the Mice started to move back to the ship. They would return that night to bring the prisoners back to Anta Dvīpa.

It is getting into night, but there is still enough of the day left to get something done. With a few gifts, offices do stay open late here. Rani has left with Vishal and Shilpa, Parminder, Lakshmi, Zeenat and Rahki to register the transfer.

Chãch, his wife and their son and daughter-in-law and three grandchildren gaze into the small box at the money that will enable them to restore their family. All of them look thin and hungry as do their last two servants, an old woman and her husband, the man who opened the door to me. Should we bring food back as well?

Basil

I think that there is a certain poetry to this. We will do the questioning in the house by the water where we had killed the servants of the Masters last time we were here. We now own it and, to me it seems appropriate and, if they know the house it may help break them to give us what we need to hear. I will send Ia back to the ship with instructions on how we will do it.

Lakshmi

Now that we are back and the title is registered, I get to deal with these six. She pulled the six bravos into a row out from the wall. *Tie a rope from hands to feet and they can only sit up.* She then put Mice behind each one of them. *It still takes quite a bit more time for them to revive...it certainly was a strong spell.* Once she was sure that they were all awake she nodded and their blindfolds were whipped off.

"Good afternoon boys." *They look properly shocked from the expressions in front of me. They are all straining against bonds and gags and their eyes are wide.* "We warned you, but it seems that you are fully unable to stay out of trouble, aren't you?" She looked at them and shook her head. She tried to keep a sorrowful expression on her face instead of laughing at their discomfort, as she felt like doing.

"We are going to leave you here for a while and then, one by one, we are going to take you aside and question you. We are going to ask your name, the name of the others and where you all live. We will then set you free after fining you everything that you have on you and I mean everything. We may leave you with enough material for a dhoti. If anyone is caught lying…well let us not consider that. It is not a nice thought."

She smiled thinly. "We warned you once by taking your purse. We warned you a second time when you found us in the street and now, we warn you a third time. I do have to say that this is your last warning. After this you will be killed immediately if we come across you just as I might step on a bug. I am not a Jain and I do not like bugs. Nod now if you understand me."

She looked over them and waited until they were all nodding like birds pecking at grain. *That did not take long at all.* "Now, you might like to consider a new career that does not involve robbing anyone as you will never know when one of your chosen victims will be someone who is under our protection. In particular it will be a very good idea for you never to go near Anta Dvīpa every again."

"We will catch you if you upset us again. It will not take long as I will take some of your hair for our mages to help them find you. You will then wake up to find yourself floating out to sea, gagged and tied fast to a piece of wood as you stare at the sky and will meditate on what you be coming back as in your next incarnation. Do you understand?" *They are getting very good at nodding.*

"It will not even help you to move to another town and try continuing your ways as we have interests outside Pavitra Phāṭaka as well. Do you all hear me now?" She kept looking at them until, once more, their heads were nodding. *It turns out that they had already been paid for this day's work and all of them have magic of some sort. By the time everything is finished, it is quite dark.*

Chapter XXI

Basil
the night of 27th Secundus

It is convenient that Chăch's house is where it is. We can move the prisoners to our new house on Anta with the saddles, all of them staying low and close to the shore. The night is fairly cloudy and, with Terror well on the wane and Panic only half full, we should be safe unless someone is looking out to sea or onto the river channel that this house is built backing on to.

We have to be honest with the old man. I hope that this does not rebound on us later, but I do not think that it will. Chăch and his family are astounded by the sight of the flying saddles. "You are obviously powerful mages," he said.

"Some of us are. The rest have other skills. You have already met my wife Ia, this is my other wife Astrid." Astrid smiled at Chăch and then at the grandchildren as she loaded a prisoner onto someone's saddle and they took off. *The little ones are staring at her cat's teeth.* "She has killed two renegade Insak-div in combat without any aid."

"You have two wives?" *Chăch has only picked up on one part of the sentence, but his son has obviously noted the other and looks impressed.* Basil sighed. "I promise you that I will explain it all when I return and we have a last game of chess." He addressed the old man. "Do you want me to leave a guard here to make sure that no-one attempts to take your money?"

Despite what has happened already, Chăch has not thought about that happening. He is almost as unworldly as Christopher was and he is much older. Thord can take the first watch and I will get Stefan to relieve him.

Lakshmi

The other, more serious, villains have been removed and I have, one by one, taken my prisoners further along the wall and asked them the questions I promised to ask. Now we will leave them in a clump of bushes near the water a little away from where a crocodile might come up and take them before they can run.

They are still with their hands tied loosely, and blindfolded and gagged, but their feet are free, very free. They have lost their sandals as well as everything else except for a loincloth. "You may free yourselves and leave now. Be sure to remember my words and," she remembered something Christopher had said, "go forth and sin no more."

Basil

The house that held the pattern is looking far more dilapidated now than when we left it. It has been thoroughly pillaged and no-one has moved in except spiders. We need to get rid of a few of them. Stains still indicate where some died, but it is obvious that the servants simply fled. While the house has been emptied of anything portable, no-one has dared to remove the lights. These still light the empty rooms when we enter.

The prisoners have been put in the cages that still line the walls of the side room. We can bring them out one by one to the room over the boatshed. When their masks are taken off it is obvious that, apart from the clerk, the first we saw, they know exactly where they are and that this is intended as the last piece of bitter gall to break down their resistance to enchantment.

It works and the questioning proceeds as expected although Theodora has to use stored mana when she enchants a prisoner. Everything is recorded carefully in case it is wanted later by a court. The young man is the first one to be questioned. He has looked around himself with fear and is keen to answer.

I do not think that we need to enchant him. None think that he is lying when he says that he is innocent. He has no reaction at all to any of the important words like 'Masters' or 'patterns' Just as Vishal was a new hired guard, he seems to be just a simple clerk. He is guiltless and after what he has heard from the others he is likely to stay so.

It appears that we have broken almost the last remnant of the organisation of the Masters in the city. The proof of that lies in them using the cutpurses. They have not yet recruited more dedicated followers, but just use these hired local ruffians when they need them. There has to be someone else around, but they are possibly only a messenger who comes and goes, as instructions arrive infrequently.

We now know where the messages are left and will keep an eye on it when we are in the city. Most of what our opponents have done over the last day has been improvised, but the plan to gain the land...none of them know why it is wanted...had arrived in a letter. It turns out that Mulraj knows exactly who he works for and he has enjoyed taking girls in the house before now.

Adara, Jennifer, Zeenat and Rahki are all interested to hear that. I think they want to give him a lingering death. The prisoner's addresses are obtained and people have been sent to search their residences. They have come back in a stream with gold and magical items and have left the doors open behind them. Now that we have left, any of their neighbours or their servants can enter and help themselves to what is left in the way of possessions.

The men had a lot of wealth between them. I think that, once they had the land, they were going to get instructions to have work done. We can now afford to leave it here to aid in buying up more land and buildings on the island. It is mainly in large coins from outside Haven and, when it is added up, it looks like it will nearly repay our outlay for the new land on the island, even without selling magic or jewels or other precious objects.

Basil
much later that night

It is all over now. By the time they have answered what we want to know, it is obvious that they cannot just be freed. The Princesses have put their heads together and decided that there is no use handing them over to the authorities. It is likely that they have powerful friends, ones who do not fully know their true nature, but friends nonetheless and even Rani has to agree that justice was notoriously both corrupt and partial in Haven.

We do not need to leave any more stains on the timbers here. We can let those who want to do so quietly strangle the prisoners. Then we can weigh down their bodies and take them far out to sea underneath saddles and dump them there. I am sure that the fish will take care of them. No-one will ever know their fate.

Chapter XXII

Christopher
early on 28th Secundus

Now we can go out, look over what we have and start to plan for the future. We can leave it up to Basil and his people to acquaint those who are living in the buildings of the new ownership and of the new obligation that they now have in actually paying rent.

As he does that, we priests get to search to find a secure place as the start of the local establishment, and another as a temporary church, but Goditha and Galla can get to work straight away on what we have.

I believe that the priests for this parish, Eustathius and Hilarion, favour Saint Paul as their patron. He is a good choice for evangelists in a strange land. They need to set up as quickly as they can and become a part of the island.

In the meantime, they can take over the house on the water, as being one in good repair, as a residence and we can all now start openly finding out if we can convert some of the locals. I am told that now, when Basil's people go out into the streets and markets, they are not only seeking to find out things, but also to spread rumours that may reach the ear of any Christians who live in the city.

Basil
later in the day

Having concluded that unpleasantness, it is time to go back, this time on foot, to Chăch's house with my wives, with Rani and Theodora, and with

Ayesha to tell the tale. The old man and his family and his, now, three servants are to receive a telling of the full tale of the Mice and what has occurred. We owe it to him to say why his land is wanted, by us at least.

They are the first in Haven to get the full story and the presence of a Kshatya battle mage and a descendant of Hrothnog as well as what their new secretary has heard serves as a guarantee of its truth. To show that the tales of the necklace are true, Puss brings it out to let them see and handle it, explaining how she had come by it and what we know of its history.

Chăch's family are marvelling over it. I think that they are almost shocked that the long-cherished family legends are true. It has been important to them that it is actually found. It gives them confidence that their fortunes are about to turn about. This finding has marked a big change for the family, but they do not seem to regret the bargain that they have made in exchanging an empty promise and the land for a new start in life for them all.

Christopher
32nd Secundus, it is the Feast Day of Saint Sophia

It has taken us several days of tidying up our new land enough to start to consider moving on, but still we wait. I am not unhappy with that. During that time we have started to have traders from Erave Town that are docked further up the wharf appear at our warehouse and Church, and even a couple of families from elsewhere in the city seeking worship.

Already some of those from the rest of Sacred Gate are moving into repairable houses from where they were. A protected enclave, near a church, will expose them to less harassment than they are accustomed to, or at least leave them closer to help if it does happen. While persecution is not an everyday affair here, it has been known to happen when someone in power, or who is desperate, wants someone to blame other than them.

We keep waiting. Apparently, we are waiting to see if there will be some official recognition of such a large transfer of property within the city. During that time we can buy furniture and fit locks to the house, as it is rapidly being cleaned and repaired. Building material is being bought for repairing other buildings. Even the shippers from Erave Town are hurrying home to bring us construction material to buy.

Food is procured and a small kitchen established by the priest's wives and their cook in an abandoned house with a very large front room using rice from the River Dragon. *It does not give free food to all, but it is made to be very cheap and affordable to anyone with an income however little it is.*

Somehow I have a feeling that of all of the Saints, Basil the Great will always be important here, as will the Saint whose day it is today. It was not hard to preach to her this morning. Once their circumstances are known, several people are no longer asked to pay.

The first family that Ia and Astrid attended have even been taken in to clean the properties and otherwise act as servants. They are still weak and feeble, scarce able to do their job yet, and will stay so for some time, but they are very glad of their change of circumstances and I am sure they will be, before long, the first of the new local converts.

Basil's wives still need to spend a lot of their spare time holding and feeding the children, whose stick thin limbs mark them as being too weak to stand for long, and in watching them cuddle and weakly play with Maeve. It will be a long time before the two can behave like normal children in any way. There are many others like them around us. I pray that they will come forward to us.

Basil and his people are making sure that the local thieves and bully-boys are made aware of a change in attitude in the area. They are being told that it will not necessarily refer to the laws of Haven, but will be far swifter and a lot less corrupt. It is likely to have more severe consequences for them.

It is taking more than a few bruises and broken bones, with a couple of people taking impromptu swims and having to avoid crocodiles, and one outright death in a fight before they start to take the point that is being made.

We own most of one of the poorest quarters, called Entertainers and another called, of all things, the Foreskin. The people that live in these places are very poor. At least, as the toughs move away from the areas we own, it does not take a lot of time for the more law-abiding inhabitants of the area to start to emerge. As people stop stealing from the poor, they can actually spend what little they have on themselves and their families.

The toughs will not mend their ways so easily, however. Most are just moving to what is called the Lost Sector. Few people live there, so perhaps they will need to feed on each other. We own quite a few places there apparently, but most of it is just vacant land so we are ignoring that area for the moment. At least we can keep them there so that they are not to be a menace to anyone who stays in our areas or who moves there. More criminals will try and move in as well and they will need to be discouraged in turn.

Astrid

Now we are getting a chance to relax a little. I have to admit that this is a good place to shop and to get things that people want to buy. We got to surprise Ia. Her face was priceless when she opened the strong box we gave her. She opened it to discover a new, and very clear, crystal ball that is over two hands across. It is the largest and clearest that we could find. It sits in the box resting in a nest of soft velvet.

She gave a cry of delight and I am glad that we temporarily have a room of our own now for the night. It may lack a good bed, but at least it is fairly sound-proof.

I am even getting a chance to just talk to people and just as well there is time. "So, Thord, we have not had much of a chance to just sit and talk before now. How is your bride-to-be? How did she take the present?" She was soon regretting asking as it was not until midnight that every detail of the visit was laid out before her by an excited and very happy Dwarf.

Shilpa

The arrival of an officious pair of Guards is the first official recognition of us being the new owners. It has taken them well over a week to come a bit over a hundred paces down Videshē ka Ghāt from their base at Pravesh Kila to where we are docked.

They swagger down and come directly to our food stall, where several people, both ours and poor locals, are openly working and they dare to make an obvious attempt to obtain some money. Only our beloved City Guard would make a threat that, unless they are paid a bribe, they will have to spend more time looking at what is happening here.

Shilpa heard this from inside and came out and upbraided them loudly. "It would be a first if you did pay attention on Anta. You have allowed all sorts of things to happen here under your noses. If making you actually perform your job properly means that we cannot bribe you, then it will be a first in this city. Usually, a bribe has to be paid to make you even pretend to work. We are acting legally as we own these buildings and can do what we want with them."

The men have hurriedly left in a much-chastened state. I do not think that it will be the last we see of them, but I think that I need to talk to the Princesses. Surely there are some poor Kshatya, ones who are honest, that we can recruit as our own Guard. It is our land after all, if we want to have house guards, none can stop us.

Perhaps we should even look at some of the lesser thieves and see if they want to reform. After all, we have. There is a girl I have seen hanging around for a couple of days with many knives for a start. She just watches what goes on and the locals seem to know her and do not act as if they are threatened by her, although they stay clear.

Rani
2nd Tertius

Shilpa may have been expecting the first visit, but this is the one I was waiting for. We get a fat and officious munshee, a senior clerk from some vague office or another who says that the buildings will be taken in by Sharan as foreigners cannot own property in the city. This is a bluff to extort money. That is not the law and never has been.

This time Shilpa, when she is fetched, points out that, even if the law changes later to make anything illegal, title already lies with citizens of Sharan, specifically herself among others, and who she allows to live in the buildings, and what she decides to charge as rents, is up to her and to her alone.

Indeed, she stresses, what she arranges to happen to trespassers is really up to her as well. She looked at the man in a significant way as she said that and he left very quickly soon afterwards. She may have been a little too direct in her threat to the man, but it seems to have worked. He looked most chastened as he hurried away.

I get to stay in the background as we see several other visitors try variations on this theme or who try to get money for permits and other minor extortions. We have thought of these tactics and Shilpa has our lawyer's written instructions citing the actual laws. If any are persistent, they are referred to his office. He is doing very well off our business.

Rani
6th Tertius

Eventually, well after mid-summer, the visits taper off. *It is good that we can finally leave. We will leave Zeenat and Rahki, with some of the other Mice as support until we manage to return. They and the priests can keep working on what we have and the rest of us will take up the next stage of our travel.*

Once again, we take the River Dragon *out to sea from Haven and only now, for the first time, it is first sailing directly towards the east in peace. This time it has holds that are full of goods on board as we seek opportunities to trade and explore.*

Chapter XXIII

Olympias
6th Tertius

I am glad to be sailing. I hated just sitting there tied up to a dock. Once more I have taken the River Dragon *sailing out of the city of Sacred Gate into a bright and sparkling morning. What is more, it is a fine day for us to sail. No longer is the stink of the city in my nose, but the fresh breezes of the ocean. The sun, rising in the east, sends shards of light bouncing off the light and choppy sea as we ride over a long low swell.*

My sister's new family additions may not share my sentiments. Maeve may have enjoyed travelling on my ship on the smooth river, but she is a lot more nervous about this heaving and bucking thing that the River Dragon *has become in the long swells of the open sea coming in from the south-west and our starboard quarter. I think that this young Ia feels much the same.*

It was good on the lake, but now we are out at sea the green-light box really does come into its own. It certainly does show exactly where we are in relation to the shore. Not only that, but it also shows any boat near us that has a sail up, even if it does not show those that are small and very low to the water. All we need is something to tell us how shallow the water is to make life perfect. I wonder if a water mage could do something about that?

It shows the saddles, if they are close, and even the larger Leatherwings. The wind lies from the west, just as the current seems to always do. Until we rounded the end of the Swamp and started to travel into Iba Bay, we got to travel briskly under the natural wind. After that turn into Iba Bay the natural wind dies off somewhat and our own wind is unleashed.

We still have a way to go, but now, still watching the box I get to make my first visit to this Flyjudge place. We will travel around the bulge of delta with the forest and swamp and I will keep the shore only a mile to the port. Using the saddles to keep track of the depth, we can work on our own charts and sail close to the land. The water below is already discoloured with dirt from the rivers and we can hear the occasional cry of distant beasts and birds.

Theodora
9th Tertius, the Feast Day of Saint Francis

We have arrived at Flyjudge and Olympias has carefully manoeuvred us behind the island to wharves that are usually used by much smaller vessels. Already we have a Father Eusebius in place here. He arrived from Southpoint the day before with Father Theophano. Theophano will not be staying here, but will be travelling on the next day to Squamawr via Bloomact.

He will be accompanied, for the first part of the trip by Mullah Walīd who has come with them and is going to consult with Mullah Uthman about where he will be most needed. Ayesha has told him, in an embarrassed voice, that he will probably be going on to Eastguard to live under the very shadow of the Caliphate and, as well, also to be almost certainly ignored by it.

At least we can give all three of the men supplies of Dadanth to keep the insects at bay until they can get their own. They have already noted that the insects are even more prolific here than they are at their home and that fewer people have access to areas with public spells set up to keep them at bay.

Shilpa has sold very little in the way of goods here, mostly only some rose-water, but she is buying large supplies of cotton of different grades, simply because it is far cheaper here than anywhere else, and she had plenty of spare space. We are not bothering to stay the night at the island, but are sailing on in the same afternoon of the day that we arrive towards Rainjig.

I do not think that I want us to overnight in Flyjudge if we can help it. I can see people looking oddly at the Havenites among the crew of the River Dragon, *as if they are assessing their worth as slaves on the cotton farms. We don't want to have to fight them, and so I have decided to remove that particular temptation from them.*

Theodora
10th Tertius, but only just

We get to sail on, leaving the muddy waters behind for travel across the dark pellucid sea. We have gone fast enough that we have been able to anchor well offshore from our next destination in the depths of the night. From the village we would only be visible as masts on a horizon, if any are keeping watch there.

Olympias is anchoring us only with sea anchors to slow our drift and she keeps a close watch on the green light box to make sure we stay well away from shore. The depth is taken regularly, but apparently, we are too far out for anything to register on the lead. What is more important is that we need to keep a good watch out from the mast for hungry marine creatures with long necks.

Astrid keeps telling Olympias of the coral reef. Her sister-in-law wants to have the visibility of full daylight before she attempts it for a first time without even a map. After a while the crew briefly sailed the *River Dragon* a little way back out to sea to make up for drift, but otherwise it was a quiet night for them all.

Astrid

it is now after breakfast

Olympias is using the saddles to plot a course to the bridge, which is also used as a landing stage for visitors. Now I get to fly onto the island with my husband and sister-wife. While most people are already on the coast staring at the River Dragon, *as it is the largest ship that they have seen, I have seen someone running towards the bridge. I know who that is.* She headed straight towards him.

"Greetings Saccius, and I have some very good news for you. We have items on board to sell here and so when Shilpa arrives you will have to negotiate some landing fees with her. She was from Haven, but she is now one of ours. Does that matter to you?"

He shrugged with his habitual grin on his face. "If someone is going to pay my wages, for once, why should I care where she comes from?" he said. "How long are you here for this time? Do I send out word to everyone?" He paused and put on a wide grin.

"We are starting to be spoilt with visitors. I suppose you know that we got a ship from Darkreach? They did mention that you sent them. They had people to take on to Flyjudge, but they promised to come back soon to actually do some more real trading." *He is unconsciously rubbing his hands together at the last phrase.*

Gradually Astrid was able to slow him down and let him know their intentions and the drums started to sound while young lads were sent out as runners to the outlying people. *Tonight we will have a market for all of the odd things that are left over from the Freehold shipment and more that were picked up in Sacred Gate.*

None of it is very special, if you happen to live in a large town, but much of it will also be hard to get, and so generally expensive, in an isolated village which lacks a full range of resident craftsmen, or even a modest range of them. I know that Shilpa had that idea partly in mind when she was been buying things for us to bring on this trip.

At least this time Ia will be far happier on this visit. Now she will be able to fully take part in the sacrifice and services with Dianan and Caractacus as she is no longer Maid, even if she is not yet fully Mother. Astrid shook her head over the thought. *Religions can be silly sometimes with their restrictions, perhaps they are silly most of the time.*

Theodora

I get to take my husband by the hand and divert her attention away from what is about to happen by going to the sea-ward side of the island as soon as I see the young bull approaching the bridge and well before it is brought over and taken towards the shrine. I don't want to have to deal with comments about cattle-killers and such all night. I want to make love.

At least, by the time she goes to sleep even my beauty has to grudgingly admit that at least some of the residents of the Swamp seem to be nice people. We are getting none of those looks directed at some of our people that we got in Flyjudge. It is just the usual looks one gets towards pretty girls anywhere.

It seems that we will leave tomorrow morning to return to Sacred Gate with a goodly supply of salt. Between what was bought by the Southport ship to go back to Darkreach and what is on board the River Dragon *there is scarce enough left in Rainjig for their own use and no barrels or boxes are left in the village for storage at all. Some of the barrels that we have taken on board with us are even filled with salted fish.*

Olympias
16th Tertius

Our return to Haven took a while running directly into a wind which has some frequent rain squalls travelling with it. Being in the south the rain is often heavy and the green-light box shows how useful it is as the visibility that we are able to get with our own eyes sometimes falls to almost nothing. Without it we would be forced to crawl along or perhaps even anchor.

Chapter XXIV

Shilpa
16th Tertius

The return to Pavitra Phāṭaka was unremarkable. Now we get to land and, even before the officious customs official can make it to the ship, we start unloading a goodly proportion of the cargo into one corner of the warehouse that is separated from the rest by a short solid fence. We still do not have the separate building roof fixed yet, apparently.

Shilpa met him at the door. "We are not selling any of this cargo here. It is, at least until we ask for bond to be taken off it, not something that we will pay duty on. You will get docking fees and little else."

She showed him the manifest. *Good girl. Rahki already has her warehouse journal in hand as well and can show how it has provision ruled up in it already for bonded goods to be held, eventually in one small separate building, for goods to be traded here, goods that will be going out of Sharan and other categories. We get to send the man away unhappy again. It is such a pleasure to pay the small docking fees in order to see his reaction to the rest.*

"I have a feeling that we will see him unhappy a lot of the time," said Zeenat. "Now, we have had our first river trader headed to us come in to the port. He was told to expect us and look out and dock where we are.

"It is a mixed load that he had and he didn't want to spend a week having to sell it himself so, after he had paid duty I bought the lot and he was able to go north again as soon as his crew had a sleep. We sold him stuff out of our store, all already with duty paid.

"Look through the journal and you can take from there when you head west. You may get better deals on it out there. There is some lovely amber jewellery, some fine woollen cloth and some good hard cooking cheese...all from Glengate... among it and, while the amber will get a good price anywhere, the cheese and wool won't sell well here unless they are buying up goods in order to do what you are about to do."

Basil

At the same time as customs dues are being assessed the Princesses are being introduced to two men by the cousins, both of whom are keeping very carefully bland and innocent-looking faces as they speak. It does not suit them. We left them and Stefan behind as protection for our new establishment. Was it a good idea? What have they cooked up between them while we were away?

"This is Maximilian," said Bryony indicating the taller. *He is a handsome and strong looking man with dark hair and a short, neat beard. He is well-groomed and neatly and tastefully clothed in Freehold style and armed with a broadsword and main-gauche as a prosperous merchant of some discernment might be.*

"...and Guy," said Adara about a shorter man. *He is very handsome and very well-groomed with a head covered in close-cropped blonde curls. He is dressed in a similar fashion to my wedding garb, but on him it is very obviously his everyday wear and not something special. He comfortably bears the two rapiers that such clothes usually have with them as an accessory instead of my shorter and wider blades.*

Although the blades have smooth and well used grips, and the leather of their harness is not new, the silver intaglio worked into the hilts shows that the blades are obviously of very fine workmanship and, from them and the gems in the rings that he bore on his hands it seems likely that he could be one of their nobles.

Bryony continued the description. "They are from Ashvaria and want to see if they can come and live with us...Guy says that he is a teacher..."

"...but Maximilian is being a little vague about what he does," Adara added, "but he says that he can do many things and will work hard. At least his hands are hard, but Guy has very soft ones, so he may indeed be a teacher, but we can be sure that at least he is not used to having to work hard for a living at all."

The men are looking from one of the women to the other. They are unsure what to make of this introduction. "They won't say why they want to come and live with us," Bryony concluded.

I have, I think, worked out exactly the same thing that the cousins have from how the men stand together. He quickly grabbed hold of his wives and sat them down on a nearby bale of cotton fabric to watch the show unfold. "I wonder how long it will take for the Princesses to work things out." *This could be very amusing.*

Now they were finished introducing the men the cousins retired to join their husband and the three perched themselves in much the same fashion as Basil and his wives were doing on the other side of the discussion.

Rani and Theodora started trying to question the two men. *It is does not take long for that to go nowhere. Both men are being fairly evasive about both their past and their plans for the future and our rulers do not know what to ask or even what to look for.*

Neither Princess is making any headway with finding out anything from the newcomers nor does it seem likely that the two men will be granted their request without saying what they are reluctant to say. Basil eventually grew tired of the sport and interrupted Guy.

"Forgive me my Lord." *Guy has inclined his head as if such were a natural form of address for him. Just so easily do people give themselves away with their habits.* "But you are going to be denied unless you admit that you are lovers and tell us your real story." *I am rewarded with four sets of astonished looks and a poked-out tongue from Bryony as she hands her cousin a coin.*

"Princesses, I know that you are used to it just one way, but it is not just two women who can love each other...look at how Maximilian stands near Guy... it is how Rani stands next to you Theodora...or for that matter Goditha near Parminder when you all think you are being secret about your relationship... now talk. We already know that Guy is a noble, a younger son I would say, or he once was at least.

"We also know that Maximilian has done hard work with his hands. He is not a merchant. What is more I strongly doubt that either is from Ashvaria originally. I am betting Trekvarna or nearby for Guy and I would say south for Maximilian..." He sat back smugly.

Personally I think that I am starting to learn the sound of the different Freehold accents quite well. Let me see if I am right. He leant onto Astrid as Ia, in turn leant back onto him.

"How..." spluttered Guy "...who?" *Maximilian has moved his right hand onto the hilt of his sword and is looking around for trouble as if he is expecting to be attacked. They have moved closer together, their backs nearly touching and both now face out against the world. The Princesses are both looking at me rather than at the men.*

Basil simply waved back at the men indicating that they should proceed. *Maximilian has seen that none except us have moved and it is he who speaks up to the Princesses.*

"He is right. We really are called Maximilian and Guy and we are lovers...

we have been for several years…we left where we grew up…" he looked down at the smaller man. *I think that he is about to be honest.*

"…I left Rubi near Dewakung to live in Ashvaria quietly in the hope to live life as I wished. Guy fled his home in Trekvarna, in the same way and we met and were living quietly together away from Court. A friend like us told us that the Dominicans were about to come and see us about our unholy alliance," he almost spat the words out.

"We quickly gathered what we could gather together and adopted disguises and fled the city just as night fell and before the gates closed. We travelled under darkness and as rapidly as we could. As we made our way eastward along the coast we heard stories about your village of…rejected ones and decided to head here." He looked around. "I can see you allow women to be together, but they do that in Freehold sometimes. Will you allow men to live together?"

"…only if they are lawfully married and have the proper regard for each other," added another voice. *That surprised the men even more as they turn to see a priest. I guess that their lives are about to become full of surprises.* "I am Bishop Christopher Palamas and I speak for our church on this matter. The more important matter is what do you, as people, offer to us as a village that would incline us to accept you?"

It turns out that Guy has been brought up well. He is the third son of the Duke of Trekvarna and has received a good education as he grew. He was expected by his family to be an ornament to the Church and a teacher, among other things, but he never felt that calling, or any other in particular.

He hid matters for a long time but eventually his father had discovered his son's attraction toward men. He also found out that his son could not change his feelings, nor was he even willing to try to do so. Guy was forced to flee his father's wrath and to hide and live under an assumed name out of sight, or so he thought.

Guy was largely supporting them in Ashvaria by tutoring children while Maximilian had, as he always had, worked at what he could get. He has a lot less education, being the son of a rural gamekeeper. His father had been as strict as Guy's, but easier to flee and hide away from. He was willing to work at anything as long as he could stay with his partner.

"Put them to work here until we return," Theodora said to Rahki and she turned to the men. "We will give you an answer when we return. Bishop Christopher is right. We don't care who your partner is…what is more important is the love that you show."

She takes Rani's hand in one of hers, raising it and kissing it gently before waving the other hand casually at our two thrupples of seated people who are looking at what is going on. The men are now looking around them. It is easy to see that their faces show confused expressions as they realise what they are seeing.

Basil

Once that is over Olympias and I get to sit the two down. Out comes my notebook and I put a new nib in my pen. From their background, these men should have some information that I want to add to my book. My sister did not take long to leave. She is interested in the navigation of an unknown area, if we go far, and all that the pair can add there is something that they think is secret…the existence of the New Found Land.

They can give me little beyond the name. It is a badly kept secret in Freehold, although neither of them knows much about it apart from the fact that it is there and that a lot of wealth comes from it, some flowing to people with no apparent connection to it. Simeon, having been born there, has told us far more about the place than we have obtained from any other source so far.

I am far more interested in what is happening in terms of the politics of Freehold and what fallout there had been from the events in Toppuddle and the gossip about the fall of the Brotherhood. It seems that having the Queen take on a base-born female lover is what has set the Dominicans on a quest to clean up the morals of Freehold and so prompted them to flee.

There is something else there that they are avoiding, but I think that I will have to gain their trust more to get at it. They are scrupulously avoiding saying who it was who told them to flee, and that may be important to us in the long run if we want to gain access to what is happening there. I can understand them wanting to protect the person, but it is not as if we are going to persecute them. We would neither be able to, nor even want to.

Other than that, by hiding themselves away from Court they lack most of the gossip that I want. The only interesting thing was Guy's reaction to seeing Bianca walk past. It was almost as if he recognised her. On the other hand, she did not react to him, so they could not have met before she left there. I will need to dig more on that matter again later as well.

Stefan and Astrid joined in as well. *Now we start questioning the two about military matters. Guy knows a lot more about that. Between us three questioners, the two men are hard pressed to keep up with the flow, turning from one to another and scarce finishing one reply before the next query arrives. By the time we are finished I am reasonably certain that nothing, but what I have noted, is being kept hidden from us.*

Ia

Should I get involved? Say something? The cousins have moved to beside me and they seem relaxed and willing to wait. "You will get used to it eventually," said Bryony. "Our Stefan used to be much easier going, but now he has a 'Captain of the North' side and, when that is switched on, he sometimes ignores everything else…even us. We still love him and it does mean that he is a very important man now in the North when we go there and that even makes us important.

"Your two have always had that sort of thing built into their character but neither has ever really noticed it because they both have it and they think that it is a normal way for people to be. Just a word though: do not get between either of them and what they see as their duty if you can. It may not be wise to make them choose between obligation and love. Even Bianca has to be careful of that with the Bishop."

Shilpa

What do we take on this leg? A load of mixed goods for the small villages, I suppose. I have lots available. I will be travelling west with relatively empty holds on the River Dragon *as it will take a lot of experience to work out what is needed on this new run and what will sell. This trip is to be more an exploration than anything else. Salt and the right cloth will sell anywhere, so that is going to be the start of a load for us.*

Eventually what she decided on was taken on board and made ready for the next day. She finished the work, wiping some sweat from her brow as she did so. *There is one other thing that we need to arrange to get here. I want some of Aine's real beer, and a place to cool it down to a proper cellar temperature. We need a tavern of our own in Sharan.*

There are no paradēśī inns on Anta and the Sharan equivalent that I am used to frequenting is not the same sort of place. You don't want to sit down in a tavern here after hard work, or a hard trade, and just relax. They are for food, for deals, for finding girls for sex, and for gambling only. If we are to be attracting foreigners, we need a proper tavern and properly chilled drinks. At least one of our mages should be able to arrange that second part.

Rani

"Princess, we may need more land off this island in time." Rani looked surprised at Christopher's words. *We have just bought a large part of a whole island. What more does he want us to have? He can see the expression on my face.*

"Not much, but we should start looking now even if we cannot do anything with it. If we do it needs to be on…what is it called?…Pūrvī Taṭa…the eastern side of the river where the caravans stop. We do not have the priests for it yet, but it is no good only looking after those who come by water.

"It may be that we will one day need land for a church and some housing there. I would think that it may be too far for most of the traders to come here, through the city although I believe that a few have found us already." *That actually makes sense once he explains what he means, but we were lucky here. I doubt we will get that luck again.*

"Shilpa has also talked to me," Christopher continued. "She says that we need a proper tavern to be built here on Anta as well. If it is good, that is if we can build something they are used to and need here, that will at least help get the merchants over to this island and, she said that it may mean that we do not need the other."

Chapter XXV

Theodora
17th Tertius, the Feast Day of Saint Patrick

The next morning we set out again, but for the first time when sailing out of Sacred Gate we are heading to the west. At first we will follow a south-west route along the coast until we have passed the Havenite town of Saltverge. Not only is this town the smallest of all of the towns of Haven, but nearly half of its people are not even Hindu and quite a few of them have pale skin.

It is the most isolated part of Haven as it is the only town not on the Rhastaputra river system. There is even a small intrusion of the Great Forest that reaches the sea between it and the rest of Haven and that further serves to isolate it and its hamlets from the rest of the Kingdom. I would venture that it used to be a part of Freehold before the Great War and the invasion at the end of the last Age.

It may be like the independent towns of the south coast in many ways, but I have been told that many, or indeed most, of the boats that we saw docked on the wharves of Anta will come here on a regular basis. It has been decided, for the moment at least, that we will ignore it. What is more Cosmas already has a church and priests based there.

Theodora
later in the day

Eventually the land that we are following turns from heading in its south-westerly direction around a slow bend into the long east-west expanse of the south coast. Once we have rounded the point to this it becomes a hard slog for the River Dragon *into a strong headwind as we headed west to Bridgecap. Even with our own wind behind the sails and opposing the one that we sail into it is best to beat along the coast as we go.*

The River Dragon *goes from being within a ballista shot from the coast out until no details can be seen apart from the coastal cliffs and the occasional clump of trees as a dot of green. Now that we are clear of Haven the saddles again come out of the hold and the riders can take to the skies to keep an eye on things and see what the green-light box cannot reach.*

We ride up and over the long swells of the sea coming from port or starboard as we tack. We can see that, to our right the forest and cultivated lands soon disappear and the even longer swells of the plains take their place. Once a caravan is seen heading west and another time there is a family group of Khitan visible but the sea around us is clear of other sails. It seems that no fishers come this way.

Theodora
much later in the day

Bridgecap does not provide much relief from the sea. If had not been for a desire on the part of Christopher and I to call on Metropolitan Demetrios and, also, to buy some of the sh-hone cloth that the village is famous for, we would not be stopping at all. As a settlement, Bridgecap lacks advantages and it requires much that other places take for granted.

For a start it gets by with only timber walls to protect it and it even lacks a port or a wharf of any sort and only small craft can run up onto the small beach that lies in a shallow cove there. There is not even a good bottom there to retrieve your anchor from. While Olympias has to anchor well out away from the hard and rocky shore that it lies on, several saddles went ashore.

At least it is not raining although, even anchored, the River Dragon *is rising and falling heavily with the long high swell. There is no protection here from that and we may as well be at sea. Olympias does not look pleased. At least, seeing we will probably be here at least some of the night, we have the green-light box to warn us if the anchors shift, a luxury no others will have.*

It is hard, given the sea state, to do more trade than just buying the sh-hone, but I have promised that we will try and again call in on our way back. We have to try to do something for the village in return for what they are doing overall. It has been a very hard few years for them.

The villages that Demetrios cares for have been under pressure from Freehold for some time and he will be sending several of his priests to Cosmas for duty in Sacred Gate and possibly even on to the Swamp. As well he has already arranged for the first file of the Basilica Anthropoi to head west. They are apparently travelling deep in the plains well away from any who might see them from the sea or who may be using magic to look along the normal track that heads into the west from here.

Their support people have formed into a group to try and look like a caravan and they are well on the way as well. It seems that they have instructions to try and look as much like traders as they can to a casual observer. Demetrios is now wondering how to find the money to build what the increased numbers of men will need when they settle in at the end of their trip.

Olympias
18th Tertius

It was well and truly night before we got to leave and we needed to use our own wind to give us the headway to even draw in the anchors and keep the ship off the rocks as we did so. I do not like this place as a place to anchor. Now the River Dragon *has had to battle all through the night against the wind, the current and the swell to head west to the village of Ooshz.*

My sister says that the village name is another of those whose odd spelling has to have been a hold-over from a former, and now long-lost, name as it was now simply called Ooze even by the people who live there. The saddle riders sighted the stone walled village in the distance with the dawn but it is still taking some time to come up to it.

At least the wind is dropping by this time, but I am unsure if I am going to risk the River Dragon *to get behind the L-shaped stone jetty and the long breakwater that can be seen coming out from the shore.* It took a trip on a saddle for her to see that the breakwater came out far enough into the sea and had been designed exactly with this westerly wind in mind.

The western wall, facing into the waves and wind, is almost as the wall of a castle, although without the battlements, and it is easy to see that it would need to be that strong if there was a gale beating the waves against it. The walkway behind is almost completely sheltered. The only tricky part is coming in behind the wall. At least it is deep enough there.

Magic must have been used long ago to place the huge stones that can be seen in the wall in water that deep as it was being built. Having cast the lead there, even at low tide I should still have at least a fathom beneath my keel when I dock near the end of the breakwater pier. We are tying up just after a squat and solid tower with room for a beacon and room for archers on the crenelated top, although our top is the same height as it is.

It still took quite some time for her to feel her way in to the small port and, by the time that the *River Dragon* was safe behind its shelter, almost the entire village was assembled and watching them. *Between my ship, one of the largest that they will have seen anchor here, and the saddles, the villagers seem fascinated.*

I am sure that these little coastal villages have little enough excitement come to them that does not involve them in raids or festivals and something novel will be appreciated. As for me, I am just looking forward to docking and having a chance for my crew to get some sleep after that last, and very long, night.

Shilpa

Here at Ooshz we first offered lots to the shopkeepers of the town before opening up what we have brought for more general sale. I was just guessing, but I thought that few would buy a whole barrel or box of salt. In the end we sold three, the largest to the general goods store admittedly, but also one each to people who make the local goat cheese.

I didn't want to empty the whole ship and then have to pack it up again. It is not as easy as having a packhorse. I let people look of the list of what we carry on board and items are only brought up if there is an interest in them. As it is we have ended up buying more than we sold with amethyst and goat cheese and some serviceable gotar cloth. We bought several types of that.

Stefan

Shilpa is negotiating hard over buying some gotar, but the wife of the seller is paying no attention to that negotiation at all. She is nervously pulling on my sleeve. I guess that she wants someone's attention and I may look to be the least strange person to her. "Pardon me," she said, "but my son, he was headed your way. Did he reach you?"

"That be right," replied Stefan. "Denny, he be coming from here does he not. You must be his mother." The woman acknowledged it nervously. *She still looks worried.* "He be about to get married to a pair of lovely girls and..." *Her mouth is now hanging open and there is an expression of shock on her face.*

"Two?" the nervous mother asked anxiously. "Did he change...? Is he now...?" *She is apprehensively inclining her head towards where Ayesha stands in her obviously Caliphate dress and wearing her hijab. I suppose that we are going to have a few moments like this.* Stefan laughed and beckoned the cousins over.

"No. It be legal for a Christian to have two wives as well. T'is be Bryony," she said hello, "...and Adara," as did she, "and t'ey be both my wives. Do you see t'at little man in black with t' shortswords? He be married both to t' young woman who holds his hand and t' big woman over t'ere with t' pole-weapon. Your son be fittin' in real fine in our village. We need his skills."

"His wives to be are sisters...both apprentice mages...lovely girls and hard-working...but I be not convincing you, be I?" *The woman is shaking her head at me. I can see that she is hearing what I am saying, but my words make no sense to her. I need...*Stefan turned around and soon saw who he was looking for. "Bishop Christopher...if you are free..."

He beckoned and Christopher turned and began to come over. *The woman is immediately looking aghast. Hopefully she does not faint. I somehow doubt that she has ever talked to a Bishop before and now one is approaching and seems to be about to talk to her about her son and his upcoming bigamous marriage.*

It took some convincing before Christopher could settle her down and convince her that Stefan had told the truth.

Theodora

There is little beyond its dock and its goats to commend the village. It is four or five times the size of Mousehole but with a lot less in the way of advantages. Although their herdsmen and farmers try their best, the village lacks the fertile fields and the mountain meadows and its amethyst, while in demand, does not fetch for them anything near the price that the rubies of Mousehole do.

Olympias has asked that we stay here overnight so as to not have to venture out again into the large rolling swells that tell of a heavy storm that is happening somewhere far off to the west. We do not know what we are going on to. Apparently she does not want to risk straining the masts. The waves crash so hard against the breakwater that spray comes over to the River Dragon *and keeps the deck moist.*

At least the delay gives us a chance to tell more about the events of the last two years than the garbled stories that have reached the village so far. They have had no direct word, but only heard from people who have heard it from others. The people of Ooshz are even unsure of the details of the Compact with the Khitan and that is information that is vital for them to know.

Astrid

19th Tertius

Now we sail on towards Jewvanda. Again the River Dragon *has to breast the swell and beat and tack as she goes. Like Ooshz the village has an odd name whose derivation is long lost and whose pronunciation differs a lot from its spelling. It is spoken of as 'U-vanda' and the village itself is only a bit over twice as big as our little Mousehole.*

Goditha

Jewvanda has suffered badly from the bandits over the years. I wonder how Robin and my old home is going. How are our parents? Will they still be alive? It is some time since we were taken from here. Now that where I came from is in sight, I am starting to understand how Rani feels. I realise now how brave it was for Theodora to so openly display her husband to her family, to a real Emperor even, not just her immediate family.

It has been so long. I worry over our parents. How will they react to seeing their daughter again? Should I acknowledge my wife to them and tell them of their many grandchildren? I am so used to being happily married and now I am going back to my old village. I could never express my feelings there, although there once was a girl I had more than a few feelings for.

In utter despair over the decision, she had to make she stood on deck looking at the approaching village and clutching Parminder to her for comfort.

Rani

I can so clearly see the misery that is etched on Goditha's face. It is easy for me to see that she is thinking of her family and what she should tell them, or if she should tell them at all. That is the face of a girl who understands what my problem is, at least to a certain extent. I wonder what will happen now.

The wind has dropped away by the time we have dropped anchor, late in the afternoon, although there is still a rising and falling of the sea coming from the east. This village of Jewvanda stands on an island of hard and rocky land standing firm in an extensive saltwater marsh that makes up the mouth of Piali Creek. It has a strong palisade, but it is one that is only made of wood.

The main defence of the village lies in its being on an island, a very long bowshot from the nearest firm ground, in a very long and quite broad quagmire. Apparently really the only way over the creek, at least for some distance, indeed for a hard day's ride north, is over the causeways and through the village.

Here, Goditha has told them, is the best gotar we are likely to find as well as carnelian and superb feta. Much better than the stuff at Ooshz, she added dismissively. We can sell what is in the hold to others and keep the good stuff from here for ourselves. When she said that to us earlier I would have thought that she was glad to return home. Now as we anchor off-shore she stands rooted to the spot and she is making no move to go ashore.

Goditha

Parminder strokes my hand. "You don't have to tell them about me," she said to Goditha softly. *She is reading my mind.* "It is not important. But you have to tell them that you and Robin are alive. I wish that I could tell my mother about Gurinder and me, but I cannot find her in Pavitra Phāṭaka and you know that I have tried. Come love..." and she pulled Goditha towards the saddles.

I love my little dove so much. Goditha shook herself. "Thou art right, and if I do not tell them about thee then I am being a coward and I doth not love thee well enough, after all, what canst they do? Throw me out of the house?" Parminder laughed. "It do be a little too late for that. Thee and me shall go be a seein' them.

"They should be a proud of thee and me and now I wish that thee and I had Melissa and Daniel with thee and me...and our Gurinder of course. She will be a mage as well." She gave her wife a kiss and together they grabbed saddles and headed towards the village with the others who would be going ashore.

Chapter XXVI

Shilpa
19th Tertius

Just as it did in Ooshz, the arrival of the River Dragon *has caused most of the people of the village to gather. They have told me that they see smaller caravels from Freehold several times a year at least, but not a ship like this. Hulagu came with me to the land first. We arrived near an hour before the ship, to assure the villagers of our peaceful intent, our desire to trade and to apprise them of what we have on board.*

The village here is really too small for a regular market and the locals just gather together from all around when a trader arrives. In the time between us being first seen and before the ship anchors the people of the area have many items that may have been of interest to us brought out for purchase and put out on display. More farmers are still arriving with small amounts of cloth.

Goditha

There are my parents. How have they gotten to look so old? Has our loss hit them so hard? She landed the saddle with the others, dismounted, and walked towards them. *They look grey. It is not just their hair but their skin as well. It is as if the entirety of their life and colour has been drained out of them with the loss of us, their surviving children. I need to be strong and to not cry.*

It is my mother who sees me first, or at least recognises the approaching sword-wearing warrior as her daughter. The woman said nothing. She just opened her mouth, tried to point and then she collapsed without a word in a faint. *It is too much for her. Perhaps she thinks that I am just a faint come to haunt her, or someone who looks a lot like me*.

"Mother." Goditha leapt over to her as her father now stood transfixed and open mouthed. He could do nothing but stand and just stare. *He now looks like he will collapse as well right beside her.* It took some time to revive her mother and then to convince the pair of them that it was in fact their long-lost daughter who was in front of them.

Despite the interest in my re-appearance from the villagers, which far overshadows a mere chance to trade, I am taking them away from the others and sitting them down on some stools. We need to talk. Parminder followed. "Please," Goditha turned and used her full voice, "I am glad to be seeing thou all and thee wilt get a full explanation of me a coming back later."

"We ha' much to say to you, but pray let we be alone for a little while... Parminder...my dove...doest thou see that man over there," she pointed "he do be a brewer. Be thou a dear and do get jugs and goblets for we all from him." She turned back to her parents and they just looked at each other for a short time while they recovered their composure.

Parminder arrived back with tankards followed by the brewer with jugs of beer on a tray. "I thanketh thou, Master Linn." She waited until he had left and they all had a tankard and had taken a sip at least before continuing. *Where do I start? Perhaps it should with the good news that will make them happy and leave the rest until later.*

"Robin be also alive as well." Her mother began weeping on her father's shoulder. *I think they are tears of joy*. "He and me be both taken by bandits and let us just say that it wasn't easy for many years. He and me be made slaves and they did use us badly." *My father is looking aghast*. "The good news be that we ha' both survived and many others didn't."

"He and me be both well and he doth be married to lovely women and they hath many children." *Now comes the hard part*. "I am sure that thou doth remember that thee could never get me interested in any of the local boys..." *Both of them nod*. "that be because I be not interested in boys at all and never have been. I don't know how else to say this to thee, but I do love a woman and what be more I be married to her proper in a church."

The happy, if slightly puzzled look on my parents' faces now turns to shock as they, one after the other, look up in gradual realisation at Parminder who is just standing there quietly in the background. My little one now moves over and puts a hand on my left shoulder as I sit here. I reach my right hand up and lay it on the hand that rests on me.

"This be Parminder and she and me have three children one of whom be adopted and the other two, let me just say that she and me had help but Melissa and Daniel, yes I did give unto them thy names, they be beautiful children who wilt grow up loved and rich, safe and happy. Robin be also married to a woman who also be once a slave and they have three adopted children and three that Eleanor hath borne to him."

I am speaking so fast, trying to get it all out while I have the courage to do so. I must slow down. "Eleanor, she be a jeweller now. We all do all live together in a village in the mountains and be very wealthy and both Parminder and I both be mages as well. As well I be now a mason and be the one who is in charge of building a grand Basilica for the church."

There, I have had gotten it all out. Now I will be quiet and we get to see what reaction they have to all of the news. My parents are yet to say a single word in interjection or praise and their faces are pictures of shock. I have turned their world upside down and inside out all at the same time. I am not sure they know what to say.

"Thou canst not marry a woman," said her father sternly "no offence be to thee young lady," he looks up at Parminder, "I be sure thou art very nice as a person...but that cannot be. Father Frederick will indeed be shocked that you think that."

Christopher

I can see the tableau unfold in front of me and do not need to hear the words. It is just as at Ooshz with Denny's mother. I suspect that this sort of thing is going to be common when the people from my odd village came back into contact with those who have known them before. It is as well that I have held myself ready to intervene, leaving Simeon to talk to the local priest. Now he came over.

"Hello." He lowered himself and sat on the ground to get to their level. "Child," he said to Parminder, "...be so good as to get me a tankard as well if you please." He looked at Daniel and Melissa. *Here are the originals. They look...tired. They are obviously wondering who I am. I am obviously a priest and one of substance, even if I am wearing travelling clothes.*

"I can see that it is time that I stepped in. My name is Christopher Palamas and I am Goditha's confessor and am also the Bishop of the Mountains, although I was just installed in that role. I consulted with Metropolitan Basil, who was my superior at the time, and we both agreed that the girls could marry. Since then we have held a Synod of every Metropolitan in The Land and our decision was confirmed by all of the Faith."

"I am happy to confirm to you that your daughter is indeed married in the sight of God and, might I say, you have several lovely grand-children whom

I have baptised myself." He waved his hand around. "In our village we have two other sets of women who are married to each other and soon, I suspect, a pair of men." He took a tankard of beer from Parminder.

"Thank you my dear. Now might I suggest that the right thing for you both to do is to drink a toast to your daughter and your son who, as the Bible tells us, are to be treasured as those who were once lost and who now return to you. Remember as well that your daughter loves you very much and that she has even named her children after you."

Goditha

Dear Saint Irene, now Father Frederick has chosen this moment to come over. How will he react to this news? At least he is my old Confessor. He is the one person here who already knows of my loves and my lusts. I hope that he has had enough time to finally come to terms with them. She scrambled hurriedly to her feet.

"I do need to congratulate thee on thy survival and I be also a hearin' that you be the master builder of a new Basilica dedicated to God and have been using that sword of thine a fightin' the battles of the Church in the North alongside the Basilica Anthropoi as well," he said jovially. *I guess that I am forgiven by him then.*

"Thy parents must indeed be very proud of you." *My parents are now just looking silently at their local priest as if he has somehow betrayed them. It is as if he has turned into a snake right in front of them. I do not know whether to laugh at the expressions on their faces, or if I should just cry with relief.*

He has obviously been more quickly accepting of the new ideas he is presented with than the part of his flock that are in front of him have been. I hope that the rest of the village are the same, if only for my parent's sake. I guess that, when it comes down to it, he is glad that this previously wayward girl is now legally wed. I could absolutely kiss him.

Goditha

It is taking some time, but eventually the love of their missing children is overcoming the prejudice of the pair of them and my little dove is being embraced, even if my parents keep looking around for a man when she says the word 'husband'. Later that night with what seemed to be the entire local area stuffed tight into the village hall the story of the Mice was told.

It is a story that leaves my mother weeping as she hugs us two tight. It embarrasses me even if my dove accepts it. During a break in the story Goditha broke free. *I leave my mother and Parminder hugging each other and crying. Parminder is quietly telling her more detail, things she has never discussed with anyone apart from me and, I presume, her confessor.*

Goditha went around and talked to the people who she grew up with. *Some are able to accept things as they are. It is mainly the men who can do that. Many have noticed my short hair and that I not only wear a sword, and a good one, but also that I am obviously used to wearing it and have the calluses on my hands to prove it.*

I suppose that I have to be amused by some of the mothers who shift their daughters away from me when I try to talk to them. My God, these are girls I grew up with and have talked to all of my life. I suppose that it will do little good to tell them that I have known their daughters all their lives and have not made love to them yet, well that applies to most of them at least. What is more, I am now a very happily married woman with children of my own to worry about.

Theodora

Although the bandits and what happened to their people has the most importance at the start of the story, the tales of the dragon and the discovery of Dwarvenholme, the actual stuff of legend, soon takes over their attention. Skrice and the Swamp are too distant and are not important enough for them but the Compact and the other battles of the North are.

During the night I have to make sure that I stress to the village about the school at Mousehole, and what it means for the people of the independent villages. With the acceptance of the girls and the Mice by their mage Nicholas and their Father Frederick it seems likely that we will one day see at least some children from this village arriving in Mousehole.

Goditha

Did Ayesha have to play my part up? I am embarrassed, but the men are really looking at me differently now. I think, from what they say that they see me as one of them now, even if a couple have slipped up and called me Robin. Now everyone gets to find out that I am now an Earth-mage, in addition to my other skills, and that my wife is a mage of the Spirit.

Old Nicholas is our sole local spell caster. He is a mage of Water and really the local leader. He has gotten all excited now and, during the next break in the tale, is dragging my little one and me outside. Parminder has to demonstrate her ability to talk with animals. I admit that it is one of the talents that people hear of from the past. He says that he has never seen it happen before his eyes, nor had he ever expected to.

I know how the people here often struggle for money. I have made sure that I tell the priests and the mage that, if they find someone who can benefit from the school, I will pay their school fees. Nicholas has agreed to start testing everyone that he can. He had felt that he is too old now and had not wanted to take on another apprentice to train, but that will be no excuse now.

By the end of the evening I can see him casting his eyes over the children running around. I wonder which of them we will see first.

Ia

20th Tertius, the Feast Day of Saint Cuthbert

The next day dawning is, apparently, the Feast Day of Saint Cuthbert, their patron of shepherds and a special day in Jewvanda as well as in many of the plains villages. We will be staying another day in the village to help them celebrate. It seems that the people of this village only see their own chief priest every few years and have never had their service conducted by a Bishop before.

I still cannot believe that my sister-wife wants me to come to all the services that she is going to and is also insisting that her god will look after me as well even if I am a pagan. I just have to hope that the Mother will do the same for her. My beliefs are not quite as elastic as those of my sister-wife seem to be.

Chapter XXVII

Rani
21st Tertius

Perhaps there is some hope for me as well. We are leaving for Growling Harbour early with a slightly less heavily laden ship and with the last of our crew, Goditha and Parminder, only coming back out to rejoin the River Dragon *when we are nearly out of sight of the village. I am jealous about how I watched it unfold for them last night.*

Now that they have returned Parminder is wearing an old necklace that is made of the local carnelian and it has a matching ring. It was given over late last night and apparently it is a family treasure to that relatively poor family and had once been meant for Goditha, but her mother Melissa has given it to Goditha's wife instead. It seems that she is now regarded as the daughter and the real daughter is a second son. Can I get my family to acknowledge my wife like that?

As she stands there, by the rail, one of her hands is absent-mindedly caressing and playing with the old stones. Parminder spends the time until Jewvanda slips out of sight, and indeed some more after that, standing cradled in the arms of her husband with both of them looking back to where their mother lives. Both of them have tears of happiness in their eyes. I want to have those tears instead of the pain. I need to have acceptance and love instead of the rejection that I fear that I will receive.

Theodora

As we sail along in the River Dragon *the saddle riders are reporting that, on the road that runs along the cliff-top that marks the edge of the plains there is to be seen a very motley looking caravan. It is headed west. It has a couple of small carts, each trailing a couple of extra horses on lead ropes, as well as a hand of people walking and a large dray.*

To their practised eyes it does not look much like a caravan of traders. For a start, although all of the people among the train are armed, it even lacks obvious guards. Hulagu has decided that there is a good chance that this is the train of servants for the Basilica Anthropoi carrying what would be needed for the start of making their new outpost.

Olympias

Apparently Growling Harbour has the best port among the independents, if the Captain of a ship knows how to enter the mouth of its harbour and has a strong enough stomach to risk its relatively narrow entry. Personally, I am glad of the help of the saddles for a first visit. I would not like to come in here in a large vessel if there were a strong cross wind running. The constant current is enough of an issue.

Although not as long as the single breakwater at Ooshz, two strong stone breakwaters run a way out to sea. Each breakwater is walled along the outside and even crenelated and about three paces wide. There is a small tower, with room for a few archers on top, at the end of each of these and a long chain runs between these towers that may be raised from the deep to close the entry to unwanted craft.

The stone walls make a good harbour. Once inside a vessel is safe from almost any sea. It is one that allows docking for around six smaller craft and one ship, usually a caravel, such as is sometimes seen along the coast, or a small brigantine like us, but nothing that is bigger has any chance of fitting in.

The settlement, about the same size as Bridgecap, is built on the bluffs around where Barrowbrah Creek enters the sea from where it rises near the isolated mountain of Dagh Ordu, the reputed home of the dragon of the Khitan, in the middle of the plains. The village takes its name from the sound of the waves on the long beach of stones that runs along the sea-cliffs that go for a long way to the east of the village.

Out on the cliff-bound headland to the west stands a large windmill taking advantage of the almost constant wind. I am not sure that I have ever been to a place that can be better described as wind-swept. What trees I can see all have a lean on them as if they are all just a little drunk and are trying hard not to show it. Some have tops that go sideways further than they are tall.

Here we are buying wine, garnets and mozzarella cheese and more sh-hone while we sell salt, some cotton, wool, hemp, and general goods. As we go along, and sell more volume than we buy, the ship is rising in the water. I am starting to wonder when I will have to add ballast for stability. I will consider it overnight. We arrive in the mid-afternoon and, once again we will stay over for a night to tell the story.

Only fragments of the tale, and not always the correct ones, are reaching this far away from where the events have unfolded and the Princesses have decided that it is important that the entire south knows of it. Hulagu also particularly wants the details of the Compact, now it has been confirmed as applying to all of the free villages, to be clear to the coastal communities so that none of them unintentionally breach it and cause it to collapse.

Theodora
22nd Tertius

The next village up the coast, and another good day's sail even with our strong magical wind behind us, is Deeryas. Thankfully the wind from the west has moderated somewhat or it would have taken us even longer to sail the distance. It is the former home of both Valeria and Jennifer and, like Jewvanda, it has suffered much from the attentions of the bandits over the last cycle in its outlying areas.

Once again there is no harbour for us to use, but at least here there is a long headland jutting out to sea to the west of the village which gives a fair degree of shelter from wind and wave. The village is built a little way up Kyogle Creek from the sea and, if any boats call there, they are usually small enough to ground in the small mouth of the creek. At least Olympias is not complaining about the bottom for anchoring.

Jennifer

This time I get to be the one to leave the ship well before we will be anchoring. I have brought both my husband and Nikephorus with me to make contact with the village. Now that is done we go firstly to where my parents live among their chickens and vegetable plots and then we go on to Valeria's old home.

Neither of us is from a rich, or even moderately well-off, family. In my case we mainly lived off what we could grow on the stony ground up the creek although my father also uses nets along a beach to trap fish. He is a very good fisherman, but he does not have a big market for what he catches. She gave her parents a large purse privately and a barrel of salt and some barrels that fish could be packed in.

My mother doesn't care about what goods or money I give her. She has a son-in-law. I am sure she has heard not a single word that I have said since I introduced him. Harnermêŝ is an unusual son-in-law for her, but he does undeniably exist and is not a story I have made up as an excuse. I wish she would not, but she keeps touching him to be sure of it.

Her daughter…me with my notorious habits, has actually settled down and with only one man. That I am now wealthy and have a new home or even that I was kidnapped are all unimportant. Jennifer eventually gave up on explanations until that night. *At least my parents will tell the outlying people who live near them. I am sure that they will all be in the village later to hear the full story.*

Nikephorus

Valeria disappeared so long ago that she has been presumed to be dead and her parents, both now bent and aged early from their work, find it hard to believe that she is not only alive, but has given them grand-children. They seem enchanted by me. They are not accustomed to the courtliness that is a part of my life as I tell them of their grandchildren Angelina and Eugenia and where I am from and how I met their daughter.

The old-seeming folk are almost silent over the idea that one of their children is now a servant to Princesses and has met an Emperor and I have great difficulty in stopping them from deferring to me as if I were a lord myself. Despite all of my efforts, I don't think that I can ever be quite sure if they really believe me when I say that I am not.

That night, after the story had been told to the villagers, Nikephorus came up to the Princesses. "These are Valeria's parents," he said introducing the bent-over and aging pair, and the young man with them "…and this is her brother James."

"They want to know if James can come with us. Apparently he grows vegetables, and does it well, but they do not have enough money to set him up well in his own farm. I gave them money for Valeria's bride price, but there are so many other things for them to spend it on, what with the older children, that they thought it best if he comes with us to seek his fortune."

"We need men," Theodora said to them, after greeting the three, "...well not me, but the village does. I am sure that Giles and Asad will be more than happy to have more farmers among us. We have none living with us yet who specialise with vegetables and so we will all welcome you in the long run. Has Nikephorus told you how we run our little village?" *I did, but did it sink in?*

He is in awe at the beauty of the Princesses. As well, having been told by me exactly who Theodora is, James can only just gulp and nod. Like his father, he stands with his grey felt hat clutched desperately in his hands as it is being massaged into shapelessness. At least he can nod in some sort of acknowledgement.

"...then we will be glad to have you join us. I am sure that we can find you a wife or two as well as some land." *The young man's face has quickly coloured at the idea of a wife...and quickly coloured even further at the idea of two. I can see that the very real poverty of his family had left him looking at a bleak future without marriage. Coming from where I do, I am not used to seeing such poverty. May God surely bless the Emperor for making sure that it does not exist. What I have seen out among the barbarians is hard to believe.*

Olympias
23rd Tertius

The last independent village that lies along the south coastal road is Saltbeach, the former home of Adrian the miner. This village also sees the last of the plains, as only a good day's ride both to the north and the west of the village is the start of the Oban Forest. You can see the trees when you are high aloft on a saddle.

The village is built high on top of a cliff around where Arden Creek widens as it reaches the sea. For me as a helmsman, perhaps even more so than in entering the port at Growling Harbour, going into the dock here looks as if it will take some fortitude. It was not a dock that was ever meant for a vessel as large as the River Dragon.

I think that if the town's fishing boats can pull up onto the outside and dock against us there will be just enough room to nose her up to the wharf that is built hard under a cliff with stairs leading up to the village. I can see that there is a winch there to lift bulk goods up and down. Our soundings tell me that the creek may be only a few times as wide as my ship, but at least it is deep.

The way the land lies, it is as if someone had once taken a giant axe and driven it hard and deep into the edge of the plains and then pulled it out again leaving a gaping wound in the sea-ward cliffs. While others make arrangements with the village to land, I survey the dock and take soundings and reassure myself that, with the use of our own wind, we will be able to make it in. On the other hand, we may need to use our anchor ropes and so warp our way backwards to get out.

She then took her saddle to where the village boats were fishing and made arrangements with them. *I have to find the one of them that belongs to Miles Fysh, the village leader.* Cautiously, under only her jib sails, and with crew ready with wool-filled fenders and with sweeps and ropes, the *River Dragon* nosed into the narrow port.

Cliffs rise high on either side of the ship and Harnermêŝ, from his station on the mainmast and keeping an eye to ensure that there is room for the ends of our spars, cannot see past them and on to the plains as we go in. They are tall cliffs indeed. At least there will be no issues with wind once we are tied up.

Looking up I can see that around us the children of the village watch and wave from where they hang around on the cliffs, their normal playground. We must be the largest ship to actually come in and dock at their village. Gradually adults are joining them in looking down over a stone fence along the edge. Ahead of us a bridge crosses the chasm left by the creek and people are peering down from it at the ship as well.

Theodora

Saltbeach is still recovering from the Burning. It still does not have a complete wall, although it is nearly finished. What it has now is all made of wood on a rampart of earth that is still incomplete. By the look of what is there, the village plans to put a more solid one on the outside of it to leave room for another street or so of houses to be built there later.

It already has provision inside the walls that they are building for flocks to be brought inside and more space for that will be added with the new walls. Once this is done it will be as secure as Warkworth is, but until then Freehold, or anyone else who wants to attack them, are a constant threat to the life of the residents. It is a village that has few assarts outside it, particularly to the west, although there are hamlets further up their river, I am told. By the look of it many people choose to travel out to their fields in the morning and then retire back to a more secure place to sleep.

Christopher

Shilpa trades with their shopkeepers. The Princesses talk to the local leaders and mages. Meantime I get to talk to the local priest. He has only received a letter about the arrival of the Basilica Anthropoi with a trader a week ago and he has difficulty believing the good fortune of the village in getting them to move here.

It may not be an army that they are gaining, but they will be more protected now. As well there will be more money coming into the village as a barracks and other facilities are built. It will put back the building of their stone wall even further but the residents have already started with hurrying to complete the wooden one so at least they will have that to fall back on.

Shilpa

It is an unusual village in many ways. The creek that runs through it a filled hand of paces below the houses cuts it squarely in half. A wide stone bridge, from the look of the rocks that make it up it is one that was built in a much earlier time, spans this gap and walls and fences extend along its rim to prevent small children and stock from falling in.

To me the bridge looks very similar to the one outside our valley in the manner of its construction. It shares the same look of age as well. It has, however, been far better maintained than its equivalent in the mountains. There are no missing stones on the edges here. The village produces salt fish and, from a mine in a hill near the sea, an hour's walk way away to the east, sapphires.

I am able to sell all of the remaining salt that I have here for a very good price. I have very carefully worked it out and I am sure of my margins on this trip, but the locals are well pleased to tell me that my price is far cheaper than they are used to paying. Mind you, they only told me that once they have paid their money over. Using a ship is, however, far cheaper than bringing it in by land, so I am probably making a better margin.

There will be some disappointed merchants for some time as they work their way along the coast. With all of the fishermen that are based here in the village, those working in the sea, in traps and nets along the creek in its tidal area, in its upstream cascades, and from traps along the coast, salt is always a constant source of a good profit for the traders who come here. There is very little flat ground near the water for them to make it themselves. I will definitely be coming back with more if I can get Olympias to bring me.

Thord

Adrian had asked for me to look out for his parents and I have done so. They are astonished that, not only has their son made it across the breadth of The Land to where he said he would go, but he is doing the work he trained for and is marrying, of all things, a miller. It seems that they heartily approve of that.

As he told me, his parents are farmers who work in the poor, dry, shallow, and sandy soil of the plains that is all that they have here. They try to grow a crop of wheat in it, and I am sure get a poor return. By their standards marrying a miller makes you prosperous straight away. I will not try and explain the way Mousehole works to them.

Thord

Now that I have discharged that obligation I am going to set about enjoying myself and making sure that some of the Mice return to my training. These are good cliffs, even if they are made of sandstone instead of the harder dolerite and basalt that we are used to at home. The village can look on as a Dwarf, a woman from the Caliphate in a hijab and trousers, and others begin to clamber up and down their cliffs and are soon even jumping down them with a rope.

Climbing is one of the few free local recreations, something I already discovered from Adrian, but they rarely see anyone else who enjoys it. To them the abseiling is unusual and not something that they do here, in fact they hardly use rope at all. I am finding that we have a line of locals, and not just the children, wanting to find out how to do it.

I am glad that I decided to use the cliff that leads to the long beach that gives the village its name as, at least, it gives sand for people to fall on instead of rock when they make their mistakes, as several do. The local blacksmith has to be shown the iron loops that make it possible and, by the time it is too dark for us to continue he has already made a hand of them. Now we are finished I will leave them with the hemp rope that I have used. I have deliberately brought a spare with me to shore and it is not my best.

They grow hemp here, so they can learn to make more long cord for themselves later, even if they do usually only use the plant for cloth. However, I have also had to leave them a couple of pairs of strong gloves as well. The isolated village lacks a good leatherworker and any gloves come in to them from Freehold and are usually more a fashion item than something with so practical a purpose.

Thord

that night

Even after we have had several drinks I gave up trying to explain about the wealth of our village to Adrian's parents. Hopefully it will sink in now. Now that all of the negotiations and other talk is done I have handed over to Adrian's mother a small pair of ruby earrings that Adrian arranged for Eleanor to make.

She may have found it hard to believe that he was able to send something as rich as these, but tonight I notice that she is wearing them now to the admiration of her neighbours. It may be the best jewellery that any here have. She may have also put on her best dress for the occasion, but it is one that has obviously seen better days.

Now we all have to sit around outside as the tale is told. At least there are no mosquitoes here. Saltbeach lacks not only a tavern, but also a hall and they even have to bring their beer from Jewvanda or Freehold, and that is expensive. Some of the farmers make their own. One taste of that has Astrid and I going back to the ship and bringing back up a barrel of the wine from Growling Harbour slung underneath two saddles.

Apparently one of the things that the locals are hoping for is that, with the Basilica Anthropoi coming to stay, they will soon have enough trade coming through to be able to attract and keep a brewer. One of their farmers is hoping that this will be the case at any rate as he seems to be making a start at building a tavern of their own.

Stefan
early morning 24th Tertius

As we prepare to depart, someone appears on top of the cliff above us calling us to come and look at what is happening. Once we are up it easy to see a file of the Basilica Anthropoi approaching the village, but from the north-west not along the coast. I guess that we need to wait until the men arrive, almost hard on the heels of their introduction letter.

They are on patrol as kynigoi. Their armour will be with the train. Behind them are remounts and pack-horses. I get to sit out with the Princesses and the village head, this fisherman Myles. After Praetor George, their leader, is told of where their servants are, he announced that he has news as well.

"Someone in Freehold is definitely looking this way in a not friendly fashion," he said. "We took three of their scouts coming out of the forest to the north."

"Could they not have been hunters?" asked Myles. *That is right, Adrian said that his village generally does not believe that anything more than what is normal is happening in the world around them. Didn't he listen to what was said last night? Why does he think that he is getting a garrison? Are they being deliberately blind to events?*

Praetor George looked at him blankly as if doubting what he has heard. "No," he said bluntly. "They had come out of the forest, where we saw plenty of game. They ignored the game around them on the plains. They fled as soon as they saw us, and when we killed them they had no pelts or meat on them. They were equipped for several weeks of a patrol and had new coin on them. They were paid to come and find things out."

He looked around and then down at the ship and its flag. "You will be the Mice that I was told of by the Metropolitan." *It is a statement rather than a question. He can see several nodding heads.* "When you get back to Bridgecap, let them know of this. It will be several weeks at least before the next file arrives." He thought for a moment. "Are you going east or west?"

We now all look at Rani. This is her call and so far she has given us no indication. At least it is not a question that has caught her unawares. She is quick to give a reply. "West," she said. "I was going to have us look at what we can see of this New Found Land of theirs."

The Praetor nodded. "If you get a chance to upset their timetable, it might be useful." He looked at Hulagu. "You are of the Mori then?" Hulagu nodded. "I have talked with the Mogoi on this trip. We know each other well. They know of my concerns and will also keep a tighter watch on the Örnödiin in the name of this Compact you made."

The Praetor is a square dour man with a short square-cut salt and pepper beard, the corners of his eyes are creased in a way that shows that he spends his life outside and peering into distances. He seems to be pleased with the idea of allies and is already grimly planning ahead and seeing what he can do to make the best of his situation.

Until more of the Basilica Anthropoi arrive and begin to settle in I suspect that his men will see little of the village they are based in as they begin to actively patrol around it and start to learn the terrain that they will perhaps be trying to defend with such a small force. They will need to know it well to overcome the disadvantage of being outnumbered. It can be done. Look what we did to the Brotherhood.

I am sure that they will find more riders to help them among the local herdsmen. Their Praetor is already talking with a pretty girl in trousers with a bow case at her hip and the look of one who rides for a living. I somehow doubt that he is chatting her up and they already appear most serious in what they say.

Rani
a little later

With this news, and with the Basilica Anthropoi already looking at where they can set up camp for now and where they will build a barracks and other buildings in the longer term, we get to cast off and slip out to sea. The crew fend us off from the wharf as a rope leads back to the wharf and is let out until the current has us far enough out. We have a jib sail picking up the ship's wind to keep us oriented. The ship rides light and high.

"Olympias, "she said, "take us well south so that no-one casually flying around is likely to see us. Keep a close watch on the green-light box…Hulagu… three fliers aloft by day and at night one. During the day keep one very, very, high and the others lower. We want to know of any ships or anything suspicious."

She looked around at the waiting listeners. "I want us to head for Camel-back, but we need to arrive well off-shore so that we will not be seen by accident from the coast or a fishing vessel. The only sailing direction that we have is north-west from there for about ten days, so that is what we will do."

Chapter XXVIII

Olympias
27th Tertius, the Feast Day of Saint Zita

We have sailed into a breeze with the green-light box just keeping contact with the shore to the north. Then in the middle of the fourth day, the line of the coast has disappeared and not come back, even though we have been moving along the same parallel the whole time. Menas was sent out, flying high, to see what the coast was actually doing.

They kept track of him, showing only as a tiny fleck of light on the green-light box, as he could not be seen. He had gone so high. He came back after an hour. "I went up until I started to find it hard to breathe," he said. "The river goes north...there is a big river there," and he pointed towards an invisible coast "and a lot of forest." He then pointed further west.

"There is an island offshore north of that which could easily be your Camel and another river north of it. I was too high to see any boats or anything else but the actual shape of the forest and land and a city up the first river. I couldn't see far up the second, but there might be one there as well."

Olympias brought the *River Dragon*'s course around to the starboard until she found land again in the green-light box and then kept it at a constant distance as she circled around it. *Camel Island is easy to detect.* Once it lay to their south-east on the screen, she turned the head of the *River Dragon* and they headed towards the north-west into the growing night. *At least the water here is that of the open ocean and even the deepest lead can find no bottom to it.*

Now that we are in these totally unknown and potentially hostile waters we will keep four saddles up, two on each side and high enough up to be just dots in the day, although I will keep them lower at night, and far enough forward that they can see well ahead of what the green-light box can tell us about from on board the ship.

They are the only dots to be seen on the screen for some time even though the natural breeze is coming in very softly and the River Dragon, *sailing only under her own wind, is travelling north-west near as fast as she ever has.*

Rani
34th Tertius, early morning

It has been very quiet so far. We have had a pleasant cruise up until now and that is all. However, now a saddle has come back to us on the River Dragon. *It looks like things are going to change. Things are about get very exciting indeed.*

"There is a ship ahead of us," said Tãriq animatedly as he pointed towards the port quarter. "It is bigger than us, far bigger, and it has four masts and is sailing more or less into our way. On each of its square sails it has an empty equal-armed cross painted in red and it streams a flag with three lions in the fly and then the same cross. Is that a Freehold flag? What do you want us to do with it?" *He is looking at me. If we do the wrong thing here we may just be about to start a conflict with Freehold. Do I want that?*

She started giving orders: "Pull everyone back down, but get as many on saddles, low and behind us, as we can as soon as it comes in sight. I want molotails on each saddle and make sure that you have enhanced arrows ready to use." *I have never run a naval battle before, but hopefully Olympias will correct me if I am doing something wrong. If I watch her while I give orders…*

"We will turn across its bow when they can see us so that we can better hide the saddles. Fly our Mouse banner and see what they do about it. Be prepared to respond with force, but hold firing until they do something. For all we know they may be friendly. Ariadne, get below and prepare the light-thrower. You will need to throw open the rear of the cabins and latch them open and I will call if you are to use it."

What else? Oh yes. "Get people ready on the ballistae with charged rocks but cover them over so that they cannot be seen. We have the four weapons, but really only two crews so be prepared to move your crew across to the weapons on the other side of the Dragon if we have to come about. I will get ready on my pattern to either attack or to cast a defensive spell. Bishop, please take a position on yours."

Olympias is looking like I am missing something. What am I missing? We are heading towards them now. What happens when we get close? What range will we be at? "I want to stay out at a maximum range for spell casting and beyond most arrow fire until we see what is going to develop…anyone who is not doing anything else but who can use magic get ready to use it." *She is turning away. That must have been it.*

"Can I take a saddle and board them?" asked Astrid innocently. "I have the magic protection amulet and the shield amulet and I should be able to distract their casting."

Rani paused before answering. *I don't want her to board them. She may think it is fun, but one person cannot take on a whole ship. She will also get in the way of us being able to target them if we need to. However, if she can fly past and cut some ropes so as to hamper their ability to manoeuvre and sail, I am sure that would be good.* Rani finally nodded.

"Take a saddle and circle low and stay well behind them," she said. "When you see them start to engage they will probably ignore anything coming up from behind them so only close up then. Otherwise remember that mages have a good chance to see you. Come in fast and see what you can do. Cutting rigging will probably be enough if you cut the right ropes.

How do I stop her being too wild? "Only go on board if you think you will be safe from us and our fire. Remember that you have children and two other people here who will miss you, so don't do anything rash. Try and keep their ship between us and you. That will at least give you some cover from our fire."

Astrid grinned. *Butter would not melt in her mouth. She was planning on boarding them.* She kissed the other two people in her life soundly before putting on her magic and disappearing. A moment later her bardiche disappeared from view and then her saddle. *Presumably she is heading out and away.*

Olympias

My eyes are glued to the green-light box while Harnermêŝ is aloft with a telescope and his eyes on the horizon. "Sail-ho," he called and pointed. That direction agrees with what is on the screen at least. Now it begins.

There is no sign of Astrid. If she still has the ring on we will not see her. If it is off, then there are occasional dots on the screen that might be her, or they might be a high breaking wave, or even an albatross turning and momentarily casting a reflection.

She brought the *River Dragon*'s head around a little so that they were going to be coming square across the bow of the other ship and the saddles moved around accordingly. Gradually more and more of it became visible.

It really is a huge vessel. It is well over thrice the length of the River

Dragon *and the top of her stern-castle is itself near as high as the top of our mainsail. The stern of the craft even has a balcony running around it with a rail that soldiers can stand on to fight from during boarding actions. How many sailors does she have?*

"Harnermêŝ, use the telescope and tell me if you can see arbalests or rockets or anywhere where something like that could be concealed."

Eventually he called down: "I cannot see anything like that, but I think that there is a person standing on a hatch, probably in a pattern like ours; just one. There are archers in the maintop, and it is a very big maintop, and I think that some have fire pots there and there are soldiers on the deck wearing armour and getting ready with crossbows. Some people seem to be putting nets up from the masts to the rails. As well there are a few people who are dressed in black like a Metropolitan but with no beard and no hat."

"Dominicans," said Simeon. "Expect no mercy from them. They do not like the Orthodox, nor witches or...well...most of Mousehole really. I tried to hide myself away and...well, before I fled, I used to be a Benedictine monk and I had to flee them. I know how intolerant most of them are to anyone who is not exactly the same as them."

"Get buckets of water ready. Tie each one with a rope to a rail so it will not be lost if we need to scoop up water." *That sends the sailors hurrying to get ready to protect their ship.*

We wait and gradually the two ships draw closer together. At four hundred paces the archers in the rigging on the other ship started shooting arrows of fire into the sky. "They have enhanced the range of their bows," said Rani approvingly. Olympias brought the helm around a little so that they missed. *It is a long way for an arrow to travel and I have the advantage of manoeuvre.*

Rani

I wish that I had thought of extending the range of shafts. It is good tactics for a bow that will be used from one ship against another ship. "I guess that they do not like us. Well, they have fired first, so now we can shoot back with a clear conscience. Aim for that mage and fire the ballistae."

Quickly the covers were pulled off the starboard pair of weapons and Deniz-kartal and Krukurb fired after taking careful aim. *Even as they do so others spring to rewind and reload.*

Olympias brought the ship further around again to avoid another flight of arrows. *I get to lean over and send our riders off.* "Stay clear of the direct path as you go. Get the archers first if you can, now go."

It is still a long range for the ballistae and one shot missed the hull, but managed to hit a rope or a stay as it sailed over the top of the craft. It exploded in the air. Even from here some faint cries can be heard. The other shot is low, as it is supposed to be. It hits the hull.

It leaves a gaping wound of near a hand of hands width and half that high in the side of the ship above the water line. The explosion has staved in some of the thick timbers of the hull. That will make it hard for them to turn without letting water into their hold.

The saddles come around the River Dragon *and start climbing, as the next flight of flaming arrows is coming in. Not wanting to have one of the riders run into the ship as they fly out restricted Olympias' steering a little and two arrows hit. We have one on the deck and one in a sail. The crew have buckets quickly in play as they are burning both hot and fast. The effect of their burning must have been enhanced as well.*

Arrows keep coming in and most are able to be dodged, but some strike the ship and one hits Mary. People sprang to and quickly put the fire out on the ship. Others hurried to draw the shaft, which leaves an ugly wound. It is dressed and Mary is given a potion for healing as she is carried aside. The next two shots from the ballistae open up a hole in a side railing and one in the huge stern-castle.

The first at least carried away several men in a back and breast cuirass from among those who lined the rails. Some can be seen tumbling into the sea. In their armour, even if the men can swim, they will have no chance. The damage from the second ball cannot be seen.

Olympias brought the helm over. "I am going to come down their port side and try and keep the range open," she said to Rani. You can see they have far more archers than us and at this range they can only fire at us with a hand of them. We will try and keep the rest useless as they probably only have normal bows. Our two ballistae do a lot more damage than their hand of archers do. If we can keep away we will take them."

It soon becomes obvious that the other ship's captain has realised the same thing and is desperately trying to close on us. His craft is more ungainly. Olympias says that he has the weather gage, but his ship is far slower and does not seem to steer as well, so we have the advantage.

The saddles are climbing and the riders are starting to shoot down at the ship. Some miss and small explosions dot the water, but it is hard to miss something that is so large and several more little explosions could be seen in sails, on the deck and on the masts.

Just then a huge ball of fire appeared flying from the other vessel. It comes from the hand of the caster on the deck and it grows as it flies. My Theo-dear has been muttering away in High Speech. She has obviously been trying to judge when a spell would come as she only takes a few more loud words and something, a distortion in the air perhaps, flies out towards the ball and they meet.

It can then be seen that, as the ball keeps flying through the air, it reverses and starts to shrink back in on itself. It finally disappears in a small puff of smoke that quickly dissipates. She had a spell of negation ready. My Princess immediately starts chanting again. Several others did the same. Maria is the first mage to cast. Her bolt of fire is much smaller than that which came from the other ship, but nothing came to oppose it.

She aimed at the helmsman, leaning on his wheel and concentrating on his sails and the wind. He saw it coming at the last moment and, in reflex, tried to leap clear. He failed, but to get that range she had sacrificed power and it struck him only as if he had been hit a glancing blow from an arrow at distance.

The effect is scant and he is soon standing again, but the real damage has already been done. In evading the bolt he has let the wheel go and it is now rotating wildly with sailors desperately trying to catch it and bring it under control.

The huge ship is now almost broadside to the wind. This causes confusion in the rigging and arrows fly in several directions. The bow of the ship is now pointed nearly directly at us and the next two shots, this time from the port ballistae, both impact near where the bowsprit emerges from the hull.

The bowsprit itself is the first casualty. With a tearing sound it falls alongside the craft into the water and begins to drag alongside the ship and slow it down. The other has hit into the deck near the forward leaning first mast. Now all of the fire coming from the other ship is masked by its own sails and it lies impotent. I was about to start my own spell. I don't think that I need to now.

Olympias is switching to our slower wind and stopping the fast one so we can stay in this position longer. Other spells began to leave the River Dragon, *one for each of the lesser mages as well as from wands. A small rock flew from Goditha, and two more of fire from others. They hit among the people trying to cut the bowsprit free. Goditha's power is getting stronger.*

The saddles are now well above the other ship and fire arrows are springing into the sky reaching for them and answering fire rains back down. Someone threw a molotail and it missed the other ship leaving a spreading sheet of fire on the water. Someone else hasn't missed with their throw. I hear the 'whomph' noise before the ball of fire ascends from the middle of the ship as a sail catches fire.

The loss of the bowsprit, and the stays that lead from it, now prove crucial. As the helmsman tried to correct from his mistake in letting go the wheel the masts can be seen to shake. The rest of the stays making the rigging rigid are starting to let go. Any sudden change or strain in the ship could now dismast them. No more fire arrows are going up. Two people suddenly leapt out of the rigging to the water below as flames are coming up to meet them.

Screams begin to be heard across the water. Another molotail hit near the bow and suddenly the people who are working there are engulfed in flame. They begin to run about, spreading the effect and more screams can be heard rising up. Panic seems to be setting in among our foe.

The ship was turning to come back on course, but suddenly it yawed again and, just as the fires suddenly all went out, the strain has proved too much for the third mast, which still has all of its sails up, and it falls with a noise like a forest giant. It is time to use the loud-talker and change our attack around. None of them should speak Darkspeech. "Switch to normal arrows. Use no more fire. Take the mages and the priests and then any archers."

She turned to Olympias after speaking, "that was right wasn't it? We will be able to take them now." Olympias nodded. *She is starting to order sails to be taken in. Another round from each of the ballistae attacks the fore-mast, just behind where the bowsprit had been. One hit it and the other must have hit into a gap in the hull. It went far under the deck before exploding. Slowly the mast begins to topple sideways.*

Now the ship only has its mainmast, standing bare of useful sail after the fires and without any stays and a small mast high in the stern with a triangular lateen sail. It doesn't seem to matter though as a group are struggling with the wheel and some can be seen leaning over the rear. The huge ship doesn't seem to be answering the helm at all, no matter what they do.

Olympias called down to Ariadne to close the rear windows and to come up on deck. *The weapon of light will not be needed in this fight. By the time she has stowed the weapon away and is up on the deck I can see no-one moving around on the other ship, although the fire is still out. Our archers in the air have now swept the enemy deck clear of sailors. There have been no prisoners taken, but then none have tried to surrender either.*

Olympias began to steer towards the other ship. "Why did the fires go out?" she asked.

"Someone on board had thought about this sort of battle," Rani replied. "They realised that fire would be used and, just as Theodora had an anti-magic spell ready, they had an anti-fire enchantment to cast. It was possibly set up like a contingency cure spell. At any rate, we need to work on one of those." She now turned to the saddles and used the loud-talker again.

"Half stay aloft and stay ready to fire and the other half board. Where is Astrid?" A lone saddle came around from under the overhang of the balcony that ran around the stern-castle and the rider waved.

"Damn," said Olympias. "That was better than cutting stays. She must have destroyed the rudder with that great axe-thing of hers."

Basil

There is a lot of ship to search, starting with the filling hold. There seem to be no combatants left, so everyone can land and start working. Gradually we can begin to take boxes back to our vessel slung under the saddles.

There are three people still on board the craft and alive, hidden under the decks. Of all the people to find on a Freehold ship, one of them is a Goblin, and he is locked in a cell. He emerges when he is freed and tries talking to us without any success.

On reaching the deck he looks around the ruins of the ship and is more than happy to be brought over to the River Dragon. *Everyone tries to speak to him, but not even Aziz could understand a word that he says. Ayesha is particularly annoyed. She is proud of actually speaking some of the Goblin tongue, but anything that she tries to say he just shakes his head at.*

The second person is a pretty girl of around thirteen or fourteen years dressed in a very full dress of rich blue velvet with silk panels. Its top is covered in pearls that are embroidered in patterns all over it. She is brought kicking and struggling up on deck by Puss, carried under her arm. Her kicking shows that she has hoops under the skirt.

She is calling us pirates and smugglers and wishing us all to go to hell. She is trying hard to escape Astrid's clutches, but it has little effect. The third person is an older woman, one who is more concerned for the young girl than for herself. She is only struggling in order to get free and to try and reach the girl.

"Shut up and behave the pair of you," said Astrid, in her sing-song accented Latin. "This ship is going to be sunk. It is already slowly sinking, and you will be taken to our ship. You cannot stop this so behave yourselves or we will leave you here to drown."

"You are not going to rape me," said the girl "I will not let you..." *She stops and her face looks taken aback in astonishment as the whole boarding party who hears her and who can speak enough Latin to understand what she said, burst into loud laughter that spreads as they translate to those who did not pick up the original complaint.*

"Oh deary, deary me" said Astrid. She has a huge smile on her face as she looks at the girl's reaction to what she provoked. "Apart from the fact that most of us are women, that is one thing you are going to be safe from. Please, when I take you over, say the same thing to the people on our ship. I am sure that they need a good laugh as well." *The girl just looks at her scornfully and tries to break free again.*

"Put me down you Kharl-woman," the girl said trying to break free. *Puss laughs again, hops on her saddle and lifts off. The girl is now face down across her lap and screaming. Her hooped skirt lifts high in the air shows off her legs cased in loose white linen breys and several layers of underskirts. She obviously didn't see how we arrived and was not expecting this.*

Very quickly she has stopped her struggling, but she screams the whole way across. At least, once the girl is off the ship the other woman only wants to follow her and rapidly consents to ride behind me without any problems at all.

Now the young girl is on board the River Dragon *and starting to rant about not being raped by pirates. She tried to grab one of the falchions from the rack. Goditha has grabbed both of her hands. She keeps struggling and yelling. Eventually she realises that almost everyone on the ship was grinning and laughing at her and becomes even more indignant. It takes her a while to begin to wind down.*

"Why do you all think that is so funny?" she asked. "Why are you all laughing at me like the Kharl-woman is?"

Theodora

"Firstly, your ship attacked us first without warning when we were just sailing innocently. So it is obvious that they were the pirates and not us. Secondly you will notice that most of our people are female and a good number of them have been captive of bandits and repeatedly raped. If there is one thing you are safe from with us it is rape."

She stopped for a moment before continuing. "If we find that you are evil and have committed crimes then we will execute you. Until then you are safe. If you give a solemn promise in the name of…" *Do the heretics have the same Saints as proper Christians do? I guess we share some things.* "…Our Lady to behave then you can stay free otherwise you will have to be bound and that is uncomfortable."

"You will kill me anyway and probably eat me," said the girl. "You have demons and Kharl and probably witches and other evil things here."

This girl is a puzzle. Is she drunk or perhaps taking a drug? "We kill demons, only Gundardasc is a real full Kharl, although several others are part-Kharl and that is no shame. Denizkartal is a Boyuk-kharl, Aziz and Krukurb are Hobgoblins and both are Christian. Thord is a Dwarf. Ia is a witch, but she is a good one not an evil one… Which one of us is supposed to be a demon?" *I admit to being puzzled over that.*

The girl is pointing at the cousins, both of whom, as usual, are displaying a lot of cleavage with very open bodices. "They are Mistress Demons with the red hair and flaunting their flesh to tempt weak men into sin and error. They are just like the one that my mother says has her hooks into my father..." *Again she stops as her words are greeted with gales of mirth.*

"Can we keep her?" Astrid asks. "We need someone in the village who can make us laugh so easily after a battle. I have been told that Princes and Kings sometimes have fools to entertain them and to make their people laugh and she is so very good at it. I think that you two, as Princesses need a fool and she does seem to have the gift of making us laugh." *The girl is looking very indignant at that.*

Gradually the girl and her nurse settle down, or at least the girl does, and we get some information from her to add into Basil's little book. The nurse keeps fussing and trying to make her young charge more comfortable. The girl ignores the nurse's fussing and stresses that she is worth a lot in ransom. She has made that very clear.

She is Virginia Norbery, the second daughter of the Duke of the New Found Land, and she is being sent back to what she calls the Old World to be shown around for marriage. Some of what they had on board was her dowry and cannot be touched it seems. As a prisoner she is very demanding and obviously used to having her own way. Her nurses name, she just called her 'nurse', is Ursula.

In time we are ready to complete the sinking of the other ship; apparently it is called the Goldentide and is the largest and newest of the three Freehold galleons. It still has most of its cargo on board but the holds of the River Dragon *are full, the saddles are all on deck and that deck has boxes and barrels all over it in such profusion that you have to walk on them, or crawl under a low sail, to get about.*

I hope that we do not encounter a storm. The River Dragon *sits very low in the water and answers its helm very sluggishly. We apparently have on board everything that is the best of the County of New Ashvaria and some from the other Counties as well, or so Simeon deduces and Ursula confirms.*

It varies from several different types of cheeses, to boxes of arrows, one of bows, two large cases and two small of fine porcelain, and even many barrels and boxes of bottles of a fine whisky. Simeon insists on bringing them all when he saw them.

There are three large boxes containing shawms, crumhorns and other instruments packed carefully in wool, spun wool of outstanding fineness, many barrels and bottles of wine, bale after bale of remarkably fine linen, and woollen cloth, and boxes of swords and maces and mail as well as jewellery and box after box after box of gold and jewels. Simeon says that some of plunder is from his old village.

There is even a large box of embroidered and couched braid, another of embroidered linen tablecloths and napkins that are suitable for a Royal Court and a large chest of fine stitched gloves of various sizes for men and women in cloth and kid. There are potions and herbs, luckily all of them seem to be labelled as to effect, and other boxes of dried dies.

We even brought some iron, gold and silver across in bars and ingots, but most of the metals, and indeed most of the weapons and cloth and almost all of the food, are still in the hold. It seems that we have managed to intercept the main tax ship of the County of New Ashvaria, with the dowry added in well over one half of the wealth for the year of the New Found Land, perhaps even more, will not reach Freehold. Praetor George wanted us to disrupt their plans. We may have done that very well indeed.

My husband has talked with Olympias. The main advantage of the River Dragon *in a fight against a larger ship lies in its speed and in being more nimble than its opponent. She has neither at present and the ship lies very low in the water now and is steering like a pregnant cow. If there is a serious storm, or really even just a mild one, we will need to jettison some rather valuable plunder in order to gain freeboard.*

It seems that we will have to return to Haven. Reluctantly, and carefully, the helm was put over and, with their strong wind set in place they headed back along to the south-east, so that they could travel along the south coast, out of sight of land, until they reached safer waters. *As we go the cargo starts to be re-organised so that the saddles can be stored away out of sight if it is needed.*

Chapter XXIX

Ia
34th Tertius

"I am closest to her age and the newest here. I will try and look after her." *The Princesses are looking at each other. I don't think that either of them thought about having someone looking after a prisoner who can roam around on the ship.*

"But you are a witch," said Rani. "You heard her."

"So, would you have Bianca who is a foundling and below notice for a noble, look after her? Would you have one of the Saints, all of whom who used to be prostitutes, Parminder, who is married to a woman, Ariadne, who is part-Kharl or Verily who is…odd? Age and newness are as close to her as we come unless Theodora looks after her."

Theodora looked at her husband… "She is right dear." And then back to Ia "Have you asked your husband and sister-wife?"

"You are right. I will do that next." Ia went over the barrels and boxes to where the two sat keeping an eye on the girl. She spoke in Darkspeech. "I have told the Princesses that I will keep an eye on this virgin, but not why I must." She stopped as she talked to them and looked at the girl and all around them. *No-one must hear this.*

"Remember I said that the face of the woman with Basil and I changed from Astrid to someone like Parminder to Ruth and so on…" *I wish this was not true. Oh Mother I wish that it was not true.* "One of the faces that I saw in that vision, the one that was like Ruth, was hers. I need to find out more about her but I don't want to tell anyone. Will you help me?"

"Little one," said Astrid. "You are married to us. If you think it is a duty or something…of course we will help. Just remember that we really do not want to have yet another wife for Basil."

It really does depend on who it is actually, but I suppose that you are right really. But what if the vision is a true one? I hope it isn't but I cannot rule it out from what I know at present. "I think that I need to make a first use of my new ball tomorrow and look to see what may lie ahead for us."

"You are a witch and an evil devil-worshipper," said Virginia to Ia. *She sits with her nose in the air in rejection as Ursula brushes her hair. She is sitting on top of a barrel of wine as if it is a throne. When she says that, it was as if what she has said is a complete and sufficient rejection of me and all that I stand for.*

"And you are a spoilt and ignorant chit of a girl who was raised to be useless and to hate or look down on anyone who is not exactly the same as you. You would even have killed that lovely Bishop who, even though he is not of my religion, I know is a holy man. You would kill me. Father Simeon says that I would be burnt alive while I was tied to a stake, and it would be because I am who I am and believe what I believe.

"You would kill my sister-wife and probably her beautiful children and the Princesses and Parminder who is so quiet and sweet and talks to horses and cats and eagles. If I have the Bishop right, and he said it in a sermon yesterday, for your God the greatest commandment and virtue is love. How can you say I am evil when you are the one who hates so much?"

As Ia spoke the expression on Virginia's face had gradually changed from shock to rage as the words sank in and she threw herself at Ia. She did not succeed, but tangled herself in her voluminous cane-hooped dress as a foot went down between casks. She fell as Ia, dressed in more practical leathers, lithely dodged away.

Her husband and sister-wife, sitting nearby to watch what happened didn't even stir although Maeve, sitting on Astrid's lap, chattered an unanswered question at Astrid.

"See, you hate me and you cannot stand to hear the truth," she turned to where Christopher was on his hatch, sitting in one of the few clear spaces with Bianca and called out. "Bishop, what was it you said in that sermon about truth from your Holy Book when we were just out of Bridgecap?"

He is thinking back. A lot has happened in the last few weeks. "It was: 'But speaking the truth in love may grow up unto him in all things, which is the head, even Christ.' Why is that, my child?" he asked.

"It is just an illustration for this seemingly hate-filled girl whose only apparent skill is to be pretty. She is being sent off far from home to eventually be sold by her parents to a man she does not know yet. They will marry and so to bear more ignorant children just like her." *Looking at Virginia it can be seen that some of those words have struck home.*

"I am more than skilled. I am often told that I am very accomplished. I play several instruments, I sing, I can embroider and paint and dance well and I have three languages that I speak well."

"You have been told that you are skilled by people who flatter you just for your father's sake or to gain your favour. I may not dance or paint and embroider, but they are only frivolous things to fill in time if you have nothing better to do anyway. I became an orphan when I was four and I am now about your age and yet I speak nine languages, more or less well.

"I can heal both animals and people. I can read the future, teach people, can mix potions that kill and cure, can make items that I have prayed over to cast spells and I can survive on my own in the jungle. On top of all of that I can use both a sword and a bow and still I can sing. I have been supporting myself by my craft and my wiles since I was just ten years of age. What makes you think that you are in the least bit accomplished?

"You have just been taught to flaunt yourself and tease men. You have been shown how to be useless and a decoration, and to waste your time and others. You could not survive on your own out in the real world for more than a day." *This time the nurse restrains the girl from leaping up, even if the expression that is on the older woman's face, where it cannot be seen by her charge, seems to agree with what I said.*

Ia
much later in the day

We have not stopped arguing, but I am far more stubborn than she is. I have had to be to survive. I will wear her down eventually. She has been raised to be compliant to authority. It was bad enough when she was fed the same food as everyone else or, as she put it, 'the common sailors', but it comes to a head now dark is starting to fall and the matter of accommodation comes up.

"There are two real beds on this ship. One is for the Captain and one is for the Princesses. You have two choices. You can roll around underfoot or you can get into a hammock and be grateful for that."

This absolute insult to her dignity is almost too much. She has exploded and then wept uncontrollably on the shoulder of her nurse. It is so obviously something that she does to gain her way with others that my cydwraig has again burst out laughing at the girl. She gets a long look of hate in return.

When it became clear that she was not going to get her way she consented to sleep in a hammock but wanted everyone to leave the room while she was assisted out of her farthingale. Astrid again burst into laughter. *Around us are men and women in various stages of undress and only Ayesha and the Muslim men seem to look the other way or even seek a token privacy in what they do.*

Rani

that evening

My Theo-dear is sitting on a hatch with a slate and her eyes are unfocussed and staring into a distance that only she can see. She is completely ignoring everything going on around her. There is a plate of food beside her. I was able to approach and sit down beside her and she only noticed me when I kissed her on the ear and laid my hand on her leg. "What are you working on now?"

"Oh...they will soon know that the ship is not coming and then they will use a spell to determine what happened to it. I am working on something that will cloud the issue and will make it harder to trace anything back to us. I think that is best, don't you? We will perform the enchantment tomorrow. It will take more mana for us to cast it then, but I think that it will not be so much more that it will not be worthwhile regaining all that we used in the battle."

If my Princess says so, I have to believe her. I may have gone to University, but she is nearly a hundred years more practised than I am. She is better at these things than I am. After making Theodora eat something Rani left. *She can keep working away in her own incomprehensible way.*

Theodora

35th Tertius

What I want out of this spell is that, to anyone that looks at the area, the Goldentide should just appear to sail into a huge bank of sea-fog and never emerge from it. The River Dragon *still has her protection from Skrice and none can scry her from afar in the present moment, but now she is also covered by the fog. Indeed most of this part of the ocean is.*

She looked all around at the greyness that now surrounded them. *It feels odd that it looks like a dense fog, and yet it is not damp at all. It is all just a vast illusion of fog. It should take a lot of luck for a searcher to find one unknown ship sailing into or out of the bank that covers the water or even the traces of a wake.*

I can see that the spell has worked. Now I need to get Olympias to change the course, to be sure that we will not make landfall at all. If we sail to a point well below the south of The Land before we turn then it will make it harder to predict where we will be. On such a course it will be even harder to find us as we are deliberately sailing to where no ship will normally sail.

Ayesha

I think that he speaks the same Goblin tongue that I have, but it is as if a Brotherhood person is speaking poor Arabic to someone from Rainjig. Neither one of them will understand the other. I can establish that his name is Yabaribaykus, but that is about all. I wish that I could write Goblin. He has got hold of a slate and wants to communicate, but I have no idea of what he is writing.

He was a prisoner on board, but whether he is a criminal or something else I do not know. He seems to be very surprised to be left free on the ship and he wanders all over it, looking at what is happening and watching our people at work. Most often he is found near Gundardasc, the person on board whom he most resembles in appearance. He has been offered clothes and a belt knife to eat with.

He seems more than content with his own very brief kilt, but is delighted with the knife. It might as well have been precious jewels. Simeon has explained to us that most of the Goblins of the New Found Land only use stone tools. Only the wealthiest among the Goblins, or those who have been successful in raids upon the settled areas, have any metal weapons or tools at all.

Ia

Astrid and Basil can keep an eye on the girl for a while. I in truth need to read my ball and see what I can see in our future. This girl truly annoys me and I am really hoping that she is not to be one with us.

When she eventually came back on deck she had a languid smile on her face. *I am still under the influence of my drugs. My eyes are wide and my voice is slurring and I just want to curl up and cuddle and slowly make love. It irks Virginia when we do it, but I need to speak in Darkspeech and low, so that no-one else can hear me.* "It is a lovely ball and so much clearer.

"There are only going to be the three of us, and Sin, but we need a new house.

We have just so many children between us. We have so many lovely children. Isn't the house next door to us still available? If we take it over, then we can make holes in the wall as doors and have it as just one large house. We will need it. We will so need it."

She turned to Basil "Our first daughter is just so beautiful. I promise that I will be the mother to all of our children that my mother could not be to me. I am going to be a mother." She hugged Astrid and Basil before returning to the fray with Virginia. *I have to concentrate on that. My mind may be more than a little slow at present, but I am more relaxed about her at least. She is not to be a sister-wife.*

Lakshmi

4th Quattro, the Feast Day of Saint Ambrose

Six more days of sailing brings Thomaïs to labour and, without Fear's help it is a more uncomfortable experience than the woman would have wanted. At least I have Ia's biscuits. Labour has taken most of the day. Curse that child for demanding that Thomaïs be kept quiet. At least she was rewarded with glares from the entire ship's company. It may have subdued her temporarily, but that is all.

Habib is soon showing his son, Isidore, named after his father and his daughter Delphinia, named from the pod of marine mammals that have accompanied us alongside the River Dragon *during the birth, around the ship proudly. They may be the first Mice to be born at sea, but one thing that seems to be fairly certain is that they will not be the last.*

Olympias

6th Quattro

It takes us another two days, running with the sea, the wind and the current before I reckon us to be somewhere well to the south of The Land. It is time to send the saddles far out to confirm this. The green light box can see nothing at all to break its sweeps. At least that means that there are no ships out there to threaten us.

They came back to say that we are apparently well south of Growling Harbour already, but they cannot agree on how far. After hearing everyone's opinion on that it will be time to take a reading with my astrolabe. That will let me bring the helm around to aim, hopefully, directly to Sacred Gate. I will correct it as we get closer if I need to.

It is useless for us to call at Bridgecap. The goods that are most of interest to sell there are now lying truly buried under everything else. When we are closer to the land some saddles can be dispatched with news for the Metropolitan.

Lakshmi

10th Quattro

"I really wish that we had Fear with us." *Sacred Gate is in sight and Irene has been in labour since the morning and has even eaten the last of the biscuits.* "I am sure that this one has a problem of some sort. She didn't when last Fear listened, but she does now." The delivery took almost until they were up to their wharf and, when the baby girl was born she lay there blue and still.

Irene has burst out in tears of anguish through her pain and Sabas holds her tight as the lifeless baby is passed to Christopher, who is waiting in the pattern. He has earlier led us in the Divine Liturgy in the preparation for the birth and even Irene has taken the wafer. We are all subdued and quieter than we normally are. It is not a time for noise.

Even the expression on the face of the Freehold girl is a mix of revulsion at the blood and pain and pity for the anguish that Irene and her husband show. "She is not all bad," Astrid noted to Ia. *She is pointing out to her sister-wife that the pity is slowly winning, and it seems to be.* "She just needs to see more of life."

Christopher held the tiny bundle close in his arms as he prayed. When he had finished and stood there unsteady there was a wail from the bundle and Polymnia, or beautiful song, was finally welcomed to the world of the living. *I praise the Lord that I have chosen the path that I have taken. He is indeed a very holy guru to follow.*

Chapter XXX

Basil

10th Quattro

As we come near the river, and the Foreigner's Wharf comes into view, I have to make Virginia clearly understand that we do not trust her not to be foresworn, and that she will remain below deck and firmly restrained until we leave again. She can object all she likes, but to my trained ear it is obvious that she was planning on breaking our trust and has an attempted escape in mind.

She is shackled fast under the deck and Ursula given the choice of being restrained as well or remaining silent. I suspect that Ursula realises that Virginia will order her to untie her. She chooses to sit restrained with her charge. At first I hear some muffled yells, but that only took pointing out that a gag will be used on her unless she stops, they ceased. Showing her the uncomfortable ball gag helped as well.

Shilpa

Our customs official is becoming tardier in his arrival. "We have a manifest, but it is incomplete as we have not had a chance to list everything in detail. Most of what we have on board will be bonded and some will be loaded back on board. You are welcome to wait and watch while I work out which is which."

The man was surprised to be given a chair. Now he sits and watches with increasing astonishment as the wealth of the cargo is unloaded before him and weights and measures taken and noted. It was as well that we arrived before lunch as it is still well after dinner before we will finish the task.

Shilpa relented enough in her dislike of Havenite officials to feed him as well when they took a break from the work. *I will admit that he has been very patient with us this time. Perhaps he did not believe all that he was seeing.*

Astrid

Some of the goods are loaded back onto the River Dragon *and, now with Guy and Maximilian on board we set off going back up the river at night. It was a nice break not to have to worry about them, but eventually we have to release Virginia and Ursula. This close to shore we have to make sure that Virginia is fastened to either Ia or me. I showed her a crocodile, but I am not sure if that will stop her if we get close enough to land.*

Once she tried to grab Ia's eating knife but she was easily disarmed and dissuaded from doing it again. In the short fight she managed to cut Ia. *My little witch-wife is easily cared for this time, but that is not going to happen ever again and it is time that Virginia learned a lesson instead of behaving like a spoilt child throwing tantrums at not getting her way. She needs to know about consequences.*

To Virginia's humiliation, and despite her best efforts to resist, Astrid promptly picked her up, put the young girl over her knee, pulled up her skirt and paddled her publicly just as if she were a small child who needed a short lesson. *From the indignation she expresses, the yells, and the look on Ursula's face, she has never had this done to her before.*

"I could never do that. She had a whipping girl," Ursula whispered confidentially to Basil, without, for once, trying to intervene "…and Virginia just didn't care what happened to her." *Ursula does not realise how good my hearing is. That is good to know though. Obviously it is something that may have an effect on her.*

Her humiliation is complete when I finish and she sits up. She can see two men, from their dress obviously from Freehold, holding hands and looking at what just happened with looks of amusement on their faces. When I introduced them she is even more mortified.

"But I was told once that, if you did not go into the church, you could possibly be the man that I was to be married to," she said. "You cannot be one of…of… them. You will be burned."

"Only if they catch us, dear child," said Guy "and once we get into the valley we are headed towards, we will only leave it for a very good reason indeed. I look forward to a lovely quiet life teaching other people's children so that they do not turn out to be the same sort of ignorant adults filled with hate that you seem to be." Guy turned to Astrid. "How can we make sure that she doesn't tell the Dominicans about us? Can one of your mages or your lover do a forget thing on her?"

"Ia cannot..." *No need to ask her, she is shaking her head,* "but if worse comes to worst I am sure that Theodora can. It is one of those things that we will see about. She will most likely not be set free for some time anyway as letting her free would make it known that someone took their ship, and we don't want that to happen until this is all over."

"But I must be set free." *She has tears of shame and rage streaming down her red and blotchy face still, but Virginia can now be seen to be completely horrified at the prospect.* "If I am not married, or at least appear in Court soon, everyone will assume that I am dead and when I return everyone will think that I have fallen and no-one will marry me as I will be soiled."

"If they think that, then they are not worth marrying anyway," said Ia shortly. There was a bitter lack of any sympathy in her voice. "I was raped by evil men who killed my mother when I was only a child and Basil knew of that when he married me. If they only care about you being a virgin, then they do not care for you at all." *She is rewarded with a look of horror from the other girl. I am not sure what part of the explanation that is due to.*

Astrid
14th Quattro, it is the Festival of Pancake Pali before Lent

We didn't stop at any of the river towns on the way upstream and only briefly called at Erave Town, with the pair below again, to sell some whisky and some of the cloth. As we crossed the lake we started transferring people and goods by saddle to the village. Those who are returning to the village are all back in it by the fourteenth of Quattro ready for the festivities of Pancake Pali.

We make sure that Virginia is shown the valley and told of the gate and how it will kill her if she tries to get out. She is shown the river and how cold, strong and quick it is. She looks very forlorn, as she cannot swim anyway. She is shown everyone at work and is dismayed to see Goditha already back working on the Basilica with Nadia. Both women are stripped to only their short kilts. To make it worse, they are singing a psalm in Latin between them as they work.

She is looking around her. She was not expecting this sort of scene from us rough pirates. All around the village fierce warriors are soon transformed as we play with children who have been left behind in the care of others. We all still carry our weapons, but no-one wears armour. It is good to be home.

Ruth

We need to see more people who can talk about their experiences in the world outside our little area. Ruth dragged Virginia into the school to talk about the New Found Land. "But it is secret," she protested. "You cannot know about it."

"Father Simeon is from there," said Ruth, "and we know of at least another four lands as well. I just want them to hear from a noble perspective what it is like to live there."

Astrid was right. She is nearly useless. It turns out that she can tell the children less about it than Simeon already has. She has lived a sheltered life in Castle Mount, the Ducal seat and knows little of life outside its walls or those of New Ashvaria and some hunting lodges.

I asked her to explain why she was being sent back the The Land. She didn't realise, until she saw shocked looks on the faces that the children regard her as being abandoned by her parents when they sent her back to be hawked around the nobility like trade goods.

I grew up in Freehold society, and can truly say that I am glad to not be there now, all things considered, but in most of the cultures of the children here a woman's family are given a substantial gift by the groom in recognition of the loss of her services to the family. They don't have to pay someone to get rid of her.

Chapter XXXI

Rani

15th Quattro, it is Ash Tetari, the rst day of Lent

Pancake Pali is over and Lent is upon us. At least this year my wife has only given up sweet pastries. Soon it will again be autumn and then winter will be coming around again as the year goes through its slow cycle of four hundred and thirty-two days. If our calculations are right then the Imam should return to Mousehole from Darkreach soon.

It will then be time for us all to make our first, and long awaited, visit to the Caliphate. Our patrols are keeping a good watch out to the north for this arrival. Now I am left to think about who should go on the trip.

Now we are safely back in the valley, where others cannot hear what is said Basil has told me what he had found out and deduced about the presence of an Adversary in the village of Ta'if. If he is still there, that is. I need to hold that in mind with my planning on how to go about this visit. It means that we cannot be as open and straightforward as I would like to be.

Thinking of the wider picture, for now we will not need to use the River Dragon. *We should allow it to be seen appearing in Haven sometimes as just a simple trader and with no connection to any untoward events that are happening around the land.*

That means that it will need to take saddles, even if just to load and unload with when it lies offshore in some of the villages of the south. After all, they are far easier to use than small boats for the purpose.

I think that we need to give the ship four of them and two can stay in the valley with the carpet to scout around and ensure that no-one sneaks up on it, and to stay in touch with the Dwarves and the Hobs. That means, unless my wife gets to work on them again, and I know that this is not yet scheduled until winter, twenty-four saddles will be available to go on to the Caliphate. That gives me my numbers.

Christopher

We need to sit down and discuss things with this Goblin. It turns out that the magic of a Darkspeech speech book does not care at all about whether the person who it is given to can even read any of it. Now that I have talked with him, if the Catholic Church in Freehold is rejecting the Goblins in the Newfoundland, then perhaps the Orthodox should reach out to them.

It had been worthwhile doing so with the Hobs. With the blessings of God, maybe we can be lucky again. I will have to take this matter up with the Metropolitans. I can get Glad to start writing up a letter to send around among them and seeking their opinions, and perhaps to gain a volunteer or two to send to the Newfoundland. It will be dangerous, but also possibly well worthwhile.

It seems that Yabaribaykus means Wild Owl. His tribe is the Guneydeolan halksulutoprak or 'The Southern People of the Watery Earth'. Their territory is west of New Trekvarna. It seems that there are a lot of swamps and jungles down there. His is one of the three tribes in contact with Humans, although his has less to do with the Duchy than the others do.

He knows, because they told him, that he was a captive being taken back to be put on display in Freehold for the nobles there and then questioned by them and the Dominicans. He is only the second to go there since contact was made. Unlike the other, a woman called Yakuţana from the Kayipkasehaliçden, he realised that he had little chance of surviving the experience.

The priests who had him captive do not think that he is a person with a soul, and they are trying to upset a treaty that another Goblin tribe, the Halkgenisovadin, had arranged with the County of Sweetwater in the far north of the territory claimed by Freehold, despite what many of the locals felt. Simeon told us all about that.

I am glad that I have Basil taking notes as Wild Owl is both talkative and well informed about what is happening in his area, if not with the other two tribes. He is also keen to learn Latin so that he can speak to the invaders of his homeland and perhaps negotiate with them. Now that we have one tongue in common it is far easier for this to happen.

His tongue is, we think, written the same as Goblin is here, but the pronunciation is so different that it may as well be a different language. At least now we priests can start taking notes on the Goblin tongue of his distant land.

Ayesha will help in that. She wants to learn how to read and write his tongue after all.

Astrid
17th Quattro

Eleanor has completed what I want for my sister-wife's jewellery. They are only meant to be worn for a formal occasion, but it means that she can then wear another set of earrings without showing her scars.

They are two long metal bracers covered in raised metal filigree in the design of flocks of butterflies. Between the wires are baked-in coloured enamels and the effect is of flocks of butterflies flying on her arms instead of the plain leather that she otherwise wears there.

Ia cried when she was given them and wanted to wear them all of the time. Eleanor showed her with a test piece just how fragile the enamel can be. After that she has put them away for good use, even if she does take them out sometimes to just gaze at them.

I think that they are the first things that our little Butterfly has ever owned that are just there to be pretty. Any effect they have on spell casting may be more accidental than intended but they are very pretty to look at.

Theodora

People quickly settle back into their routines while we wait. Our new farmer, James, is happily looking at the soil and preparing land to plant his winter crop of vegetables. The idea of re-building of the bridge across the stream is rapidly becoming more and more important as we need more and more space just to grow things in the valley itself.

Guy is now, even more happily, helping Ruth and looking after some of the little ones whom he will eventually teach while Atã, although he does not quite know how to accept his sexuality, is delighted to discover that Maximilian is not only a strong man but he is also glad to take the bottom end of the saw in a pit and, what is more, has done so before. Our supply of sawn timber is starting to grow and more and more of it is being put aside in stacks to season.

Of all of the people that we have in the valley only Virginia refuses to do any work. We may as well lock her up all of the time. She considers work to be beneath her and, what is more, she refuses to even allow Ursula to do anything except fuss over her. She even upbraided the poor woman when she discovered Ursula helping in the kitchen one afternoon.

I thought that I was almost useless when I decided to run away from Ardlark. It seems that I was just almost terminally bored. I think that I would have killed someone if it had meant being given something useful to do.

Ia

I am beginning to regret taking on the care of Virginia. The girl has to be confined each night to sleep in one of the cells as no-one trusts her word. She has already tried to steal the jewellery that opens the gate once she saw it used and has been caught hiding weapons when she has been forbidden to have even an eating knife when she is away from the table.

She has to be searched each night before being put into her cell. Not only is she untrustworthy, but she is bad at it. Each time that she has been caught Astrid has publicly spanked her, not as hard as a real flogging, but just enough to make her a little sore. It is meant mainly to humiliate her and it seems to at the time, but she forgets it overnight.

Like a stubborn child she will not learn and flounces and pouts afterwards as if it is all Astrid's fault or mine and not hers at all. I have talked to the girl, who is exactly my age to the day. I have argued with her. I have tried reasoning with her. I have had Ayesha tell her all about what has happened up to now and nothing has an effect.

She is set in the ways her mother has guided her into. She doesn't even believe what she is told about Baron Toppuddle, even when Guy confirmed what she is told. She met the 'lovely handsome man' when he visited her father's castle a few years ago and her mother has said openly that she thinks that he was one of the best men in Freehold and perhaps its hope in the war against the unbelievers that is coming. I guess that means against us.

There is one thing that I am sure of and that is, whatever the potential of that vision four years ago, there is no way that fate would have been so unkind as to make me fall in love with someone so shallow and so spoilt. I am glad that first Astrid, and now Basil, have my heart in their hands. The Mother is definitely looking over my future.

Chapter XXXII

Rani
19th Quattro

Why is Parminder running up to me? She looks worried and she has hurried from where she has been working. She has flour on her breasts and even on her nose. She has been making bread I will warrant. "Princess, an eagle has told me of a man near its eerie." *She is pointing towards the cliffs that lie behind the valley and that formed its defence and yet prevent escape except by the two paths.*

"She wants me to get rid of him for her. She is worried for her nest. I looked through her eyes and he is not here yet. He is still some way back from the edge of the valley, but he is close enough to us that he could come down tonight if he wanted to, or he could do what that horrible flail man did and just watch us."

"Someone fetch Astrid and Ayesha with their rings." *They are quickly beside me although Astrid is still doing up clothes after having come from a class.* Ia, who was still wearing only a lop-sided and hurriedly-donned 'dress' made of two small pieces of chamois hanging from a belt at the front and back and tied at the side, was carrying Astrid's bardiche as her wife dressed herself. *It must weigh half what she does.*

*An irrelevant thought, but she really is a very pretty girl. I wonder what I would have done if my readings had been about a girl from the Swamp. It would still be an older and a younger person…*she dismissed the thought. *My life with my wife could not be better and dharma would not be so cruel as to pair me with one of the cattle-killers.*

Ia ran away again as Rani gave instructions. *I can hear her calling to Basil as she nears their house. Now she is running back, breasts jiggling. She gave a wand to Astrid while Basil arrives with a couple of sets of shackles and a gag for her to stop the man biting his tongue or grinding his teeth. I didn't think of that.*

He then gave another two sets to Ayesha. Rani prepared to send them out and turned to Parminder. "Check with your eagle again child and point out exactly where he is."

Parminder closed her eyes for a few minutes. *She has her eyes closed and points, pauses briefly and then changes the direction slightly.* "He is still back at least a filled hand from the edge and is creeping slowly forward as if he expects to be watched as he moves. He is very good. Perhaps only an eagle would see him."

Astrid

Looking up I can see the bird wheeling high in the sky. It must have looked at Parminder as well as at the man to correct her aim like that. Now I need to take careful note of exactly where she pointed. It is along a bit from where the Flail of God tried to come in. Ayesha and Astrid quickly kissed respective spouses and sister-wives and jumped on the saddles and were soon out of the gate.

"Everyone try and look as if all is normal," Rani called out loudly. "Ia…go and look out for that idiotic child of yours. She is likely to think that he is a rescuer and do something stupid."

And she is. I can see from here that she is trying to light a fire. Poor Ia. Mind you, I think that Make was worse than Virginia is and Make eventually reformed and so there is still hope for the girl or maybe we just have to sit out her captivity until we can safely release her back to the life that she craves. At least we will not be marrying her.

The two women flew out of the gate and headed around to the south. *He is coming in nearly directly above the mine and to the north of where we picked up Vengeance. By accident or design he has chosen one of the better cliffs to tackle, if he can make it through the shield that is. This sometimes seems to be possible where there is a natural gap. After all, we did it. The cliff there has several fissures that run all the way up and down it like chimneys without the fourth side.*

Thord has proved that these are sufficient to enable a confident person to use them just like that. They may also serve as a gap, as the gap in the cliff did when we first attacked the valley. On the other hand, we can fly most of the way while we are visible and still talk as we do it. The man wouldn't actually have a chance to see us until we are directly behind him and only a few hundred metres away.

That gives us a chance to lay out what we want to do. Once they went invisible Astrid moved forward, first at a slow walk speed, keeping up a soft continual update of what she could see as they held the rope between them. "I see him." She stopped. *That sudden soft jolt tells me that Ayesha has run into my saddle. Stop talking now.* She felt the rope move to her right and she started to move forward again.

They were a filled hand from the edge of the cliff and half that from the man who was inching forward along the ground. *Parminder was right. From the sky only an eagle would have seen him. Our sentinels must already have missed him on at least one of our regular sweeps. It would not have been hard. He is dressed all in grey and green and will not stand out in any way.*

The rope gave a wiggle. *That is our agreed signal.* Astrid landed. Leaving her weapon on the saddle…*if the man happens to look back he will see us, but there is nowhere here for us to hide our mounts, at least there is enough wind to cover small noises…*Astrid dismounted and they moved cautiously forward on foot. *I cannot afford to make a noise.* They were only a pace behind him when Ayesha dropped her end of the rope.

Astrid had been slowly taking it in. *We cannot be much more than a pace apart.* She finished winding it up. *If I drop it then it will become visible and make a noise.* She readied the wand. *I am not used to wands but my sister-wife has made sure I know exactly how long it gives us to act. Ayesha is waiting on my action before she moves on him. It is time to move.*

She used it and jumped forward as the man slumped. *My job is just to hold him still. She took one of the man's forearms in each of hers. A suicide-gag has appeared on his head as he starts to come back awake. He cannot bite himself now. His feet suddenly have a shackle on them as he begins to kick and thrash around. He is a strong man, but against my strength, now with all my magic, he has not the slightest chance.*

She felt something against her. *That should be Ayesha.* She moved his hands to behind his back and held them together until shackles appeared on his wrists. She now took one of her shackles and pulled his arms back and grabbed his legs as they kicked up and then fastened one to the other. Astrid looked up. *Ayesha is visible.* She took her own charm off. She was sitting on the pinioned man as he lay on the ground under her.

"Hello Sayf," said Ayesha, looking down at the man. "As you can see, by the will of Allah, the Strong, I have learnt well from you. Has my sponsor lost her influence or are you acting on your own? That is right…you cannot speak. Don't worry we will soon fix that. Meet my colleague Astrid…just nod politely. She will be carrying you."

Astrid had stood and now picked the man up by the shackles. *Obviously, he must be a ghazi as well. This could be very interesting.* They walked back to the saddles with the man hanging beside her like a saddlebag. Astrid had to send Ayesha back while she used the last shackle to suspend him from a hard fastening point meant for holding cargo.

I have dropped Ia's wand and we have to find it. Once that was done they took off and returned round to the south to come in again at the gate. *It has taken less than an hour from when Parminder had first found him for us to get out here, take him and return back to the village with our captive.*

The mages are ready and a curious crowd is gathering around. Several are still in work clothes and the man's eyes are bulging at seeing so many near-naked women, some with blades strapped about their bodies, others with an apron worn over otherwise bare breasts and often with tools hanging off belts. Still others wear a dress and a hijab. Astrid unhitched him and, still with just one hand, carried him over to the frame.

Despite his attempts to resist he was soon strapped up in it. She then went over to Ia, who was still only wearing a kilt, and gave her a kiss as she gave the wand back. "It worked beautifully. I will be glad when you can make it to last a little longer, but it does make it so much easier." She turned to Basil who stood waiting. "It is over to you now. Which mage is it this time?"

Basil gestured. *It seems that Goditha, the Earth Mage, will cast the spell.*

Rani

Her elemental area of Earth governs truth. Goditha has mainly been practising spells of binding in her work up to now, but it is time she extended herself on something new. She stands there nervously, in a pattern with her wife. She has her mana store clutched in her hand. She is about to channel three times her normal mana, getting one third from that mana store and the rest of it from her wife.

I have thought about Ia, her young age, and yet her strength. I have decided that, in order for the apprentices to grow, just as if they are doing physical exercise to build the muscles of their body, the lesser mages need to do what the young witch has done and start stretching themselves when it can be made fairly safe for them to do so.

Sayf abd Allah

This man in black is standing beside me as if he is about to do something, but I cannot get my eyes off the sight in front of me. There is a tall, beautiful near naked woman in front of me. She is short haired like a man, but very obviously a woman despite her sturdy work boots and full apron. She is sweaty and streaked with dust, but she is also obviously a mage standing in her pattern.

As well, the one assisting her is obviously also a mage, even if her dark skin is covered in patches of what looks like flour. She even has some on the end of her nose. He looked sidewise. *Apart from Ayesha, there are several other women here wearing a hijab and also men in Caliphate dress, but none of them look at me as if I am a friend. Even the one who I know personally is standing with a barbarian of the plains and she is looking at me very coldly.*

I am supposed to kill myself rather than reveal anything, but that option has been quickly taken from me by the big blonde woman who tossed me around as if I was a child's stuffed toy animal. She now stands there holding the little dark near-naked woman with a tattooed stomach as if they are lovers and yet both have kissed the man who is on the other side of me. I am confused.

"My name is Basil and I am a tribune in the Antikataskopeía of Darkreach and I also have sort of the same role here in Mousehole. You have already met one of my wives. She is the larger one of those who brought you in. Over there are our Princesses Rani and Theodora. Theodora is the cousin of your Princess Miriam who sent Ayesha, with the blessing of the Caliph, to protect her."

Despite my discipline, I can feel sweat breaking out on my brow. What have I gotten myself into? This is not what I was told that I would find. "We are fighting a fight; I think that you may call it al-jihad al-Akbar against some of the seytani. First, we freed this village from their servants, then we found Dwarvenholme and killed some of the lesser seytani themselves.

"Since then we have been travelling around The Land and fighting them and killing their servants. So far the real seytanyi, the chief ones that is, have evaded us. I think you have been sent here by one of them and I want to find out a lot more about you mission and who it was that sent you from your lips.

"The woman mage over there, she is dressed like that as she has not had a chance to change from her other job as a mason, is about to enchant you to talk to me and I will ask you questions and you will answer.

"My other wife, the one who has taken all of her life to discover that she actually likes running around half-naked showing her lovely breasts off to the world even when she had more than enough time to put clothes on," *The little near-naked one has smiled at that and blown him a kiss.* "...she will write down everything that you say. After that we will decide what to do with you.

"This may just be to hold you as a prisoner until we have done what we need to or it may be to execute you. We are waiting on a representative of the Ayatollah Uzma Alĩ ibn Yũsuf al Mãr to go up to the Caliphate and try and find the seytani and kill him."

I know now that things are definitely not as I was told they would be. I have been thrown into something that is completely different to what I expected. For a start I well know the name of the leader of the Faithful in Darkreach. It seems that I am acting against him as well as these people. In front of me I can hear the mage starting her chant.

"I have been told that you are not an evil man, and so you may survive this experience. Many who have been where you are now have not. Now, I will talk to you again in a few moments...and you will then be able to talk to me as well," he concluded and stood aside to wait allowing Sayf to clearly see the mage in front of him. *What can I do?*

Sayf looked at the man beside him, the little near-naked girl, *Such a lack of modesty, does she flaunt herself to lead me to error and distract me from my duty?* the big blonde woman holding her, *look at her teeth,* the mage, *I am to be enchanted by a near naked woman,* Ayesha and lastly the woman with golden eyes, *the Princess does have the same eyes,* and then back again.

I need to stop this. I am trying to work my mouth around the gag. I desperately need to bite my tongue and kill myself. It is what I was ordered to do, but there is something projecting into my mouth and all I can do is swallow nervously. This is not supposed to happen. This may not be what I was told to expect, but I do have my orders.

Basil

Goditha has finished her enchantment and almost collapsed from the strain. Her wife and the other apprentices help her out of the pattern and she is brought a tankard of ale and fed sweets delicately by her wife.

Cautiously Basil gave his instructions to Sayf and then removed the gag. *The man hasn't tried to kill himself so the spell must have worked. Christopher stands ready in case some other spell has been set in place to cause him to die. Now we start the questions.* Basil set to work as Ia wrote down everything that the man said. *I think that Butterfly's breasts sitting before his eyes are almost a final insult for him.*

His name is Sayf abd Allah and he is a senior instructor at Misr al-Mãr. Ayesha has already confirmed that. The head of the school, Mullah Mughĩra abd Allah, has assigned him to a mission at Ta'if. Naturally he has not asked any questions, but has done as he was bid. A man, whose face he had not seen, but who had a very deep voice, had told him to come here.

He had to be very careful in his approach and he had to find two objects: a jade mouse and a golden horse. I suppose that those were predictable targets, but how did they become known, that is the question. He had to return with them to Ta'if. He was told to very slowly come over the cliffs at night and to bring no magic with him. We need to keep a better eye up there now.

It will be very dangerous and probably the hardest task that he has ever faced. That is right, and he failed, but I admit that he could not have expected an eagle to tell on him. Without it he may have gotten in. If any interrupt him he is to kill them and if it looks like he would be captured he is to kill himself so that he could not be made to talk. Again those count as failures.

Under no circumstances is he to tell anyone what his mission was. That is a total fail. As he speaks, the sweat can be seen standing out on his forehead as his mind fights fruitlessly against the enchantment that has control of his body and his voice. Goditha did a good job on him. It matters not what else I ask or how it is phrased, that is the entirety of what he has to say apart from the trivial details of getting here.

When asked what he will do if we let him free, he confirms that he will, of course, do his best to complete his mission as he was instructed to do. He will then report his failure to keep silent when he returns and no doubt be punished for that. It is a penance that he will gladly accept. Will he kill himself now if is locked up? He will no longer need to do that, he has no more to give away. He has told me everything.

Ayesha confirms what she can of that so we are finished with him. Basil turned to the Princesses. "What do you want to do with him?"

Theodora spoke up. "Christopher has told us that he is not an evil man. He has done nothing to us yet and committed no crimes here, or elsewhere. We will hold him and, to give him something to do, we will let him read our story as Ayesha and Ruth have written it. When we return from the Caliphate then we will decide what to do with him."

While he was still under the effect of the spell Basil stripped him, put him in a cell and gave him a cloth kilt that was too weak a weave for him to hang himself with, or to use as a garrotte on another. *I think that it is best if he is to be allowed nothing that can be used as a weapon and has to eat with his hands. At least that should not be an issue.*

"He needs a bowl of flat pebbles and a bucket in his cell for them once they have been used," said Ayesha. Everyone just looked at her. She looked back. "Trust me on this."

Chapter XXXIII

Theodora

20th Quattro

Last night on the first eve of autumn the watch reported an early campfire clearly visible in the north. Now, in the morning a saddle reports a fast-moving column of kynigoi in Caliphate clothing accompanying the Imam. It seems that in a few days we will be heading out again. It is time to spread the word that the people heading out should get ready and prepare by spending a last few days in the village getting as much done as they can.

Most are just doing things they have been meaning to do for a while or that they will not have time to do for a while. Astrid goes fishing in our little river. Adara and Bryony leave Stefan to look after the children and go out to do some hunting. Ia heads up the valley to work on her shrine with Goditha. Several others just sit around and relax in the last warm sun they might have to relax in for some time.

As for me, once I get some more casting done, I intend to spend as much of the next day in bed with my husband as I can get away with. We will be away for weeks and I will miss making love in our own bed, assuming we get any privacy at all while we are away.

Hulagu

Soon after lunch Neon, who is on watch outside, reports Bryony running up the road towards him. She is waving frantically. I guess that means the end of sitting in the sun and relaxing. Hulagu took his junior wives, who were also there, and went out on a saddle.

"Adara has been taken," Bryony gasped. "I don't know who has done it but, by the tracks, there are four of them at least." *We need to gather everyone. This could be the prelude to an attack.* Hulagu turned and looked at Alaine. *She nods and is off back to the village.*

"Show us." Bryony hopped up behind Aigiarn on the saddle and, now with bows in hands, they flew off. Hulagu looked around for an ambush while Aigiarn followed Bryony's directions. *We head south for a little way and then up hill. There is a largish hopper lying dead in a clearing.*

"I killed this and then called for her. She didn't answer and I started looking." Bryony pointed the way and, keeping low, they flew further up the slope and over a ridge that lay further to the south. *Where the hopper lies is now some distance behind them and, with the normal bush noise, it would have been easy to miss hearing anything.*

"I found this..." she pointed to a scene of struggle. *It is against a large free-standing rock. It would have provided a good place to conduct an ambush. The struggle was strong enough to clear and break some of the shrubs.*

There is some blood on the ground, two patches actually. Neither shows enough blood to indicate that someone has bled to death. Marks on the ground lead away from the site. A short distance away, tossed under bushes, we can see Adara's bow and spear. Whoever has taken her has taken her arrows as well.

"Go up," Hulagu pointed to the sky. "Look for the others. They should be along soon, but watch ahead of me, get Astrid." He brought the saddle down close to the ground and, heedless of the noise of shrubs bending and breaking away from him looked intently at the tracks and where they led.

From what I can see one walks ahead. They are bleeding, but not seriously. Next come two others carrying something, probably Adara. The person being carried is bleeding more than the first person and then come a fourth person who occasionally turns to look behind. There is a small spot of blood on a rock there that clearly shows them turning as they stood on it.

There are no easily seen tracks leading in to the site so the attackers, possibly all male from what I see of their pace length, are experienced enough, when they have enough time, to leave none behind. That is bad. At present they are in a rush to get clear. We need to catch up with them quickly before they can settle back to their normal practice.

Hulagu kept following the tracks. *First the lead person shows no more blood and then the person being carried stops bleeding. I have to assume that is Adara.* A glint under a bush showed why. Discarded, and almost concealed, lay a small potion bottle. *I will put it away in a pouch in case it can tell something to a mage; that is a more experienced mage than I am.*

He sensed someone behind him and whirled the saddle around. It is Ayesha and Astrid. He nodded at them and told them what he had seen and showed them the tracks.

Astrid

"This is where I get off this and start going on foot. Ayesha, as we agreed, stay invisible and just behind and above me. Hulagu, the rest of the saddles are behind us and some ride double. Gather them up. Get someone to take my saddle. Go high and form a wide circle around the entire area and begin coming in from well out of arrow range."

"If Ayesha and I cannot safely take them then we need to drive them to where we want them to be. We have to assume that they will not kill her out of hand, but if we can stop them then we can get her back. Make sure you re-assure Stefan and Bryony that she is still alive, they are both nearly frantic with concern."

Astrid began running. *I can leave my bow on my saddle. It has only a limited use in the lower storey of the mountain forest at this level and leaving it will let me use my bardiche unhindered.* As she loped along she looked from the ground to ahead of her and then back to the ground.

None of the four walkers show any sign of turning aside, but, if they do and ambush me it will at least bring the attackers out in the open and someone will be watching me anyway. I have a contingency cure and potions and a priest is not too far away if I am badly hurt. Astrid may have been running, in a bent over position so she could keep looking at the ground, but she moved as near as quickly and quietly as any of the great cats would have.

Occasionally her eyes flicked up and ahead as she ran. *The creek-line I am following is rising towards what sounds like a small waterfall. Someone just cursed. I don't speak Arabic, but that is what it sounds like, the sort of involuntary curse that a person makes when they fall or trip.* In case anyone was watching her who understood her hand signs she indicated enemy ahead and slowed down.

Now that I have heard them I can almost ignore the tracks. I need to be alert for a trap, but there is no need to look for sign. As the valley grows more confined the air feels damper and the normal shrubs begin to disappear from the lower storey.

I am wending my way over a thick layer of fallen bark and soft mosses, through ferns of different sizes and over fallen trees covered in different fungi and more moss. There is the smell of damp and of rotting wood.

Little insects scuttle around. There is one of the little round hoppers, a pademelon, peering at me through a ground fern. Peering ahead, through the clearing under-storey, she could see the waterfall. *It is only a small one, but it provides a serious obstacle to anyone travelling along the creek line. The idiots must be used to following valleys to reach a pass. Don't they have any idea about our mountains?*

In most places this works, but on the slopes around Mousehole the valleys always end in cliffs and you follow the ridges to get through the ranges. Now, stuck in the confines of this valley, they are struggling up the waterfall. Adara is not helping in that regard. She is bound but conscious. Her trousers are torn and there is blood on one thigh and in her hair and she is struggling hard.

The four men are trying to attach a rope to her but she wriggles and struggles and makes it difficult for them. That kick to his groin will delay him for a while. He is on the ground and they sound like curses. Her reward is a hard hit to the head. She has gone limp. If I had brought the bow they would all be mine by now.

She pulled back a little way and put her hand on top of her head. It was an agreed signal and Ayesha appeared.

"I will hang on to your saddle and we will disappear," Astrid said. "Lift me up until we are well ahead of them and then come down. You will feel me let go. Then we take them. You go behind and take the last after I take the first. We then take the two with their hands full. Try and keep at least one of them alive."

Ayesha

It is a good plan. Astrid disappears and my saddle settles. Ayesha put her ring back on and they rose up. *We are just in time. The four have just succeeded in getting Adara up to the top of the low falls, although one stopped briefly to grope at her breasts and feel their size. I don't think that I will be telling Stefan what the man just said, although I am sure that the cousins will probably regard it as a compliment.*

The cousins have developed a very robust sense of humour about sex and both are very proud of their breasts. Ayesha flew ahead and up the side of the creek bed. *It looks like the men are going to walk in the creek for a time to help disguise their tracks.* Ayesha settled down beside a large rock in the middle of the stream. *We shall take them here, Inshallah.*

Ayesha felt the saddle shift and rock and waited a bit to give Astrid time to get clear. She lifted up to rise and fly back behind the men to where she could leave the saddle without it being seen. *That boulder there, they are nearly up to it and, when they have passed it there will be more than enough room behind it to hide several saddles.*

I am already glad that we are invisible. I have recognised all four men. The first, Surayi, has stopped and is looking about him. The others likewise come to a halt and they all start peering in every direction. Perhaps he is sensing that they are about to be ambushed but, as hard as he looks and listens, there is nothing. "Can you hear something?" *Rãfi will be their leader.*

"La a'ref y." *Surayi does not believe his senses and keeps going.* Once they were past her and with the front man perhaps a filled hand from Astrid she dismounted and drew a throwing blade and her kindjal.

First and last have bows. The other two have no weapons out. I have shackles and so does Astrid. This is the second attack from the Caliphate and is completely separate to that by Sayf as he was directly asked about any others coming. In the name of Allah, the All-Wise, we need to know more about what is happening before we go up into the mountains.

Are there others on the way? Is an attack about to come? What about my sworn duty? She looked ahead. *I need to catch up. I have to move along the bank and I am not as good in the bush as Astrid is. Just as they are, I will leave things swaying behind me.* Ayesha tried her best but the one in the rear chose the moment that she brushed against a fern to turn and look behind.

He opened his mouth to yell as she threw. *It really doesn't matter. Surayi's head sprang off his shoulders and his body fell sideways into the water. Astrid has struck out.* The man at the rear, Hamid, fired at where the bush swayed and the knife now in his gut had appeared from. Ayesha had expected that and had jumped to the left across the narrow creek.

He is getting another arrow out, bad mistake, fatal. She leapt forward and into the water as her kindjal rose under his chin to his brain. His yell became a gurgling scream as he fell face down in the water and was muted as he briefly thrashed about. *The other two have dropped Adara and are getting swords and daggers out.*

The front man falls back onto the second as if he had been struck by a giant, and in effect he has. The second dropped his sword as he tried to regain his feet but it was too late. Astrid collided with me. We are each trying to hold him down to put shackles on his hands. He is struggling in the water trying to breathe. Ayesha dropped her shackles and pulled out a gag.

I am relieved to see shackles appear on the man's arms. Ayesha put a pair of shackles on his legs, dragged his head clear of where he was spluttering underwater and possibly drowning in the stream and turned. *The one that was struck is groaning, for an instant. A gag has appeared in his mouth as Astrid moves on to another task. Praise to Allah, the Protector, we have freed her.*

Ayesha stood up and removed her ring, stooping to pull Adara out of where she floated in the water and started cutting her bonds. When the other man was bound Astrid reappeared as well. *We both look up to signal. None of the riders that have to be above us can see a thing. The canopy of whitey-wood and hop bush meet overhead creating a tunnel of cool green where everything has happened.*

"I'll get the saddle." Ayesha ran back. Astrid hauled the captives and the bodies up on to the bank and began the task of disarming the captives.

Astrid

The bodies of Hamid and Surayi are going to be left lying by the stream to be picked up when we can. Ubãda is going straight back to be put in the frame. He and Rãfi can answer a few questions for us. Rãfi can stay out of earshot for the present. Ayesha introduced them. "Hamid and Ubãda were in my class. Surayi was a senior and experienced man and Rãfi is another instructor."

"Ubãda didn't like me profaning Misr al-Mãr with my presence and it is a pleasure for me to be the one to take him captive." *I am not mentioning him feeling Adara's breasts and tweaking her nipples, nor will I mention what he had said about her when she was unconscious. They will add to his ithim that is tallied on qiyamah, Judgement Day.*

Today Goditha is again the first to perform an enchantment. She casts on the junior man Ubãda and it is noticeable that she is both far more confident this time around and that she recovers quicker. The story Ubãda gives is remarkable only in its brevity. He has done what Rãfi has told him to do. They were to attempt to kidnap someone, it did not matter who, and bring them back to be questioned.

This time, however, the travel details are not trivial. They have been in place for a week and a carpet has checked on them every night. He is told to watch the darkness to make sure that none creep up on them and so he does not know the recognition signals, but they were all looking forward to going home. That will not happen now, al-Ḥamdu Lillãh.

I didn't have to tell anyone about his lustful thoughts about Adara. The men were promised any woman they brought back to be a slave between them. He admits his lust and his desire to use Adara when he wanted. He even admitted to handling her during the escape. Stefan has to be restrained by Adara herself and by Bryony. They point out that he is taken now.

Basil asked Ubãda about killing himself and he looks surprised at the notion. He obviously does not know much and had not been given any instructions like that.

Astrid
a little later

Naeve is the next most senior of the Earth mages, the ones most suited to finding truth, in the village and she performs the second casting. So far most of her spells had been done to aid the grass growing and to increase milk and ensure the production, fertility and health of her flocks. They are the same sort of spells that many Earth mages use and are similar to those miracles cast by priests.

Just as it had been for Goditha, this is something completely new. She has set everything up as carefully as she can and has written the spell out in large letters so that she does not need her book in her hand but can read it out from where Goditha holds it for her. Naeve has support from Lamentations and from Hand, another of the Brotherhood girls, both of whom also hold to the element of Earth.

The milkmaid has been proud of how far she has come, but this casting is far in excess of anything she has done to this time. After it is over she may have had to be carried to where her husband waits with a sweet yoghurt drink for her, but as she is carried, she has a proud smile on her face.

She has already said that she hopes, one day, to be able to show her mother how much their family has risen. Now one of her daughters can actually cast major spells instead of just being of use to milk a cow.

Ayesha

Rãfi has a lot more to tell. For a start, as I thought, he is the leader of the group and is able to give the signals for the carpet. Once we have all of the details my husband can quickly round up an air group and, taking Pass as an Air mage to control the carpet and Rani and I to control the mage who is to be taken, we can all head off into the afternoon for the rendezvous point with some others to act as decoys to draw in their target.

Rãfi had received the same instructions to kill himself so as to not reveal anything as Sayf had and gave the same responses about killing himself. He is also not an evil man. I would have been very surprised if he was. He would have used his slave simply as a slave. He regards it as wrong to have sex with a slave unless she also wants to do so.

However, he has kidnapped and done violence to one of the Mice, so Theodora orders him to also be put into their jail under the same conditions as Sayf. The two have a cell empty between them. She will not cast judgement yet, but will wait until our next excursion is all over to see what we should do with him. He will have to wait for adl, justice, to come.

The healers are not making the same mistake again and the bodies of the two who died are brought in and both are going to be thoroughly dissected by the apprentice physikers. It is unfortunate that both of the dead are men, but it at least does give them a start at seeing how the body is put together,

Chapter XXXIV

Theodora (20th Quattro)

It is polite for me to meet them outside the gate. Iyãd has two Omáda, patrols, of kynigoi with him under a Tourmachos Perissótero, a *senior Tourmachos, as well as a junior Tourmachos who is also a Fire mage, and two junior clerics who will be staying on in the Swamp when this is all over if they are needed. They even have a small train of remounts for each man and pack-horses so as to be as self-sufficient and rapid on the move as it is possible for them to be.*

The men, more used to the cities and the roads of Darkreach that stretch through largely flat dry terrain, continually look around them in wonder at our timber-clad mountains and valleys. Now we are inside, they look around even more when they see the people of Mousehole at work, but they have obviously been warned about this village, or at least are polite, as they try not to stare.

Such partial nudity is also more of a custom in Darkreach than elsewhere, when it is needed and, of course, in the Arena, but there are several men who are obviously relieved to see several women wearing the hijab when we get to be near the stables and in the actual village.

I think that the Imam was expecting to be greeted by Ayesha and not by me. He is looking now that we are inside as if seeking her. "The Sayyeda is not here?" *I was right. This is where it could get difficult. She is with the prisoners.*

Theodora had to explain what was happening. *As the men are settling into the barracks, Basil can take him to see the prisoners so that he can start questioning them and talking to them over matters of faith and obedience. I suspect that he will be with them for some time. Let us see what he can add to what we have.*

Theodora

Basil has left him there and reported back. Already it seems that the prisoners, and in particular the two senior men, are not happy with the way the conversation is going. Although they all knew the Qur'an, the Imam is a hāfiz, he knows it by heart, and he has also been trained in rhetoric and argument rather than in the use of weapons. They do not have a chance.

The two different interpretations: of love and of obedience are apparently being played out in the gaol. Ubāda is almost excluded from this and Basil says that he sits bored even while he pretends to listen. He was brought along on the mission for his physical skills and his ability to obey without any question, not for his grasp of theology.

Iyād ibn Walīd

We will let them think on my words while we perform the Maghreb prayer. Again I see Basil and this time his wives...his wives! I was carried up by the moment and have not immediately done as I was charged to do. I must correct that. He hurried over to the people concerned and asked to see them straight after prayer.

Iyād
a little later

Now to complete my task. "I will be back in a moment." He went to a pack that had been left near the door of the stable and returned.

"I am not sure what is in here, but the Emperor himself entrusted it to me." He handed over a long flat chest of fine workmanship to the three who were sitting outside the Hall of Mice with a small animal on the little Human woman's lap. "I am very sorry. I was supposed to give this to you straight away. The Emperor has learnt of your marriage and sends you all wedding presents."

"Thank you very much for bringing these." *The Insakharl woman, Astrid, looks surprised.* "I would not worry about being late. He cannot see what happens here. It is one of the few places that he cannot watch." *She turns to Basil.*

"I am still not sure whether to be flattered or not that he keeps such a close watch on us, and now on Ia I suppose. I hope we have not shocked him with what we get up to..." she thought for a moment "...just as I know something of him I suppose." *Her head is cocked to the side. She is thinking about something.*

"He must have seen our progress along the south coast and heard the explanations that we gave to the people there. That means he possibly also knows of what we did to the Goldentide. How sweet of him it was to send us presents."

I am not sure that I want to hear the Emperor described as 'sweet'. He quickly gave a look in Astrid's direction. *I am even more unsure about someone who would use that word for him. I briefly met her at the Synod and I have heard the stories about her, but I spent more time with the other ecclesiastics than with the non-Muslim villagers.*

I am aware of her husband's rank, of course, but this Insakharl woman from among the barbarians of the lost towns of Northern Darkreach speaks more than familiarly about the Emperor, a person who I only met personally to speak to for the first time when I was given this commission.

I wonder what she is, and who the little girl who is snuggled up to Basil really is. She was not here last time. She seems to be only a pale-skinned elf-like child, even if she is armed and, from the look of her pouches, carrying several different sorts of wands. The strange animal adds to the mystery by moving around between the legs of the three people.

The three sat straight down on the veranda and opened up the box. Inside are a sword, a main-gauche, three books and a small package. All of the books are obviously magical tomes and each has a name and a picture on the front. Astrid's has a bardiche, Basil has two shortswords and the little woman has a sword and a main-gauche. The weapons are all labelled 'Ia', that must be her name, and there is a note on them.

Astrid sighed. "He knows our little family so well." she said.

Ia first picked up a small package that lay on top of everything else and looked at it. It had a name and a note attached to it. Ia read the name and kept the note. Giving the package to Maeve, she told her: "Astrid is right. He is such a considerate man. He even sends something as a present for you. You can open it now while I see what it is."

I am not sure if it is worse to hear the Emperor referred to as 'considerate' or if 'sweet' was harder to hear. What is more the girl seems to expect the little creature to understand her. He looked down again. *The beast obviously does. It is untying the ribbon that wraps the package up and laying opening a package that was not food at all.*

It has unwrapped the package very neatly, even folding the cloth and putting it to one side before making a chattering sound. Ia is reading the note by then and keeps talking to the beast as if it has talked to her. "No, it is not just a pretty collar. It is a charm to protect you from being hurt." *She looks up at Astrid.* "Sister, I love this Emperor of yours already even before you take me to see him."

She is turning to me with a sweet smile. I feel even more shocked at how he is being referred to now. "Please thank him for us all when you see him next," she said as she was fastening the charm around the neck of the beast and making sure that it was comfortable. "Now," she continued to Iyãd as she stood up and reached for the weapons and their note, "…if you do not mind. I think that we have some reading to do and then I want to try these out."

"You should do it the other way around," said Basil as they started walking away. "That way you will know just how much of the effect is from you changing and how much of it is just from the weapons."

Chapter XXXV

Rani
the night of the 20th Quattro

"I am sure that he will check for magic before he comes close," said Rani. "With what we carry, we will all glow like beacons to him."

"In that case we will leave Ayesha and some others, with only the amount of magic that the men he is expecting had at the site and the rest of us will be elsewhere," said Hulagu. "My wife will be undetectable and he will only pick up four men and a captive." *He looks around the terrain in the afternoon light.*

"He will be coming from the east or south-east and, if he is sensible, he will check the area from far away. So, if the rest of us sit under that cliff," he points, "...and close to the base then we should be sheltered from his detection magic. We will be too far away for him to pick us up with his own senses and even if he turns around and detect us after he is past, we will still be between him and his home and we are the ones who move faster."

Rani looked at the points Hulagu had indicated. *That is quite a good plan.* She nodded. "You are right. That should work well." Hulagu gave the orders that sent them all to their places. *Dusk is coming up quickly. We are only a few days into autumn. Not yet far enough for us to have no leaf cover to hide within, but already it is chilly,*

Rani looked at the notes that she had written for herself before the light went. *Ia's sleep spell has already shown itself to be very useful in taking people safely and I really should have sent my wife along if that is the spell to be used. Sleep is a Water spell. I am a Fire mage and Fire is the opposite of Water and so it will be more expensive for me to cast.*

Theo-dear struggled to hold Ahmed when we first took Mousehole and I will not have a diagram to work in if I stay aloft, even though I am now stronger. I am working with opposed magic as well, and I do not know how strong the one

I am facing will be to oppose me. Rather than hold him, I think that it would be best to just knock him out and let Ayesha restrain him.

I can do the range...one person...best make it two in case he has a companion...compel...boost the mana with all of my stored power to overcome his resistance. I need to land so that I can use my cloth and charge it. She landed and went to her saddlebag. *I have a big penalty on casting for a new spell and a lesser one for the elemental opposition, but I can still try and stack some things in my favour.*

I need to work out the best way to say what I intend and then to practice and learn what I want to say. I will not be able to read it out in the dark. She looked up. *Dobun is watching what I am doing.* She explained the logic behind what she was doing and he nodded in agreement.

The Khitan shamen also use the element of Fire. He has realised that he might one day have to do the same sort of casting. He will use very different mental patterns to accomplish what he wants, but the concepts behind them are similar for mages and for priests of any sort.

A mile away a small fire began to faintly glimmer in the growing dark. *It is the first part of the signal that will tell a watching carpet-rider that the kidnap has been successful.* They settled down to wait.

Rani

After an hour or so Alaine, who was sitting on her saddle near the pattern, made a small noise quietly in her throat. Rani turned and looked at her. *She is pointing into the air to our left and forward.* Rani looked up and then around. *The carpet is a small blot of blackness that is sometimes obscuring the stars. It is almost half way to the fire already.*

Those waiting out at the fire must have seen the signal they are waiting for as the fire disappears, then appears again. Disappears and then appears and stays visible, the flame turning green now. That is the signal for success. The carpet began to descend and Rani began chanting. Around me I can sense saddles lifting off and spreading out along and under the cliff keeping cover behind the trees where they can.

If my target escapes my spell then they will cut him off. It is harder to see him now that he is no longer outlined against the stars but Terror is still almost full and Panic is waxing so the night is near as bright as it can be. He came down to the ground. *The men down there all speak Arabic. Hopefully he will not notice Darkreach accents. I have to time it right to cast...now.*

"Done." Rani called loudly. *The saddles are darting forward rapidly towards the fire*. She scrambled to gently and safely let the charge out of her cloth and then to pack it away. By the time she was down at the fire it was all over.

"If you don't mind me saying it like this," said Ayesha, "but it worked like a charm. He is still out and we have a new carpet for the valley."

Stefan

There is only one man and he is left bound for the night with a guard upon him while he sleeps the spell off. They have bound his hands flat, stopped his ears, and blindfolded him as well. They didn't put him with the ghazi. That way the other captives will not be able to speak to him and he will not know exactly what has happened to him.

Eventually he gets to wake up to spend an uncomfortable night up here on the roof with the watch. He has been left lying naked in a clear space with a piece of wood over a pace long holding his legs apart, another the same length for his hands over his head and two more running down his sides to stop him bending or turning. He has the typical build of a mage who relies on his magic instead of being well-rounded.

He has tested his bonds several times, straining as hard as he can, but Basil does not make mistakes on a matter like that and his straining has no effect at all. There is a blanket here to cover him in case it gets too cold, but it seems that it will be unnecessary. The night stays mild enough and what discomfort there is for him will be useful tomorrow to lower his resistance. The gag will add to his discomfort as well.

Theodora
21st Quattro, in the morning

The next morning, after breakfast and prayers, the watchers are assembled, including Sayf, brought from the gaol and bound tight, to act as a witness. He can pass on what is said to the other ghazi. When all is ready the man is brought down. He is a mage and so it will be harder to force him to talk than the other three were. I will perform this casting myself.

We at least have a name and it is probably the real one. While he was unconscious clippings were taken of hair from his head and his groin, some blood and some fingernails. He does not know that. Keeping his fingers flat and with the gag, blindfold and ear coverings in place he is put into the frame by Basil and Astrid. He tries to struggle but Astrid holds him while Basil fastens him and makes it tight.

Try as he will, even as his muscles bulge with the strain, he cannot make Astrid budge in the slightest. We will leave his earmuffs on for the moment. If he can not hear he will be more disoriented and it will make it harder for him to brace himself to resist a spell that he probably expects. However, he will not be sure exactly when it is coming.

To distract him further Astrid has a sharp blade in one hand. She is running the blade around his body as if she is about to start torturing him with it. At this range even I can smell his nervousness. As she runs the blade around him and he tries to flinch away from it, I can see sweat start to appear on his body. He flinches and his penis, not a large one to start with, shrivels up further as the blade goes between his legs and pauses.

Ia is using a feather as a counter distraction. It seems that he is ticklish as well. Between the actions of the two women you can see him wriggling and flinching. He has no chance. She nodded. *He is well and truly ripe for the plucking and his concentration for resistance to anything would be very low due both to his fear and the feather and where it goes. Mind you, I think that I would prefer the knife to the feather myself.*

Theodora began to drone out the spell in a low voice so as to not penetrate the earmuffs as Astrid and Ia kept up the attention on him. *It is a powerful and much enhanced spell; in essence the same as Naeve and Goditha used, but further reinforced and with extra control over the target built in. Now that I am finished, Basil can remove the earmuffs and begin to give instructions. When he finishes that, he began the slow process of seeing if the mage is really controlled and then getting him to exhaust his mana.*

When that is done Basil begins to talk to him as his junior wife takes notes. "Uqba, tell us all about why you are here," he said. *Basil has planned his questioning carefully. He has gotten as much as he can out of the man before giving a sign to our Bishop and then he starts his prayer before signing back to Basil.*

Only now does Uba get asked what we think will be the first vital question. We suspect what will happen next and, unlike in Warkworth, the preparations to deal with it have now been put in place. Basil is given the go ahead that all was ready.

"Who sent you?" he asked. *The words are barely out of his lips before the man begins to choke as if his heart is stopping, but this time Christopher is ready and he finishes the prayer that he has worked out after Warkworth for just this purpose.* Uqba begins to breathe again and Basil let him know what happened to him and again asked the question.

"I do not know his name," Uqba said. *It looks like there is only one trap enchantment place on him. It was all that would normally be needed after all.* "I think that I have been granted a boon from Allah, the Victorious, and that I have met an Archangel."

"Blasphemy," said Iyād vehemently. He is simply the first. Several among the watchers angrily echo him. They are all shushed.

Uqba continues: "I just did what Mullah Mughīra abd Allah told me to do and I placed myself at his command. The Archangel touched me and, just with his touch, he gave me a vision of Paradise and a sense of perfect happiness. The vision of God was too much for my frail body and I became unconscious." *I hear more unhappy murmurs from several people.*

"When I awoke it was a day later and my body had been translated to Ta'if. I am forever his to command. I believe in my heart that, like the Prophet, I have been blessed more than other mortals and have both seen and been touched by an Archangel. I will do whatever he asks of me and I know that I am already destined to go to Paradise when I die." *Even under my spell, that is his unshakeable belief.*

Basil finds out what else he can and concludes the planned questions by asking Uqba what he will do if he is detained in a gaol or set free and he receives the expected response. This man is too dangerous and too fanatical to be allowed to live long. Even while he is supposedly under complete magical control there is a light of madness in his eyes.

We were going to finish there, but Basil has decided to explore some new areas and asked him about his past and what he has done for his Master. It turns out that his master has, over the last few months, used Uqba and his carpet to kidnap a young girl each week or so from the areas around Rebelkill and Doro and Third Tower in Darkreach.

He has brought them to the house in Ta'if, at least we now know exactly which one, and Uqba has explained to the terrified victims what was about to happen to them and how their soul will be in torment and eaten. They are kept gagged so that none might hear their frantic screams and they are bound to minimise their struggles and increase their sense of helplessness.

He had then used one of the obsidian blades on them, had drunk a potion and then raped and tortured them over a night before they are dispatched and have their heart taken from their body while they are still alive. His master, the so-called Archangel, has stood beside him the whole time. There is one girl at the house now. She is waiting for his return before she dies.

Theodora turned to the Imam. "I was in some doubt what we should do with him before I heard him. Now I know. He dies."

"He had to die anyway," said Iyād. "His soul is owned now by Iblīs. He is the ultimate blasphemer and speaks words that cannot be forgiven. He is speaking the deepest profanation, and he was fated for death due to that alone."

Lakshmi

Once again, now that he has been bled out, I am allowed to cut his body up to allow my students to see where everything is. Some of the senior ones can have a turn doing it now. This time the younger students of the school are allowed to watch as well and to ask questions. At least no-one is upset with the process of cutting open a body.

Uqba was not a healthy man at all. Laksmi and Ayesha pointed out the disease that was growing in his vitals and also in his brain. There is a growth through his liver and something the size of a fist that was eating his brain up. "Physiking is less exact than magic. It is more an art than anything else. Sometimes though you have no choice, even to cut into a person like this."

Rani

Sayf is put back in his cell now, and Iyãd has left straight after the execution with his troop. They will have to ride hard to the south. It is a long way to Ta'if and the only way that any of us surely know of to get there, unless they somehow learn to fly, is through the land of the Bear Folk to Bathmawr and then go straight up the Ziyanda Rũdh to its source.

Some of the Mice need to fly ahead to let everyone know that the column is no threat to them and Iyãd has been given a letter of introduction in case he meets anyone on the road who has not been warned. Thus Theo-dear and I have six people standing in front of us.

"That means us flying," said Ia.

"And us," added Bryony.

I think that Theodora and I agree. Despite the risk of letting Astrid out on her own like this with people somewhere out there that she might want to kill, there is really no other choice. The two thrupples can shepherd Iyãd and his men and call the rest of us once they are on the way up the road on the slope to the Caliphate from Eastguard.

Until then we can use the time to better prepare for what is to come at home. We will be making more magic, greater or lesser, for a start. As well others will keep doing the exercises that Astrid has taught them and also practising with their weapons. Somehow I feel that we will be going into serious trouble on this trip.

Astrid

"Do you think that we should stop her doing that?" Maeve jumped from a roof and hit the cobbled courtyard once again. *We are just sitting on the veranda of the Hall of Mice waiting for Basil who is seeing to the prisoners in the gaol. So far they have behaved themselves but he knows how good Ayesha is and two of these men were her instructors.*

"It is my fault," said Ia. "I was too good at explaining what the collar did and she wanted to see it and so she jumped off our roof. A fall that far would normally leave her limping at least and I told her that the protection will have limits. She knows that I will cure her if she comes to harm.

"She actually has a contingency in place the same as I do and similar to what I gave to you and Basil. Now she is trying to find the limits. I think that she is off now to jump from the top of the Hall. Once she has done that, unless she tries a cliff, and I don't think that she is that silly, that is as high as she can go in the village."

It wasn't long before a furry bundle hit the ground with an indignant squeak. Briefly it looks like Maeve is limping before she shakes herself and comes over and chatters at Ia. "That is the limit," she said. "I will have to put the contingency back into place now. From the top of these two stories and onto stone is the limit for her protection." The two women went into the courtyard and looked up and down a few times. *How much damage will a fall from that high do to a raccoon?*

"I would say that a good blow from a sword won't hurt her much. She is wearing better armour than you and Basil are and near as good as I wear." Ia agreed about Basil but pointed out that her main-gauche now had a charm as strong as Maeve's seemed to be on it.

Basil appeared then. *Now we take him home to spend some time together before we are again back out into the harsh and nasty world with its severe lack of large and comfortable beds. Maeve and the children get to spend the night in the bedrooms of the house next door with Sin to look after them all. We still have to get Goditha to make the two houses into one. Sometimes that is useful.*

Chapter XXXVI

Khabbāb ibn Zubayr
22nd Quattro

A day later, after Dhurhr and while eating, Khabbāb sat and thought about what lay ahead. *The Bear Folk are just legends to me. None from Darkreach have seen any of them for many years, if they have ever seen any of them at all. I am not only about to see them, but I will then go on to visit the Swamp and then the Caliphate.*

Despite the note that we have been given, and what I have been told, I still wonder about the reception that we soldiers from Darkreach, of the True Religion, will receive among the people we are about to travel among. Most particularly when we get to the Caliphate. We have two Omáda of the Orphanos under their Tourmachos and his second. Our very name represents the final defeat of the Caliphate armies. Will they know that?

They were near finished eating when the mage heard a soft voice. "Don't be alarmed," it said. *It sounds like the large Insakharl woman who thinks that she is an Insak-div.* He looked around slowly. *I think that perhaps I can see where she is, but not fully. There is only the suggestion of a blurred outline of a person almost like a heat haze.*

The voice continued. "Get Iyād and meet me by that rock." *The vague shape may have pointed.* "Damn. I keep doing that, on the mountain side of the track just past the guard."

Khabbāb did as he was bid and they waited. *She will speak when she is ready.* "You have ridden hard. You will be in Birchdingle before night. I will wait for you near the turn-off, which will be soon before dusk. Make sure that your scouts expect me to speak to them as they ride. I will be doing this a lot and, if it is not me, it will be someone else who is using my magic.

"The Tribune and my sister-wife are with me and also Stefan and the cousins.

Seeing that you will travel through the Swamp we thought it best if the girls from there do most of the introductions and, besides, in some areas that you are going to they will be too scared of me to dare to provoke me, even if they do not like you being there."

I guess that answers my doubt in the Swamp then, but should the Orphans need the protection of just one Insakharl woman? For that matter, why would they be more scared of her than of us?

Iyād

24th Quattro

I am not disappointed. Birchdingle, and then Ivyshroud, are revelations to all of us Darkreach men. We have been greeted warmly despite our hosts being mushriq, pagans with many gods.

They are like the Church of the Living God in many ways but also very different. Animals sit around the village and play with children but like the raccoon from Mousehole they seem to be a part of a family and not wild at all, that is until a large cat or a bear looks at you and then you know their wildness is still inside and you feel far less safe.

Astrid seems to have some sort of cat on her lap the whole time she is seated. Some are larger than her sister wife and once, when I turned around she had one great black cat licking her and she was licking it back and giggling.

For once the small creature, Maeve, stays close to one of its family, but from there it chatters loudly at several of the other beasts and once it seemed to be talking to a small golden bear that terrified our horses so much when we met it just off the path. It looks back at the little beast and growls and snuffles at it.

Iyād

26th Quattro

Now we are in Bathmawr. We are probably the first unit from Darkreach to enter the Swamp during this Age and, while we are not welcomed with open arms, we are at least met more with curiosity than with hostility. If anything we are proving to be a disappointment to the people there. With their Hobgoblins the Mice are much more exotic to the locals than the people who actually come from Darkreach. My escort is just made up of Human men.

Not all of them are Human, some are Insakharl, but none of them can go near to matching Aziz in their appearance. The cousins have warned us about leaving anything unattended here and Ia has coached us more on how to behave and so our visit passes without incident. I would hate to see a fight break out. My men may just look like mercenaries, but I am told, admittedly mainly by their officers, that they are the best in the Army.

Stefan
28th Quattro

We three arrive at Dolbarden, leaving Basil and the other two to shadow the riders and we are immediately greeted by Hulagu and the rest of the Khitan.

"We bring magic," he said, before continuing in explanation. "It is like the nails on the ships only with a smaller area. Each saddle is going to have one soon so that no-one will be able to look at any of us with magic if we are within two paces of a saddle. They will have to use their eyes." He handed nails over and three were put in the saddles immediately. *There are three more for when the others arrive.*

"We will stay the night," said Ayesha. "I need to talk to Iyãd about Rani's plans.

As usual, the military base is quite relaxed about a foreign military force. It seems that those who are most prepared in this regard are in many ways the most tolerant and the least likely to suspect an invasion or other incursion unless they have been given some real cause to worry. That is very evidently not the case here.

Astrid
29th Quattro

Basil is with our Orphans, It seems a silly name for an Army unit. I wonder why they have it. That means that Ia and I get to tell Rising Mud about our visit. The guard on the bridge greets Ia warmly but she is very polite to me and then stays out of reach. Well, she thinks that she is. She isn't really, but why tell her that?

"You got what you wanted then?" *the guard asks Ia as she looks at me. Her eyes are going up and down my body appreciatively. She likes girls then.* Astrid carefully looked back at her. *It is the girl who kissed Ia farewell. Perhaps she was worried for a different reason. She needn't fear me being jealous, but she would not know that.*

Ia smiles. "I did. My foretelling was right as usual. I have a husband and a sister-lover and, if I am right, a child already on the way. I will have many more of them," she said smugly. *At least we have made her happy in her family.*

Basil has now joined us. Ia can go to pay her respects at the shrine while we take rooms for us all, deliver a note to Urfai, and then go off to see Father Kessog. Goditha has given us strict instructions to report back on what is happening with the Church and its rebuilding and I am not sure that I dare disobey that one.

It is nice to be remembered. Wherever I go walking around the village there is a large clear space all around me that is devoid of men, although all of the women seem more than happy to talk to me. It really does seem that Ith had not been popular among them at all.

Seeing that most of the buildings here are only made of timber and wattle and daub, even the larger ones, the church is nearly complete. It is far larger and more impressive than is needed in Rising Mud for the few Orthodox parishioners that are left. At least now it shows any visitors where it is with its timber spire already in place and surmounted by a crucifix, even if the walls are still being filled in.

Kessog now even has a guard to give him protection, an older married man, who is there also to double as his Deacon. From the scar on his face and those on his bare arms it is obvious that he has come to his second career later on in a very active life.

His wife is introduced and it is easy to see that she is far younger than he is. It is also very obvious that, like many others have done before him, he is settling down from working the caravans as a guard for a quieter life of marriage and family now that he has some wealth put aside for his bride. She is already pregnant and showing, but she still carries a blade.

She may need that. How quiet they will find it working to protect the Church in Rising Mud is, of course, an interesting question. She just has a sword and dagger, but he openly wears his sword and mail, a padded mail coif was tucked in his belt and a bow and shield are not too far away in the entry.

When they arrived the men of the Darkreach column had to lead their horses across the bridge to Rising Mud. *It may not have been the first river that they have crossed, but the horses are sensible and regard the fragile-looking bridge with the same suspicion that I do and have to be gently coaxed over it to the amusement of the locals.*

Stefan and his wives left early the next day. *They are to fly straight back to Mousehole and return with the rest of the Mice. The Orphans left even earlier. With their remounts and, at the fast pace that the Tourmachos is making his little column ride; they will possibly even be in Eastguard before lunch. Even Hulagu is impressed with their speed.*

The Mice will be joining us next morning somewhere not too far short of the village of Ta'if. The Darkreach people will rest and travel slower once they are actually in the mountains, but for the moment they are on the road and pushing as hard as they can possibly be doing. Sleep will come later for men as well as rest for their horses.

Basil

30th Quattro

At Eastguard Tower, once again there is a note to be delivered from the Princesses to the Reeve Blanid. It allows us to find out that there has been no sighting of Figel or of any of the men who fled with him. It is thought that he did not enter the Caliphate, but no-one is sure on that. He had experienced men with him and they could easily have covered their tracks.

What is more no-one has been able to find them with magic. That is always suspicious when they have left plenty of things behind them to allow the Law of Contagion to help in the location of their owners. It possibly means that there has been the intervention of powerful magic by someone on their behalf to prevent them being traced.

Iyãd

My Tourmachos only wants to let his people have lunch and attend the Dhuhr prayer at the site of the new mosque that Mullah Walīd, who has already arrived after his trip from Southpoint, was setting up in the village. There was, apparently, some difficulty with him doing that, and it is only that he had a letter of introduction from the Princesses that he was allowed to proceed.

He thinks that a lot of the reason that he is resented is that allowing him to be here removes a lot of the reason for the existence of the garrison. He has pointed out to me the local resentment that the many slaves that are in the Caliphate from the Swamp have no priests or, and he uses the word reluctantly, priestesses to look after them.

It is true that, as slaves, they are now Dhimmis and should have their own priests. At least that is how it would be at home. This is understandably a source of tension between him and the local people. He has been speaking openly, even if in Arabic, but a druid who is listening in from nearby has drawn near and is supporting him in this.

"We allow priests from any religion who want to set up to set up..." he said "most of us are reasonably tolerant of your false beliefs, even if the cattle worshippers do not like us, but your people do not allow us to do the same. You will be going to see their Caliph. You need to take one of us with you or you must press our case yourself." *It seems that they look to Darkreach to solve the issue.*

This is going to be a major issue locally. The whole issue of setting up here seems to hinge on it. He sent one of his men to find Basil and his wives and asked the druid to gather his people. *It turns out that he has already sent a young man to do that. We can all sit on the growing walls of the mosque and get to know each other.* Once all were gathered they began to discuss the situation.

In the end they accept Ia as their envoy and she is given letters to carry. I have had to point out that, while Walīd may listen to me, the people in the Caliphate will regard anything I say like that as Darkreach interference. It will work against them, despite, or perhaps because, we are the same religion. The request is much better made by one of their own people, which Ia is.

Tourmachos Ikrimah ibn Fida

Even though the river goes north-east from the village and Ta'if is to the east, the road from Eastguard first heads due north. As it does it immediately begins to climb a ridge by a steep road not meant for wagons or anything with wheels. The Ziyanda Rũdh goes for some way further into an increasingly deep valley before reaching a huge waterfall called the Kabeer Ma'a, which marks the northern edge of The Wall.

There are two ways up into the Kũm Kaysãn from the village and the one following the ridge to the north may be longer, but it is also far easier for someone who is mounted and who wishes to stay that way. According to my maps, the other involves a path beside the waterfall that is, in places, almost a climb. If nothing else I am able to add to our knowledge of this area in case it is needed and the hudna breaks.

The delay in Eastguard has cost us time and it is well past dark before my exhausted riders reach a campsite at the head of the path. We have reached a road that runs from Yãqũsa to the left to Tai'f to the south. A person with a horse and a few remounts ridden hard can perhaps travel the distance in a long day, but anyone with laden pack animals or on foot would take several to cover the same distance.

There has been no sign of the Mice until this time. Even now we only hear Astrid's voice. We have all heard the disembodied voice of this Cat so many times that my entire unit is now used to it when they hear it. She is a good scout. She knows what to look for and tell us about so that we can ride fast. We no longer jump or look around for her. Only Khabbãb sometimes sees her, or at least has an idea where she is.

"Hello," she said. "We think that, unless they have a talisman like me or Ayesha, there are none near enough to see you, but someone could well be using magic to keep an eye out on you. None of us can be seen by magic now, but if we appear a watcher will see you talking to the air, so the rest will stay hidden. We gathered some timber for you during the day in small pieces so that it was not conspicuous.

"There is no-one else visible in the area and, after an hour or so travelling along this ridge tomorrow you will come to the end of it. The road then drops back down to the plain of the Sawãd, with its river and the village. Take your time and travel slowly then. Stop there at the top and look out over the valley and I will talk to you again. Do you have anything to ask me?"

"Yes," said Iyãd. *An observer would think that he is talking to me.* "The plan stays the same? Everyone is here including your Princesses?"

"Everyone," said Astrid. "We have representatives of all four of our religions, we have mages of every element, and we have a supply of Princesses. Once we have seen what it is that is in Ta'if we will make a very official looking party to go on to Dimashq. Unless something changes, the Princesses still want to avoid Misr al-Mãr and its Mullah at the moment."

"He represents a problem for us," said Iyãd, "if he is doing as it seems he is and committing zandaqa. I will need to talk with the Caliph about him. They brought the books of testimony didn't they?" *I am a simple soldier. I do not like this talk at all. May Mohammed, Peace Be Unto Him, bless us in what we do.*

"They did and my husband is ready to swear under enchantment as to the truth of what was said and my sister-wife to swear that she wrote down the words that she heard faithfully. It should all turn out well." *If it does not, then the hudna breaks down here and now and we get to do what we Orphans do best…get our information home at all costs.*

“Inshallah,” Iy‹d said. “In that case I will see you tomorrow, or at least hear from you.”

Chapter XXXVII

Ikrimah

32nd Quattro

The morning dawns in a clear bright manner. There is, in the light around us, the clarity that only mornings high in the mountains can have. The sun first appears around the peaks of the distant Grey Virgin Range, to the Caliphate the Kũm Hejaz. Lying on the plain behind those peaks is Doro where the rest of my Orphans wait for us to return to their base.

Fajr prayers were over and the camp had eaten their breakfast and packed to continue and they were soon on the way. *Ahead in the far distance, as if serving as a pointer for us, is the bulk of Snowcap, to the people here Kartala. It rises high above the other peaks of the whole mountains. To its left is Jabal Tahat, much shorter but still impressive. Nestled down on their flanks at the lowest point is the village of Bab al-Abwãb.*

Even travelling at a walk it does not take long to reach the spot Astrid indicated and, as any cautious group would in unfamiliar territory, we draw rein and look out over the vast valley of the Sawãd spread out below us. So near we are to home and yet to get here it seems that we have travelled over half of the world. The last time the Orphans were this deep into the Sawãd, we earned our name and left more than half of our men and women behind us.

Iyãd and I are using telescopes to look around. First we look at Ta'if below us, and then at the small range of hills lying in the middle of the valley. It is the Kũm Hadramawt and I fancy that I can see the trees around the well of Badr, whose name we bear on our banner, in the dip there. We patrol there regularly. You can no longer see the scars of the fires three years ago.

Beyond that is stretched out the valley of the Tãb Rũdh. Near the head of that, and straight ahead, is the plateau of Misr al-Mãr rising up in a long prominence before the main range. That area, and the road that leads to it, we do not go anywhere near.

"Big…isn't it?" came the voice of Astrid. "Ayesha is with me. We thought we would let you see it all before I said anything. A long while ago now we came up Snowcap and looked around. If you look east you can see the mouth of the valley and Darkreach. Princess Theodora calls it Wheoh Grass." *I know it all so well, and yet I have never been here before and seen it from this perspective. This is almost sacred soil to me.*

"I am betting that if we were able to look back in time the whole fight between Darkreach and the Caliphate came about over who controls the grazing in that valley." *That is well thought out. You are more than just an Insak-div indeed.* "I might ask Hrothnog about that when next we visit. Bits of it look a little dry, but it is fertile despite that and it looks far wetter than the Beneen Plain below it is supposed to be."

"I know the land and history of the Sawãd very well," Ikrimah replied. "Some of our people use it for grazing, as do some of theirs. It is good grazing. We patrol some of it and they patrol some. You are right in what you say. Now, where are we going now?" Astrid told them what she knows of Ta'if and then confirms the plan.

We do not know how the Sheik of the little town feels, but for the moment we will assume that he is innocent. The rest of the Mice are still out of sight behind us, but Astrid and Ayesha will follow close behind my men. They will be invisible and with their magic masked behind ours. It should work.

Ta'if is a small village. It lies open below us with even smaller hamlets dotted around it. The Ziyanda Rũdh runs down from Jabal Umm through it and down to the Swamp over the waterfall. Even where we are now an alert person with a glass could make us out. We need to be open in our approach and yet be ready to protect the Imam.

Ikrimah gave the signal and a green banner with writing in Arabic on it was unfurled to flap lazily in the breeze and the riders in their column moved down and off the ridge along the long winding road down to the valley. *It is the first Darkreach banner to fly here for two cycles. If any read it, the names on it are for half of the features of this valley, but still we are best being open.*

For once on this trip we are moving casually and slowly. I am trying to time our movements down the road so that it will be near the hour for the midday prayers of Dhurhr by the time we come to the village. Our Mullah has decided that this is the least threatening time to enter, and I agree with him. Our bows are strung, but in their cases, and we do not ride in a battle formation.

Ikrimah
several hours later

As we approach over the ford it can be seen that Ta'if shows all of the signs of a new village. Few women can be seen in the streets or fields, perhaps even less than expected. The wall is only half built and we could leap over most of it with our horses. The busiest people here are the builders. Several houses are obviously under construction.

My Orphans fit in so well that it is not until we are starting to pick our way slowly through the village streets that anyone notices that we are not from the Caliphate. The differences are minor in many ways and major in others. Apart from our banner, the largest is that, although it is obviously based on civilian garb, the bulk of my riders are in a uniform. Few in the Caliphate wear those, and then only on ceremonial occasions.

The minor ones vary from the way our robes are tucked to details of tack on the horses. It looks like that young boy ahead of us is the first to realise that we are foreigners. He has started running up the street ahead of us. He keeps on running until he disappears into a large house in the centre of the village that is sitting beside the mosque. I guess that we should head there.

I can hear him calling out as he runs inside, but his words cannot be made out. The house is far larger than most of the rest of the buildings in Ta'if. It does not take long before a man hurriedly emerges from it, looking at us as he does so. At least, if he is unfriendly we will get clear easy enough. I see no soldiers and few enough people with weapons. Still, now it is up to Imam Iyād to make sure we are accepted.

Iyād

I have decided, as we approach the village, that this structure has to be an important building of some sort. Ikrimah obviously thinks the same. We are travelling at a slow walk as we do so as to let people realise about their arrival. All our weapons are away. We have timed it well. The men part to let me go forward just as the man looks like he is ready to speak.

"You are not from the Caliphate," the man said abruptly, but with a note of curiosity in his voice. "Who are you and why are you here?"

"As-Salāmu 'Alaykum. I am Iyād ibn Walīd and I have the honour of being the Imam of the Imperial Mosque in Ardlark. I am here following a Synod of the Christians which discussed matters of the faith on both sides of the Mountains, at which I was an observer for Dar al-Islam. After I reported back, the most holy and revered Ayatollah Uzma Alĩ ibn Yũsuf al Mãr decided to send me here to the Caliphate on a similar mission.

"If the kãfirũn could have a meeting like this, should the itaqu do less?" He waved around at the men behind him. "His Imperial Majesty found favour in this idea and he graciously gave me an escort to see me safe through the lands of the unbelievers." He stopped, ingenuously waiting for a response. The man in front of him looked a little stunned with the answer.

"Wa-'Alaykum us-Salãm wa-Raḥmatullãhi wa-Barakãtuhu...Marhaba!" *He took a while, but he finally came out with the standard response. I think that I surprised him.* "I am also named Iyãd...Iyãd ibn Hãritha al-Shaybãn al-Ta'if, and I am the newly appointed Bitrĩq of this humble village..." *I suppose that coincidence added to his surprise a little.*

He started to say something else and then has stopped as if a thought has suddenly struck him. After a pause he cautiously continued: "Does the Ayatollah Uzma claim jurisdiction and rule over the Faithful of the Caliphate?" *This is where I need to start being very diplomatic.*

"Unless you have an Ayatollah Uzma then he is the only one currently among the Faithful. This is why I am here. We wish to see what the attitude is here, and most importantly that we have a Dar as-Sulh, a domain of agreement, again. It is stupid for the Mullahs and Imams not to talk on matters of religion if the Emperor and the Caliph are talking on matters of state. After all, which is the more important?"

The other man nods in reply to such a self-evident question. Now I need to sound conciliatory. It is peaceful now, but it could all still come apart. "Our Ayatollah is a holy and peaceful man and does not wish to force anything upon you that you do not want. I do know that, like the Emperor, he does not wish to rule you physically. You already have a Caliph to do that." *And he started our last conflict with raids on us and still none know why.*

"The Ayatollah also does not want to rule you spiritually. He is merely interested that, with the grace of Allah, the Peaceful, that matters of the Faith stay...consistent...within Dar al-Islam. But come, let us attend midday prayer. I hear your Mu'adhdhin issuing the ãdhãn, and after that, then you can show me around your village and we can talk." *Let us see what you say about the place we seek.*

Ikrimah

It has taken some time, but by the time he has showed off his village, and what is being done in it, Bitrīq Iyād is beginning to warm to Imam Iyād, who is praising their work of building. The latter has made it clear that he wants to spend the night in the village with my men and the column are set up to stay in the caravanserai. I have the men beginning to disperse around the village talking to the locals.

I have them staying in groups of at least three out of caution. They will keep their weapons on them. Soon we are all glad to discover that someone talented has decided that a trade route was a good way to get wealthy and a maqhaa, far better than my men are used to, is the social hub of the village. I have left Khabbāb meeting his counterpart here, Yāqūt al-Shahīd.

It has not taken long for us to be shown everything that there is to see, even being introduced to a beautiful girl who is introduced as a dancer, but in the knowing fashion that indicated that the wealth that she is accumulating will lead to such a large amount of money that she could bring to the marriage that any mahr of her man would be insignificant and the way she has earned it will be overlooked.

I wonder where the two Mice are, and indeed the others. We have seen all around the village and even been near the house that will be our target. It lies well outside the wall that is being built and obviously belongs to a very wealthy man. It is larger than that of the Bitrīq. Most interestingly he has entirely failed to mention it or even who lives there.

The Imam is not seeking to force him to try and acknowledge it. I am glad, that might be dangerous. I just follow silently and watch him and to me, watching his eyes, the Bitrīq seems to not even notice the house where it lies up the river from the village. His eyes seem somehow to avoid it whatever happens. I will need to talk to Khabbāb, but I think that he is ensorcelled in some way.

Khabbāb

To my eyes the old man, one of the oldest-looking people that I have ever met, has to be a veteran of the wars against us. He was obviously trained during the Burning. At home a man of such age would be long retired and living in comfort with his family instead of still having charge of the enchantments for a village, even one as small as this.

His best days are noticeably long over and his mind tends to wander easily.

He seems to think that the village is being invaded, but I am not sure that he means by us. Does he, in his rambling mind, sense that there is another threat that he cannot actually see?

His devoted apprentice seems to be as much a servant as he is anything else and he is far too junior in his abilities to take over the duties of being the sole mage in an isolated village on his own if the old man either retires or dies. I think that a new mage may need to be in residence here before very much longer.

Ikrimah

Darkness falls and we observe Maghreb. My two patrols do as they were supposed to and keep the village and its forces occupied in conversation. We eat dinner, observe Isha and then sit back. The dancer, Buthayna, has proved that, whatever her other skills, she is also a very good dancer. It appears that the Bitrĩq wants to be hospitable and her services have been reserved for the evening for the Imam or Khabbãb or myself.

That somewhat shocks the Imam. It is not the way he is used to things being done and I think that my wife would not forgive me easily. Before anything else more physical is arranged the Imam takes us for a walk. Ostensibly we discuss what we plan to do on the next day. I think that Khabbãb regrets that we have to leave her behind, but then he is a single man.

It was quite amusing seeing the junior Mullahs, both of them un-married men, try and take over the conversation with the Bitrĩq. The younger is more wide-eyed over the dancer than he is attentive to his task at hand. At least my Starşiyrang Perissótero, my senior serge*ant, can keep an eye on them while the three of us are away. Hopefully they will not embarrass us.*

Ikrimah

Ayesha is visible and meets us on the edge of the village nearest the house. "We are all ready," she said. "The rest of us are waiting just over that ridge." *She points at the last outcropping on the road as it comes down the hillside that we descended from to the village.* "They are watching us and, when we are nearly there they will descend and we will take the house. Inshallah."

"Inshallah" the three men replied.

"We will now move behind you once you are in the open. Hopefully anyone detecting magic will only think of you and, if they are to see through our enchantment, then we hope that you are in the way of them seeing us with their eyes as well." *She puts her ring on and fades from sight.*

The three men walked along, deep in conversation and seemingly not paying attention to where they went. *The other two have both switched to reciting, in one case a prayer and in the other a spell. I am fingering my sword and wishing for my bow. We are not supposed to take part in the combat, but one never knows what will happen once a battle is joined.*

It is Khabbãb who notices the saddles coming in and has casually touched our hands to bring them to our attention. They cover the ground far quicker than my horses can.

I can feel something brush past me. Soon after, a few paces from the door, Astrid comes into view clutching that bardiche. So does Ayesha, who is walking beside the Imam. "Visible," Ayesha calls softly. *She waves at the saddles. The nearest is now only two hands away.*

It is the Havenite Princess and she immediately points at the building. She has obviously been preparing the cast as she rides in. Whatever the spell is that she casts, there is no visible effect. Astrid may have heard Ayesha, but she just keeps going and, just before she reached the door, the Imperial Princess points a wand at it and it shatters. Astrid continues and hits the remains of the door hard.

It flies apart before her mail-clad shoulder and she nearly falls as she goes inside through its ruins. The Antikataskopeía Tribune has done this sort of thing before. He just stands and barks orders and these Mice pour through the door with weapons, with shackles and with wands. Instead of being able to help we are left standing with weapons in hand and spells ready to cast at opposition and there is none of that that we can see.

Even before everyone is inside there is the sound of one apparent fight going on, and then several loud banging noises can be heard one after the other but from the rest of the building, and the out-buildings behind it, there is silence. We are simply not going to be needed and the others can let their enchantment and miracle go incomplete. My sword can go away.

Astrid

I have uttered my prayers to Saint Kessog as we approach. Now I just rush into the building. Behind me I can hear my husband giving orders. I get to take on anyone that is still standing after Rani's spell. There is a small courtyard with a fountain visible ahead through a doorway. Ignoring the doors that lead off the passage she hurried through and ran across it lightly.

Ayesha has said that most important people live, or at least spend their early evenings, straight opposite the main door. She kicked the door in. *On the floor is a man. He is unconscious and there is a platter of food scattered around him. Another man stands behind him on the bare floor. A rug has been pulled back to expose a pattern of some sort and he already stands in it chanting.*

He has golden eyes and, now that I know the relation, there is a family resemblance to the Imperial family that will come as a shock to Theodora. Without interrupting the chant he pointed a wand at her and a lightning bolt came from it. *I anticipated that.* She dodged quickly to the side. *Someone who is behind me is not so lucky.* She heard that someone, in a man's voice, cry out in pain.

She leapt closer like a striking cat, hitting out with her bardiche. The man had no choice but to leap out of the pattern lest he be pierced and his blood spill over the symbols on the floor.

In the process of his sidewise dance he drops the wand. I am happy with that. He said something that I don't recognise. I will bet he swore. As he dodges around the pattern away from me he whips out a small thing. It is like a hand-crossbow, but without the bow, in one hand, and a sword in the other.

He pointed the thing at her. *There is an explosion and that hurts a lot. Fuck you.* She attacked and the man parried with his sword as he backed up widdershins. *He isn't very good with his blade, but I can already feel blood flowing from a wound in my side.* The thing exploded again and again. *Dear Saint Kessog. That was in my chest. My mail seems to have had little effect on it. I am having trouble breathing. It hurts.*

He muttered again and she could feel herself growing weaker but she still struck out. *I am supposed to try and make him captive, but fuck that.* This time the man failed to parry and he lost his sword and most of the arm that held it. *He still makes the thing in the other hand explode again even as he screams in pain. It hits me in the leg, but that…I am having difficulty…Oh look…the floor.* She slumped down unconscious.

Basil

Like it or not, my place is here in the courtyard taking charge. It was my job to make sure that the house is saturated with people as quickly as possible and, though I itch to be with my impulsive wife, I know that the one with the experience has to co-ordinate the attack and make sure all is done as it should be.

A fight has erupted from where Astrid has gone and Thord, who I sent behind Astrid, has cried out in pain and fallen back. There are voices and explosions and then a piercing scream. I think it is the cry of a man. It all goes silent and then another scream erupts in the same voice and it is cut short.

Ia

I follow behind Thord and Astrid. I might be short, but I am taller than the Dwarf. I saw the wand being raised as Astrid dodged. She tried to call a warning and Thord dodged to one side as she had dodged back behind the doorway. The sharp smell of a lightning bolt filled the air and she heard something. *That sounded very much like Old Speech.*

She leapt back around. *Thord is against a wall reaching for a potion. I am in time to see my cat-wife hit and hit again with something. It makes her stagger each time it hits, but she keeps attacking. I have no time to cast and it is too close anyway.* She drew her new blades and leapt sun-wise around the pattern to the fight.

Astrid is down but the man has his back to me. I am not losing my lover to a murdering bastard like you. He is unsteadily pointing something at where Astrid lies unmoving as blood streams from his severed arm.

Ia stepped forward and thrust with both blades where her healing training had told her that the kidneys were and twisted both weapons as she plunged them into the torso in front of her. *My new sword slides right through his body. The man screams in agony. I like that.* She withdrew her weapons and stepped back.

He starts to turn. Someone outside has been waiting for a clear shot and an arrow streaks into the room and buries itself in his guts and explodes. I have his blood all over me. He has a shocked expression on his face as he beings to fall. Now we wait. Yes, it is obvious that, like most mages, he has a contingency in place.

His cure kicks in but the one that I put on my cat-wife has had time to do its work now and she is active first and both the archer and I are waiting. Another arrow explodes in the same place on his body as I thrust forward with my sword into his chest. He screams briefly, a gurgling scream as blood is already filling his lungs, before a quickly rising and bloody Astrid removes his head cleanly with her bardiche. She is weak and unsteady though and nearly falls as she does so.

Basil

All through the house it has gone quiet except for the sounds of Mice scurrying through the building. Bodies and other things, presumably magic and other plunder, are already starting to collect in the courtyard. I need to start to move around the house and order searches be made on things of interest.

First I send Rani, who is just standing there after spending her mana in the enchantment that had sent most of the building into unconsciousness, to let the Imam and his mage know what has happened and to send them back to the Bitrĩq with explanations if they are needed. We need to get the saddles inside and prepare to move on if it is essential.

Ia

Hulagu was the archer. He still has his bow in hand as he comes in to admire his handiwork. It takes confidence to fire into a fight where friends are. "Thank you. We needed that."

Ia looked to her sister-wife and made sure that she drank some potions. *She will be fine, even if her armour has holes in it.*

She then began to search the man. *There is a bracelet on each wrist. One has numbers on a glass plate.* As she looked, the last number changed upward. *The other, on the severed arm, is smooth. It looks to be made of mithril.* She pocketed these. *In one pouch he has a small metal box that opens and which has a small glass screen and buttons.*

That can also go into my pouch. Another pouch is empty and, by the shape of it, it looks like it should hold the crossbow-stock thing that hurt Astrid. It has another pouch on the outside of the main one that smells oily and had two little metal boxes in it with round-nosed things made of two metals in them.

Ariadne

I was brought along just in case there is more of the not-magic here. She had immediately started searching the rooms. It was not long before she sent Menas out to Basil and Theodora with news. *Well, surprise, surprise, I have opened a locked door with a magic chisel and found a whole room of not-magic. A light comes on as I enter and it goes out again when I step out again, but that could just be magic.*

There are several flat surfaces made of stuff like the green-light box, sitting on a bench-desk, even if none of them glow. There is a seat in front of them. On a bench is a sort of helmet that covers the eyes. I am not putting that on. It might be dangerous. Even the bench and the seat seem to be covered in that slippery stuff, even if it isn't actually very slippery there.

In a cupboard there are boxes that hold two long things that are sort of like the light thrower. However they are smaller and far lighter. There are also four of the hand-crossbow stock things without the bow like Ia has already shown me. In another cupboard, also locked and in a metal box, there are many stiff paper boxes of little shiny brass and lead objects that smell faintly of oil, and also like the ingredients that make a rocket fly and explode. They all smell of Antdrudge.

They are the same as the ones in little metal boxes in the pouch. The whole room is full of the faint smell of lightning and it is cool and dry. In another cupboard are boxes of tools, some of which I have never seen before and more boxes of those green cards with metal on them and writing. She rubbed her hands together. *These were going to be fun to play with when I get the time.*

Some of the screwdrivers are smaller than I would have imagined possible and there are even two round glasses on stands that make tiny things seem huge. Eleanor will want one of them for doing jewellery. I get the other one. There is a bin sitting under the desk. She looked in that. *It has several of the green card things in it and they look partly melted. They look just like some of the ones I saw before the green-light box and the light thrower were repaired.*

Basil

I have everyone sorted now. I can check on Puss. She is recovering from several wounds that she assures me are only light. It is a poor lie. I can see the holes and the blood and Butterfly, who is standing behind where she sits, is shaking her head at me from where Puss cannot see her.

A naked and pretty girl, with bracelets on her ankles and wrists, solid ones that are meant to attach to chains, is carried in by Stefan. He lays her unbound on a divan, and calls the cousins over to look after her, instead of putting her beside the other unconscious people. I have a hand of prisoners lying bound as if they are all mages, in front of me.

"She was locked up in an outbuilding," said Stefan. "She has been abused." *He points at the red marks that are left by healing wounds. They are the marks that only fade a few days after healing.* "I would say whipped and tortured regularly, probably raped as well. She could have been waiting on someone to take Uqba's place to kill her, or perhaps they need a new carpet to be able to get a fresh victim when she dies. I think that she could end up coming home with us."

Ia

After the Mice who had been injured in the attack are cured and back on their feet some spend the rest of the night reviving prisoners and questioning them. Others take turns to rest and keep watch. I now get the opportunity to show the mages how I can control a person. It is very different to what they do, but it works, at least much of the time.

She waited until one of the men was awake and sat him up still bound and then began idly and absent-mindedly swinging a jewel back and forward reflecting light of it as she gently talked to him. *Soon I have him dreamily answering questions as if he has smoked several pipes of hashish. I am lucky that it has worked so well. I am still not an expert at this.*

Praise the Goddess. By great good fortune he is the one who knows the most. I made sure to give him an instruction to try and counter anything he may have been told about dying. The Christian priest is ready though, just in case. It turns out that Jamal abd Allah is yet another ghazi and his master's bodyguard.

He has been with his master Maarshtrin, it is actually one of the Adversaries that we have killed, for some time. He calls Maarshtrin a demi-god and an Archangel and speaks reverentially of a thing Qiyamah, some sort of end time. Maarshtrin used the room that Ariadne found to talk to other demi-gods in a language he did not understand. He says it is the language of Heaven. I say it is Old Speech or perhaps Daveen.

It seems that Maarshtrin is not a very strong mage, but he has machines that amplify and do magic for him. Jamal speaks of a bracelet that tells time and another that protects him from spells. Ia produced the ones that she had taken and he confirmed what they were. *The room has not worked properly for some time. It has only just been repaired after an accident and they were celebrating its repair tonight.*

Maarshtrin has not been able to talk to the others of his kind, or to see over the world as he usually does, for some time. The villagers will not hear or see anything unusual about the house. They have a spell cast over them that ensures that they do not even see it unless it is directly pointed out to them. Even if that is done then they will soon forget it again.

They have grown concerned as all of the beautiful girls of the village gradually disappeared, but cannot work out where they are going. Then all of the young ones started to disappear, regardless of their beauty. We people of the Swamp are somehow being blamed. Why does everyone always blame us? The dancer has been kept alive for something special.

She was going to disappear tonight, but the arrival of the Darkreach men disrupted that. When Ia had finished asking all that she wanted to ask at his time she made sure that she gave him an instruction that should have him answering and obeying whenever she needed him to.

As he spoke his words were recorded. Ia smiled. *Ayesha has spoken of a Book of Records that her God keeps on everyone. We have our own by now.* The servants were questioned as well, but the last, a mage, was just tightly secured. *He will be questioned tomorrow.*

None of those questioned can give any clue as to the role that the master of Misr al-Mãr played. Ghazi are sent here for a while or assigned here, but the Mullah himself has never once appeared in the village.

Astrid
33rd Quattro

I ache and my healing wounds itch like mad, but the worst is my nose and what is coming to it. The body of Maarshtrin is beginning to smell already. In a few hours it has begun to smell as if it has been dead for a few days. She took up the body and moved it well outside the house wall, before washing herself.

Good. With luck the Princesses will not ask after it for another couple of hours and the family resemblance will have gone completely by then. It is not rotting away as quickly as a demon does, but it is decomposing far faster than anything else made of just normal flesh should do. If he was as old as I think that he was, then I suspect that he is doing all of his ageing at once.

During the night the woman woke and immediately started screaming and trying to escape. *Having woken up in the house she is expecting to again be raped and tortured, as she always is.*

She spent the rest of the night sobbing and being comforted by the cousins and other former slaves among the Mice. *She is a Muslim girl from a farm outside Third Tower and Stefan was right. Despite what had happened to her not being her fault, she feels that she cannot go home again. She has been shamed and her family will disown her. Idiots.*

Theodora

There is something wrong about the death of Maarshtrin. Now that I think about it, I am not happy with the way it took place. I expected more. I have gone over the details of what everyone has told me of the fight and he died very easily; too easily. I would have thought that an Adversary would be as hard to kill as, well a dragon, a small one at least.

Instead he died as if he were just a normal man and, although he was surprised, he did not even show as much magical skill as I expected. This is a being who Dobun had thought could trap him in the Spirit world and one or more of them had cast a fog over the spirit world and stopped the shamen of the Khitan and the seers of Haven from seeing the future.

As she thought she realised the answer. *Somehow he relies on machines and not real magic. He had magic, otherwise he would not have been in the pattern, but not enough to make even a good wand. He had to use those metal things that injured Astrid. Ariadne said that there are all of those green things in a bin and the ghazi had said that his machine was broken.*

He might not have even talked to the other Adversaries for some time and he lacks the magic that I used to repair the green-light box and the light throwers. Perhaps he even uses something like Ia does to control people. In other words something else that does not use magic either. That room that Ariadne wants to take home is what made him strong and the same, possibly, will apply to the others of his kind.

Maybe the helmet thing is his way of controlling the machines and perhaps even of seeing into the spirit worlds. At any rate, with his machines it seems that he was an Adversary and a deadly opponent. Without them he had been a weak mage and really only a mediocre armsman. He relied on servants rather than exerting himself. Having decided on that, I am now far happier with what has happened.

Chapter XXXVIII

Rani

33rd Quattro

While the Muslims are all busy with their prayer, it seems to be the right time to cast the next major enchantment. Goditha will be performing a new casting. Earth mages are good at both making magic permanent and at dispelling it. She can use the pattern in the house to aid her. It is a normal magical pattern and has not been disrupted by having blood or anything else break its patterns.

It is her first ever disenchantment spell to cast. Having her do it will leave my wife and I, the two stronger mages, free in case we are needed later in the day. Learning to cast a disenchantment on a fixed object is key to her learning how to cast a strong defensive spell in battle. When the villagers emerge from their Fajr prayer they will see and remember the house for the first time since the enchantment was placed on them.

Ayesha has already alerted Imam Iyãd and he will be bringing Bitrĩq Iyãd and some others out to see the house and what we found here. Here they will witness the questioning of the mage and then will be able to read the books of questioning. Then they can see the rest of what is here and be able to talk to the prisoners. After that, how they react and what they do is up to them.

Ayesha

The Bitrĩq brings his Mullah, the ancient mage and his apprentice and one of his retainers, who serves as a guard commander. The Imam brings Ikrimah,

Khabbãb, and his junior Mullahs. I bring the dancer. The girl has a right to know how close she came to a horrible fate and what has happened to so many of her friends and other women. She needs to give thanks to Allah, the Compassionate, for her life.

Questioning the mage gives us nothing new, but a combination of what he says, as well as what Ia has gotten her man to say, and what Reema, the girl from Third Tower has said, has left a look of horror on the face of the Bitrĩq. He has come to realise that he has not been the one who has been ruling this village for quite some time. He knows now that zalimun had been freely having their way here.

This Adversary has been the one controlling everything from his building hidden out in plain sight. Only now do some of the things that visitors have said in passing make sense to him and the others from Ta'if. Glances often pass between them during the testimonies. It is only now do they understand what has happened to all of their women. Now they have to go and talk to their people and allow families to be able to properly grieve.

We Mice can now enter the village and be made welcome. Once the prisoners have been put in the charge of the Bitrĩq, we get to spend the day in rest. Today I sip kaf in a proper maqhaa and tonight I will tell the story of the Mice and the events in the world. The people of this village need to realise that they have a very personal stake in this tale.

It is good to see that this Bitrĩq Iyãd is a dutiful man. He has immediately gathered his people together and explained what has happened just outside their wall. In the name of Allah, the Just, he has decided to keep the man Ia has under a trance alive, in case his testimony is needed later, and promptly and publicly had the heads struck off the rest.

Ia

Now that it is all over I once again talk to my prisoner. This time their Governor is present. I can take the opportunity to reinforce my control over him and also make sure that he will obey this village headman from now on. He can still possibly break free, if we are unlucky and the man has a strong will, so they need to make sure that he is kept under guard and shackled at all times.

After that I get a chance to renew my lover's spell of healing. Last night did not go the way I would have wanted. I think that I need to look ahead instead of putting my family at needless risk. Ia took advantage of the day of rest to look deeply into her globe and, when it was nearing dusk, Astrid brought her before the Princesses. "You need to hear this," she said.

I am bid to proceed. My mind is still hazy and I know that my speech is slow from the drug, but I must be clear in what I say. "I like to check on what is likely to occur. I had not looked before we came up here because my last reading was still coming true and, as a result, my sister-wife was put in grave danger, so I decided to look. There is great danger ahead of us here in the Caliphate.

"I see an old man, a very evil old man. He will try and isolate us and cut us off. What is more there is something about the house where the Adversary was living. It is hard to see what it is, but the building itself is best left alone. I think that there is a trap in it, and it is a vast trap that could swallow all of us up in death. It is strong enough to take the whole village at once in a storm of fire. I think that we can take the contents, but nothing that is fixed."

There was something else in my visions that I need to talk about. What was it? Oh yes, the visions of evil people hiding behind fair masks. "The last thing that I see for this trip is that we will soon meet many people who seem to have good intent towards us. They will, in fact, be evil despite seeming to be good."

"The rings…it sounds like the rings," interjected Astrid and the Princesses nod. *It makes sense to them then. That is good. I know that the Goddess has granted me a strong vision, but not everyone accepts these things straight away.*

"At the end of my vision I saw that, when we return from here we will come to have both a very long voyage and then a coming together in resolution."

"We need to get everyone to do a reading when we return to Mousehole." *Rani turns to her wife and Theodora agrees.*

Now, once my head has cleared a little, and before the night of storytelling starts, I need to do as we agreed with the druids and witches down at Eastguard. I need to take our Muslim priest with us and talk to the local headman about the matter of the slaves here and their worship. This is very important.

Ia

a little later

I am glad that it seems that he is a good man at heart. Between our role in what has just occurred here, and with the strong backing of the Imam, this is one town of the Caliphate that will at least be open to a discrete presence. Now it will be a matter of selecting the right person for the role and that is a delicate matter.

My people have been given a status here as something called 'dhimmis'. *I will at least have one success to report back. I think that I will suggest a follower of the Mother be sent. I don't think that they would allow a Circle to be built here. On the other hand, I think they will approve of someone whose first act will be to plant trees.*

Ariadne

The others can sit back and rest, but I need to prepare to move on at the house. We cannot take much of what is in here. To my regret I cannot work out how to shift the entire, fascinating, room back to Mousehole in one piece.

Coming on top of what Ia has said it is easy to get the Princesses to have the Bitrĩq agree to seal it up tight and place a guard on it as well. No-one will be allowed to enter the room, or even the house, until we return to see what we can do to take away the trap that Ia feels certain is here. It can all wait.

In the meantime Ayesha tells me that all that is here is legitimate ghanimah. I can take what I want from the building. I was going to anyway, but it is nice to know that the local people will not object to what I am doing. I need not hide my activity and I can choose what I wish to go with me now without having to hide the rest.

The things that are not actually a part of the room should be safe to move. I have packed all of the tools, the light throwers and the hand-crossbow things and the small boxes of metal things. I have determined that the things explode in the hand-crossbow like rockets and hurl their little lead darts around that with a lot of force. It is enough to go through good mail. I have the ones that came out of Astrid when she was healed.

I ache to be able to test the light throwers and do more with the hand-crossbow things, but I am not going to be separated from at least one of the objects. I made it go off during our first night and it left a dart shattered and flat in a crater in a wall and, at least now, have worked out what the little lever on the left-hand side does as well as the button that makes the metal box of lead things drop out.

I now have several pouches that each holds one of the hand-crossbow things. I cannot keep calling them that. There has to be a better name for them. A few of the filled metal boxes go into each one as well. One of these pouches can go onto my belt to that I can keep it close to me while I work out more about it.

There is also a very solid square box in another locked section that, when opened reveals tubes of stiff paper with metal ends. In each of them is an egg-shaped object, three times as long as a real egg and made of dark-green painted metal. Each has little bits of machinery attached to them and each has the same characters painted on them in yellow. To me they look like something that is meant to blow up.

Similar things are sometimes made at Antdrudge, but it is too hard to, without magic, determine when they will explode. I want to make some tests, but that will have to wait until I am at home. She put two of them in a saddle bag. *I will think about them on the way.* She made sure that the rest, those that she could not take with her, were kept in a safe and guarded place for when they returned this way.

Chapter XXXIX

Hulagu
34th Quattro

We move briskly on to the village of Yarmũk. Although Yarmũk is close to Misr al-Mãr, the Princesses have decided we will now move more openly with the Mice flying all around the column of moriid, but not going so high as to be very visible. Where we are going we cannot be physically seen from Misr al-Mãr and our magic should keep us safe from any other gaze.

Between the Princesses they have decided that the rest of the Adversaries will be unlikely to look here for us as they will expect Maarshtrin to look after the area. For the most part, except for the scouts, we travel at mori height. From ground level the Sawãd shows itself to be as fertile as we thought when we looked down on it from on high.

Long grass covers its floor and, except that it lies as a bowl within surrounding mountains that fringe the skyline with white tips, and we have to ride through a pass in a small central range, it might as well have been the plains that we cross. After the Burning and the long war between Darkreach and the Caliphate it seems to be lying empty and just waiting to be filled.

We Mori all feel at home. Our upper meadow at Mousehole is good, indeed the grass here is not as green, as plentiful, or as long, but this is far better in terms of its expanse. What is more, it will not be as easily subject to snow, indeed, it is quite warm for this time of year as we move into the autumn.

Once again the Darkreach kynigoi travel hard. Along the way we pass several caravanserais that are for the passing trade. There is a lot of that. Most carry goods around the Caliphate and there are a fair number of these traders around as well and we overtake some and pass several others who are coming towards us.

It is as well that we have the Darkreach people with us so that we have least a measure of familiarity to the other travellers. We still nearly panic people as we approach them and still leave much astonishment in our wake after we pass and we leave them trailing behind us.

Ayesha

It is different coming through here like this instead of on a horse. Now we approach Yarmũk. It lies where the Tãb Rũdh bends back on itself like a snake to form a steep-sided gorge that is better for defence than any castle moat. Steps lead down to the fast-flowing river and a waterfall on it that drops the river even further and the wells inside the village have to be very deep.

When its location is added to its strong stone walls and, with everything in the entire town being made of stone, brick, and tile, it is almost impregnable, even to us flying on our saddles. If everything inside the walls were to be taken inside the buildings, there would be very little left there in the town to burn.

Yarmũk is so rugged that the streets need to have steps in them to save people slipping on the sloped roads when it rains or is frosty and, although they build carts here, no wheeled vehicle can easily pass through it. They have to be unloaded and moved empty through the village while the goods from them are taken to the other side of the village by people or by donkeys.

This both hinders trade between Dimashq and the north of the Caliphate and makes a lot of money for the town. Another disadvantage to its location is that it is home to over two thousand people who are very tightly packed within its walls. Even with stone houses that are up to four storeys high, people are starting to have to build on the far side of its bridges to the north or along the road to Dimashq.

Not only is the town starting to spread out beyond its defences, but even more the two mosques in the town cannot even hold all of the villagers and they always have people outside of them worshipping in the streets during services. At least no-one is trying to pass through the town during a service. They need a new wall at the very least.

Sheik Muhammed al-Fud l al-Khawlãn

I am not quite sure how to welcome these people. The Iman, of course is welcome any time, but if I read the banner of his escort correctly, I fought them at Badr when I was a younger man. Their commander has the eyes of a professional. They stopped us for a while and few of them escaped to tell of our trap and turn it back on us. Without them we would have taken all of their southern armies and their towns on the plain would now be ours. Inshallah.

I am not sure what to make of the other group that the Imam travels with. Its mix of men and women, one of whom wears a hijab, but who behaves like a man and who is married to a Khitan is more than strange. What is more; the different religions of the group and the naked power that they all represent are a worry to me. Still, al-Ḥamdu Lillāh, we are in a hudna where none need die and trade is opening up, so we tolerate them.

Sheik Muhammed

a little later

Having heard their story I am now even more concerned about them. I travelled as a young man and saw Peace Tower. It was strong. To have made up a force that defeated the Brotherhood and brought it all down speaks of a major effort. I am glad that they are here among us in peace. Let it stay that way.

I do, however, worry about these women Princesses of theirs, even if one is an offspring of the Emperor of al-Īmbiraturiat al-Dhakina, Darkreach, but at least they seem to have proper marriages for the important men, which I did not expect of the al-Masihiiyn. This Umra al-Harb, the one who kills dragons, he has two beautiful wives who attend to him.

On the other hand, this al-Nisa al-Hayawan may be a concern. The women here look at a woman who can kill al-Quizam al-zalam with large eyes. She may be married in a proper marriage, but she is a bad example to them and she does not seem to put that huge weapon down. My mages tell me that she has more magic on her than I have.

I was enjoined to say nothing to Misr al-Mār about the visit and, on reflection, I agreed that, not only is this a good idea, but I will forbid anyone from my town from going up to the fortress until the whole matter is cleared up. If Ta'if can be taken over, so can my town and, as a father with three young and, at least in my eyes, beautiful daughters. Inshallah, we shall stay apart from it all until it resolves itself.

Astrid

From our point of view of the Mice, I am very happy to stay here for a quiet night. At least this village has a well-established bathhouse and I am delighted in being able to use that to relax in. The attendants, on the other hand, seem to be more than a little worried by armed women keeping their weapons beside them even as they bathe, but my weapons do not leave my sight. I will clean and oil them carefully before we go to bed.

Ia and Basil are delightfully attentive to me. I find it hard to admit that I am still tired from my curing and the healing scars on my body are still livid. I will not say this aloud, but I came very close to dying. My healing spell would not have worked unless I was nearly lost to them. If Maarshtrin had managed to use his hand-machine one more time on me after my healing had started then I would almost certainly not be here.

Rani

35th Quattro

Our next village will be Bab al-Abwãb in its high pass and so, tied as we are to the speed of the horses, we have decided to spend the night in one of the caravanserai along the road. It does not take long to decide that the River's Head, in the Darkreach Gap, may be just as new, but the owner of that establishment knows a lot more about comfort and hospitality than the host of this place will ever have even if he re-incarnates several times here.

It was fairly obvious that only traders, soldiers and the poorer people travelled on the ground. The richer people, those who might demand more from a host, fly more rapidly backwards and forwards directly to the towns on carpets and did not have to frequent such establishments. This Fayyum has an oasis and one day it will become a village, but until then it is best avoided.

I wish that we could fly directly on up the slope to Bab al-Abwãb, but it is obvious that my wife is right in this. She did not have to work too hard to convince me of why it is a bad idea to travel without the Imam and his men. Even with them our reception at Yarmũk could be best described as strained.

Ayesha

36th Quattro, the Feast Day of Saint Cephas

The Bitrĩq of Bab al-Abwãb is Khãzim ibn Azĩz al-Mudar and his village is even more incomplete than Ta'if. Ta'if at least had some parts that existed there before the Burning. There had probably been a village once where Bab al-Abwãb now stands, it is too important a spot for this not to be the case, but a powerful mage, or perhaps even more than one of them, must have caught the insanity of the Burning plague here.

I have been through here many times. There is nothing now standing here from that time apart from shards of pottery, or occasional pieces of rusted metal, or even old coins dug up when someone is working. Some of the rocks lying around the pass can be seen as having once been shaped, but what they were a part of, only Allah is Wise enough to know.

The Bitrĩq is a young man full of energy and although he has an architect and a builder to help him, his mosque is small and he only has one junior mage based in the village. Like Goditha he is an Earth mage and a mason and he is having the unusual experience of sitting and indulging in shop talk with a woman who understands exactly the issues that he deals with daily.

Everything here seems to be directed to building the village itself, mining the nearby crystal and polishing it, or else looking after travellers. Although there are chickens running around, his village even brings most of its food in, and what is produced locally is mainly produced by some of the few women and children. The settlement is so small that our audience tonight all have to sit outside. They are wrapped in robes and with their breath steaming in the chill air to hear me tell our story.

The village men were reluctant to allow the women out to have this happen, but give way to the visiting Imam and the strange woman who is obviously related to their own Princess, and so perhaps one of the rare women to be obeyed. They have watched the blonde al-Nisa al-Hayawan go through her exercises as well and, from their faces, Astrid seems to be someone, perhaps not to be respected, but at least to be feared, as well.

As the tale is told the Mice who are not involved can stand outside the village in its pass and look across the high mountain plain of Rãhit and the lake of Buhairet Tabariyya to Dimashq, the magic of its outdoor lights showing its location clearly in the still night air. It is so long since I have been there.

By the time we have finished it appears that Reema, the kidnapped Dark-reach woman, will not be coming back to Mousehole with us after all. This village lacks women. Anyone can see that it would be hard to attract one to live here in chill pass. However Atã and Tãriq have already had their, now usual, conversation with the men who live here.

It seems that, if Reema stays here she will have a choice of husbands who are more than willing to overlook something that is not her fault in return for a beautiful wife. What is more, not only is she beautiful, but she has experience with looking after goats, and can spin and weave their fleece as well.

None of the people here are rich, but they are all working as hard as they can to overcome that minor problem. Here, with her skills, she is to be regarded as a great asset as a first wife for any man who wants to get ahead. Khãzim has agreed to look after her until she has made up her mind. I will leave some mahr with him for the groom to give to his wife as a surprise.

I am very much enjoying, for the first time in my life, being able to freely indulge in sadaqah, the charity that lies beyond the fourth pillar of tithing. Astrid has got me to find the woman whose role in matchmaking in the village is the same as hers and they have already talked. We can leave confident that Reema will have a number of good men to choose between.

Chapter XL

Rani
Ist Quinque

It is a long, slow and tedious process moving down off the ridge towards Dimashq. Just as it was when it came down the ridge to Ta'if and again up the saddle to Bab al-Abwãb, the road switches backwards and forwards in curves like a dead snake on an ant's nest and even though the column rides hard, we are only just reached the floor of the Rãhit by the time it is dark.

The caravans must take far longer. We passed two caravanserais evenly spaced on the way down and several traders going up or down the road. I am glad that we did not to have to stop at either of the stations on the slope. Both, although obviously already in use, are still equally as obviously just being built. They are still merely stone and adobe shells. Really just enclosed yards for animals to be penned in while their owners sleep beside them and with an actual building still being worked on for more than a kitchen.

We cannot avoid staying at the one at the bottom of the descent however. They call the little settlement Shabwa and, although it looks to be far better set up than the other two are; it is as yet far from luxurious and lacks the blessings of Pusan in any way. At least the host of the caravanserai here is very conscious of this fact and apologetically offers his own bed up for us.

My wife has thanked him, but we have politely declined. To me he doesn't seem to be prosperous enough to afford to have a permanent de-lousing spell cast on his establishment. I prefer to sleep in a simpler bed, one where our herbs should provide at least some protection from the vermin that infect such places.

We need something portable to cope with this problem. It is yet another spell I need to think about. I will add it to the growing list of charms and enchantments that eventually all of our travellers should sooner or later be carrying when they leave the valley. Everyone needs to have a bracelet with charms on it for all eventualities that may arise.

Ayesha
2nd Quinque

Now we ride and fly through the lush fields that occupy the flat spots in the Rãhit. In the low and sheltered places there are gardens full of flowers and vegetables. Trees line the slopes of the hills. The Hawrãn Rũdh brings water from Kartala and the Litani Rũdh from Jabal Tahat to water the soil. The Rãhit is a fertile valley. Holes in the gentle slopes show that qanat add to the greenery as they bring even more water underground from the aquifers of the mountains out to the plain.

Dotted through the whole area, often at the end of the lines of the qanat, are hamlets. Some are only the size that can be managed by a single family, but others are approaching being villages in their own right. Roads are shaded by palms and other trees and canals spread the water to where it is needed after it is brought to the surface by wind-mills or magical devices.

We travel slowly through a lush and prosperous land. It is so much larger than our little valley, so much richer and more peaceful. Beside the roads are flocks of goats, sheep, llama and other animals. We share the road with people moving food and other goods around. Allah, the Peaceful, looks over it all with a beneficial smile.

Dimashq grows before us as our column moves up the broad isthmus that connects the flat plateau of the city with the rest of the plain. The city sits at the end of the land with the lake acting as a giant moat for the town. The wall that faces us is not as strong as that of Ardlark, but it is far taller and mightier than most of the others that we have seen.

I have never really viewed it like this before. A great tower stands at each end of it and another two flank the entry. A huge double-sided iron-clad timber gate stands in the centre, so large that even one of the great lizards of the Swamp could perhaps enter it. The wall runs for only a hand of filled hands of paces on either side of the gate, from water to water, but it is also over a filled hand of paces high. Above the wall can be seen the minarets of the town's six great mosques.

We have given the Imam the honour of entering first. However, for some reason the gate closed as we came up to it. There are a few hands of men outside, but it is solidly closed. "You and your men can come inside," the guard said to him, "but I have strict instructions that the others with you have to leave their flying things outside and must enter on foot."

"They will refuse to do that," said Iyãd. *That is correct.*

"Then they cannot enter." *This is where it will get interesting. I am trying to not push my way forward. It is almost a reflex for a daughter of my father given those words. Luckily we have Astrid with her heavily accented and sing-song version of Arabic to say what needs to be said. Hopefully they can understand her.*

Alã al-Sadiq

I have done as I was told and now there is a large pale haired al-Nisa al-Hayawan standing in front of me. She holds a weapon that I never seen. She is larger than I am and her weapon is larger still. She wears mail that has seen battle recently. It has holes in it. Links hang loose and her aketon has dried blood on it around the holes.

She has been pierced several times through the chest and other parts by some weapon and yet she is still standing there alive in front of me. She holds her weapon lightly and grounded on its butt plate as she smiles down at me. I do not like that smile. I feel like a mouse looking at a hungry cat. Women should not have weapons at all, but in particular this one should be barred.

"Let me get this right." *Her accent is hard to understand.* "We have flying things that will go over your wall and you think that you can stop us because you have a gate closed against us."

If I am nodding nervously it is simply because I am actually very nervous. Exactly the same thought had occurred to me, but it had not seemed like the right time to bring it up when I was given those orders by the man who instructed me. Now it seems even more stupid than it did then and I do not have him to back me up.

"You do realise that if we were hostile we would fly over you and do to your town what we have already done to Peace Tower? You may have heard that the Brotherhood has fallen. You may not have heard that we are the ones who destroyed its main citadel."

I heard that it had fallen, but not how or by whom. In the name of Allah, the Merciful, please somehow let me get out of this alive. I have a wives and children who I am sure would miss me. Alã swallowed and looked at her teeth. *It is slightly easier as a view than looking at her weapon. I pray that I do not feel them at my throat.*

I know that I have my firqa and more support on the wall behind me, but it doesn't seem to be much of a consolation at present. Inshallah it will work out, but from the look she gives me I feel as if I am date sugar that she is looking at that someone has tried to sell as imported cane. She is saying nothing. What am I supposed to do now?

"Do you have a reason to give us, when you have not even asked who we are?" *At least I can give an answer to that.*

"Under ahl al-dhimma, you cannot be armed inside the city and you are too dangerous to be allowed to enter. What is more you are infidels who would defile the city with your presence."

I was told that, and although I was not told to say it, no-one told me not to. Some explanation had seemed like a good idea and the truth of the matter seemed like the best thing to say before I spoke the words out loud and laid it out like that. Now, looking at her, I think that I may have been able to say it better.

She has gone silent and is looking at me again. This time it is just like a cat looks at a mouse. "We shall ignore your law, whatever that is, but you are right about us being dangerous if you were to make us your enemies, but wrong about the second. We have the Imam Iyãd of the main mosque of Ardlark with us, and even I, who do not share his faith, think that he is a good and holy man. We have his men and several others of your people in our group." She stopped, stood beside him and looked behind her. *That makes me feel even smaller.*

"I tell you what, the Imam and his men will come in and they can ask the Princess Miriam to come out to see us. That is, after all, who we are here to visit." The guard looked at her. *I am suspicious about her agreeing with what I was told to tell them. There will be a hidden trap in her words.* "You see the two women looking very regal and who are not armoured…"

I can see two beautiful women, ones that are wearing no armour, just clothes. One is from Darkreach, by what she wears and the other is a dark-skinned beauty showing a lot of her skin. She ignores all of the concepts of 'awrah, but she would also fetch a lot of money as a slave.

"Not the Hindi one with the bare stomach you idiot, the other, more fully clothed one with the golden eyes. Does she remind you of anyone?" *Did she read my mind? Astaghfirullāh, that one looks to be of the same family as the wife of the Caliph's third son.*

She notices my confusion and she nods. I knew there was a trap. "Now, how about you go and tell the Princess that you, personally, have denied her favourite cousin entry to see her after more than four years of them being kept apart by life. If she is as good a mage as our Princess is then I think that you should duck fast as there will be a spell coming your way."

"Now," *she is back to sounding reasonable* "we are going to go back down the road a little way. There we will set up camp until someone inside decides to get sensible." *Where is the trap?* "We will be telling our story to all of the passers-by and, when it gets to the part about seytani starting to rule parts of the Caliphate until we killed them, I am sure that there will be a lot of interest." *There it is. Now it closes fast and tight on me.*

Now she turns to this man beside her who must be the Imam Iyãd. He has let her do the speaking while he is still sitting there on his horse. She must be the leader of their firqa. A woman is in charge of his guard. I have no choice but to let him in and I will need to pass a message to the Calat. That will not make my superiors happy, but I have no choice.

"Go and talk to your Ayatollah. I hope that he is as nice as Bishop Christopher and Ayesha tell me yours is...but somehow I doubt it if he has idiots like this one at the gate. He is worse than the gate guard on my first visit to Ardlark. I promise that we will wait quietly outside for a month or so before I get impatient and start tearing walls down. Please stay in touch with us."

Was she in jest about tearing walls down? Somehow, I am not so sure. At least she is promising to sit quietly.

Astrid

He is unsure what to do next. I have been looking at him just as Mũsã used to look at me in Hrothnog's entry room. It works on him much better even than it worked on me. One more withering look and I get to watch him squirm for a little while more before I put myself back on my saddle and leave him to open the gate for the Imam.

A few waves of the hand gather the Mice up and move us all back down the road. We will make sure that we are far out of range of the several ballistae that I can see on the wall. There is a caravanserai that I can see. From the look of the pens it caters to people driving stock to the markets. My husband can check it and its kitchen over and then we will settle down to wait.

As Astrid had promised, Ayesha, Theodora and even Astrid herself started to take turns telling their story. *The road outside is soon blocked as people gather around to hear the tale. I should have expected that they will like storytellers. The parts where ghazi attempt to kidnap Mice, and what happened in Ta'if receive frequent mention in between the other parts of the tale.*

That this story is told by a ghazi, and a female one, the daughter of a Sheik no less, makes it even more interesting. People hurry away to the town after hearing it and others come out in return. None are accused but I make sure to note how wrong it is that the Princesses are not allowed to see each other, and how curious it is that this comes on top of all of the other things that we have found wrong since entering the Caliphate.

Basil

Not only are we Mice gaining popularity by entertaining them, but we are adding to it by buying food from the kitchens and from vendors who have arrived to take advantage of this gathering, even from inside the town. Not only do we feed ourselves, but also we begin to feed the crowd of listeners. They look well on us, and even on the disrespect that Puss shows to their rulers.

In Ardlark I would be keeping a very close watch here. As I pass through the throng there is a lot of muttering in the crowd that is very disrespectful of the Caliph. What is more I am hearing that the Imam and his men have already been reported as giving alms to the city beggars and the poor as soon as they went inside. Others have noted the words that are embordered on their banner and know what they mean.

The behaviour of our two foreign groups is being compared with the local rulers and, in addition, the Orphanos, whose story I grew up with, whether by accident or not, and I suspect not, include a couple of storytellers in their ranks and they have been telling similar stories to those of the Mice in the town itself. They even explain their banner if they are asked and talk of the fire a few years ago. That should all be interesting.

In the meantime we talk to anyone who will listen at the caravanserai that we have taken for ourselves. From what I hear, and here gossip flows like the waters of the Rhastaputra, the Imam has yet to go near the Calat, the fortress of the Caliph, beyond the Mosque of Sulieman in its forecourt, where he and the Orphans were just among the worshippers.

Finally there are a number of well-armed men gathering in the crowd. None of them wear their arms openly. None seem to be very good at trying to blend in. They are not as well trained in this as Antikataskopeía would be. I have stolen blades from two of them to show to Ayesha quietly. "These look the same as yours. Does everyone use blades like these, or are they just for ghazi?"

"Just for ghazi," she replied. "No others have the skills to use them. You stole…" he shrugged and quietly he showed her where the men were. *The two are actually very obvious when you knew what to look for as they have discovered that they are missing something.* "I know several of them," she said and they went and told the Princesses.

Astrid
just before sunset

A man has appeared in front of where we are. He has some guards with him, I suppose to provide support. They do not look very happy in their role and the crowd do not look pleased with them. It is time to again practice the look that I receive from Mũsã as he tries to get in to see the Theodora. He does not mention Rani.

He was an unctuous man and almost as soon as he opens his mouth Bianca is speaking quietly in Darkspeech. "I sense that he is not as he seems. He is a treacherous man and intends something very bad to happen to us." *What to do? Behind me are several of the other Mice waiting, but the Princesses are still inside.*

"And yet," the Bishop chimes in, speaking the same tongue, "to me he seems a good person, one who is perhaps too good, and I see that he wears several rings." *I know what we need to do now. They are not getting near the Princesses.*

Astrid now smiled the smile of a waiting cat at the man and then, moving her gaze around, spread the smile around his guards as she kept her silence for a little while. *Several are starting to shift from foot to foot nervously. That will do.* "You will not be seeing the Princess. You will be dealing with me and I see no reason to change what we are doing."

The unctuous man, who does not introduce himself, changes his tack and now wants us to enter the town and stay at the Calat. This message I will allow to be relayed. The Princesses sent a message back out to agree and this Astrid did. They paid the host of the caravanserai generously as if they had actually stayed the whole night and moved off on their saddles.

Bianca has already spread the word of what she and Christopher felt and I have the Mice all spread out to make it harder for any one spell to catch all of us. We will all keep both our weapons and our wands handy for treachery.

Astrid rode directly behind the man and his guard and a little over their heads. *Let us liven this up.* As they went ahead of her through the crowds she wove back and forward on the saddle and made little barking noises as if she were a dog herding sheep.

The crowd around them is getting the joke and they are laughing at it. The man at the front of the procession takes the point as well, but he just glares back at me. Every time he does I smile at him again and bark once more.

The guards leading us look increasingly sheepish and nervous about the whole affair. They may not realise it, but they are drawing together into a tighter clump. Some stare grimly ahead but others keep glancing around nervously or look shame-faced. Yet others glare out at the crowd's laughter and grip their weapons tighter.

Astrid

Now we have arrived at this Calat and the unctuous man is trying to direct the men in one direction and the women in another. Like getting us to give up our saddles and weapons, this is a total failure. The man is obviously very uncomfortable dealing with me. He had better get used to it. I will make no concession to him however.

Behind me I can hear Theodora, I have practice making her nervous and she is not letting her husband interfere and split us up. "A Princess just graciously waits and seems not to notice that anything is awry while their major-domo or their guard commander sorts these things out," Theodora said in Darkspeech. *She can be sensible sometimes.*

"We just sit here and pretend nothing is happening…now smile and wave at the nice people who want to see if we have two heads or are really just women who have entered their city with shamelessly displayed naked hair, and in your case a naked belly-button. You did that deliberately didn't you?"

In the end we are both going to be inflexible. Screw him. Leaving the man open mouthed and in mid-sentence, Astrid again wheeled them around and went to find a place to stay. *I have certain requirements.* She soon found a corner building, a storey taller than its neighbours and, like many others in the city, with a flat roof where the saddles could be put.

I like this place. It has only one entry point on the ground level and it has a top floor where we can all stay with a staircase that can be guarded. The top floor usually houses the host and his family, but a sufficiently generous purse for his inconvenience convinces him to hurriedly vacate with his family and move them below to a lower floor.

We will be sharing rooms and beds once again, but we are well and truly used to that by now. Having an easy place to defend is far more important than having plenty of rooms. This place almost qualifies as a small fortress, for a tavern. It even has lovely thick brick walls all covered in plaster that would be hard to bring down.

Basil

With our defence as the first thing in mind we get to set up for the night. Butterfly and her familiar come with me to visit the kitchens. I was just looking but Ia emphasises that we can check for poisons and any other contaminant in the food but, by leaving a few gold coins behind, also manages to imply that we can be generous if we are happy.

"Can you actually find out if food is poisonous?"

"Haven't I mentioned it? Either with a spell or another of my wands," she said, "but again I am not really powerful enough. My wand will only last a few days if we test every meal. I wish that my spells worked the same as the Princesses do. It would be good to be able to teach others the spells that I use."

"Maeve can also sniff poison," Ia continued. "Her nose is very good. It is one of the things you do with familiars, you teach them things and they can then tell you what they find. She can tell us if there is Waxbad, Mordorwyrhta, Wolfsbane, or several others. It is usually better though if people think that it is all being done with magic."

Chapter XLI

Ayesha
2nd Quinque

Stefan has taken charge of making the building secure, although I am checking his arrangements. He is still not used to people like me. He has set two guards up on the roof and another pair at the top of the stairs, where there is a door that we can close and lock at night.

During the night watches, Astrid's and my magic, as well as the bracelet that we got as ghanimah from Ta'if, will be passed around among those on watch, but during the day we will all be very visible.

Luckily there are no buildings too close to us that are of a similar or taller level. People can still shoot at our roof guards from below on the street or another building, but they will lack the advantage of height and our people will have cover. It is also a very long throw for a grapnel to the roof. You can climb the outside anyway, but it is far harder without a rope, especially since the walls are plastered.

They had just had a communal dinner in their largest room when there was a commotion at the head of the stairs. *Two men in bronze lamellar armour and equipped much as Hulagu are confronting Menas and Neon, who wear even more complete iron armour and also have the advantage of position.* "They tried to force their way up," said Menas.

"They should have had the brains to say who they have to protect." She turned to the men on the stairs: "Sulaym, Tũlũn, as-Salāmu 'Alaykum. Your Princess is below I take it?"

The men nod somewhat sheepishly in answer to my question. They are not used to having to ask permission. People generally realise that they have someone important who wants to go somewhere and just give way. This will not apply to Darkreach-trained kataphractoi though. They have their own Princess to protect.

"Then bring her up. My Princess is here as well and I am sure that they really do want to see each other." A woman soon appeared. *She has a hijab and veil but the unmistakeable eyes tell anyone of her descent. She and Theodora rush into each other's arms and begin exchanging the kisses and embraces of long-parted and fond relations. The ghazi can leave them alone. They can come into the room where we have just finished eating and be given food and kaf.*

"It has all been checked for poison. Your Princess is our responsibility while she is here. Now sit and let me introduce you to my husband and the rest and you can hear our stories. I suspect that you may be waiting here for quite a long while."

Ayesha
3rd Quinque

I was right about the length of this visit. Several of the Mice, those who have later watches, have already gone to sleep and it is well past midnight by the time the Princess has left.

Basil has already noted to me that, despite my training that is better than his in so many ways, there are other areas where a simple street guard is far better equipped than I am. He has found it straightforward, as the two men relaxed, to find out many things from them. He said that they were so easy to be put at ease.

They had expected our Mice to be very different to them and to be offered proper hospitality, and then to discover something as simple as several of the men having more than one wife, even if the wives are not very deferential to them, makes our men seem more than half way to being just like any other successful man that they know. We even have the same roles of protection.

Astrid

Before they leave, Miriam is introduced to the rest of us Mice, something that she is obviously uncomfortable with. She has been brought up a Princess and has married a Prince. Unlike Theodora who moved out into the larger world before she again became a Royal, she has simply moved from one Palace to another. The poor girl is shocked enough at the details of her cousin's marriage and how she came by a child.

You can see on her face that to be introduced to one of the Antikataskopeía, as if he is her equal, along with his wives the child-witch and the barbarian Insakharl and even our pet animal is almost too much for her sensibilities. I can see this discomfort so clearly. I think that the right thing to do is to add to it a little with a few cheery words. "The last time I had a chat with your Granther he looked well.

"The marriage suits him. Do you have anything that you want me to tell him personally when I see him for kaf next? He keeps asking after my family. It will be good to tell him of how some of his own is." *The Princess' eyes are almost bulging out at my seemingly offhand question. Her guards are even giving me an odd look as if they are suddenly re-evaluating me.*

I have a feeling that, like their Princess, and despite knowing Ayesha themselves, they do not take the idea of a female warrior very seriously and so had discounted me and what I can do. It is also perhaps quite likely that they can more easily accept a woman with political connections than one who is a warrior.

Theodora has not seen her cousin's face and unintentionally makes her reaction worse. She reached out and laid her hand on her cousin's arm to draw her attention and said: "Astrid actually arranged his marriage for him behind all of our backs. She even seems to see him far more than I do, not that she or Basil talk much about it, but Palace servants do talk when you ask them in the right way.

"Granther even sent all three of them wedding presents, which I didn't get when I got married, and Astrid always kisses him farewell when she says goodbye to him and when we leave Ardlark. I would never be able to do that and I think that he likes me." *The eyes of the guards and of their charge all seem to bulge a little more at this additional piece of news. Somehow I don't think that Miriam has ever kissed her ancestor.*

Basil

Once the Princess is gone I take my wives and get to go and see the Princesses. "Her guards are very uneasy and nervous. For the last few weeks there has been something very wrong with the Caliph. He went to visit Misr al-Mar and has not been the same since then. He does not even visit the harem and spends most of his time in the mosque or with a few others."

"They did not like having the Princess coming alone to visit with us here.

Bianca says that the Princess' guards intend no treachery to us, but I think that they are uneasy over our presence. Not from us being a threat, they don't see us like that now, but they expect something to happen to us and did not want her to be here when it happens. I could get nothing else from them. I have alerted everyone and I expect us to be attacked."

That surprised them after the visit went so well. "I expect that it will probably even be tonight before we can see anyone else. I will not go to sleep at night while we are here and all of the doors between rooms need to stay open. I will be checking all the rooms continually. Astrid and Ia will stay up with me as well. We will sleep during the day."

"You are truly concerned?" Theodora asked.

How do I put this? "I think that we have walked into a lion's den and are lying down to sleep in it. What I hope is that the lions will discover they are attacking a nest of pack-hunters. I am sure that neither you nor I have ever seen lions win against pack-hunters in the arena no matter how great an advantage of numbers they have."

Theodora

He has a look of concern on his face. It was so good to see Miriam again that I was starting to relax. She has gotten a little stuffier here, but mostly it was a fun visit and she did not mention any problems. Still if Basil is as worried as he looks, there must be something in it. It is his job to know about such things after all.

Theodora nodded and gave Ia two air wands. *They are my most powerful. Ia will use them only if they are needed. I will not trust Astrid with one of them. Who knows if the woman will use one when she is bored just to see what it does, or even as a practical joke?* ÒTonight at least we shall all sleep with our weapons handy then."

Chapter XLII

Ariadne
3rd Quinque

According to the time device that I now have on my wrist, the attack is coming at a fraction after four in the morning. I know that because I am just looking up from checking it. Luckily I have the explosive hand thing in my hand and am idly amusing myself by pointing it at things when I whirl around to point at the air and realise that I am actually pointing it at someone climbing over the wall to the roof from the adjacent lower building.

They are dressed in dark clothes and only their head and upper torso are visible coming over the waist-high edge. I pull the lever bit at the back and quickly push the other little lever with my right hand. It is a pity that it seems to have been made for a right-handed person. It would have been far easier to just use my thumb to do that. Now I point and pull the trigger.

There was an explosion and a flash of light in the night and she nearly dropped the thing. *The person has disappeared.* She moved towards the edge, intending to look over but an arrow skimmed her shoulder and she dropped to where she could not be seen. She looked back at the others on the roof. *Ia, Basil and Astrid have been circulating between the roof and the floor below.*

Ia is currently up top with me. Bianca is also here and Asticus is the fully armoured man. He is already crouched low and is moving over to where a grapple can now be seen. I heard something. Ariadne quickly turned around. *There is another grapnel on the other side facing a building and a man is already half way over it.* She pulled the trigger again.

It missed and she quickly pulled it a second time. *That hit, along with a knife from Bianca but this man has fallen inside onto the roof and is reaching for something on his belt. No you don't.* She ran over and put the thing to his head and pulled the trigger again. *That may have covered me in gore, but he certainly isn't moving again.* She pulled out a dagger with her right hand and clumsily sawed at the rope.

Arrows started to come in and, as she sawed, she could feel the rope. *There is someone else on it.* She leant over and saw a person two paces below. An arrow missed her. She pulled the trigger and, at that range could scarce miss. With a prolonged scream he fell to the ground to lie there in a broken-looking shape. *With his weight off the rope I can abandon cutting it and just pull it up.* She had just gotten it up when an arrow hit her and exploded. In agony she fell to the ground.

Ia

Mother! What is that noise. She turned and saw Ariadne with her new toy and watched her with a wand ready in her hand. *Ariadne has eliminated first one climber and then, apparently, another two before falling to the ground with a gaping wound to the shoulder. This I can deal with.* She leapt across and started pouring potion into Ariadne's mouth. *Now, for good measure, some goes into her wound. It was a deep one.*

Behind her she heard Bianca. "I have the other rope," she said.

Asticus then spoke up. "You will have to hold the roof. I am going to try to get into the sky to take the archers from above. We need to use our advantage, we own the air." *He is already on his saddle. It now leaps up into the sky as arrows try to reach after it. His fast move has ensured that he has surprise on his side. He needs it. Even in the dark I can see that the sky is thick with arrows.*

As he flies he is weaving around and this makes him hard to hit. Even in the low light of the night arrows can be seen arching up and reaching for him. Bianca and I have to hold the roof? Bianca is already stringing a bow herself. Ia put Ariadne's metal thing near her for when she had recovered enough to use it and backed herself into the corner that projected most into the street. *I have two wands out and ready. Here I can see if someone is trying to climb up any of the walls or put up another rope.*

Basil

There is an explosion from above me and a cry from the passage. He was about to go to see what was up when he heard a noise as someone fell and he quickly ran into the Princess's room. *It faces the street. They are the only ones with a room of their own, if you don't count Nikephorus sleeping at their feet.*

Their servant has obviously woken or been awake and has tried to do something, but he is down and clutching his chest and coughing as a man stands over him looking around. Basil already had his short swords out and quickly flew into the attack.

The man facing me has a kindjal in each hand. It will be a nearly even fight in terms of weapons then. It only remains for us to see who has the most skill. At least I have dark behind me and he has the window.

Aziz

What is that? Aziz had just used the night pot and was about to lie down again when he saw the shutter beside him beginning to open quietly from the outside. With a smile he leant down and with one hand picked up his scimitar, while with his other he shook his wife hard.

He straightened without waiting to see if she woke up, grabbing his shield as he did so. *Lucky I listened to what Basil said and have worn my mail when I went to my rest on the floor.*

A man has appeared in the window and is peering into the gloom of the room. *A heavy scimitar is certainly not meant to thrust, but it can be clumsily used for that purpose if that is all you have.* He stepped forward and put his strength behind the blow. *It has gone into the man's throat at the base of the neck.* With a gurgling scream he fell back out into the street.

Aziz stepped forward and an arrow exploded on his shield. Quickly he stepped back into the room as the sounds of combat erupted from behind and above him.

Astrid

What is he indicating? Astrid was near the door that led down the stairs to the rooms below. She had been talking quietly with Hulagu and Stefan when Stefan held his finger to his lips and pointed at the door. She looked down. *Slowly the handle is turning.* Astrid waved the other two back and stepped to the opening side, making herself as flat against the wall as was possible and started a quick silent prayer to Saint Kessog.

I knew that I took the anti-magic thing from Maarshtrin for a reason. This will be fun. I will stay visible. It will be more intimidating that way and my friends are less likely to hit me by mistake. As the door slowly opened she nodded to Stefan, on the other side of the door. *He has taken my meaning. He reaches out and grasps the handle from his side.*

Quickly he pulled the door open. *A man is still holding on to the handle on the other side and he falls forward into the room. As he does Hulagu brings his mace down on his head and leaves it a bloody ruin.* Astrid, without looking, thrust down the stairs as she came around the corner to see what was there. *From the resistance and the scream there was at least one more person close behind the door opener.*

She kicked out as she reached the top of the stairs and a body fell back off the point of her weapon. *Above me on the roof there is the noise of that cursed thing that Maarshtrin used on me. I am glad that I am not meeting it here.*

Now to intimidate them with good cheer. "Greetings" *There are several men facing me on the stairs. Their faces are in shock as they support the man who is already dying in their arms, his chest gaping open as blood spurts out to cover them.* "I hope that your god loves you, because you are now about to meet him." *The stairs are full of a close-packed group of men who were expecting surprise to be on their side.*

Despite the unwieldiness of my weapon in such close proximity, these men are even more hampered and they begin to die. All are only wearing leather and they carry parrying weapons, not shields. Whatever magic of protection they wear is inadequate to counter my weapon or my enhanced strength and speed.

I aim to just use the point to thrust deep in chest or groin, or to remove heads and limbs with a quick flick of my wrists. As they fall, often screaming, I kick them back onto their friends and they generally help clear them back and then I kill them as their hands are engaged.

Once she had to start carefully stepping over their bodies she yelled to Stefan and Hulagu to drag them clear so that she did not trip. Some feet went up the stairs from in front of me, so it looks like the two men are doing that. She came around a corner of the stairs and a man...*he looks like a mage*...pointed a wand at her and a fireball erupted from it.

I feel cold, even though I have just been hit squarely in the chest by the ball of flame. I feel surprised. He looks surprised. We are all surprised. He is not a fast learner and keeps firing at me. I can safely ignore the idiot. She moved into the passage of the next floor and killed the man in front of her. Out of the corner of her eye she saw Stefan kill a man on the other side.

Now for the mage. He is still using his wand uselessly as flames flickered over her and disappeared, but he is also clumsily starting to draw out a sword. He cannot retreat, although he is trying to. More men are coming up the other stairs from below and this blocks his retreat. Down the corridor a door opens and a head pokes out. The person there sees what is happening and the door quickly closes again.

She dispatched the mage. *He will almost certainly be back, but I can leave him for one of the men behind me to kill him again.* She heard that happen noisily as she took on the next two. *They are not as good as Ayesha is, although they are equipped in the same way.*

Perhaps this is just not their sort of fight, but I am killing them easily. Now down the next set of stairs. They are starting to thin out in their numbers. I only had to kill three to go down that flight, even if I left the stairs a little slippery afterwards with their blood. Suddenly I am down on the open ground floor.

Rani

Something is happening. Rani came awake. *My wife made me sleep fully dressed tonight. It is uncomfortable, but now I am glad of it. Basil is fighting someone in the middle of the room and another man is already in the room through the open window and looking for an opening. I have been keeping a wand strapped to my arm in the same fashion as Bianca and Ayesha always carry knives, even at night. It is time for me to use it.*

The man standing near the window erupted in fire and began screaming and running around trying to put himself out as the blast of fire set alight to anything flammable on him. *Already the smell of his roasting flesh and the sound of his screams fills the room. I don't want to fire at him again lest I set the room on fire.*

Luckily her wife now had a wand out and the man flew back against the wall and slid down it. *The flames on him, like his cries, are snuffed out and extinguished by the violence of the air blast. There is noise elsewhere outside the room but things are busy enough here.* Rani looked at the window. *Another man is outlined there against the sky.*

She fired at him and his head and shoulders were wreathed in flame as his face took the bolt in its centre. *He screams all of the way to the ground.* An arrow came through the window and exploded against the far wall. She saw Theodora edge around the fight towards Nikephorus and start giving him a potion. Basil took his man and suddenly their room went quiet.

Nothing more to see here, and if anything happens, those two will look after it. She went to see what was happening in the other rooms.

Asticus

It is easier being in a formation charge. Asticus soared into the sky drawing his bow from its quiver. Seeing that he was on watch it was already strung. Between his dodging through the sky, the shield amulet and his armour he was only hit by a couple of the volley of arrows aimed at him…*but being in a solid wall of riders is not as much fun.*

One of them exploded, but I am lucky. My armour will need a lot of work as lames now hang loose on my chest and the aketon I wear over it is in smouldering tatters, but I seem to be fine. He looked below. *There seem to be archers on roofs in all four directions.* He chose a direction at random as he rose and started duelling with the archers there.

They have the advantage of numbers, but I am a moving target and they are getting further and further below me. It took all of my explosive arrows, but I have cleared that roof as arrows, now at the top of their arc from the other roofs, fall around me without reaching my height. Some explode when they hit roofs below. What to do next? He looked around.

Much of Dimashq is lit at night by magic, but that is mainly near their citadel and the mosques and we seem to be in one of the darker patches. Still there is more than enough light to see the movement of men on roofs. I only have one molotail and that roof has a lot of people on it. The men on that roof didn't see the attack coming and the night sky of Dimashq suddenly erupted in flame and rang with the screams of human torches.

The parapet of the roof edge is acting nicely as a well to contain the fire within it. Flames lick around the roof as anything flammable there catches. First one man, and then others, throw themselves off and fall to the ground as flaming comets to lie limp in their own private funeral pyre. Very effective. I can see why the Engineers like them.

Two more can be seen still on the roof. They are rolling around in their bath of flame, their attempts to extinguish the flame ultimately futile as they scream their life away. Undoubtedly, even as they scream they are breathing in flame and perhaps even the hugron pir itself. This is not a good death for them.

Something is rising from the roof where we are staying. He went to fire and stopped. *Others among the Mice have now made it up to the roof and they are starting to dive onto saddles and come up into the sky.* He moved over and began yelling instructions to them. As they rose up to meet him be began pointing out where the targets were and one by one their attackers died.

Stefan

I just get to come down the stairs behind Astrid. I am taking no part in the actual combat, I just pull bodies away. I have even sheathed my sword, although I still have my shield, the better to clear the stairs. These are almost slippery with the blood that is on them. Who would have believed that so much could be shed in such a small area?

I have sparred against Astrid since our last visit to Ardlark, but she has obviously been holding something back. She is far deadlier now than either of those Insak-div were. I might be good, but to face her in serious single combat now is to die. Her opponents are brave but stupid to keep pressing forward as they do. They must realise just how many people she has killed in order to get to them.

Astrid

Now at the bottom of the stairs there is a whole room full of armed men. They are edging around to better place themselves. Time to un-nerve them a little with more cheerful talk.

Again she felt a mage's spell wash over her as a lightning bolt grounded itself. She ignored the spell as if it had not happened. "If any of you want to surrender now, just throw down your weapons and lie flat on the floor with your arms out. The rest of you I am going to kill one by one."

She heard movement on the stairs behind her and a yell. *This mage is smarter than the first in trying for another target*. Another lightning bolt sizzled past her. *It is time for me to move*. She started in the mage's direction and felt people try and get around behind her but the noise indicated that she had back-up there.

My enemy are dying in front of me and suddenly some are trying to get out of the door. One escaped outside to be struck down and then, after a few more have died, the mage flees. She could see outside past the man she was killing. *The mage only made it out for a few paces and then suddenly he fell very flat and didn't move again.*

Ariadne

There are some explosions below. Ariadne and Ia looked over the edge. *I still feel weak, but it is my right shoulder that was hit and so I can use my left hand with its weapon satisfactorily. My right shoulder can keep healing under the influence of strong potions. It seems that Asticus has drawn all of the fire from the other roofs. Good.*

Ariadne ran around to the different sides and looked down. She fired another explosion and stab of light at a man climbing into a window and another two at a man below him on the ground. *The man on the rope has dropped and the other has fallen clutching his shoulder.*

Ia has used a silent wand at another building. Four men were standing there firing into the sky at Asticus. The two toward the rear fell from a strong air bolt and the others do not seem to notice even though the parapet of the building has partly crumbled behind them.

Behind us people have started to come out onto the roof and, quickly beginning to string their bows, making ready to head into the air. The two went back to look down again and suddenly a man came out of the doorway below and began running. *Ia now has a wand in each hand and he falls over from one of them.*

Ariadne fired. *This thing doesn't seem to be very accurate at even that small a range, but the man lies stationary and so I am able to hit him. He drops, but again starts to crawl away. It takes another four explosions to stop him, only two of which seem to hit.*

After the last explosion the thing locked itself open with a click and Ariadne looked at it for a bit before she realised that it would not fire again. She pushed the other button on it and the metal box fell out. She carefully put it away and removed another one that was full from her pouch and put it in the handle, releasing the top part.

I really need to practice this. Now the whole thing really smells like the Megas Fabrika. I am sure that I reek of al-kīmiyā as well. It is such a familiar smell and it reminds me so much of home. She smiled. *I am getting homesick in the middle of a battle. Who would have expected that to happen?*

I am fairly certain now how it all works, even if I lacked the machines to make one myself. I wonder if I can get together with a mage and make something similar that is suited to me, perhaps we could turn this one around to be left-handed, even a simpler version could perhaps be useful. Wait until we get home.

Ia has fired the other wand at another man who ran out from below. He lies limp and broken-looking and, well, flat against the cobbles. Around the streets heads are appearing and disappearing as people wake up and briefly look outside to decide that they want no part of what is happening.

To the south, a few houses away, a roof explodes in fire. Someone has used a molotail on the people on it as the Mice on our roof begin to find their way into the sky, bows in hand. Screams fill the night sky. None seem to be from our people and that is good. I can see people jumping off the roof as flaming balls. Four storeys will not be good for them, but then they are on fire anyway.

Astrid

It is done and all over for the moment. Astrid stood and looked around. *I can see Stefan on his feet with a cut on his forehead and with Hulagu, looking more than a trifle singed from a bolt, beside him. Behind them are the cousins, both are just in trousers with bare and bloody feet and bare breasts. They fought just as they had slept in their furs. Each is wielding a spear.*

I thought that my last couple of men were a bit distracted as I killed them. Those four breasts bouncing around are enough to distract anyone. It is time to look over the bodies and work out who could, or perhaps even should, be saved. Now I need Ayesha and Christopher and Aziz and my sister-wife.

Now that the energy of battle is wearing off I can feel blood trickling down my left arm. Looking down she saw that her armour again gaped open. *It has served its job once again. I think that I need a new set though.* She flexed her arm. *The wound is messy looking but it hardly hampers me. I can still fight if it is needed.*

Ayesha

I have checked all of the areas upstairs. That is where danger still lies if any are still alive there. It is what ghazi are best at, attacking from surprise. I know. I am one of them. I recognise several that lie near the head of the stairs. Basil has managed to kill the head of the Palace Guard in his room. It seems that Basil has come a very long way since we first attacked Mousehole.

That man used to test all new ghazi and, to the best of my knowledge, had never had a practice blade laid on him. Nikephorus is still slumped against a wall holding his healing chest.

"This certainly does not happen in the Palace in Ardlark." *He is complaining as he tries to feebly beat off the ministrations of his Princess. Whether he is talking about his wounds or being served by his Princess is quite unclear. I think that I would bet on it being the second as being more important to him.*

Ayesha went down the stairs and pushed past the cousins towards her husband. *He has been hit by magic, but is cheerful about it.* After making sure that he had drunk a potion for his wounds she started to move around looking at the faces. *I am again seeing many that I know.* "They are all from the Caliph's guard."

She moved over to where Christopher was tending an older man, "… except him. That is the Caliph. Ia…" she quickly moved over to the stairs. "Ia, bring your bauble. You still have work." *I cannot believe that the Caliph has been corrupted. All of my life I have been brought up to revere and obey the man. There has to be an explanation and we cannot let him just die.*

We will not get out of the Caliphate alive, despite all of our strength, if he dies here. We have to assume that he is enchanted in some way. She searched him for weapons and other items and then Ia arrived and between them they propped up the older man and Ia began to start swinging the little crystal bead backwards and forwards as she droned on.

Rani

Lastly, there is the roof. I first checked downstairs and all I had to do was reassure the frightened people on the floor below, including our host and his family. Before I went down below I ordered people up into the air and then heard explosions from outside. Now I want to see what is actually happening up there.

Ariadne is now alone there on the roof and stinks like my old alchemy room with an acrid smell. She is missing much of the cloth and leather that used to cover her right shoulder and breast. Bare and new skin shows there. Her normal colouration makes it hard to see, in this light, how much damage she has sustained. In her left hand she holds one of the explosive things.

She has spun around to point it at me. Suddenly I feel weak at the knees. I saw what it did to Astrid, but thankfully she quickly recognises me and moves her aiming point away along with where her eyes are looking.

"We have won," Ariadne said waving her free right hand to where riders were coming back. *She points into the sky.* "Bianca is keeping some in the air just in case." *Already some are landing and comparing notes. A little way away a rooftop still burns, but there are people on it now trying to put it out.*

Rani nearly fell over. *Something has just slipped away under my feet with a clinking metallic sound.* She looked down. *There are all of these little hollow brass tubes*. She stooped to pick one up. *It was very warm and it smells of that smell. They must be from the hand bow thing that explodes.*

"I may not be much good in close combat," said Ariadne, "but using this I killed at least three." She waved the metal thing in the air. "It needed a name. I am going to call this thing a Thunderer. It makes a noise like thunder and it strikes out just like lightning."

Rani looked over the edge. *Except for a few bodies, two still burning and adding their unique stench to the air, there is nothing below, but it will not be long before the guard come from the wall to see what has happened in the middle of their city. It might be best not to have Astrid deal with them. She might take that idea a little literally now that she is all excited.*

"You have done well," said Rani. "Stay on guard, particularly look for anything that flies, that is not ours that is, while I go and check on the rest."

Chapter XLIII

Rani

We are efficient at this. Bodies have already been brought from other buildings and dragged inside. Atã has even left money with the people whose roof had caught fire and he says that they seemed more than happy with the amount that they were given. Four men lie tied up and secured in a row for later questioning and the Caliph is already answering questions.

"Someone has already hypnotised him," said Ia. "That has made what I have done easier. I am not sure what you want me to do with him now. I don't think that he will kill himself if we question him, but I am also not sure what will happen if I make him go back to being himself."

She seems uncertain. "Sometimes," she continued, "people just keep doing what they have been told, even if they would not have done so before." *She looks at us and we look at each other. I wish there was an instruction book for this sort of thing.*

Bianca called down from the roof that someone was coming and they looked out. *A group of men are coming towards our building in a block ready for trouble. They have their weapons out and their shields in hand and in front of them. Before Rani could say anything Astrid had already slipped outside.*

It is unlikely to ever happen, but Ganesh please grant her at least a little wisdom. She is waving her weapon around in one hand and looks extremely dishevelled and bloody. This time some of the blood even looks as if it may be hers.

Astrid

I can go back to having fun. I recognise this lot. Astrid strode into the square outside. "You…" she waved her bardiche in the direction of the one leading them. *Heads are beginning to appear from windows and doors now that the noise of battle has died down and I am talking to the spectators as much as I am to the man I am addressing and his other guards.*

"…the one from the gate who didn't dare give his name. What sort of town do you have that people can be attacked in their beds? We might have been badly hurt. As it is we have had to kill over fifty of your people and have had our sleep disrupted and some of us got slightly hurt." *I don't think that I was expected. They are confused. They have just stopped.*

They are still at the other side of the small plaza with their shields up as if waiting to be attacked and the others of the group have drawn away a little from their leader, the man I addressed. He now stands with a good pace of clear ground between him and his men to his left. The men beside him are looking at him rather at me.

She continued. "Come on. Speak up. I am waiting for your explanation. It is your job to keep order isn't it?"

"What do you mean fifty people attacked you?" said the guard leader. *He is trying to sound brave.* "If fifty of us had attacked you kãfirũn you would have died. You must have assaulted some innocent people and set fire to buildings. We would have been better keeping you out." *I have to make sure that I don't give them an excuse to attack us. I need to stay clear and just talk.*

"You can come and look if you want." *I need to be loud. Again I am addressing the wider audience that are in the surrounding buildings. They will spread the news to the rest of the city.* "You can ask the people who watched out of their windows as to who attacked who. But you need to prepare yourself for a shock. These attackers were ghazi,"

Now I wait and let that sink in. I can hear murmurs from the windows. "…and we killed almost all of them, and at least two mages, and now we have their leader captive. The question is, having attacked us after letting us in; does that mean that he has breached ikraam? I am told that the concept is important to you, even if I cannot see it in operation.

"If he has so breached something important, do we kill the leader out of hand or do we let him live and just hit him on the head with a shoe?" *Now people are coming out of the buildings and the square is filling.* She looked around at the gathering people. "Any of you can come inside and see that he is still alive if you want."

"Why would I want to see a bandit?" asked the guard.

Now to sound puzzled. This bit is very important. "Did I say he was a bandit? Oh dear no. Who else could lead fifty ghazis to battle in the middle of the city of Dimashq? We have the Caliph as a captive inside after he tried to kill us while we slept. We think that the seytani that we have told people about outside the Gate have taken over his mind."

She grinned widely as the whole square drew a collective breath. *With that many people listening in to what I say the indrawn breath is very clearly audible. Except for the gap between the guard and me, the square is now nearly full with onlookers.* "You might like to send for his senior son and the Mullahs."

Behind her Astrid heard Ayesha's voice: "you will not find either him or his second brother. Send instead for Miriam and her husband Hassan. He has become the heir through the madness and possession of their father."

Rani

I have to admit being surprised at how well Astrid handled that. Now Fajr has come and gone and it is the middle of the morning. The bodies have gone, the floors are being scrubbed around us and we have as our guest Hassan ibn Abdul, the now senior son, as well as Batrīq al-Akk, the Sheik of Dimashq and as many other dignitaries, secular and religious as can fit in the room.

The Caliph is lying on a mattress, but he is dying. That much is clear to everyone. The wounds Astrid gave him have been healed and prayed over, but all agree that he is a broken man grieving over what he has done under the influence of another. According to Ayesha he fears that he is now mufsidūn, one who wages a false holy war.

His last words are being written down as he speaks. He has, for the last few months, believed that the events in the Brotherhood and the fight that the Mice have undertaken presaged the turmoil before the Day of Judgement. For advice he had gone to see the Amīr al-Ghazi, the commander of the ghazis, about this. He came back as if he was another man.

Not only was he convinced that the man, Mughīra abd Allah, is al-Mahdi, the final prophet who has to be obeyed, but his entire person changed. He says that he ordered the death of two of his sons when he told them of his plans and they disagreed with him and threatened to tell the Ayatollah and others. Al-Amīr al-Ghazi had told him that we are a threat and had to be eliminated and we are sure that Maarshtrin is behind that.

Once we were dead al-Mahdi was to be proclaimed and a new al-jihad al-Akbar, the great struggle, proclaimed. Archangels will be on their side to sweep all before them. That explains Maashtrin's weapons of light.

We have heard this all before. It is just what we heard from the captives from the Brotherhood, but for the Ayatollah, Bishal ibn Mũsa, and the others who are listening in to his words it is all new and they are horrified at what he says. They had better get used to it. Wait until they hear what we have to say.

Batrĩq al-Akk has the support of the son Hassan and they both wish to swoop upon Misr al-Mãr with all of their forces and to level it. Now horror appears on many faces for a different reason. Not only is it a holy site, in fact their most holy, but so much of the Caliphate and its history is stored in the libraries and other rooms of the keep as it is the most secure place that they have. They could even lose objects and writing that have managed to survive through the Burning from earlier times.

Thankfully Imam Iyãd insists on being listened to. He has pointed out that we have perhaps three days before word of what has transpires gets back to the Amĩr al-Ghazi, unless someone leaves on a carpet. Runners were quickly despatched with guards and every flying carpet in the town is secured. The unctuous man is taken trying to get hold of one. He did not wait to be questioned, but killed himself immediately once he realised that he had failed.

The Imam points out that, to assemble enough people to take the citadel would take weeks and that in that time everything will be destroyed and their enemy successfully fled. They all agree with that. He next proposes that they listen to the women who have been conducting the fight against the Adversaries up to that time. We have sat quietly up until now and the looks my wife and I get show why that was a good idea.

He argues hard for us. It is getting harder and harder to stay silent over the idea that the assembled men will not listen to what we say simply because we are women. Astrid also looks nearly ready to explode. Ia and Basil are taking her out to calm her down. In the end common sense prevails, and with food and kaf being brought to everyone, the tale of the Mice up to that time is told to the men.

It takes the rest of the day and several of the Mice leave in shifts to get sleep and otherwise to relax for a time after the fight. After it is finished, and all brought up to date with the latest addition of the events in Ta'if and the night before, Ayesha can hardly speak. Christopher has already made her drink mild healing potions twice for her throat.

We still have not said anything. The other listeners sit in silence for some time after she has finished. Each is sunk deep in his own thoughts. It is the Ayatollah who finally breaks the silence. His first words are; I am sure, revolutionary in their own way. "What do you recommend that we do?" he asks us as we sit to the side in chairs holding hands.

I have been thinking about that exact question all day. Using what Ayesha has told me about the place as a basis of action, if we are to be allowed an open hand, I might have an answer to the question. It is bold and audacious and dangerous, but it should work despite the ten times four hands of ghazi that will be there in the Fortress. She looked at the men in front of her.

The question is whether, despite the evidence that is still being cleared up around them, these men will consent to allow their fate to be decided by a group largely made up of women and not only that, but women who would be taking on a fight in their holiest place. I need to be at my most convincing when I start to speak.

Chapter XLIV

Theodora
4th Quinque, the Feast Day of Saint Mary Magdalene

Now we set out. All of our armour is repaired, except for Astrid's. Hers had to be completely replaced as it would have taken far too long to repair it fully. However, apparently she now has a better set from the Caliph's armouries. How long it will last in that condition is another question. Most people tear shirts. All of our clothing is washed and sewn up and we are all well fed and rested.

I have taken ample time with my cousin and seen her son, who I do not think to be as handsome as my beautiful daughter although, in the long run, he is a potential husband for her or even for Fear, even if he is far younger than her. We have all of our saddles at this stage and even carry some extras from among the Darkreach people, including Imam Iyãd.

Behind us come a column with the rest of the Orphanos and a mufriza of Caliphate men. They have many remounts with them and will ride hard to take over Misr al-Mãr from the Mice if it is freed. More men will be coming forward on carpets, not enough to take the place if the first assault fails, but enough to help hold it for a while from another assault.

We will spend the rest of the day, and the beginning of the night, at Bab al-Abwãb resting further. Later that night we will fly on, leaving some of our people behind to firstly guard some of the saddles. Later we will start shuffling them forward.

Theodora

5th Quinque, the Feast Day of Saint Thomas

It is a very serious group of people that wake from slumber to eat, pray and then, for those who could, go back to sleep again. The people of the village were concerned about the unexpected presence of giant cats for some time before those of the Mice who are awake reassure them with smiles on their faces.

Now that we are all awake and setting out, most of the saddles are carrying double with those among the Mice that can abseil being passengers on another's saddle. Thord, Ayesha, Ariadne, Aziz, Verily and Krukurb will be the second wave of our assault and ride with those who will stay in the air to give cover with their arrows. Most of the Mice are to stay hidden in a gully that leads up behind to the great keep.

We will stay concealed there until all of the sentries are dispatched. It is, apparently, little regarded by the defenders as an approach, except during training exercises. As a way in it is very exposed and there is also a hard climb out of it, even for an experienced climber. As well, one of the sentries looks down into its bare walls for most of his round.

He will be the first to die and, after that, the back door will, hopefully, be wide open. All that we have to do then is to keep our element of surprise through the entire attack, which, I admit, will be a military miracle of the first water. Hopefully the magic of the Horse statue will help a little with this, but we will try and avoid relying on it.

At least, looking at the plans of this place that I have seen, I think that my husband has worked out a good plan that should work, given that we get that element of surprise. We only really need a little bit of luck.

Ayesha

My husband and I have the two concealing devices with us and we are the first part of the attack. Hulagu flies the saddle. He has my device, while I have Astrid's. That means I can whisper directions in his ear. She looked down from where they were flying in the sky above the keep. *Al-Ḥamdu Lillāh, the guards are where they are supposed to be.*

One walks around the inner keep and the Courtyard of the Qabbala with its stone covered in a cloth intricately embroidered with āyāt. This backs onto the ravine and is regarded as the quietest and safest watch post. Two more men walk on either side of the outer keep that contains the mosque and the Prophet's Well. Their paths nearly meet at the main gatehouse.

The last guard has a position in one of the minarets of the mosque. His task is to look into the distance at people approaching across the plateau or coming up the road that leads from Yarmũk. If he has been alert he had a small chance of seeing us as we all flew in from Bab al-Abwãb, but we tried to minimise that. We stayed close to the mountainside and, as soon as we could, used the height of the plateau to keep below his line of sight, once we were closer.

Looking at him now, he shows no sign of having glimpsed us. Once again, our saddles have made obsolete the classic defences of the Land. Normally it would have been impossible to move that far on land without being seen. The sentries are changed every two hours to keep them fresh and I now have the wrist-band that tells time so that I can strike soon after change.

The first sentry is easy to kill. The man is even standing for a while with his back to the ravine on one of the corner towers where he cannot be seen from the minaret as he looks over the entire courtyard. Hulagu landed and Ayesha dismounted. Her victim started to move away from her. She slid behind him and covered his mouth hard with one hand while, with the other, she drew a blade across his throat to kill him, near severing his neck.

Despite his struggles Ayesha kept hold of him, to prevent noise, as he died. She then threw the body into the ravine, removed the ring of concealment and waved down into the darkness. *They can start to move up now.* Putting the ring back on, she then started feeling for the saddle.

Hulagu kept an eye on the man in the minaret and only landed to take their next target when the man there went out of sight. *We have to be quick here. My target is only a young and beardless lad, obviously a new trainee, who is hardly able to put up a struggle as he dies. When next the man in the minaret came round his small circuit he does not even glance across to where the young man should have been.*

I know this next one and he is far more experienced than the other two were. He will be much harder for me to take. She whispered her instructions to her husband and he gripped her leg to acknowledge them before landing and letting her dismount. As the guard moved towards the gatehouse she followed behind.

His second set of senses must be hard at work. He turned once with a puzzled expression and gave a long look at the seemingly vacant wall walk. *Even with Terror and Panic giving almost their lowest light of the month, there is enough light for him to clearly see that nothing moves behind him and there are no shadows that should not be there.*

He waves at the guard in the minaret, who is watching him, and then makes an exaggerated shrug at him before continuing on his path. He will only be out of sight of the minaret for two hands of paces, so I follow close behind and strike. Again she covered his mouth, but this time, as he was stronger than her, she plunged the dagger into his brain from under his chin. *It might be a little noisier, but it is also a lot quicker.*

We now have to move very fast. The man in the minaret is probably already suspicious. She ran back and, feeling for where it was, she jumped on her husband's saddle and they took off. *There is no room for us to land now, but my husband has his lasso ready with one end attached to his saddle with a half hitch and he is ready to keep it tight once it is used. Inshallah, this will work.*

Although the plainsmen mainly used their lassoes for stock, they were also readily usable on people and Hulagu proved this to be the case as he dropped one end around the man's neck and took off so quickly that it tightened and the man began choking as they lifted without him being able to make much more that a quickly-muted sound.

The saddle is not meant to carry this much weight and goes down slowly as we fly. The man is struggling to free himself and, once we are over the ravine I aid him by releasing the rope from its restraints on the saddle. We can recover the rope later. With a strangled and much muted sound from his crushed throat the sentry fell into the chasm to his death and the freed saddle again leapt up into the sky.

It is now time to gather the people for the next wave of the attack. We remove our concealing magic so that the others, concealed and waiting as they are, can see that we have succeeded in our first tasks and that they can now move into place and play their part.

Theodora

Now I land on top of the gate to the inner courtyard with Basil. The secret of this whole attack is to be as quiet and stealthy as we can. We do not want to fight anyone if we can help it. However we do want to take as many of the garrison and students out of action as we can before anyone can realise that an attack is even happening.

Once I am set up I will cast the strongest sleep spell that I can. With the blessing of Saint Michael, it should send most of the junior ghazi and priests into a deep and enchanted slumber for enough time for us to accomplish what we have to do.

Casting an enchantment like this will mean that I will be able to cast nothing else all night. If it means that there are a few filled hands of swords, or even of junior priests, and of servants, at the very start who no-one will have to actually fight, it will make our life a lot easier and less risky. The more people we have to fight, the greater the chance there is that someone will get hurt and hurt badly. It only takes one thrust.

Like all of the mages and priests who are involved in the attack I have a supply of Rest Potion with me in case I need to refresh my mana, but we all hope that it will not be needed. She set up the cloth with her pattern on it and began to recite the spell that she had adapted for the purpose. *This will take a while to say and I must not be disturbed.*

If anything goes wrong Basil is here on the roof to protect me. Already he has his shortswords out and has prowled around the roof checking its access before settling quietly near the rooftop approach from the room beneath. Anyone coming out through that will most likely die as they climb up the ladder and before they even know that he is there.

Astrid

I now land in the courtyard with Imam Iyād. Butterfly is beside me with Ikrimah and with Maeve. Once Theodora signals it is time to do so, it will be our responsibility to take care of an entire barracks. I may have made light of this earlier when I was asked if it was possible, but now I can admit quietly and privately to myself that I am a little nervous about this.

Saint Kessog, there are candles coming to you...lots of them. Apparently the bottom floor is where most of the junior ghazi, the trainees and those who are simply guards and the lower ranks, live. They should hopefully be insensible to the world for some time if Theodora casts rightly so I will not have to kill them.

The senior ghazi lives on the top floors and they will be the last ones for me to meet. I had to have a special dispensation in order to get to kill them. Normally it is a death sentence for one not of their faith to enter this enclosure and getting the agreement of the Ayatollah on this took Ayesha nearly a full day of our preparation and it is one of the reasons the Imam is with us.

They landed and put the saddles to one side before settling near the door to wait. *Others are landing outside the guardhouse and the quarters of most of the junior priests and teachers.* Astrid began praying quietly to Saint Kessog. *In two other languages I can hear the Imam and Butterfly doing the same sort of preparation. When in doubt before a battle, prayer helps.*

Ayesha

There is one building that has rooms for the Ayatollah and the Caliph when they visit. It also houses the senior mullahs and the Amīr al-Ghazi. There are six of us in the assault here and there should be seven targets. Unfortunate that, but it is the way it works out. In addition it is usual that there will be guards in the corridor.

What this means for our attack is that even Verily will have to kill at least one experienced person on her own. Inshallah I have trained her well enough. One of us, at least, assuming we all make our first kill, will be doubling up. It is certain that nothing goes to plan, let us just hope that this goes at least sort of to plan.

Except for Astrid, who is needed elsewhere, we are the only six people among the Mice on this trip who know how to use a rope in the manner that will be needed. There is no space for the saddles to land outside the windows and so, while the saddles bearing us stay in the air above the building, we get to lower ourselves down on ropes, just as we have been training to do on cliffs and in the mine.

The openings we will enter at are over three times a filled hand of paces in the air and, as I expected, the shutters of the building have been left open for the cooling breeze. After we all look at each other to check readiness, I give the signal and we all carefully climb inside, pushing aside drapes in order to do so.

Ariadne

Only one of the six of us has real experience at this sort of attack and it is certainly not me. At least Aziz and Krukurb have experience as hunters, I am an engineer. I kill people from a distance, not from right up close. I am terrified that my target will wake up, but at least I am able to steer myself towards him guided easily by his snores. My chosen weapon is my Thunderer, but it is noisy. It is very noisy.

I used a couple of metal darts in Dimashq to find out how to overcome this, and all I need now is to find a pillow in a bedroom. There is one. She pressed it over the end of her weapon and put it near the man's head and pulled the trigger. As she had been told to do she waited for a count of four, to allow his body to heal if it were going to, before she pulled it again. *It may not have been as quiet as a knife, but it is not too bad. At least he is not going anywhere now.*

Thord

It is just like being back in the Hall of Mice on that first night, but now I know a lot more about what I am doing and I am already inside the door of the room where my victim lies sleeping. It isn't fair to do this at all, but I am trying to win a battle, not have a game of hnefatafl. Fairness has nothing to do with fighting. It is the winning that is important.

He stood over the man as he stirred in his sleep. Thord's hammer swung and fell hard on the head in front of him.

It is like striking a melon, but with blood everywhere instead of juice as the body spasms. I expected to have to do this again and I am right. The skull knits together in front of my eyes. He heard a dull popping sound from next door where Ariadne was and then he struck again. *That is it. He stays dead this time. I will wait a little more to be sure.*

Verily

I am very nervous about this. Yes, Ayesha has been training me, but I have never actually used these skills in a real attack. So far it has all been practice and play acting. That ends now. I have decided that distraction is better than the little protection that my clothes offer and I am going in with my blades strapped to my bare torso.

I do have large and well-shaped breasts and anyone waking to see them swaying above him is sure to lose a second or two to confusion before he takes action, particularly seeing that these men supposedly see very little in the way of women. The man is on his back and so I will do everything as I was taught.

I can use both hands equally well and so have a pesh-kabz in my right that will seek his heart and a kindjal in my left to plunge down into the brain. She acted and both stuck home.

There was just a faint noise…is that Ariadne? She pulled the kindjal out of the man's head as his body shook in a spasm and his eyes and mouth opened. *I was right. Even in his pain, as his head heals, his eyes are fixed on my large nipples dangling over him. I know that they are erect in the slight breeze and perhaps in a bit of excitement. He is confused.*

Now she pulled her pesh-kabz out of his heart. *His face takes on a look of anguish as his hands clutch at his chest and blood can be seen spreading quickly out on his clothing as his heart collapses. I will finish it now.* She brought the kindjal back down again through the mouth that had opened in pain.

She waited for a while more in case of another cure being in place. *Now he dies without ever making a sound beyond the thrashing of his corpse. I am pleased with myself. It has all gone exactly as my teacher said that it would. I am glad now of the endless hours of practice. Let us see what else is before us.*

Krukurb

Aziz and I, in our respective rooms, are not going to be subtle. We have agreed on the same method. We have each kept our shields on our backs and use our scimitars to remove our victim's head and our free hand to then grab it and fling it away so that, when the curing spell is activated, it leaves the body seeking ineffectively for a head that is several paces away and glaring futilely. Mine lands so that it must be glaring at the lush carpet on the wall.

Now I make a second stroke to cut open the healing skin and reopen the neck wound and so allow the body to rapidly bleed out. Wait a little and check there are no more cures in place, and so it is time to move on. Krukurb moved to the door of his room and moved his shield from his back to his arm. *Now we get to attend to the guards. That may be more than a bit harder.*

Ayesha

Inshallah, I have left the hardest for myself. I have to kill the Amīr al-Ghazi himself. This man is not only a ghazi, but he is also allegedly the most powerful priest in the entire Land and is one of the few alive today, if not the only one, who can make a carpet fly well. She moved quietly and moved straight into the shadows between windows and her caution was rewarded.

The man either sleeps like a cat or he has some sort of warning system in place. Suddenly he sat up and looked around him. *I am visible, but I stay still and he does not seem to see me in the gloom. There is a faint noise from next door. That will be Ariadne's Thunderer and al-Ḥamdu Lillāh, it provides the distraction that I am looking for.*

The Amīr rose from his bed and headed for a door, grabbing a belt with weapons hanging from it as he did so. *He apparently sleeps only in a loincloth.* She was quick to take advantage of this as she struck from behind. *As I told*

Verily to do, I use my pesh-kabz to the heart and my other blade into a kidney where I rotate it before withdrawing it quickly and stepping back.

The Amīr turned. *A look of hate appears on his face when he sees who is attacking him.* Ayesha took another step forward and plunged her blades in again, or at least tried to. He deflected the blow to his face with the pesh-kabz with his hands, although the strike to his stomach struck home. *He then starts to feel the effect of the previous blows and cries out as his cure takes hold.*

I do not wait to see what will happen. She rained blow after blow to different parts of his body. *He deflects some and it seems that he has more than one cure in place. He calls for help and tries to draw a blade.* The noise of battle filled the room as steel clashed against steel and the man cried out in pain for help.

Gradually though he grows feebler, as I kill him over and over again and his body tries to recover through the increasing weakness that anyone naturally feels after a cure had taken effect. How many does he have in place? Who has more than one or, at most two?

He dies a fourth or fifth time but again he is coming back. Behind me I can hear the door opening but I ignore it. This man has to die. If he survives the attack and escapes then all else that happens here is a complete waste of time. My own survival tonight is not as important as this man's full and complete death beyond any revival. I place my fate in the hands of Allah, the Merciful.

Thord

I come out of my door to see four men about to enter a room. Kruburb and Aziz are on the far side of them. Cries and the sound of a fight can be heard coming from the room. The men are not looking at us and we all charge to the attack. Aziz and I are closest and we strike out unopposed. We are both rewarded with screams of pain and the door is soon forgotten as the tableau in the corridor dissolves into a melee.

Ariadne

The corridor is empty still. Verily should be beside me and we are supposed to tackle the next man together. She came out of her room and waited. *There she is.* The near-naked girl also emerged. Ariadne grinned. *I don't think that I would ever have the same effect on a human man that Verily does, even if Krukub does like what I have. Even I am distracted and I don't like girls like that.*

Together they approached the next door and Verily opened it while Ariadne looked around the corner, her Thunderer at the ready. *There is a man, already armed, with a sword in one hand and a wand in the other only a few paces away. The wand is moving to point towards me. No time to be silent.* She pulled the trigger, waited for the blast and then, bringing it back to point at him, pulled again.

In the closed area it is almost too loud but the man has fallen back, letting go of both items. To be sure that he was dead she marched over and pulled the trigger twice more as he lay on the ground. *He could be shuddering in death or it could be a cure taking effect, but I am going to make sure.*

She waited until the body of the man was finished with its twitching before leaving and joining Verily outside the room. *It looks like the men have finished with their four as Ayesha joins us in the corridor.*

Theodora

I have been slowly intoning the words I need as I stand in my unfolded travelling pattern rug. Now, finally, that is the sound of explosions from Ariadne's Thunderer. It has been agreed that, if nothing else has happened before that sound, it will serve as a signal for all of us others to go ahead with our parts of the attack.

Theodora completed her spell and felt it take effect as the mana flowed out of her. *Within myself I feel that it was a good casting, but not a critical one. Still, it will have done what it was supposed to do. A lot will now be deep in an enchanted sleep. They will not waken for a long time. Hopefully we will have succeeded by then.*

Drawing one of her wands that had long range spells in it that would strike near as far as a bow would, she moved off to the edge of the roof to use those spells on anything that may present itself as a target if it was needed. *As I look out I can see my people starting to now go into buildings through various doors around the two courtyards.*

Ayesha

It has all gone to plan. Ayesha felt relief as she took the lead. Suddenly a door opened ahead of her and a man emerged. *It is the chief instructor. He must have taken to sleeping up here with the mullahs. I may well die here. She brought her blades up. The man's two long curved blades have begun to whirl around in two arcs that almost seem to hum as he advances.*

She was intent on his approach and was only intent on looking to how she would try to block his blades. Suddenly she was nearly deafened as Ariadne's Thunderer spoke near her ear not just once, but twice and then three times. *She has missed once, but the other two impacts have spun the man around and he has fallen down with a look of astonishment on his face. Allãhu Akbar.*

Ariadne brushes past the rest of us. The al-Nisa al-Hayawan might already be used to the noise of her weapon, but no-one else is and the noise slows us all down as our heads ring with the sound. Ariadne is aiming again. The man throws a sword at her from where he writhes on the floor. At the same time he is attempting to open a pouch with his other hand.

The blade glances off her as she moves, hits the wall, and falls harmless in a clatter on the stone floor. She steps closer and fires from close up into the man's head as he snarls at her. The back of his skull shatters as its contents cover the floor and the foot of the wall.

Ariadne grinned at the others around her teeth. "I think that they know we are here," she said as she turns to me. "I hope that you didn't mind that I interfered."

She seems concerned that I would be upset that I could not kill him. Ayesha shook her head both to try and clear the ringing noise from it and to signal that she did not. *Al-Ḥamdu Lillāh I do not mind at all not having to fight him. This way I get to live.*

Again they went on. *This time I will, much more sensibly, let two of the armoured men take the lead and the third take the rear place as we work our way through the building.*

Stefan

I lead the charge into the guard barracks area with my wives behind me taking up a corridor. If anyone comes at us they will have to face two spears to get near my sword. My job is to hold them and try and catch arrows with my shield while my wives kill them. Now as people emerge and throw themselves forward in ones and twos, it seems to be working.

Asticus, Neon and Menas face the other way and Rani stands in the centre of us all with wands at the ready and with two of Ikrimah's men, armed with bows, standing beside her. They hold the only doorway out and if any want to get out of the building by it then they will have to go first through us, and then through them.

Christopher

I wait nervously in the outer courtyard with my wife and with Lakshmi. We wait until someone calls for us. Personally I hope that does not happen because, if we are called it means that one of our people is very badly hurt. That is, they are hurt beyond the power of just a potion or one of their contingency cures to fix. I do so wish that we could avoid battles entirely. Perhaps one day we will be able to.

Astrid

That has to be Ariadne. Astrid ran through the corridors of the barracks. *Iyād and Ikrimah get to hold the door and hopefully Butterfly and I will be able to eliminate anyone before they have a chance to test the two who are left behind. I don't think that either of them has been tested in serious hand-to-hand battle before. At least there is someone there in case we fail.*

The ground floor contains rooms full of men who hopefully will not stir. We throw open door after door to reveal, with relief, that each holds a hand of men who are not noticing anything for some time.

We go up the stairs and here is our first opponent. He is dressed in the leather that seems usual here. She fenced at him with the point of her weapon as he dodged and deflected. *He is good and, what is more, he has a lot more room to dodge than the ones in the inn. It is like trying to kill a mosquito with a harpoon.*

By the time she had killed him there were three others behind him and Ia had eliminated another who had come from behind with one of Theodora's wands. *The three press me hard and there are loose rings on my new mail by the time they are gone and another man, this one in mail himself, stands in their place.*

He is the best so far. Butterfly is using her wand, when she can, to take out several new people. Seeing that the spells in it are meant for buildings, it only requires one casting to kill a person, but she must be up to the second wand by now. Astrid fought her way forward over broken-looking men lying on the floor. The man died. *Another has already appeared behind him.*

Hulagu

I was not happy to be left in the sky with the rest of the Mori, but I see now why the zürkh setgelee gartaa barisan khün wanted it that way. These people are trained the same as she is and they regard a window as a fairly normal way to get into or out of a building if other ways are not easily available to them. Soon the Mice in the sky were firing continuously as people tried to get out of the building or else trying to fire at them.

It is just as well that we have several quivers of arrows each as it looks like we will use as many shafts as one would in a running battle on the plains. Soon we all have damage ourselves, mainly due to arrows in the legs, and one by one I get them to briefly pull out and go high to remove the shafts and drink potions.

It does not take long for us to have to pull out a second time either. Cures may fix the damage, but my legs will ache for a long time and I should not try to run for a while. It is well that I am sitting and not trying to run. I doubt that I could even stand my legs feel so weak.

Rani

I am using my wands to back up their weapons now as groups come rushing at one side of our position or the other. I thank Kartikeya that I have plenty. The archers are firing down the sides of the corridor and I am using my height so that I can fire blasts over and around the trios in front of me. Suddenly someone on the other side fires an actual spell, a ball of fire, heedless of who they hit. The corridor is filled with flame.

My resistance helps me, but Stefan and the cousins, along with their current opponents, are felled by the blast. The corridor on that side is empty now. The person at the far end has killed his own people, or at least brought them down in his rashness. The archers and I all let go at once. One of the archers has used an explosive arrow and I have my own fireball ready.

The mage was knocked over and, as he tried to raise his wand again, they all fired a second time. *He might have dodged one, but not all of us together and this time when he goes down he does not rise again. Once again to be sure.*

Christopher

There are a series of loud explosions, we had heard some before, but his time there is a loud cry. "Bishop." *That is Rani's voice. The three headed inside. Oh Dear God preserve us, what carnage. Bodies litter the floor, some only as pieces, and Rani is already pouring potion into the mouth of one of the cousins*. Lakshmi leapt to the other while Christopher moved towards Stefan.

The girls were obviously behind Stefan and are still moving but I would say that Stefan was in the centre of the explosion. He may have caught some on his shield, but he is not responding at all. He does not show a pulse. I cannot feel the spark of life within him.

Christopher dragged his body back towards the door. *There is some clear space here. Lakshmi helps me, while my wife takes up a position to fight.*

Quickly he laid out his cloth with a pattern ready drawn on it. Lakshmi helped him lift Stefan into the centre before he stepped out again, lit some incense and drew out his Gospel and began praying, using the small icon of Saint Anne that he had obtained in Ardlark, hoping never to need it, and making his other preparations.

At least Stefan is Orthodox. That will help and I need all the help that I can get here. Beside me I can see the cousins holding each other and crying as Lakshmi tries to bind wounds on them that are not yet fully healed. Adara is reaching out a hand towards where their husband lies on the pattern. All of his visible skin is burnt off and he is not a good sight.

When I acted on Ayesha I took more time, but I lack a consecrated area here and so it is best acting as quickly as I can. I hope that I have grown enough to perform this miracle better than I did the last time. Mind you, it is also my second time to pray for it and that should help. Now it is time to get started. "In nomine Patris et fillii et Spritus Sancti."

Theodora

There is one that seems to have escaped everyone's notice. Theodora aimed her wand carefully. *He is near my maximum range even with these wands. It is just as well that the inner courtyard is much higher than the outer and that the gatehouse I am standing on is taller still. I can just see over the entire mosque except for the dome and the man is nearly up to the opposite gatehouse in the corner of two walls.*

That is why no-one has seen him. He is going up instead of down. She fired and he fell back. *I must not have hit him fully as he survived the spell's effects. He screamed as he plummeted down, still trying to futilely grab hold of the wall, to lie limp and twisted on the cobbles. He only moved for a little while longer before going still at least.*

Astrid

As we have gotten higher up in the building I think that the opponents have gotten far tougher. There cannot be many left. Butterfly has made me drink some potions. In fact she made me drain an entire bottle. I must have been hurt worse than I realised. It is amazing how battle keeps you going. I never seem to notice the wounds until we are finished. Perhaps that is why I need a wife to look after me.

The draught, added to the exhilaration of battle makes me feel light-headed. She looked over her body. *From the rents in my armour and the tears in the padding underneath I am to add more scars to my body from this trip to the Caliphate than I have collected so far in my entire life. Mind you, I have also faced and killed far more people on this trip than ever before as well.*

Also both Ia and Maeve have been hit with arrows and buffeted by explosions, and once Butterfly had to fight on her own behalf with a blade and kill a person who came out of hiding. Maeve even used her teeth and claws on that one's leg near his groin. He screamed at that and tried to beat her off. She may have had teeth in more than his leg. It certainly was enough of a distraction to allow my relatively inexperienced new wife to kill him.

Both Butterfly and Maeve are, however, still unhurt, and that is important. I hope that Hrothnog is watching the show that we are providing and is pleased with seeing how his gifts are helping us.

Ayesha

We stalk the halls of the building going down towards the ground. From what we face it seems to be mainly mullahs and other clerics living here. Some have a little skill at arms but most are so unused to battle that they die before they can even pray up some battle magic. I hate to admit it, but Verily's display of 'awrah is even helping more than a little as a distraction.

One mullah, probably the most prepared so far, was chanting something when he noticed her breasts and completely forgot to say the last few words to complete his miracle before he died. It looks as if they were expecting help to come from the floors above, not an attack.

Some of them use wands and several of my group now show signs of wounds and having taken damage from them. All of our ears hurt from the noise of the Thunderer going off. Ariadne has changed the metal boxes of darts twice more now and she reeks of al-kīmiyā. We probably all do to tell the truth.

They reached the ground level. *It looks like our building has been cleared now.* Ayesha waved her hand cautiously out of the doorway before looking out and then letting them emerge. *Looking at the al-Nisa al-Hayawan and her wide grin, I think that I can see in which tribe Astrid's ancestry probably lies. There is the resemblance of distant cousins there if you look hard.*

Astrid

It is nearly time to turn around and go back down. We have reached the top of the building and all of the rooms are empty, but something makes me nervous. She shifted to the side to look at things differently. *Maeve is chattering for the first time.*

Quickly, but cautiously, Astrid swivelled and backed up against a carpeted wall. *Butterfly has gasped.* With a thump, a body landed on the floor beside her. Astrid began spluttering as she was covered in plaster from the ornamented roof that fell all around them. *I cannot see to hit him with this dust in my eyes.*

Ia stabbed him with the point of her sword in the base of the throat and then waited. He shuddered and began to move. Ia used a wand on the man and moved back looking up as she did so to check if the ceiling above her was empty. It was and she again looked at the man on the floor. "How did you know he was there?" she asked.

"He must have been clinging to the ceiling. Maeve only noticed him when you moved around. He must have moved then to try and drop on to you and the ceiling gave way." Astrid shrugged as she brushed plaster dust off her.

"I just had a feeling," she said.

Cautiously they began to retrace their steps. *Butterfly is now devoting all of her attention to the ceiling of the corridors. Perhaps we should have done that more on the way up. We may have been lucky.*

Now we are at the bottom and Ikrimah and Iyād have a hand of bodies in front of them from men who managed to get past us to the door, but were not able to go any further. The fun is now over. Now it is time to get rope and go back and remove all of the unconscious ones and search and bind them securely until they wake up and we can examine them.

Christopher

I get to slump in my wife's arms, my head against her breasts. He looked up at her. "Sorry, I forgot to kiss you first." He smiled at her. *I am weak and drained, but at least I am not unconscious this time. Lakshmi is already pouring potion into Stefan and he is coughing. He is back alive and already there is new skin that is showing beneath that which was burnt.*

He was not as deeply sunk into death nor absent from his body for as long as Ayesha was and he will probably recover quicker. Quickly my wife has dragged him clear and got one of the archers to look for Aziz while she checks his pulse. She nods to me. It is strong and his breathing is easy. The Hob is now the senior Orthodox priest present if one is needed until I have rested. I need a good rest. I can go to sleep now.

Chapter XLV

Ayesha
6th Quinque

It takes all of us working together to bring out the sleeping men and tie them up securely. There are new ghazis who lie here, there are servants, and there are even some religious trainees. In total Theodora's enchantment has knocked out well over two hands by two hands of people, all of the younger and less experienced people in the citadel.

Still, that left the same number, or perhaps even more, that had to be killed in battle and they were the stronger ones. Al-Ḥamdu Lillāh we prevailed. It seems that we were lucky and Allah, the Just, appeared to favour our cause. I give thanks.

Now we start to assemble the bodies on the other side of the outer courtyard. That number grows and grows. Some are dead. However others are still just alive, just badly injured. Unless they try to attack someone these are bound and given a potion until they can be examined. I pray to Allah, the Merciful that we can spare them.

As people wake up they are lined up for Ia to examine with her hypnosis. If she fails at this, then they are taken to a mage or a mullah, but there are so many that need to be seen to that we are trying to avoid using up mana unless we have to.

The first ones to be looked at are the cooks and the servants. After all, with this many people, both us and the captives, not to mention those who will start arriving soon, it is important for all to be fed. Unfortunately her talent shows that all of the servants that lodge within the building are too deeply sunk into their belief to be redeemable.

At present they are kept bound and locked into a room that can be sealed if needed, but this cannot last as more and more of the younger occupants join them. Eventually one of them will be able to undo another and then we will have a problem. Someone must watch them the whole time. Stefan and his wives, he with the peeling skin, and them with their breasts are given the task.

It seems that, although there has been a lot of recent recruiting, the ones that they have enlisted are the direst of the fanatics and, in many cases, ones who have already committed physical crimes or are sunk into such blasphemy that they are regarded as being unredeemable. Strangely, and thankfully, it is the four older and more senior men who were badly wounded, but who survived who are among the few who can be freed.

Servants and attendants are brought from among those who live outside the citadel. With what has happened here the halls of the stronghold will echo emptily for many years to come as it looks like it will be only those four and another four junior ghazi out of the entire garrison who will escape execution tonight. I curse the Iblīs for what they have done to my people.

Ayesha
a few hours later

The carpets begin to arrive at Misr al-Mãr soon after dawn. The first are from Dimashq but, seeing that none that have spoken have so far implicated anyone in Yarmũk, we are soon bringing people up from there as well. By the time that the rising sun bathes the golden stone of the keep in a glow of honey-coloured light, Misr al-Mãr, is well and truly back under control.

Christopher

The dawn also saw the return of Christopher to his body. As soon as the word of this spread he was smothered in kisses from the cousins. *I am embarrassed and my wife is far too amused by this.* A still weak Stefan also came and wrapped him in a hug. *That I can more easily accept. It is good to see the man is still with us.*

Christopher looked around at his people all still working away. *It seems to be a pity that we have not been able to take any of the senior people alive, but it also seems likely that we have eliminated our problems in the Caliphate, at least for a while. Apparently none has been found so far, but we must still check for a Pattern before we leave here. It could be hidden in a room. They must have some way to talk to each other.*

Ariadne

As the only one who understands them at all, it is my duty to spend the day searching the buildings for anything in the way of machines. The only one I have found so far is in the room of the second to the Amĩr al-Ghazi. In an ornate box on a table beside his bed he has one of the small boxes with buttons and the small glass screen that I found at Ta'if.

I still have no concrete idea about what it does. However, when I get home, I will be playing with them both. Two identical little boxes have to be significant in some way. I wonder if they are some way of talking to each other as they have no obvious use as a weapon of any sort. Talkers, such as the ones we use in the valley, and the pair from Skrice, always come as a set of matched items. These two could be the same sort of thing but using machines instead of honest magic.

Theodora

The next day I again cast my sleep spell over the filled room of doomed prisoners. Since 'repentance destroys sins' all, even those sunk deepest in sin and apostasy, had been given a chance to repent and recant and all, knowing that they would not be able to lie, had refused. Now they are to be given no chance to overwhelm us.

The sleeping men are brought out of the room one by one and, also one by one, have their veins opened so that they quietly and painlessly bleed to death. Their bodies are disposed of in the ravine for the present along with the bodies of those killed in the battle itself. Many of the men who perform this task are weeping by the end of it as, time after time, they kill men that they know and, in some cases, are even related to.

Theodora
sometime later

The saddles that we left there are gradually brought up to us from Bab al-Abw‹b. At the same time the rest of the Orphanos ride hard to bring all of their men and horses back together and we prepare to move on. It is a slow process but gradually control of the massive fortress is returned to the men of the Caliphate. Soon we will be able to leave.

Chapter XLVI

Ayesha
8th Quinque

It has apparently been decided that one of the Darkreach clerics, the one who is the first to go to his new home, is to be installed in the tiny community of Rainjig, not just for the few local believers, but mainly to look after any traders who arrive from Darkreach. He already has a second piece of paper, if any ask for it, which introduces him as a consul for Darkreach.

While the saddles are still being brought up for the others, he is being taken down over The Wall by Basil, Astrid and Ia, so that he can be introduced properly to the locals there by a priestess of their own belief. We all hope that, if that thrupple, and particularly Ia, do the introduction, it will lessen any feeling that they might have that he was being forced on them.

At least, now they have returned the fact that he is also a leatherworker and tanner and is willing to work at those trades as well as being a priest seems to go over well with the community. Although many people can make do with leather, if they wanted something better than an amateur effort it had to be ordered in from elsewhere. Having someone local to do the work makes him a happy choice for the job.

Ayesha
9th Quinque

Now we leave Misr al-Mãr. We will have one more stop to make within the Caliphate, and that is my family home of Yãqũsa. We have already said farewell to Imam Iyãd, who will return on horseback down the Tãb Rũdh to Rebelkill and thence Garthcurr and around the coast to Ardlark. He will spread the news of what has happened as he goes.

Going along with us, and so riding double behind someone, will be the second of the junior clerics that Iyãd brought with him. He will go on with us to Bloomact.

We bear letters from the new Caliph, for the old died a few days ago, and we have a commission to examine any person we choose to in order to make sure that they are not corrupted in the same way. I am loath to admit it to the others, but I am in great fear that some of those I have grown up with could have been corrupted by now and so be shown to be followers of the Iblīsi. Inshallah it shall not be.

Ayesha

much later in the afternoon

With just the saddles and no-one holding us back by travelling slowly on the ground we move quickly. Even though we dropped down to Ta'if to let Sheik Iyãd know what has transpired and to have lunch, it is an easy day's travel to Yãqũsa through the chill blue sky of the mountains. After Ta'if everyone has bags and boxes hanging off their saddles. We picked up a lot more of what Ariadne left there. I think that we have everything that is portable with us now.

As we go we fly over the heads of traders and caravans. None of them give any sign of even seeing us flyers in the sky far above them. I am amazed at how much I have missed the sight that unfolds ahead of me. We fly in over fields of tobacco on the plains, kaf bushes on the slopes and opium in the higher fields. I am home.

I point out the quarry, eating its way into a hill to the east of the town, and where most of the fine marble in The Land is mined and shipped in blocks and slabs to as far away as Freehold. The town itself comes into view almost at the same time. It is surrounded by its strong wall and stands beside its ford on the Khũbũr Rũdh. The river flows quickly, winding away from the town, through its wadĩ in the Kũm Kaysãn.

Approaching on her own and well ahead of the rest of the Mice, Ayesha was nearly shot by an archer, but she dodged. Rumours had somehow reached the little town of disturbance and warfare and the nervous guard had let his shaft slip. She stopped then, in the air by a few paces but still well away from the walls, and called out loudly for her father and her mother.

It was not long before the Mice had been welcomed inside. *I was long ago given up as lost by my parents and my sisters, but at least they are all still alive.*

I had not realised how nervous I would be introducing Hulagu until the time came and I opened my mouth. It is, at least, made easier by being able to point out that my husband is the Tar-khan of a Khitan tribe, and thus at least equivalent to a Sheik and that he has more than sufficient mahr for me.

I will not point out that all of the members of the tribe, except for the children, are present in front of them and that I have not actually asked for any mahr. In particular I will make no mention of how our relationship started. It also helps to be able to introduce to my mother my junior sister-wives and so to show that I am the senior wife of an important man.

My father is even more gratified to discover that he has a strong and healthy grandson who has been named after him. Perhaps more practically, my mother quickly points out that, with my new connections, I still have a sister and a half-sister who are still unmarried and although both are pious girls, they do not have all of my advantages. What do I say to that?

Astrid

Ayesha obviously does not know what to say to that, but I do. That is, after all, my self-appointed job when I am not killing things or people and it is almost as much fun and far more relaxing. It is time for me to have some fun. While Ayesha was still searching for an answer Astrid thrust herself forward dragging a young man with her.

"This is Hãshim." *Ayesha's parents look surprised at this interruption from a large and loud kãfirũn woman who they have yet to be introduced to. They will get over it. Everyone does.* "He is one of your priests from Ardlark and he is favoured by the Imam of the main mosque there and has been sent here directly by Alĩ ibn Yũsuf al Mãr, the Ayatollah Uzma of Darkreach.

"He is most likely destined to serve in the growing mosque at Bloomact. I am sure that you will agree that, for a man in his position, it would be best to have a wife beside him. What is more, the young Imam of that mosque, who will probably soon end up as the Mullah of the entire area, also lacks a wife and I have met him and he is both a hard-working and a pious man."

She looked directly at Ayesha's mother and at Hãritha's other wives who had appeared and was listening intently to what was being said. *The others are gathering around as well, but presumably the one who is closest is the mother of the other girl.* "If you are agreeable, then we shall begin to discuss what mahr shall be due."

The older women are both looking surprised at the suddenly appearing idea, but behind them I can see a girl around Ayesha's age, who has to be one of the sisters whose fate seems to be now under discussion, is looking quite appraisingly at the young man that I still have in tow. She has caught on quickly.

He, in turn is looking at me with his mouth open in astonishment. Why bother consulting him? He will do as he is told. Beside the first girl another has appeared, with flour on the end of her nose, and she has grabbed the hand of the first one. She is probably the second girl to be married off. She looks like a younger version of Ayesha so she will be the full sister.

"This is Astrid the Cat," Ayesha said to her father and his wives by way of explanation. "She is the one who arranged the marriage of the Emperor of Darkreach to a woman of the Faith." *The women now look much more appraisingly at me. I am now to be seen by the women, despite the arms I bear and use, as one whose role they understand full well. Not only that, but I am also, apparently, a woman of connection.*

Hãritha is sizing up the man that I have behind me. I think that he is a likely prospect and no others are in view, or are available. If the girls are still unmarried at this age, then they have nearly given up on making the sisters more than a junior wife to an older man. He looks at his daughters. They do not seem displeased with the idea either.

"It is good," Hãritha said. "Talk then and, as long as it proper nikah and not nikah al-mut'ah, the permanent and not the temporary marriage, then we will look at what he has to offer to my daughter and at his mahr. Can you speak for this other imam as well?"

Beside me the young man's mouth opens to speak. That is not needed. We cannot have any sort of display of indecision being made on his part. Ayesha and Astrid looked at each other. *What is needed from home now is just acceptance of what is happening.* Astrid gave him a look and his mouth closed.

"He has sufficient mahr." Ayesha nodded. "He does–they both do," she continued.

The young cleric is still looking at us in surprise. I have his story. He has been given some money for his keep until he earns money himself, but anything else is news to him. One of the reasons he was willing to leave Darkreach is that his family is poor and he hoped to find a wife who would not require mahr.

Here I am lining him up with the daughter of a sheik who is far beyond what a diligent, but poor, scholar such as he could ever expect to aspire to. It is a good match for both of them. As for Mullah Uthman in Bloomact, I am sure that he will see it the same way after I have a few words with him. He had better. He is a sensible and practical man.

Ayesha

After Astrid's intervention, the introduction of the Princesses and, belatedly, of the other Mice is a very poor second in my parent's eyes. At least I am finally able to tell my parents what task I was assigned to and, although they are very unsure over the marriage of Theodora and Rani, they are reassured by their status as rulers and that their daughter had not been assigned to some other task, such as the one that they had feared.

That night Yãqũsa has the tale of the Mice told to them by a daughter of the Sheik, and by others, and my father finds himself in the unusual position of basking in the glory reflected from the deeds of his daughter. I have to admit that this is a pleasant feeling for me.

The carpet makers of the area are not sure what to do though. They are good at their work, but Mughĩra abd Allah had been the only person who could enchant a flying carpet with both good speed and lift. He charged very highly for his services and they make very little profit from what they made and so they only made a few of them.

Now they will have to see who else might be able to take over the role. I think that, with what we did at Misr al-M‹r, there will be no others for quite some time. The carpets that come from here will be sold on the strength of their beauty for many years to come. They will still fetch a good price, but carpets that can fly well will have to be carefully looked after for some time to come.

Chapter XLVII

Ia
12th Quinque

We get to stay on in this small town for several days, through what my sister-wife calls the feast of the Saints Cyril and Methodius. I would like to put this behind us, get home and make a proper prediction made for what will happen next. At least the inn here in Yãqũsa has nice beds, even if it is not as good as having our own.

At any rate, now we are in Caer Gwyliwr Ddwyrain, we get to tell the people there of the events that took place in the Caliphate and what befell us. I admit that, even though I lived through it all I still find it difficult to understand everything that happened to us. How much harder is it for them to just believe what we say?

At least while we are here I am able to relate to the druids and wiccan priests and priestesses that I have obtained permission for a priest and priestess to set up quietly in Dimashq and more openly in both Ta'if and Yãqũsa. It is now up to the people here to arrange for this and to take their place on the plateau above.

Ayesha
13th Quinque, the Havenite Festival of Rath Yatra

Now we fly on to Bloomact to deliver Hãshim to Mullah Uthman as his assistant to, among other things, to travel through the Swamp looking for itaqu. Inshallah, they will be found among the kãfirũn. Hãshim has with him his new wife, my sister, ready to start their new life together. I am happy to see that my sister is pleased with her new husband and that he seems to be equally taken with her.

Imam Uthman is quite surprised, but not at all displeased, to discover that a wife has also been arranged for him by Astrid as well. It only took one long look from her before he hurriedly agreed to the various arrangements that were made in his name. He had better if he is to keep running his little maqhaa and mosque.

I am sure that he realises, although he is marrying the daughter of a Caliphate sheik, who is also my sister, which is an elevated link that I am sure he had not thought to ever have; he is really getting tied by very strong ties of debt to the Faith in Darkreach instead of in the Caliphate. I really do need, before we go any further, to sit my sisters down and make sure they understand what their situation is.

They may not realise it yet, but whether they like it or not, they will have to play the whole political game here, but at least in this they have some training. It would have been just a part of normal life if they had stayed in the Caliphate, but here it will be a matter not just of custom, but also of survival. They also have to adjust to dealing with the other wives we arranged locally, and their past as slaves.

Ayesha
14th Quinque, the Feast Day of Saint Bonaventura

The next day we can leave Bloomact for our home. I am glad to leave the damp and the mosquitoes behind. It will be a very long flight that is ahead of us today. Luckily it will be through a clear sky. We will break it only for a few short stops to make ourselves more comfortable and to eat, but we will be back in Mousehole two days before the Christian Feast of Easter.

Unfortunately I fear that we will only get to have a short break in our own beds and with our children. It will be a relief while it lasts, but all too soon, I am afraid to say, it will start all over again.

Glossary

'awrah: an Arabic word for those parts of the body that must be covered in public.

Adl: an Arabic word 'justice.'

Adversaries: the major protagonists behind the evil that is infesting Vhast.

Agatha, Saint: a Christian Saint, Feast Day 3rd Secundus, she is the patron of victims of rape and torture and is invoked against fire and earthquakes. Her Order run shelters for abused women.

Ahl al-dhimma: an Arabic phrase, literally 'law of the protected people.'

Aketon: a padded garment, usually of cotton, worn under armour.

Al-Ḥamdu Lillāh: an Arabic phrase, 'Praise be to God.'

Al-Īmbiraturiat al-Dhakina: Darkreach, literally 'the Dark Empire.

Al-jihad al-Akbar: an Arabic phrase, literally 'the Great Struggle' that the Faithful are engaged in.

Al-kīmiyā: an Arabic word that gives us both 'chemicals' and 'alchemy.'

Al-Mahdi: the last prophet of Islam, who is destined to appear just before the final battles and the victory of the Faith.

Al-Masihiiyn: Arabic for a Christian.

Al-Nisa al-Hayawan: an Arabic phrase for a female Kharl or part-Kharl.

Al-Quizam al-zalam: an Arabic phrase for 'Insak Div.'

Allãh wadhu: an Arabic expression, literally 'the one God.'

Allãhu Akbar: an Arabic expression, literally 'Allah is the Greatest.'

Amand, Saint: Christian Saint, his Feast Day is 2nd Secundus, he is patron of the wine trade.

Ambrose, Saint: a Christian Saint, Feast Day 4th Quattro, he is patron of doctrinal purity and beekeepers.

Anne, Saint: Christian Saint, her Feast Day is 25th October and she is the patron both of those who slay the undead and those who return from the dead.

Anta Dvīpa: Hindi for 'End Island,' it is in Pavitra Phāṭaka and the home of Harijani and foreigners.

Antdrudge: a town in the north of Darkreach where molotails and other explosive items are made.

Antikataskopeía: the Darkreach 'secret police,' an arm of the military who are concerned both with criminal investigation and treason.

Arden Creek: the most western of the major creek draining the southern plains. Saltbeach lies where it enters the sea.

Ardlark: a major city, the largest in The Land, and also the capital of Darkreach.

As-Salāmu 'Alaykum: an Arabic phrase 'Peace be unto you' that is used in greeting.

Ashuḍh ke Pul: Hindi for the 'Bridge of the Unclean;' it runs from Vyāpārī to Anta.

Ashvaria: 86,000 people and the capital city of Freehold.

Asr: a Muslim prayer time an hour and a half before sundown.

Astaghfirullāh: an Arabic phrase, literally 'I seek forgiveness from God.'

Aśud'dha: the Hindi word best translated as 'unclean.'

Aśud'dha paradēśī: a Hindi phrase, literally it is 'unclean outsiders.'

Ayatollah Uzma: an Arabic phrase for the chief Ayatollah, equivalent to a Metropolitan.

Ā<u>dhān</u>: the Muslim call to prayer.

Ānanda Dvīpa: Hindi for The 'Pleasure Island,' the home of food, prostitution and gambling in Pavitra Phāṭaka.

Āyāt: Arabic word for verses from the Qur'an.

Bab al-Abwâb: in Arabic literally 'gate of gates.' It is a strategic mountain village that guards the access to the heart of the Caliphate, the Rãhit.

Badr: a well and oasis in the Sawãd and the site of a major battle in the not very distant past.

Bardiche: a pole weapon with a very long blade that is joined, at one end, to the shaft and at the other forms a spear-like point.

Barrowbrah Creek: one of the large creeks draining the south of the plains. Growling Harbour is at its mouth and Dagh Ordu is its source.

Basil the Great, Saint: a Christian Saint, Feast Day 1st Primus, his patronage is to almsgivers.

Basilica Anthropoi: a Holy Order of warrior monks of the Orthodox Church west of the mountains. They are heavily armed and ride as kataphractoi or kynigoi depending on their role. They bear the Chi-Rho on their shields and the leader of a group will have a painted icon there as well.

Bathmawr: a village in the Swamp on the Buccleah River.

Bear-folk: a group of humanoids who have a high number of bear-based shape-shifters among their number. They live just north of the Swamp.

Beneen: a large plain in the south of Darkreach scattered with towns and villages of herdsmen.

Birchdingle: a Bear-folk settlement.

Bitrĩq: an Arabic word 'Governor.'

Bloomact: although only a small town, it is the capital of the Swamp.

Bonaventura: a Christian Saint, Feast Day 14th Quinque, patron of negotiators.

Boyuk-kharl: the largest and most intelligent of the Kharl races. They are often found in independent units and at sea.

Brahmin: the Hindu priestly caste, also found as bankers and moneylenders with others handling the actual money to avoid touching anything a Harijan may have touched.

Bridgecap: a village on the south coast of The Land and the base for an Orthodox Metropolitan.

Brotherhood, The: the Brotherhood of All Believers were militant semi-Christians of an extreme Puritan type with a focus on literal truth and rigid obedience. They have been wiped out.

Buccleah River: a large tributary of the Tulky Wash in the Swamp. In Arabic, in the Caliphate, it is known as the Ziyanda Rũdh.

Buhairet Tabariyya: a large mountain lake in the Caliphate.

Burning, the: a dread disease that causes people to go mad and destroy things. Less than one person in twenty survived the years that it raged.

Caer Gwyliwr Ddwyrain: see Eastguard Tower.

Calat, the: the fortress and Palace of the Caliph.

Caliphate: a Muslim Kingdom nestled high in the south of the Great Range.

Camelback: an island of the coast of Freehold that is on the main coastal shipping route.

Castle Mount: the seat of the Dukes of the New Found Land. It is in the County of New Ashvaria.

Cephas, Saint: a Christian Saint, Feast Day 36 Quattro. He is patron of cobblers, net makers and bridge builders.

Chamadee (the Foreskin): an area of Anta at its tip. Although this area is formally known as Mandir Kshetr (the Temple Sector), almost everyone calls it by this name.

Chevda: a mix of dried foods such as fried lentils, peanuts, chickpea flour noodles, flaked rice, fried onion, peas and curry leaves. It is often called bhuja mix.

Choli: the blouse top worn by women under a sari; it usually has short sleeves and is buttoned at the front, leaving a bare midriff. It can also have long sleeves or cover more midriff.

Confederation of the Free: a very loose alliance of villages and towns spread through the jungles and bogs that lie between Haven and the mountains.

Copper Cat, The: a tavern in Eastguard Tower.

Cuthbert, Saint: a Christian Saint, Feast Day 20th Tertius, he is the patron of shepherds.

Cydwraig: the Faen word for a sister-wife, literally 'co-wife.'

Cyril and Methodius, Saints: Orthodox Saints, Feast Day 11th Quinque, patrons of translators and of conversion of the heathen and defence of the faith.

Dadanth: a jungle fungus that can be made into an unguent that repels insects.

Dagh Ordu: a large rock feature in the sourthern plains. It is a holy place for the Khitan.

Dar al-Islam: an Arabic phrase, 'the abode of Islam.'

Dar as-Sulh: An Arabic phrase, 'Domain of Agreement.'

Darada: a plains tree whose seeds can be made into a potion or paste to get rid of internal worms.

Darkreach: this is a multi-racial Empire that takes up the eastern third of The Land east of the Great Range. It is ruled (and has been since known time began) by Hrothnog.

Dating: years run over a 48-year cycle; with the twelve zodiacal signs that are used on Vhast along with the elements of Earth, Air, Fire and Water. There are twelve months of equal length, each having six weeks of six days. The first parts of the story take part on the Year of the Water Dog. A year thus has 432 days so a year on Vhast is nearly a fifth longer than a Terran year. A person who is fifteen on Vhast will be eighteen on Earth.

Days: the six days of the week are Firstday, Deutera, Pali, Tetarti, Dithlau and Krondag.

Deeryas: A town on the southern fringe of the plains on Kyogle Creek.

Delta River: a braided and meandering river that drains much of the Swamp. Sometimes it disappears into marsh and reforms on the other side.

Demaresque Creek: the stream, more a small river than a creek, that Southpoint lies on.

Devi: For the Hindu, she is the female principle, the mother Goddess.

Devil-beast: a marsupial scavenger from the Swamp, it often used as a familiar there.

Dewakung: A town on the south coast of Freehold.

Dhargev: a Hobgoblin town in the Southern Mountains, the original home of Aziz.

Dharma: a Hindu concept, the shape or destiny laid out for us.

Dhimmis: Arabic word, a 'protected person,' an unbeliever who has some rights in the Caliphate society.

Dhoti: a male garment that is basically a loincloth.

Dhurhr: a Musim time of prayer, just after midday.

Dimashq: the capital of the Caliphate.

Dolbarden: a fortified village and trading port in the north of the Swamp. It guards the way up the Buccleah River where the Bellingen joins it.

Dominicans: a Catholic Order whose duties include the Inquisition. They are often referred to as 'The Black Crows' due to the habit that they wear.

Doro: a mining village in the south of Darkreach close to the base of the Southern Mountains.

Durga: Hindu goddess, the root cause of creation, preservation and annihilation. She rides a tiger and has ten arms.

Dwarf (Dwarves/Dwarven): a race of humanoids that tend to live below ground. Most people cannot tell if there are female dwarves as all of them are bearded and similar in appearance. They are skilled miners and artisans.

Dwarvenholme: the long-lost main city of the Dwarves, recently found and being re-built.

Easter: the main Christian Festival of the year, celebrating the rising of Christ from the dead.

Eastguard Tower: more properly Caer Gwyliwr Ddwyrain, this is a well-fortified large village in the north-east of the Swamp.

Emeel amidarch baigaa khümüüs: a Khitan phrase describing themselves. It literally means 'people who live in a saddle.'

Erave, Lake: this is almost a small sea and lies on the Rhastaputra River to the west of the mountains.

Erave Town: an independent trading town on the southern shore of Lake Erave.

Ergüül: the smallest Khitan unit size, it has no fixed number of people in it, but there will usually be at least a hand.

Evilhalt: a town at the very northern tip of Lake Erave and a focus for trade.

Faen: the language of the Swamp.

Fagus trees: a short deciduous tree of the mountain slopes. On earth they are Nothofagus (sin Fuscospora) gunii.

Fayyum: A caravanserai and oasis on the Sawãd.

Fergus, Saint: a Christian Saint, Feast Day 27th November, his patronage is all matters involving 'greenskins.'

Firqa: Arabic for a small infantry or guard unit.

Flails of God: the Inquisitors and scouts of the Brotherhood of Believers, they are taken from among orphans and some selected children of slaves as infants and then raised as fanatic believers.

Flyjudge: an island village in the east of the delta at the head of Iba Bay in the Swamp.

Forest Watch: a Darkreach outpost on a small, isolated mountain deep in the Great Forest. On a clear day it has a view of most of much of the central mountains area and, in particular, the approaches to the Darkreach Gap.

Fosgitoscilfach: the Faen name for Mosquito Creek, an insect paradise near Rainjig.

Fragrant Bean, The: a kaf house in Bloomact.

Freehold: a Kingdom that takes up the south-west of The Land.

Freeport: the major settlement on Gil-Gand-Rask, this is the literal translation of its name Þãrnþoş (pron Thaamthosh).

Ganesh: an elephant-headed Hindu God, god of wisdom and knowledge. He is often called the 'remover of obstacles.'

Garthang Keep: the most northerly settlement of Haven. It is a strong fortification.

Garthcurr: a large town in the south of Darkreach.

Gasparin: a very hot spice found on the mountain slopes.

George, Saint: a Christian Saint, Feast Day 23rd Quattro, patron of cavalry and those who fight against demons and dragons.

Ghanimah: the Arabic word for the spoils of war or booty.

Ghazi: Holy warriors of the Caliphate. We would call them assassins, but they are mostly guards and scouts.

Giant's Drop: a tall mountain in the southern mountains. It gets its name from the tall cliffs on its slopes as well as from some of the inhabitants.

Gil-Gand-Rask: a large island in the Southern Seas. Gil-Gand is name of the abandoned city on it.

Gildas, Saint: a Christian Saint, his Feast Dayis 29th Primus and his patronage is to those who combat monsters of the sea, and of annalists.

Glengate: a large independent village on the east of the plains that is a nexus for trade.

Goblin: a long-lived, small and lightly built humanoid with a skin that looks more like a snake than a Human, although it is as soft as Human skin.

Goldentide, The: a Freehold galleon taken and sunk by the *River Dragon*.

Gotar: the general name for any of the cloths made out of goat fleeces.

Greenskin: a slang term sometimes used in a derogatory way, for anyone of the Kharl races (even the Hobgoblins, who are grey).

Grey Virgins Range: a mountain range north of the Sawãd. In Arabic it is Kũm Hejaz.

Growling Harbour: a village on the south coast of the Plains on Barrowbrah Creek.

Guneydeolan halksulutoprak: also just Halksulutoprak, a Goblin tribal name, it means 'The Southern People of the Watery Earth.' They are located to the west of New Trekvarna.

Gupta ke Dvīpa: Hindi for 'Gupta's Isle;' a home for the rich, it is park-like and green.

Guthog's Bessing: a grass found on the plains of The Land. It is made into a wash to rid people and animals of ticks, fleas, and lice.

Hāfiz: an Arabic word, 'memoriser,' it is applied to someone who knows the entire Qur'an by heart.

Halkgenisovadin: a Goblin tribe near Sweetwater. Their name means 'The People of the Wide Valley.' They have signed the Scutari Treaty and may now be part of the Duchy of the New Found Land.

Hand: as a basic unit of measure it is made up of six fingers (1.7cm each) and so is 10.2cm long. Six make a cubit. A hand is six, a hand of hands (or a filled hand) is thirty-six.

Happy Man, The: a tavern in Southpoint.

Harijan: the lowest Hindu caste; often referred to as Untouchables, those who deal with the dead and with liminal products. They are often beggars, thieves, and criminals, and not by choice.

Haven: a nation at the mouth of the Rhastaputra River. Its inhabitants refer to it as Sharan.

Hawrãn Rũdh: a river that runs down from Kartala (Snowcap) to Buhairet Tabariyya through the Rãhit.

Hāthī Dvīpa: or Elephant Island in Pavitra Phāṭaka. It houses the Royal Elephants, among other things.

Hesperinos: performed at sundown, this is the beginning of the liturgical day for the Orthodox.

Hit on the head with a shoe: in the Caliphate, to strike the head of a person, or their image, with the sole of a shoe is the ultimate statement of contempt.

Hnefatafl: a board game shared by the Dwarves and the people of Wolfneck.

Hob or Hobgoblin: one of the larger humanoid races of Vhast. They have hard grey skin and are very strong and are, to Humans, quite ugly.

Holy Trinity: the Orthodox church in Southpoint.

Hudna: an Arabic word for 'truce' or a temporary peace.

Hugron pir: a hypergolic liquid, we could call it Greek Fire or napalm.

Humans: the most common intelligent race on Vhast. They have a wide variety of original origins but, despite when they come from, seem to have been on Vhast for about the same amount of time.

Iba Bay: a broad and deep bay formed to the east of the vast delta of the Swamp rivers.

Iblīs: Arabic for an Adversary.

Ikraam: an Arabic word that roughly translates as hospitality and generosity, but has more force.

In nomine Patris et fillii et Spritus Sancti: a Latin phrase, 'In the name of the Father, the Son, and the Holy Spirit.'

Insakharl: this is not a distinct race, but a name given to those who have part-Human and any form of part-Kharl ancestry.

Insak-div: the largest of the Darkreach races, and often referred to in the West as Dark Trolls (although they are largely dark green in colour). They are over twice as tall as a Human and a lot broader.

Irene, Saint: a Christian Saint, Feast Day 32nd Duodecimus, she is the patron of masons, miners and quarrymen.

Isha: a Muslim prayer time and hour and a half after sunset.

Inshallah: an Arabic word that best translates as 'if God wills it.'

Itaqu: an Arabic word meaning 'the faithful.'

Ithim: an Arabic word, it means 'the negative reward for bad deeds that is tallied on qiyamah (Judgement Day).'

Ivyshroud: a village of the Bear Folk.

Jabal Umm: a mountain where the Ziyanda Rũdh starts in meltwater.

Jabal Tahat: a mountain above Bab al-Abwãb.

Jain: a Hindu sect who, among other things, offer no violence to any creature.

Jewvanda (pron U-vanda): a village on the south coast on Piali Creek.

John the Apostle, Saint: a Christian Saint, Feast Day 6th Secundus, patron of love, booksellers and publishers, he is also invoked against poison & burns.

Kabeer Ma'a: a waterfall on the Ziyanda Rũdh, possibly the tallest major fall in The Land.

Kali: a Hindu aspect of the Goddess Durga, responsible for change and preservation, destruction of evil, and time, she is regarded as a force of balance.

Kartala: see Snowcap.

Kartikeya: the Hindu God of War.

Kayipkasehaliçden: a Goblin tribe of the Newfoundland, their name means 'Lost Bowl of the Rivermouth' and the area they live in is the one most overlapping with Humans.

Kãfirũn: an Arabic word 'Unbelievers.'

Kessog, Saint: a Christian Saint, Feast Day 10th Tertius, the patron of those who fight monsters on land. He is taken as a Patron Saint by Astrid.

Kharl: one of the races of Vaast. They are the most common form of humanoid after Humans. They vary greatly in appearance, but often have some animalistic features. There are several distinct tribes among them.

Khitan or Kara-Khitan: a group of mounted tribes who claim and occupy most of the plains, they are best thought of as Mongols.

Khoya Kshetr: literally the 'Lost Sector,' it is an area largely destroyed in The Burning. Its proper name is lost.

Khũbũr Rũdh: a river that runs from near Yãqũsa to the Beneen Plain where it is known as the North Lost River.

Kilā Dvīpa: or Fort Island, the major fortification of Pavitra Phāṭaka with granaries. It is meant as a final refuge for a large number of the city people.

Köle: a Khitan word that toughly translates as slave or captive.

Kshatya: the Hindu caste of the warriors, it includes most mages and rulers.

Kũm Hadramawt: a range of low hills in the middle of the Sawãd.

Kũm Hejaz: see Grey Virgins Range.

Kũm Kaysãn: Arabic for the Southern Mountains

Kurta: a very long male shirt that often comes down to the knees. It is always worn with trousers of some sort. It is put on over the head.

Kynigoi: riders with any level of armour riding unarmoured horses. Their primary role is skirmishing and harassing as well as scouting. They mainly use bows in combat.

Kyogle Creek: a long creek of the southern plains emptying into the sea at Deeryas.

La a'ref: an Arabic phrase 'I don't know.'

Leatherwings: a furred flying reptile, they come in almost all sizes up to huge.

Leidauesgynedig: see Rising Mud.

Lent: the Christian Holy Month in which something treasured is given up in the lead-up to Easter.

Litani Rũdh: a river on the Rãhit running from Jabal Tahat.

Llosyfyndd yr Aderyndân: the Faen name for the large volcano in the far south of the Southern Mountains.

Long Realm: the largest continent on Vhast, it runs nearly from pole to pole.

Maghreb: a Muslim prayer time a few minutes after sunset.

Mahr: bridal money paid by a groom to the wife or the wife's family.

Manoranjan Ke (Entertainer's): a section of Anta Dvīpa. Musicians, jugglers, tumblers and other entertainers are not high caste occupations. Most of them live in this area of Anta and it is often regarded as a place of genteel poverty where whole families can respectably starve to death.

Maqhaa: an Arabic word, literally 'a café.

Marchnaty, The: a large stone building in Bloomact where most of the business of the town is done.

Mary Magdalene, Saint: a Christian Saint, her Feast Day is the 4th of Quinque and her patronage is to sinners and those hoping for redemption.

Masters, the: a group of Undead who once had control over Dwarvenholme.

Megas Fabrika: the Great Factory of Antdrudge where explosives and flame weapons are made for the armies of Darkreach.

Metropolitan: the title of an Orthodox arch-bishop. Unless a Patriarch is created, it is the highest rank in the Orthodox faith and a Metropolitan, although still subject to a Synod, is theologically supreme in their area.

Mice: the name the inhabitants of Mousehole refer to themselves by.

Michael, Saint: a Christian Saint, Feast Day is 1st Undecim and he is patron of both graveyards and victory.

Misr al-Mār: a monastery and school in the Caliphate. It is the training base for the Ghazi.

Mistledross: a village in the south of Darkreach, the next largish settlement to the north of Southpoint.

Mogoi: a Khitan word for the animal and clan of the Snake.

Molotail: these are glass containers of hugron pir.

Money of Haven: the base coin is the Anna. It is made of tin and weighs 20g. The smaller coins are the Dam (copper, 2.5g, A1/100th) and Ten-dam (copper, 25g, A1/10th). Larger are Four Anna (bronze, 26.67g, A4), Rupiya (silver, 2.67g, A16), Ten Rupiya (silver, 26.67g, A160), Tanka (gold, 5g, A450), Mohur (gold, 20g, A1,800) and the rare 100 Mohur (mithril, ie titanium 180g, A18,000).

Money of the Swamp: the base coin is the ten-mote piece. It is made of tin and weighs 20g. Smaller than it is the mote (copper, 25g, 1/10th ten-mote). Larger arc a farthing (bronze, 25g, m3.75), a penny (silver/copper alloy, 100g, m15), tenpenny (silver, 25g, m150), guinea (gold 33g, m3,300, and ten guinea (platinum, 36.67g, m33,000).

Mordorwyrhta: a mountain shrub that provides a variable, but usually very strong, poison.

Mori: a Khitan word for both the animal and clan of the Horse. Moriid is the plural form.

Mosque of Sulieman: the largest and most important mosque in Dimashq.

Mousehole: a free village in the Mountains ruled by the Princesses Rani and Theodora. The inhabitants refer to themselves as Mice.

Mu'adhdhin: an Arabic word, theyare the person who issues the call to prayer or ādhān.

Mufriza: a small Arabic military unit of cavalry, up to a company in size.

Mufsidūn: an evildoer who wages jihad not in accordance with the Qur'an.

Munshee: the Hindi word for a scribe or clerk.

Mushriq: Arabic word for a pagan.

Nekulturny: an insulting word in the Darkspeech of Wolfneck that means, literally, that a person is uncultured.

Neron Island: the most northerly known inhabited island off the coast of The Land.

New Ashvaria: both the main and central County of the Newfoundland and the name of its largest town.

New Trekvarna: both the most westerly County of the Newfoundland and its major town

Newfoundland or New Found Land: A continent to the north-west of Freehold and a colony of theirs.

Nikah: Arabic for marriage.

Nikah al-mut'ah: an Arabic term for a temporary marriage.

Oban Forest: the major forest of Freehold.

Omáda: a Darkreach unit of twelve people.

Ooshz (pron Ooze): a small village on the south coast of The Land.

Orphanos: the Orphans are an elite tourma (squadron) of Darkreach kynigoi. Some of their story is told in the novella *A Brief Encounter*.

Örnödiin: the Khitan word for a Freeholder (lit. westerner).

Pack-hunters: feathered bipedal carnivorous dinosaurs with a large slashing claw central on their foot.

Pancake Pali: a fun Christian festival on 14th Quattro that marks the start of period of Lent.

Panic: the name of the smaller moon of Vhast.

Paradēśī: one Hindi word for foreigner.

Paul, Saint: a Christian Saint, Feast Day 7th December, his patronage is to evangelism.

Pavitra Phāṭaka: the Hindi for the capital of Haven, it is often called Sacred Gate.

Peace Tower: the major fortification of the, now destroyed, Brotherhood.

Peelfall: a town in the north of Haven.

Phocas, Saint: a Christian Saint, Feast Day 14th Sixtus, his patronage is to farmers and gardeners. One of the churches in Southpoint is named from him.

Piali Creek: a long, but not strong, waterway leading from a marsh on the coast deep into the southern plains. Jewvanda is built at its mouth.

Pravesh Kila: a fortification on Anta that dominates the docks. Literally it is 'Entry Fort.'

Presbytera: The title of a wife of an Orthodox priest or Metropolitan.

Pure Doe, The: a good tavern in Bloomact.

Pūrvī Taṭa: Hindi for the eastern shore of the Rhastputra

Pusan: the Hindu God of travellers, herdsmen and roads.

Pyjamas: very loose trousers held up with a drawstring.

Qabbala: a block of black rock that is the most sacred site of Islam and an object of pilgrimage.

Qanat: small underground artificial rivers used to bring water into drier areas for irrigation.

Qiyamah: an Arabic word, 'Judgement Day.'

Quiethaven: a river and the bay it forms at the base of the volcano Llosyfyndd yr Aderyndân. It is the only real shelter in the area from storms.

Randē: a word for a common prostitute in Hindi

Rainjig: a very small village in the south-east of the Swamp. In Faen it is called Glawdans.

Rath Yatra: 13th Quinque, a Festival associated with Jagganath, an aspect of Vishnu, also called the Festival of Chariots.

Rhastaputra River: the main river draining the mountains and area just to the west of them in the south.

Rãhit: the fertile plain in the mountain valley where Dimashq is built.

Rājā kē Dvīpa: Hindi for the 'Rajah's Isle' it has the palace as well as much of the upper caste housing and shopping in Pavitra Phāṭaka.

Rebelkill: a fortress village in Darkreach that guards a vital gap in the southern mountains from the Tãb Rũdh. It was once known as Lacedemonia.

Reeve: the title of a community leader in the Swamp.

Rest Potion: a potion made from Sleepwell that gives the imbiber all of the benefits of a full night's sleep, it is very addictive.

Rising Mud (or Leidauesgynedig): a village in the Swamp built on islands of mud behind wooden walls.

River Dragon: a brigantine owned by the Mice. It has Olympias as its Captain. It is gradually being equipped with formidable magic.

River's Head Inn: a new tavern in the Darkreach Gap near the head of the Methul River.

Rubi: a small village outside Dewakung in Freehold.

Sacred Gate: see Pavitra Phāṭaka.

Sadaqah: an Arabic word that roughly means charity.

Saltbeach: an independent village on the southern edge of the plains it is the closest to Freehold. It is built around Arden Creek.

Saltverge: the smallest and most isolated of the towns of Haven.

Sawãd: the name of plains of the Tãb Rũdh.

Sayyeda/Sayyidĩ: Arabic, literally 'my lady' or 'my lord.'

Scutari: a small village in the County of Sweetwater in the Newfoundland where an agreement has been struck between Goblins and Humans that may bring peace after hundreds of years of strife.

Sethji: a Hindi word, it is a male honourific for a person of wealth and wisdom. It is not the right one for Basil to have used in this context.

Seytani: an Arabic word for the Adversaries and their allies.

Sh-hone: a soft and strong cloth made out of fibres from the retted fibres of a seaweed of the same name.

Sharan: see Haven.

Shabwa: a very small hamlet at the base of the climb up to Bab al-Abwãb from the Rãhit.

Shelike: a large town in Haven.

Sherwani: a knee-length, front buttoning male coat with long sleeves.

Skrice: a village in the north on Neron Island.

Snowcap: the tallest mountain in the south of the mountains. In Arabic, Kartala.

Snowcap Rivulet: a small and fast river that starts in a glacier on top of Snowcap and ends near Rainjig.

Sophia, Saint: an Orthodox Saint, Feast Day 32nd Secundus, she is the patron of charity and sacrifice for others. The Basilica at Erave Town is dedicated to her.

Southpoint: the southernmost town in Darkreach.

Squamawr: a village in the west of the Swamp.

Starşiyrang: roughly a Sergeant or Warrant Officer, there are several grades in Darkreach.

Steerbord: *the side of a northern boat that the steering oar is on,* the right-hand side.

Sudra: the Hindu caste of labourers and workers, which includes merchants and most of the profitable crafts.

Swamp, The: the common name for the Confederation of the Free.

Sweetwater: both the most northerly County of the Newfoundland and its main town.

Ta'if: a new and small village in the Caliphate.

Tãb Rũdh: a river in the Caliphate that flows into Darkreach and becomes the Garthcurr River there.

Tempter, The: an isolated mountain near Southpoint.

Terror: the name of the larger moon of Vhast.

Third Tower: a Darkreach village on the edge of the Southern Mountains.

Thomas: Saint: a Christian Saint, Feast day 5th Quinque. He is the patron of those who seek answers.

Three Sisters: a row of mountains (East, Middle and West) in the far south of the main range. The Wiccans refer to them as the Crone, the Mother, and the Maid.

Tor Karoso: a very tall mountain on the island of Gil-Gand-Rask.

Tourmachos: a Darkreach military rank of cavalry. A senior Tourmachos (Tourmachos Perissótero) commands a Tourmos (Company), the senior mage of the same unit will be a junior Tourmachos and second in command.

Trekvarna: the second largest and most important city in Freehold.

Twelvth Night: a feast night for all Christians, held twelve days after Christmas.

Umra al-Harb: an Arabic phrase, 'warlord.'

Ülgeriin baatar: a Khitan phrase, literally 'hero from tales.'

Veshya: a Hindi word for a courtesan or high-end prostitute.

Videshē ka Ghāt: Foreigner's Wharf on Anta.

Vidēśiyōṁ: a Hindi word for alien and foreign.

Vilāsita ka Mārg: the 'Path of Luxury,' a road near the coast that runs from Pravesh Kila to Lamba Rāsta.

Vinice: a very large town in Haven.

Vyāpārī Bridge: the bridge leading from Rājā kē Dvīpa to Vyāpārī Dvīpa.

Vyāpārī Dvīpa: 'Merchant's Island;' where much of the commerce of Pavitra Phāṭaka happens and home to many tradesmen and shops as well as permanent markets.

Wa-'Alaykum us-Salām wa-Raḥmatullāhi wa-Barakātuhu...Marhaba!: an Arabic phrase returning a greeting. 'And on you be the Peace and Mercy of God and His Blessing. Welcome.'

Wadī: an Arabic word for a river valley.

Wall, The: a long ridge of small mountains that rise abruptly to the east of the Swamp.

Warkworth: a free village in the west of The Land. It lies on a sea-cliff between Amity and Freehold.

Waxbad: a low-level poison derived from a jungle herb.

Week: each week on Vhast has six days. Generally, across The Land, these are given the names: Firstday, Deutera, Pali, Tetarti, Dithlau and Krondag. Kron is the name given to the sun. The definitions and roots of some of these names are unknown.

Wheoh: a small Darkreach hamlet that sits in the entrance to the Sawãd.

Wolfsbane: a common herb that makes a deadly poison.

Yarmũk: a village in the Caliphate.

Yãqũsa: northernmost village of the Caliphate.

Zalimun: an Arabic word for evil-doers and the unjust.

Zandaqa: an Arabic word that means 'deep heresy.'

Zita, Saint: a Christian Saint, Feast Day 27th Tertius, patron of housewives and servants.

Ziyanda Rũdh: see Buccleah River.

Zürkh setgelee gartaa barisan khün: a Khitan phrase, (literally 'One who holds my heart in her hands') for a deep love.

Cast

Aaron Skynner: a tanner and widower from Glengate, comes to Mousehole seeking a wife. He marries Aine.

Abdul Mohammed ibn Hasid al-Rahmãn: Caliph of the Faithful.

Adara verch Glynis: a cousin of Bryony from Rising Mud and in love with her. She was rescued from the Master's servants in Pavitra Phāṭaka. She marries Stefan in an arrangement that allows her to share her co-wife with him.

Adrian Digge: a young miner from Saltbeach who travels to Mousehole and marries Verina.

Ahmed: a bandit mage who was captured and then executed when Mousehole was first freed.

Aigiarn: late of the Lion Clan, marries Hulagu.

Aikaterine: daughter of Theodora and Rani (courtesy of Rani's unknowing brother).

Aine verch Liban: a former slave from Bloomact in The Swamp, she is now the brewer and distiller for Mousehole. She marries Aaron.

Alã al-Sadiq: a guard commander at Dimashq.

Alaine: late of the Eagle clan, marries Hulagu.

Alĩ ibn Yũsuf al Mãr: Ayatollah Uzma or Grand Ayatollah of Darkreach

Anahita: a Khitan girl from Mousehole and Hulagu's köle, she is the mother of two of his children. She becomes one of the Clan of the Horse and marries Dobun along with Kãhina.

Anna Akritina: the mother of Basil and the customs official at Southpoint.

Anne: the new name of one of the prostitutes rescued from Warkworth. She is now a sailor on the River Dragon, one of the Saints and eventually wife of Marianus Gerontas.

Ariadne Nepina: an Insakharl (part Alat-kharl) from Antdrudge. She is partly trained as an engineer but wanted a quieter life as a brick and tile maker and layer after her parents are killed in an accident. She moves to Mousehole and marries the Hob Krukurb. Their daughter is Nikê.

Arthur Garden: a farmer and youngest son from Evilhalt. He comes to Mousehole seeking land and a wife. He marries Make.

Asad ibn Sayf: a widower from Doro. He is a farmer and becomes the husband of Hagar and Rabi'ah. Asticus Tzimisces: one of three kataphractoi (heavy cavalry) from Darkreach who comes to join Mousehole and is sent straight into the fray against the Brothers. He marries Zoë.

Astrid Tostisdottir (the Cat): an Insakharl from Wolfneck, in the far north of The Land. She is married to Basil. Her youngest brother is Thorstein, now a priest.

Atã ibn Rãfi: a widower from Mistledross. He is a timber-feller. He becomes the husband of Umm and Zafirah. Athgal Dewin: an air mage of Rising Mud and friend of Glyn and Ith. He attempts to kill Astrid and is executed after confessing.

Ayesha: an ghazi of the Caliphate assigned by a Princess to guard Theodora. She is a minor daughter of Hãritha, the Sheik of Yãqũsa. She eventually marries Hulagu as his senior wife.

Aziz (Azizsevgili or Brave Lover): a Hobgoblin who is captured during the attack on Mousehole. He falls in love with Verily and converts to the Orthodox faith, marries her, and becomes a priest.Basil Akritas or Kutsulbalik (his nickname from great-grandfather): he is mostly human (one sixteenth Kharl) and an experienced officer of the Antikataskopeía. He is married to Astrid and living in Mousehole and assigned to guard Theodora by Hrothnog. His sister is Olympias.

Batrĩq al-Akk: the Sheik of Dimashq.

Bianca Palama: a former foundling from Freehold now living in Mousehole and married to Bishop Christopher. Bilqĩs al-Yarmũk: a tiny girl, from a trade background in the Caliphate, she now lives in Mousehole as an apprentice mage. She has some ability as a glassblower. She marries Tãriq as his senior wife. Bishal ibn Mũsa: the Ayatollah in Dimashq.

Blanid verch Barita: a Wiccan priestess and the Reeve of Eastguard Tower in the Swamp. Brica: Murdered mother of Ia.

Bridget: the new name of one of the prostitutes rescued from Warkworth. She is now a sailor on the River Dragon, one of the Saints and eventually a wife of Marianus Gerontas.

Bryony verch Dafydd: a freckled red-head from Rising Mud in the Swamp. Her husband (Conan ap Reardon) and father (Dafydd ap Comyn) were killed at her wedding and she was brought to Mousehole as a slave. She is now married to Stefan. She is cousin, lover and sister-wife to Adara.

Buthayna: A dancer and prostitute in Ta'if.

Caractacus ap Comyn: Druid at Rainjig in the Swamp and brother of its wiccan priestess Dianan verch Erin. Catherine: the new name of one of the prostitutes rescued from Warkworth. She is now a sailor on the River Dragon, one of the Saints and eventually a wife of Marianus Gerontas.

Cecilia: the new name of one of the prostitutes rescued from Warkworth. She is now a sailor on the River Dragon, one of the Saints and eventually a wife of Marianus Gerontas.

Chãch Ghoshal: an older Brahmin that the Mice buy land from in Sacred Gate.

Christopher Palamas, Bishop: the suffragan Orthodox Bishop of the Mountains based in Mousehole and husband of Bianca. He is a very holy, but diplomatic, man and a dedicated healer.

Conaire ap Molloy: the Reeve of Squamawr.

Conan ap Reardon: the first husband of Bryony who was killed on their marriage night.

Conrad: a mage from The Swamp sent to Mousehole after the Hobs have supposedly cleared it. He is executed. Cosmas Camaterus: Metropolitan of the Orthodox Church for the south-east of The Land west of the mountains (from Evilhalt south and including Haven and the Swamp). He is based in Erave Town.

Crida verch Ninne: Wiccan priestess at Erave Town. Her husband and senior priest is Fiachu ap Maglorix. Cuthbert: a bandit armsman from The Swamp sent to Mousehole after the Hobs have supposedly cleared it. He is executed.

Cynric the Smith: the Mayor of Erave Town

Cyril: the first ordained Hobgoblin Orthodox priest, he was the last druid apprentice of his tribe.

Dafydd ap Comyn: Bryony's murdered father.

Danelis Alvarez: A former slave originally from Warkworth, she now lives in Mousehole. She marries Father Simeon.

Daniel: Father of Goditha and Robin.

Daniel Mason: second child of Goditha and Parminder.

Delphinia: (of the dolphins) daughter of Habib and Thomaïs and sister of Isidore.

Demetrios Choumnos: Orthodox Metropolitan responsible for the southern independent villages. He is based at Bridgcap.

Denizkartal (or sea eagle): Boyuk-kharl and Olympias's bosun on the *River Dragon* and her eventual husband. Denny Pollard: a young shearer from Ooshz who travels to Mousehole. He marries both Lamentations and Pass. Dianan verch Erin: the Wiccan priestess at Rainjig, sister of Caractacus ap Comyn.

Dobun: late of the Axe-beaks, becomes shaman of the Horse and marries Anahita and Kãhina.

Dulcie o Bathmawr: A former slave from Bathmawr in The Swamp. She is now the Mousehole carpenter and marries Jordan.

Eleanor Fournier: caravan guard from Topwin in Freehold then a slave, she now lives in Mousehole and works as a jeweller. She is married to Robin Fletcher and is one of the first in the village to fall pregnant. They have also adopted several children.

Erika Whittaker: girl from Warkworth. She marries Nadia and becomes an assistant to Kaliope.

Eusebius, Father: A priest from Southpoint who goes to Flyjudge.

Eustathius: a priest from Erave Town who goes to Sacred Gate as a priest.

Fear (or Fear the Lord Your God) Thatcher: 10 years old, she is the adopted daughter of Rani and Theodora.

Fiachu ap Maglorix: Wiccan priest at Erave Town. His wife and priestess is Crida ferch Ninne. Fire: see Kaliope.

Figel ap Machute: former guard captain in Eastguard Tower

Fortunata Esposito: A former slave from Ashvaria and now dressmaker and embroiderer for Mousehole, also a mage. She is the first wife of Norbert along with Sajãh and her son is Valentine and younger twins are Bryan and Alice.

Francesco: the merchant whose caravan Bianca was first a part of. The caravan was attacked and everyone died but her. One of Bianca's children is named after him.

Frederick Russell, Father: Orthodox priest of Jewvanda.

Galla Narchina: Insakharl sailor and sailmaker/carpenter added to the crew of the River Dragon in Southpoint. She is married to Gundardasc.

Gamil: the Chief Predestinator on the Vhast project. She set in motion her people's side of the events that are described in these books.

George, Praetor: The leader of the first file of the Basilica Anthropoi to be based at Saltbeach.

Georgios Anoteron Akritas: (the senior) Basil's father and husband of Anna. Guard commander at Southpoint. Giles Ploughman: former slave and farmer at Mousehole. He is married to Naeve. He also makes cheese. Glad: name by which We Declare Unto You Glad Tidings is known. She is a former Brotherhood slave girl who becomes Christopher's clerk.

Glyn ap Tristan: a mage in Rising Mud and servant of the Masters. He had one of their patterns in one of his outbuildings. He was killed the last time the Mice were there.

Goditha Mason: a former slave from Jewvanda. She is sister to Robin Fletcher and married to Parminder. She is the mason of Mousehole and an Earth mage.

Gowan the Enchanting: the Reeve of Bloomact and Chairman of the Council of the Free and thus 'ruler' of the Swamp. He is a second cousin to Ia.

Gundardasc Narches: a Kichic-kharl cook and sailor added to the River Dragon in Southpoint. His wife is Galla.

Gurinder: sixteen-year old sister of Parminder and also a mage apprentice.

Guy Rossignol: A refugee from Freehold and partner of Maximilian. He is the third son of the Duke of Trekvarna.

Gwillam: a bandit armsman from The Swamp sent to Mousehole after the Hobs have supposedly cleared it. He is executed.

Habib: Insakharl sailor sent from Darkreach to help crew the *River Dragon*. He is married to Thomaïs.

Hagar al-Jamila: former slave from a farming family outside Dimashq in the Caliphate, she lives in Mousehole as the village butcher. She becomes senior wife to Asad along with Rabi'ah.

Hamid: A ghazi killed by Ayesha when they captured Adara.

Hand: in full 'I Lift Up My Hand to Heaven', a Brotherhood slave freed at One Tree Hill. She becomes an apprentice Earth mage and an assistant to Naeve and Goditha.

Harald Pitt: former slave and miner at Mousehole. He marries Lakshmi.

Harnermêŝ: (Har-ner-meess): a young man from Gil-Gand-Rask. He becomes Jennifer's lover and joins the River Dragon.

Hassan ibn Abdul: third son of the Caliph, a former adventurer who married Princess Miriam on his travels. Hãritha al-Yãqũsa: Sheik of Yãqũsa and father of Ayesha.

Hãshim: Muslim cleric from Darkreach sent to Bloomact. He marries Ayesha's half sister.

Hilarion: a priest from Erave Town who goes to Sacred Gate as a priest.

Hrothnog: The immortal God-King of Darkreach and great-great-grandfather of Theodora. He is now married to Fãtima. At the start of the books his race is unknown, but is definitely not Human.

Hulagu (Togotak Hulagu): a Khitan tribesman. His tribe and totem was the Dire Wolf. He becomes a part of Mousehole and becomes Tar-Khan of the reborn Clan of the Horse (or Mori). He marries Ayesha, Aigiarn, and Alaine.

Ia verch Brica: a young and very beautiful Wiccan priestess chosen as a sacrifice by Athgal in Rising Mud. She has a raccoon familiar called Maeve. She eventually marries Basil and becomes a sister-wife to Astrid. Ikrimah ibn Fida: Tourmachos of the Orphanos. He is in charge of Iyãd's escort.

Irene: Insakharl sailor sent from Darkreach to help crew the *River Dragon*. She is married to Sabas. Isidore: son of Habib and Thomaïs and brother of Delphinia.

Ith ap Tristan: the brother of Glyn in Rising Mud. He was out of the village on the first raid is killed by Astrid on the second visit.

Iyãd ibn Hãritha al-Shaybãn: sheik of Ta'if. Shaybãn is a tribal affiliation. Iyãd ibn Walĩd: the Mullah of the main mosque in Ardlark.

Jamal abd Allah: A ghazi and bodyguard for Maarshtrin.

James Lobb: The brother of Valeria. He comes to Mousehole to farm.

Jennifer Wagg: young woman, guard, and sailor, from Deeryas. She was rescued from the Master's servants in Pavitra Phãṭaka where she was brought as a sacrifice. She ends up married to Harnermêŝ.

Jordan Croker: a journeyman potter from Greensin. No more potters are needed there and he came seeking a place to settle and a wife. He marries Dulcie. Their daughter is Rebecca.

Kalliope: (beautiful voice) the name taken by In Flaming Fire Take Vengeance on Them That Know Not God when she is baptised. She is the 16 year old widow of a Brotherhood priest taken captive at Peace Tower and brought back to Mousehole. There she marries Thorstein.

Kãhina: once Hulagu's köle and mother of two of his children. She becomes one of the Clan of the Horse and marries Dobun along with Anahita.

Kessog, Father: the Orthodox priest in Rising Mud.

Khabbãb ibn Zubayr: The Darkreach mage who accompanies Iyãd and the Mice to the Caliphate.

Khãzim ibn Azĩz al-Mudar: Bitrĩq or governor of Bab al-Abwãb

Kostas: a priest from Erave Town who goes to Bloomact as a priest.

Krukurb: (Strong Frog) one of the Hobs who join the Mice for the campaign in the North. He later marries Ariadne.

Lamentations: A slave girl from the Brotherhood brought to Camel Island to be sacrificed to establish a master pattern. Originally known as 'There Shall Be Lamentations', Bianca thought that her name was 'There Shall Be Lemons'.

Lakshmi Brar: Former Havenite and a slave, she has converted and is now Orthodox and married to Harald Pitt. She is the apothecary and midwife for Mousehole.

Lãdi al Yarmũk: Former slave from the Caliphate, she is the chief cook at Mousehole and very skilled. She marries Nathanael.

Leo: mosaic and tile worker brought to Mousehole during the Synod to work on Saint George's Basilica. Linn, Master: The brewer at Jewvanda.

Maarshtrin: One of the Adversaries. He is killed at Ta'if.

Maeve: a raccoon and the familiar of Ia.

Make Me To Know My Transgressions: young woman from the Brotherhood brought as a slave to restock Mousehole. She is usually called Make. She marries Arthur.

Maria Beman: a kidnapped woman from Greensin, brought to Mousehole by slavers after it was freed. She is now learning to be a Fire mage and marries Menas.

Maro, Father: priest in charge the Church of the Holy Trinity in Southpoint.

Mary: the new name of one of the prostitutes rescued from Warkworth. She is now a sailor on the River Dragon, one of the Saints and eventually a wife of Marianus Gerontas.

Maximilian Keep: A refugee from Rubi in Freehold and partner of Guy Melissa: the mother of Robin and Goditha.

Melissa Mason: daughter of Goditha and Parminder, elder sister to Daniel.

Menas Philokales: one of three kataphractoi (heavy cavalry) from Darkreach who comes to join Mousehole and is sent straight into the fray against the Brothers. He marries Maria.

Michael, Father: chief missionary priest to the Cenubarkincilari. Married to Sophronia.

Miriam do Hrothnog: cousin of Theodora who is now married to the third son of the Caliph, Hassan ibn Abdul in the Caliphate.

Mughĩra abd Allah: Mullah and the Amĩr al-Ghazi, commander of the ghazi and head of their school at Misr al-Mãr.

Muhammed al-Fudũl al-Khawlãn: sheik of Yarmũk.

Mulraj: agent of Chãch and also his betrayer.

Mũsã ibn Nasr: Secretary to Hrothnog.

Myles Fysh: The village leader of Saltbeach.

Nadia Everett: a girl from Warkworth, she marries Erika and becomes a mason.

Naeve Milker: Former Freehold dairymaid and former slave who now runs the herds of Mousehole. She becomes an apprentice mage and marries Giles.

Nathanael Ktenas: an Orthodox pastrycook from Ardlark who comes to Mousehole for Lãdi.

Neon Chrysoloras: one of three kataphractoi (heavy cavalry) from Darkreach who comes to join Mousehole and is sent straight into the fray against the Brothers. He marries Tabitha.

Niam verch Firlan: the Reeve of Flyjudge in the Swamp.

Nicholas Chiller: a Water mage at Jewvanda and their village leader.

Nikephorus Cheilas: a senior Palace servant from Ardlark who moves to Mousehole, he is now married to Valeria.

Norbert Black: He is skilled as a blacksmith, weapons smith and armourer and kept as a slave in Mousehole. When he gets free he marries both Fortunata and Sajãh.

Olympias Akritina: Basil's sister, a junior officer in the navy in charge of a small fast scout and messenger boat. She becomes Captain of the *River Dragon* while still holding the rank of a Darkreach Epilarch (small-unit commander) in charge of all Darkreach vessels beyond the Great Range. She marries Denizkartal.

Parminder: a former slave, she is an assistant cook and sometimes dressmaker at Mousehole, she marries Goditha and is sister to Gurinder. She becomes an apprentice mage and is a xeno-telepath.

Pass: A slave girl from the Brotherhood brought to Camel Island to be sacrificed to establish a master pattern. In full 'It Shall Come to Pass'. She become an Air mage. She marries Denny.

Patrick, Saint: a Christian Saint, his Feast Day it the 17th of Tertius and he is the called upon for dominion over serpents.

Polymnia: (beautiful song) the daughter of Sabas and Irene

Rabi'ah al-Raqisa: a poor spinner and weaver from Ardlark. Her drunken father sold her into slavery. She is sent by her Imam to Mousehole. She marries Asad.

Rãfi: son of Rabi'ah and Asad.

Ragnilde Hrolfrssen: the eldest daughter of Baron Hrolfr Strongarm of Oldike and betrothed of Thord.

Rahki Johar: a Harijan servant from Haven who was made captive. She was rescued from the Master's servants in Pavitra Phāṭaka.

Rani Rai: a former Havenite Battle Mage and now co-Princess of Mousehole. She has broken caste and is married to Theodora and has adopted Fear and is regarded as the father of Aikaterine.

Rãfi: a ghazi captured when Adara was captured.

Reema: A girl from Third Tower held and tortured in Ta'if.

Rhea: the moneylender in Southpoint.

Robin Fletcher: A former slave, he is the fletcher, and bowyer for Mousehole. He is married to Eleanor and they have adopted several children. He is the brother of Godítha.

Rosa: an animal handler on Francesco's caravan who was raped and murdered. One of Bianca's children is named after her.

Ruth Hawker: a former Freehold merchant and now teacher of the village children in Mousehole. She is married to Father Theodule.

Sabas: Insakharl sailor sent from Darkreach to help crew the *River Dragon*. He is married to Irene. Saccius ap Nemglan: general factotum in Rainjig.

Sajãh bint Javed: from the Caliphate, she is the Seneschal of Mousehole under the Princesses. She is second wife of Norbert Black. Adopted mother of Roxanna and Ruhayma and mother of Bishal & Huma.

Samthann ap Dufgal: a mage and the Reeve for Rainjig.

Sayf abd Allah: A ghazi who is sent to investigate Mousehole.

Shilpa Sodaagar: Former Havenite trader and slave and now assistant smith in Mousehole. She takes Vishal as her partner.

Siglevi the Short: the Human Baron of Evilhalt.

Simeon Alvarez, Father: Catholic cleric and werewolf who is born in Xanthia in the Newfoundland. He flees from there and ends up in Mousehole through the Bear Folk. He converts to being Orthodox and marries Danelis.

Stefan Ostrogski: a young soldier from Evilhalt. He is now in charge of the militia of Mousehole and is married to Bryony and her cousin Adara. He is also a leatherworker and has an inherited magical sword called Smiter and another, anti-dragon sword called Wrath.

Sin: more fully They Shall Confess Their Sin. A former Brotherhood slave girl, she becomes the domestic and child minder for Astrid and Basil.

Sofronia: wife of Father Michael in Dhargev.

Sughdĩ: son of Zafirah and Atã.

Sulaym: A ghazi assigned to the Princess Miriam.

Surayi: a ghazi killed by Astrid when Adara is kidnapped.

Tabitha Chrysolora: born in a farming hamlet near Erave Town and a former slave, she now lives in Mousehole as an assistant carpenter and cook. She has one green eye and one blue one. She marries Neon.

Tãriq ibn Kasĩla: a quarryman from Silentochre. He becomes husband of Bilqĩs and Yumn.

Theodora do Hrothnog: a great-great-granddaughter of Hrothnog. She is not entirely human, a mage and, at over 130 years, is far older than the late teens that she appears to have. She is now Princess of Mousehole with her husband, Rani and their adopted daughter Fear and daughter Aikaterine. Cousin of Miriam.

Theodule Panaretos, Father: a former monk and now assistant to Father Christopher at Mousehole. He marries Ruth.

Theophano, Father: A priest from Southpoint who goes to Squamor.

Thomaïs: Insakharl sailor sent from Darkreach to help crew the *River Dragon*. She is married to Habib.

Thord Arnorsson: A shorter and broad humanoid of the species locally known as a Dwarf. He comes from Kharlsbane in the Northern Mountains, but is now Mousehole's Ambassador to the Dwarves. He rides a sheep called Hillstrider. He is known as the Crown-finder to the Dwarves and is engaged to Ragnilde.

Thorstein Tostisson, Father: priest and youngest brother of Astrid. He moves to Mousehole and marries Kaliope. Their twin daughters are Berenike and Iris.

Trystan ap Dafydd ap Comyn: Bryony's murdered brother.

Tũlũn: A ghazi assigned to the Princess Miriam.

Ubãda: A ghazi captured during the attempt to capture Adara.

Umm bint Wã'il: Slave of the bandits from a poor farming family in the Caliphate, she is now a spinner and weaver in Mousehole and helps in the kitchen. She is now the senior wife of Atã ibn Rãfi.

Uqba: a Caliphate mage captured during the attempted kidnapping of Adara.

Urfai ap Carel: an elderly and powerful Water mage and now Reeve of Rising Mud. He opposed the war. Ursula: nurse of Virginia Norbery. She is taken captive from the Goldentide.

Uthman ibn Hakim: the Mullah of the small mosque at Bloomact in the Swamp.

Valeria Cheila (nee Lobb): from Deeryas on the south coast, she is now the servant of Rani and Theodora and has married Nikephorus. Mother of Angelina and Eugenia Cheilas. Her brother, James, joins her in the valley.

Vengeance (The Vengeance of the Lord is Mine Quester): Brotherhood scout and Inquisitor from the Flails of God who comes to Mousehole to spy on it. He is executed.

Verily I Rejoice in the Lord Tiller (Verily): a former Brotherhood slave and then slave in Mousehole, now an assistant cook and apprentice mage in Mousehole. She can 'smell' magic and has married Aziz.

Verina Gabala: an Orthodox miller from Mistledross. She leaves Darkreach after she loses her family in an earthquake and ends up in Mousehole married to Adrian Digge.

Virginia Norbery: Second daughter of the Duke of the New Found Land, she is taken captive with the sinking of the Goldentide.

Vishal Kapur: young armsman from Haven. In the pay of the Master's servants, he is captured and then joins the Mice. He is taken as a partner by Shilpa.

Walīd: A Mullah from Southpoint sent to set up a mosque in Eastguard.

Winifred: the new name of one of the prostitutes rescued from Warkworth. She is now a sailor on the River Dragon, one of the Saints and eventually a wife of Marianus Gerontas.

Yabaribaykus: A Goblin freed from *The Goldentide*, his name means Wild Owl.

Yakuţana: A Goblin woman from the time of the 'discovery' of the New Found Land, her name means 'Ruby Dawn'. The 'ţ' is pronounced 'th'.

Yãqũt al-Shahīd: an elderly mage living in Ta'if.

Yumn al-Yatim: an orphan carpet maker from Ardlark who became a prostitute to either raise a dowry or get enough for a loom. She is sent by her Imam to Mousehole. She becomes junior wife to Tãriq.

Zafirah al-Matie: a poor spinner and weaver from Ardlark who sells herself into slavery to pay the family debts. She is sent by her Mullah to Mousehole. She becomes junior wife to Atã.

Zainab: the daughter of Tariq and Bilquis.

Zeenat Koirala: a Harijan and former prostitute from Haven, rescued and brought to Mousehole.

Zoë Anicia: an Orthodox baker from Mistledross. She loses her family in an earthquake and ends up in Mousehole married to Asticus

Details of Mousehole

Explanation: All shops and trades will have a quality associated with them denoting level of service, how good their items are etc. As an example Mousehole has Norbert Black. He has blacksmith Q5, weaponsmith Q5, and armourer Q5. He is a generalist and can do most work using iron. He is not particularly good, but he is competent in all his areas.

A craft or vocation followed by a number indicates the competencies that the person holds. Norbert is has six competencies in Trades. The vocations mentioned are Trades (any actual Craft), Vagus (an unspecialised general category), Professional (indicates some formal education), Illicit (made their living beyond the, usually as a thief and/or prostitute), Armsman (a soldier or guard), Scout (a person who seeks paths and usually is an archer), Cleric, and Mage. Clerics and Mages have their Piety or Psychic Ability listed and, for mages, their Element and Moon (where known). Characters often have skills listed after a colon. Anything of 3 or above is at a level where a person can make a living at it.

Sometimes more detail is given. For instance there is Rani Rai (Mage $C9^{19FD}$). This means that she is currently a 9 competency mage (which is fairly powerful for a village enchanter), that she has a Psychic Ability of 19 (which is a high level) and that she is a Fire mage of the sign of the Dragon. This indicates her area of specialty in her spells (which is destruction and war).

Mousehole

This is a very small village of less than 65 inhabitants on the track from Mouthgard down to the Swamp. It was a bandit hideout, but is now free. The rulers are the most powerful mages in the area and there are minor mages. It produces dark rubies, antimony, Healbush, Sweet Ali and Lying Miriam. Potions are available. There are many more women there than men and the women come from all parts of The Lland and all are beautiful.

The Village of Mousehole

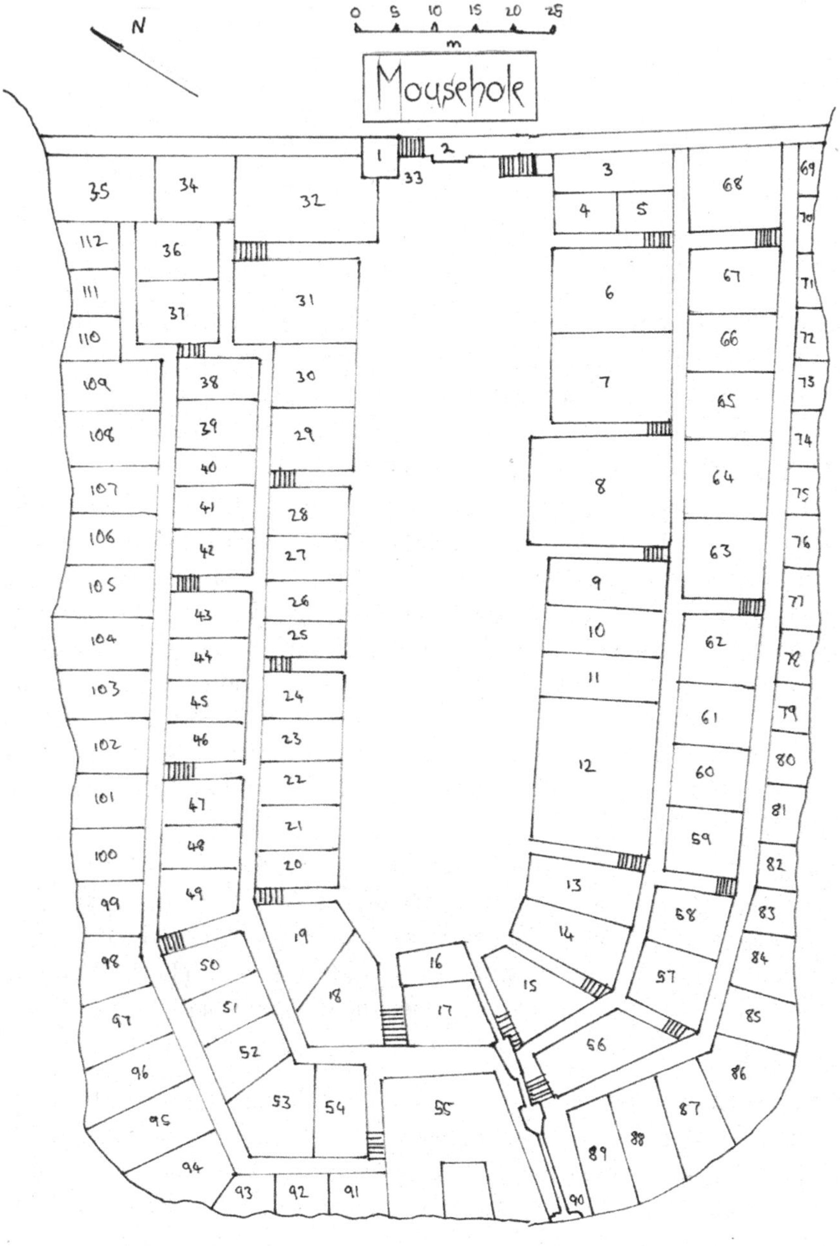

There are many children who are not mentioned. The Inn is the Mouse Hall and the villagers call themselves Mice. They use a compulsory militia to defend themselves. This militia includes a flying carpet and many saddles and rings of invisibility. The local cheese is a cheddar variety. It was known in Old Speech as Muzel. In the hills two days north of the village is a supply of gypsum that has not been mined since The Burning at least. There are no shops, as such, although items are available for purchase at workshops.

All of houses backing the surrounding cliff will extend into the cliff. Some go back a very long way and will be used, eventually, for maturing cheese and other activities that need a constant temperature. There is around 3m of elevation between levels. All of the buildings in the front and middle rows have two levels. Very few of the houses of the last row are of more than one level, but may be the same size due to going back into the cliff.

This mostly illustrates the village as it is by the end of *Engaging Evil*. Most of the people not mentioned here are still living in the Hall of Mice or in the old barracks as are most of the single people. Most of the houses are empty at this stage and only those listed are repaired enough to be lived in.

1. Watchtower on the wall
2. Wider section of wall around gate
3. Smithy: Norbert Black (Trades 6: Blacksmith Q5, Weaponsmith Q5, Armourer Q5), Sajãh bint Javed (Vagus 7: Housekeeper Q9, Administration Q3), Fortunata Belluci (Vagus 5: Dressmaker Q6, Embroiderer Q5, workshop at #23)
6. Stable (extends under next level)
7. Bandit Barracks
8. Mages building/ Hall of Mice: Orthodox priests (Father Christopher Palamas, Cleric 6^{23} and Presbytera Bianca, Vagus 4), (Father Theodule Philes, Cleric 7^{15} and Presbytera Ruth Hawker, Trade 6, Professional 1: Sage 6F36, Teacher 4)
11. Kitchens: under Lãdi al-Yarmũk (Trade 2, Vagus 7: Cook 9, Sex Appeal 5, Dance 6)
12. Village hall
16. Pool of fresh water
19. Apothecary and healing chapel: used by the priests and Lakshmi
21. (by this book) Pastrycook: Nathanael Ktenas (Trade 8), an Orthodox pastrycook from Ardlark who comes to the village for Lãdi
22. Leatherwork: Stefan Ostrogski (Armsman 5, Trade 4: Leatherworker 4) and Bryony verch Dafydd, (Scout 4, Vagus 1)
23. Dressmaking and tailoring (used by Fortunata and Astrid)
26. Miner & physician (residence): Harald Pitt (Trade 7: Miner 9, Value

Gems 4), Lakshmi Brar (Vagus 5, Illicit 2: Physician 4, Value Gems 2, Sage E400)

27.Farmer and Dairy: Giles Ploughman (Vagus 6: Farmer 4, Husbander 4, Cheesemaker 4, makes cheese at # 110) and Naeve Milker (Vagus 4: Husbander 5)

28.Bows: Robin Fletcher (Trade 5: Bowyer 5, Fletcher 6), and Eleanor Fournier (Armsman 5: Jeweller 7)

29.Brewery: Aine Bragwr (Trade 6, Vagus 2: Brewer 7, Distiller 3, Vintner 3)

30.(by now) Bakehouse: Zoë Anicia (T4: Baker 6, Pastrycook 3)

31.Barracks originally used as slave quarters

32.Guard room

53.Goditha Mason (Vagus 5, Mage 2[17E?]: Mason 3, Carpenter 1) and Parminder Sen (Vagus 3, Mage C2[16S]), Goditha is unsure as to her exact birth date and is self-taught in her crafts. Parminder is a rare Spirit Mage.

55.Princess' House: Theodora do Hrothnog (Mage 11[20AB], Noble 5, Bard 4: Rhetoric 6, Gambling 10, Sex Appeal 6, Courtier 5, Music 10 – in various instruments) and Rani Rai (Mage C9[19FD]: Astrologer 7, Teacher 7, Alchemist 4)

57.also Basil and Astrid

58.Basil and Astrid: Basil Akritas (Armsman 4, Vagus 8: Athlete 4, Courtier 4, Physician 4, Housekeeper 4, Cook 4, Tracker 4), Astrid the Cat (Scout 5: Sailor 3, Tailor 4, Bushwise 2, Wilderness Survival 2, Tracker 4, Hunter 3)

59.Father Thorstein Tostisson (Cleric 2) and Kaliope (Vagus 2: Linenmaker 5, Housekeeper 3, Cook 3, Play Organ 4)

62.Verily I Rejoice in the Lord (Vagus 4, Mage C2[21F?], Illicit 1: Juggler 4, Sex Appeal 3, Cook 3, Music 6) and Azizsevgili (Armsman 4: Mountaineer 4, Wilderness Survival 2, Tracker 2, Trapper 2, Bushwise 2). Verily is very unsure of her birth date.

90.Spring emerging from cliff

110.Cheesemaking and storage for Giles.